*TAKE WING AND FLY HERE*

To Clementine

TAKE *WING* AND *FLY* HERE

a novel by

**Priyanka Kumar**

Happy Birding!
Priyanka

SHERMAN ASHER PUBLISHING · Santa Fe

For Michael

ISBN: 978-1-890932-44-2  (paperback edition)
ISBN: 978-1-890932-46-6  (e-Book edition)

Library of Congress Control Number:  2013934574
Sherman Asher Publishing
126 Candelario St.
Santa Fe, NM 87501
www.shermanasher.com

*Design by Jim Mafchir*
*Cover Photo by Priyanka Kumar*

*Manufactured in Canada*

*TAKE WING AND FLY HERE*

*1*

THE NEWS THAT ANNE MARIE WAS FLYING out to see him transformed J.K. into an unstable combination of joy and despair. He missed his
girlfriend and would have liked to draw her into his arms, but his weekends were
even more crammed than his weekdays, devoted as they were to his Big Year.

He had planned to improve his shorebird count this weekend. Saturday,
and any time he could squeeze out on Sunday, were his only chances to boost
his lackluster August count. Anne Marie tolerated his "craziness" as best she
could, but she lost patience when he interrupted their dates to bird.

All summer long, J.K.'s lanky figure had crisscrossed fields, mountains,
nature centers, even the backs of restaurants, with binoculars slung over one
arm and a spotting scope over the other shoulder, looking for birds for his Big
Year. The Swarovski scope was his only luxury possession.

J.K. hurriedly tidied up his cubbyhole pending Anne Marie's arrival. She
was right to call his place a cubbyhole. At three hundred square feet, it was a
closet by California standards, crammed with a futon and desk. In the mornings,
he could swing open the refrigerator with his foot without getting out of bed.
The spiders and he had a pact: they were allowed to have webs on the walls as
long as they didn't get into his bed or his shower or the kitchen sink, but if they
trespassed on one of those places, they faced merciless execution. The pact
had worked well, though Anne Marie screamed whenever she saw a spider, and
they were similarly terrified of her.

J.K. spent Friday evening in his Birdmobile, stuck in gridlocked traffic
from the Los Angeles airport, trying to reassure Anne Marie that her twenties
were not "evaporating in a long-distance relationship."

With one hand on the wheel, J.K. touched Anne Marie's cheek. She was
starting her junior year at Rutgers, and there were a handful of good universities
for his research within a 300-mile radius of where she lived in New Brunswick.
Among them, he had his heart set on a postdoctoral position at Princeton.

"It'll happen, right?" Anne Marie said. "You'll get a postdoc in a school
that's close to me?" She was radiant in a navy dress speckled with tiny stars.

She was the kind of girl who *would* travel in pretty clothes. Both were too strapped for funds to fly cross-country more often than once every couple months. He hated their long-distance relationship, but she was well worth the effort.

He tousled her straight, long hair. He had worried that she'd act distant after weeks of not seeing him. But when they saw each other at baggage claim, their attraction was irresistible. J.K. knew he had a stabilizing effect on her, which she acknowledged. With two or three precious days together, it wouldn't matter that they'd spend the rest of the month apart. She told him once that his clear and honest heart, reflected perfectly in his eyes, worked as an antidote to city life and her savvy, self-important friends. Nonetheless, she often lost patience with his clear and honest heart for neglecting practical matters.

A cloudless August sky hovered and the day's light lingered. At her suggestion, they picked up a bottle of red wine and, as an indulgence, a Trader Joe's cheesecake. J.K. knew Anne Marie liked to eat out, but his graduate student stipend couldn't keep up with her taste for luxuries. Instead, he cooked them dinner under the pretext that he wanted her to try out his Chinese cooking.

"It's delicious," Anne Marie said about the stir-fry. "You'll cook for me when you move to Jersey?"

"Sure, I'll cook for you."

"That's nice," she said, letting him see her sweet smile. "Even my dad doesn't do that."

"He lets the help handle it?" J.K. said.

She looked at him questioningly. Maybe she didn't like what he said. After they put the plates away, he pulled her into a leisurely kiss. She smelled of some French perfume that could probably pay a month's worth of his rent. They moved to the narrow futon, where they lay pressed together, kissing.

"We need some time off, for ourselves," she said, moving away. She stretched her delicate arms over a pillow.

Tempted by the desire to go birding with her, J.K. said, "How about we travel next summer, before I start my postdoc? A wild, carefree trip."

"A European trip?" she said, lighting up. "Jake!" She was the only one who called him by that name. It was ironic that he'd been named after his father.

"How does South America strike you?"

"South America? That sounds fabulous." Her mind was racing with images of Argentina—colorful clothing, European architecture, tango lessons, dulce de leche. "That time my dad took me to England—I mean it was cool to count castles, but I was thinking that Italy would be fun, or even Argentina. Our cook is from Argentina."

"I was thinking of hitting some bird-friendly places while we're down there."

Anne Marie's mind came to a complete halt, and an uneasy expression formed in her eyes. "I don't know if the pharmacy will let me off," she said. She was backing out of the whole trip. "You'll be absorbed with looking for birds the entire trip. What will I do? We'll probably have to live on anchovies, which is all you want to eat while birding."

"So you don't wanna come?"

"Don't make me out to be mean," her face hardened.

J.K. knew the look. A fight was coming. "What's wrong?"

"I don't know." She considered a tear in a graying pillow, with poly-some-thing spilling out. "I had a bad dream on the plane."

"What?"

"No, forget it. It was disgustingly dark."

"Just tell me."

"You want me to?" She sat up in bed. Her eyes flashed, then drifted into midair. "You were at my . . . funeral. Even though I was dead, I was thinking—*now* he'll take a day off for me. Today. That's the most time we'll have spent to-gether in a while—at my funeral. Tomorrow, he'll go back to work." Anne Marie began to sob, and then she nearly choked, which caused her to laugh.

"Don't think like that!" J.K. said. "You're too young to think of dying." His chest tightened. He thought of his sister; she'd been too young to die. He grew silent.

Anne Marie felt the need to explain her outburst. "Lately, you don't talk about anything interesting. You know, anything entertaining. It's birding or physics. Physics or birding."

It was true. Work was everything to him. He was a physics graduate student first. In his free time, he birded. That was his passion. "What do you want me to talk about?"

"I don't know. It's not like my schoolwork isn't intense. To get into vet school—you think that's not competitive? But I still find time to be . . . I try to be . . . well-rounded."

Feeling restless, he leapt out of bed and opened the sole window of the cubbyhole. A couple of years ago, in a childish delirium, she'd said, "The day we make our third anniversary, I'll let you buy me an engagement ring!" Back then he had balked inwardly at the thought of marrying so young. Lately, the running around for the Big Year, as exhilarating as it was, had left him feeling unmoored. Anne Marie lived far enough away—he didn't want her to grow any more distant. Their bond had survived three years despite the continent separating them. She made him feel that his place in the universe was intact. That third anniversary was coming up in a month anyway.

"When we start living together," he said, "things will be easier. We'll know more about each other's lives, and there'll be more to talk about."

"I wonder about that. When will we *ever* live together?"

"We can move in right away!" he said. They both laughed.

"Married and living together, or just living together?"

"And the point of getting married is . . . ? Half the people who get married get divorced anyway. We have our commitment—that's what counts."

"So there won't be a proposal with a ring? That's too obsolete?"

A ring. That hadn't occurred to him. Why did a ring matter? Their intent to commit to each other was the important thing. Anything else was just for show. He *could* get her a ring from a campus bazaar, as long as she didn't insist upon some real jewelry that would bankrupt him for good. If only girls, like birds, preferred songs to rings!

"A ring? Do you care about that?" he asked.

Anne Marie nodded, exasperated by his response. This fight, leading to their muddled discussion of marriage, did not portend well for him, but had gotten her juices flowing. She looked at J.K. with fresh perspective. His ratty finances and closet apartment were a definite bummer. Worse, he showed no interest in ever having money. She wished she didn't have a weakness for his eyes, which were radiant with knowledge. He understood the language of birds. There was something about him, an understated dignity, as though he were the prince of a secret kingdom. A flutter of wings and a remote call was all he needed to make an identification. So far, Anne Marie had observed this obsession with a mixture of frustration and awe, not knowing what to make of his feats in a field that was as realistic to her as a fairy-tale kingdom.

Now she kissed him with kisses that were at once confused and insistent. Only the kingdom of love was theirs together, and they shut themselves in it, unable to wait any longer.

While she was in the shower, J.K. stared out the window. A hummingbird was sucking nectar at a tree whose curvaceous trunk resembled an old lady's doo-dad vase. The late summer evening was darkening into night. The hummingbird should have been asleep by now, but like him, it was having trouble sleeping. The hummingbird's greedy hunger got it stuck in a fuchsia flower. It flapped in panic, like a butterfly trapped in a spider's web.

Just as the hummingbird could not stop sucking nectar, neither could J.K.

resist the compelling lure of birding. This attraction had gotten him ensnared in a Big Year race to find the greatest number of bird species in Los Angeles County in a twelve-month stretch.

Normally, the only exceptions he made to his weekend birding timetable were the field trips he lead as Trip Chair of the Alpena Bird Society, and this was the weekend before the Piute Ponds trip.

"Rick is picking up a ton of shorebirds," J.K. told Anne Marie.

"Is he going to beat you?" Anne Marie said, emerging from the shower in a silk kimono, under which he could make out the outline of her narrow hips.

"I hope not," J.K. said. The scent of her lavender lotion had changed the personality of the cubbyhole. "Rick takes himself too seriously. I'd rather feud with Pete." He missed this high school pal. Last Christmas, J.K. got into an argument with Pete, who was working in Arizona. J.K. speculated that he could find more bird species in Los Angeles County in a year than Pete could in the entire so-called "birder heaven" state of Arizona. The argument ended in a bet and both friends began to "bird their asses off" beginning New Year's Day. In April, for personal reasons, Pete moved back home to New Jersey and called off the bet. But J.K. had crossed the 200 species mark. He couldn't stop now. He decided to go for the L.A. County record.

Anne Marie was combing her hair. "You spend too much time on the Big Year," she said. "You need to focus on getting that postdoc in Princeton."

J.K. didn't like the way she spoke of his Big Year, as though it weren't important. It felt more important than anything he'd ever done before—more important than that silly ring she wanted. "Yeah, I worry about that Princeton postdoc, . . . whether I'll get it," he said finally.

"Don't say that. Of course you will!" She didn't like him in his doubting mood, and she got cranky if he worried about the outcome of his job search. Anne Marie convinced herself that things would magically get better after he got his Ph.D.

"It's a probability game," J.K. said. "Same goes for the Big Year."

J.K. was torn between the desire to play host to Anne Marie and his need to sneak out Saturday morning to look for rare shorebirds while she slept. He recalled how Ed McCoy quit his job to do his Big Year, living with his pregnant wife in a studio in the Ballona Wetlands area. His wife was claustrophobic in their tiny studio, but Ed calmed her down by pointing out that she saw him more during his Big Year than when he worked at an office.

J.K. felt better knowing that he had never asked Anne Marie to sacrifice anywhere near that much for his sake. Ed went on to win the Big Year that year, breaking the L.A. County record by two birds and becoming an icon in the birding community.

They lingered in bed. J.K. watched as a trickling stream of sunlight lit Anne Marie's bare arms. Her dark, expressive eyes looked into his, and they both burst into mischievous smiles. He let his finger trace the outline of her fragile nose, brush past her pink lips, and pause at her soft white throat.

Later, she wanted to be taken out and entertained. "And it can't be nature-related," she stipulated.

"That's tough," he said. If only he could escape to look for shorebirds! But he'd have to write the morning off and hope to make it up somehow. He couldn't disappoint her today. It was a frightening thought, but she was his only intimate friend. He had buddies in the birding world, but that was mostly casual stuff. They were bound by their devotion to birding, but it was much the same for rock climbers and dog-show enthusiasts. People no longer had religion in common or geographical roots. Americans were good at doing business with each other, and always had been, but they no longer seemed to hang out in each other's living rooms. Maybe he was wrong, but he couldn't remember anyone ever inviting Anne Marie and him to their home. When Charles Darwin had been in college, his professors had him over for dinner, or went on walks with him, mentoring him and such. J.K. wondered if a sense of community were a thing of the past, if the only people who would see you through a rough patch now were a lover or a parent. His mother had rock-solid connections to her Italian siblings, who all had about a dozen kids each, but he felt alienated from that crowd.

Unable to think of anyplace else, they walked a mile to Leaves Café on that muggy day. He had dated a couple of other girls before Anne Marie, but she was different. She was smart and well put together and she inspired him to be his best. He could picture a life with her. He would have preferred that she be more into birding, but maybe he shouldn't mind that she was normal. Maybe it was a good thing that she balanced him out.

At the café, dotted with pine tables and chairs, they glanced at the photo exhibit—which changed monthly—of tea plantations in Sri Lanka.

"Mo' tea, Mister Ph.D.?" Luna said. There was a shade of blueberry, something wild, in her eyes.

"Yep, my usual. How's it going?"

Anne Marie was intrigued to see him comfortably chatting with another girl. Luna hid herself in grungy clothes and untidy hair, but Anne Marie's sharp eyes observed that Luna's face had the charm of a classical Greek goddess.

Paul Little walked by and said a gruff hello. J.K. had seen him before at Leaves, but he was surprised that Paul Little seemed to know Luna, too.

"We had the same guitar teacher a few years ago," Luna explained, bursting into a smile. "Paul found out recently that I work here. I slip him free coffee when I can . . . and gelato. We're both headed on the music track."

"Really?" J.K. said.

"Oh, yeah. Paul likes to write songs about the environment. He's on a mission, like me. We're both out to change the world, except I'm like twenty-four, and he's like, what, double that age?" she laughed. "I keep in touch with whoever I can 'cause my best friends are scattered around the country."

"It's sort of the same situation with me," J.K. said.

Anne Marie giggled.

The glass walls of Leaves Café offered an unforgettable view of the San Gabriel Mountains, and J.K. longed to drive into the mountains to try his luck. He could show Anne Marie a memorable sunset, while keeping an eye out for birds. Borrowing her cell phone, he checked the Bird Hotline. A vagrant yellow-bellied sapsucker had been spotted at the Benedictine Monastery. Antelope Valley was a two-hour drive north, and if they started now, they could get to the monastery while there was enough light to see the bird. He had also been meaning to get the Lewis's woodpeckers hanging out in the yard of a nearby state-prison facility. The woodpeckers could be relied upon to stay put until next weekend, but the sapsucker, likely blown west by some freak winds from Texas, might take offense at the rowdy dogs at the monastery and the too frequent chiming of bells, and decide to head home.

"Is there a club around here that's good?" Anne Marie asked Luna.

"Yeah, sure . . . like if you go downtown."

"What's this about?" J.K. said.

"I'd love to go dancing," Anne Marie said, "*if* you guys have a night life here!"

"I was thinking of taking you to the Benedictine monastery," J.K. said.

"Oh?" Anne Marie said. Then a glint entered her eye. "Is something going on that I don't know about?"

Luna was making tea for a customer, but J.K. sensed that Luna was also listening to their conversation, and assessing Anne Marie with half-closed eyes. Over Anne Marie's shoulder was a black leather handbag with PRADA stenciled in silver. Had Luna looked at it with envy or pity?

"There's this sapsucker at the monastery . . . " he began.

At mention of the bird, Anne Marie's smile dropped. J.K. figured that it would be too hard to sell her on the state-prison facility and accepted grudgingly that he'd have to sacrifice the whole day to love. He decided to take her to the monastery anyway, but mainly show her the gardens and the scenery.

"I wish sometimes that the rest of the world would leave us alone," Anne Marie said on the long drive there.

"You mean my friends?"

"Yeah. For sure. And my dad. I'm up to here with course work," her hand slicing its way over her head.

"What about your dad?" J.K. said.

Anne Marie shook her head. "He thinks I need stronger financial planning."

"You mean like more money?"

"He wants me to take another job in addition to my pharmacy job." She paused, hesitant. "Dad's not so hot about our relationship. He doesn't think you'll ever make real money."

"That doesn't surprise me," J.K. said, bristling. "Your dad's obsessed with bank balances." He'd once challenged her father, an economist who consulted for McDonalds, on the importance of money as a measure of happiness. But the economist overpowered the physics graduate student with his number crunching.

"He's now gonna start telling you who to go out with?" J.K. said.

Anne Marie again shook her head. "He just doesn't approve of . . . "

"Doesn't approve of me? Great. Because I don't approve of him!"

J.K. didn't dare ask why she didn't move to a smaller apartment instead of taking on another job. Stretched over two jobs, how would she ever travel with him in the summer? He knew better than to discuss money with her, though. She'd spent the money to fly here, after all, and in any case, the last time he brought up the subject of downsizing, she'd said, "You expect me to live in a cubbyhole, too?"

## 2

The Piute Ponds trip began on the last Saturday morning in August. The freeway buzzed with engines and gusts of exhaust fumes, though it was barely 6 a.m. J.K. drove his Birdmobile on this field trip, his childlike gray eyes sparkling. He was tanned after a long summer's birding. His bronze hair stood up in the wind with Bart Simpson ends. Despite his anxieties, in those days, J.K. had an easygoing air. Back then he assumed, as many twenty-some-things do, that he had a "safety net." He didn't know exactly what he meant by the term; he hadn't defined it as a physicist might. But he felt that if he were to make some real mistake, the fall would be cushioned. This protective cocoon, he guessed, was woven by people such as his parents, physics supervisor, bird society members, and even his girlfriend, who knew his potential and would give him what support he needed to realize it.

Rick Silverman's battered pickup whizzed by. J.K. accelerated to catch up, his lumberjack shirt flapping about him. They met at the same gas station, as planned. J.K. had with him anchovies and hardboiled eggs and needed only to buy a six-pack of Coke. He fished dollar bills out of his weathered jeans while Rick, a clean-shaven man in his forties, picked out snacks. Rick's body still had the tautness of his bicycle racing days, but a belly had formed under his waistline due to his love of steak.

"To heck with the rest of the trip," Rick told him. "Let's just focus on the sandpiper."

J.K. looked at him. All Rick wanted was his Big Year bird and to get on with it. To hell with the rest of the members on the trip.

"How's the count?" J.K. said.

"Terrible. Can't seem to find a decent bird. Anyhow, getting that sandpiper is what's gonna make or break this trip."

J.K. got back on the road and drove north to Joss Canyon, but he couldn't shake off his unease. At any other time, J.K. wouldn't have minded helping Rick, but they were in a Big Year race, and J.K felt that Rick was parasitizing on his work. Rick always wanted to know what bird J.K. had seen lately and then became obsessed with finding that particular bird. J.K. figured Rick was three or four birds behind him, but Rick kept his own Big Year count a mystery. Rick was like a scrub jay—a sharp, territorial bird, not shy about guarding its interests. J.K. had a well-meaning, collegial nature, and he let Rick benefit from his scouting, but he wondered now if he could afford this generosity. The members of the Alpena Bird Society thought it natural that J.K. was doing a Big Year to smash the old record. What they didn't know was that the timing couldn't be worse for him. It was his last year in graduate school, and he must belt out enough physics papers to earn the Ph.D. he needed to land a coveted job as a postdoctoral researcher.

A Big Year is a race against time, and never in J.K.'s life was time scarcer than now. He didn't have time to be Trip Chair. He meant this trip to be the last one he led. But how to break the news to the members? If Blake weren't only ten years old, he could take over as Trip Chair. Maybe the biologist, Robert Kern, could be co-Chair with Blake? But then someone else would have to re-place Kern as vice-president. A shuffle was inevitable. But how could J.K. trig-ger it? People were too damn cozy with things as they were. And "things as they were" no longer worked for him—this did not leave him enough time for either physics or the Big Year. He sacrificed precious free time to plan these trips for the bird society. He'd driven over an hour to the Air Force base to scope out birds for the Piute Ponds trip, but that's when he'd had a rare sighting of a Baird's sandpiper. Now Rick was dying to see the bird.

Rick led pelagic tours off the Channel Islands and was amassing a hoard of shorebird sightings. Would that J.K. had such leisure! Curiously, Rick made public that he was doing a Big Year soon after J.K.'s quest became known. Was this a coincidence, or was Rick trying to upstage him? Like a jay, Rick stayed in the background until he perceived a threat. J.K. had seen how a jay would squawk and squawk until the bird it saw as a threat left the premises. Did it upset Rick that a Big Year win would make J.K. the King of Southern Califor-nia's birding community?

"You'd think only Texans are stupid enough to do this," Karen muttered.

"Mom!" Blake said, with a child's instinct that something was wrong.

The cowbird trap was five feet tall and made of green mesh. Karen was sur-prised to spot the contraption so close to the parking lot. When her ten-year-old son approached it, the trapped birds flapped in panic, smashing against the wire to escape. She had driven her son to Joss Canyon, where the bird society members were to congregate for the Piute Ponds trip, but they found the parking lot empty.

"Oh no, they've left already!" Blake said, jumping out of the jeep.

"Good," Karen said. "Now we can go back to sleep." She wished he would be willing to go back home and badger his father into cooking them pancakes.

Blake stood in the empty parking lot in his bird society sweater. The logo on the top right was a line drawing of a perched vireo framed by the society's name. "Did J.K. email us directions to the Base?" he said with the impatience of a boy to whom the trip meant everything in the world.

Karen shook her head and tucked her hair behind one ear. In the old days, Rick might have left a note on the door of the Nature Center, but fire had gutted the structure, and in its place was a lone trailer, seldom manned, with the nameplate: BILLY GRIMSBY, DIRECTOR. An investigation of the fire was ongoing. Meanwhile, Joss Canyon was neglected. The bare hills above were all burnt grass. Around her, poison oak thrived, the leaves tinged with a red shine. Castor beans grew wild, spreading toxic seeds.

On the cowbird trap was a sign: DO NOT DISTURB. ENDANGERED SPECIES MANAGEMENT PROGRAM. A male cowbird with its chocolate head and shiny black body hovered around the lid of the trap, chattering with its imprisoned mate, trying to find a way out. Other prisoners—two song sparrows, a towhee, and a finch—flew from perch to perch in a frantic circle. Water and seeds were provided, but the birds only wanted freedom.

Blake watched as the chocolate-headed male cowbird also entered the trap and became a captive.

"Come on!" Karen said, horrified. She'd vaguely heard about the traps, but it was the first time she'd seen one. In the jeep she unscrewed a thermos of coffee. She gulped some and gave a sip to Blake.

At the sound of a passing car, Blake swung around, and the camera hanging from his neck swayed in the air before thudding to his chest. J.K.'s Birdmobile screeched in, tailed by Rick's shabby pickup. Karen poked her son in the stomach. Blake grinned. It was a cool dawn, the only time of day in August that Karen could stand to be outside. But her cherub loved nothing better than to kill a day birding.

"Hi there," Rick said, coming up to Karen. "You look awake-ish."

"Thanks," she said. "That really improves my confidence." They considered each other pals who make a habit of outdoing each other's jokes. She gave in to the impulse to hug him, and noted that he held on a few seconds longer than necessary. "Want to carpool with us?" she asked him.

"Absolutely," Rick said. He hurried to transfer his things to her jeep.

"Did you see that cowbird trap?" she called after him.

"Two more up in the canyon," he said. "They'll let the others go and kill the cowbirds."

"That's smart."

"They parasitize the nests of vireos."

"So Billy thinks it's okay to kill one bird to save another?"

Rick shrugged as though he'd rather she didn't bring up dreary stuff right before an important birding trip. "It's great we have a small group," he said, returning with his scope. "Let's go, gang. If the others come late, too bad!" When this jovial ring entered Rick's voice, his melancholy eyes brightened, and he switched from a legal administrator into a birding buddy.

Karen made her way to J.K. as he sprung out of his Birdmobile. A set of bird feathers hung from the car's rear view mirror.

"Let's get off our butts and do something about these traps," she said. "I can't believe we let Billy get away with this."

"I don't like the traps either," J.K. said. "Cowbirds get a bad rap as egg-laying machines—they lay two to thirty eggs at a time, but typically only one or two hatch." Seeing that he had as witnesses Karen, a board member, and Rick, the president, trailing her, he added, "I don't seem to have any time these days. I think you'll have to look for a new Trip Chair."

"Can't do without you," Karen said.

"I'm already doing service as president in a Centennial year," Rick said.

"But I really don't have the time," J.K. said.

"Oh, you're young," Rick said. "You've got lots of time."

J.K. felt uneasy. Rick, as usual, was guilt-tripping him.

A dozen people materialized around their leader to receive directions to the Air Force base. About half of the group was old ladies; this reflected the bird society's demographic, which ranged from tall, angular Zanne McDonald to petite, nearly invisible Jean Savant. Among the others were the biologist, Robert Kern, in khakis, ready for a safari; Dana Leeds, a terrific "birder by ear," trailed by her retired husband, Frank, and board secretary, Patty Cole; *Los Angeles Times* reporter, Anissa Montez—aloof, but knew her warblers inside out; Wynn, a schoolteacher, just back from a summer working in Alaskan fisheries.

"I have a special permit to get in," J.K. said, surveying his flock. "But it's important that we all enter and exit at the same time. They'll shoot the stragglers."

Rick adjusted his cowboy hat and repeated the directions for the old ladies who cast about confused looks. The Air Force base was over an hour away, and Karen had brought her newly washed jeep instead of her husband's scruffy little Toyota. She needed the trunk space for their food, binoculars, spotting scope and tripod, and "doo-dads"—as J.K. called them—that came in handy during an expedition.

Doors were slammed and the procession threaded out of Joss Canyon. J.K.'s Birdmobile was in the lead, followed by Professor Kern's SUV and Karen's jeep. In the middle of the caravan were the schoolteacher's beat-up Ford, Dana and Frank's Subaru, and Annisa Montez's Prius. The old ladies trailed.

As she drove, Karen admitted that she still felt sleepy.

"So I was right," Rick said, "as I always am."

Karen thought herself a paragon of virtue, and certainly was not considering cheating on her husband, but she could not help flirting with Rick. She gave him a sidelong smile—a knowing smile, set in a face with high cheekbones.

They drove past Antelope Valley, past rows of lookalike pink houses on scraped-bare fields and hills punctuated by shopping complexes and billboards advertising more development. "We took long drives here when I was a child," Karen said. "That was before my parents divorced." Then there were endless fields of saltbush and tangled masses of junipers. The bark of Joshua trees was topped with green stars. Karen thought about how neglected she'd felt when she was Blake's age, because her divorced parents no longer had the inclination to indulge her.

"J.K. said we're almost guaranteed to see a Baird's sandpiper," Blake said. It was the tenth time he had brought this up. He was on his 299th "life bird" as he headed for his eleventh birthday on Tuesday, and he hoped to bag a life bird during this trip to round out his statistics to an even 300. "Mom, you think we'll find the Baird's?"

"You don't have to keep repeating that question," Karen said.

"I have to. Otherwise my brain goes crazy." He ducked as his mother's hand shot out to swat him.

"How did you like *Spiderman Two*?" she asked. Her husband, Oscar, had taken the kids to the film yesterday.

"It was good. But there was gross stuff in it."

She smiled, knowing that he meant the kiss between Toby McGuire and Kirsten Dunst. "You look away when Marge and Homer kiss on the Simpsons!" she teased.

"It's gross." He flipped to the sandpiper pages in his *Sibley Bird Guide*.

"You better not be complaining about that. That's the way you came into this world. The human race depends on the fact that people like to kiss each other."

The boy saw Rick laughing at him and blushed purple.

J.K. opened a side gate of the Edwards Air Force Base with a secret code that he punched into a metal panel. They drove in past a "VEHICLES WITH

EXPLOSIVES" sign, guarded by a raven, to another that read, "THIS AREA IS OFF LIMITS TO ALL PERSONNEL BY ORDER OF THE BASE COM-MANDER." Karen negotiated the jeep over a bumpy gravel path, flanked by arid fields of saltbush, brickle bush, and burnt devil's lettuce.

In the rearview mirror, Karen saw a figure in a raggedy military outfit racing after her. How did that vagrant Paul Little hitchhike this far out? Here was a man who looked as if he were ready to explode. It wasn't just his stomach. His disgruntled attitude and his habit of shadowing Blake unsettled her. She wished J.K. had not let him in the gate. She had happened upon him on the last birding trip, staring at Blake with that glinty look. Some of the others thought Paul Little was a pacifist, out to change the world; others believed he had the mak-ings of a terrorist and that he had set fire to Joss Canyon because he hated Billy Grimsby's plans for an expanded building complex in the Nature Center. Who could blame Karen for not wanting a suspicious character to hover around her son? She reached for her coffee. "When you have kids," she said to Blake, "you'll realize how much your mom loves you."

"I'll never have kids," Blake said. His eyes were everywhere all at once in case a sage thrasher was about. The other drivers were discussing the thrasher on walkie-talkies, but Blake could not get his walkie-talkie to settle on the right frequency. When they drove up to the cluster of little lakes known as Piute Ponds, Blake opened the window and his head nearly fell out.

"You'll never find a girl you like?" Karen said.

Blake shook his head and tumbled out of the jeep the second it stopped. With a thrill of anticipation, he grabbed his spotting scope and binoculars and trotted after J.K. to the edge of the first pond.

"Let me guess," Blake said. "305?"

"Three hundred and six." J.K. set up his spotting scope on a dirt road next to the reeds.

Two yellow-headed blackbirds, the velvety black and yellow intensely sat-urated in the morning light, passed overhead. J.K. and Blake instantly zeroed-in their binoculars on them.

The boy calculated J.K.'s score against last year's all-time-high Big Year record of 346. "Forty more to go," he said. "You wanna know Rick's score?"

J.K. said nothing. The Piute Ponds, crowned by the San Gabriel Mountains on their south end, reflected the blue and pink of the morning light. Skirting them was a column of reeds, brittle and brown.

"Last week he was at 301. My mom told me."

"I'm hoping I'll get a semi-palm today for my count," J.K. said. "It's a hot race."

"You'll beat him!" Blake gazed up at J.K.'s six-foot tall figure and swelled with pride thinking about J.K.'s heroic quest. "I'll do a Big Year one day," Blake added.

"That doesn't surprise me." J.K. knew who the hardcores were because they stuck with him to the end of his trips. And his birding trips almost never ended. There were would-be birders who came along one time and never came back. They couldn't take the heat. Karen would have been one of those if it weren't for her son.

"So you think we'll get the Baird's?" Blake asked, studying J.K.'s face. "It's my birthday next week and I've got to get to 300." True, his 300 would only be a life count, not a Big Year count like J.K.'s. But still, the Baird's would be as much a treat as birthday cake.

J.K. let out a smile. The boy took it to mean yes. He whooped and dashed to convey the good news to his mother.

In such moments, J.K.'s resolve to quit as Trip Chair faded. Why was it that his mind saw only the birds his flock needed? Why did he study obsessively the permutations of locations he must hit to find those birds? Next August, J.K. would leave for wherever he got a postdoc, but he knew that if there were one place where he wanted to do a Big Year, it was here. This had always been his dream. A couple of weeks ago he squeezed out some cash to go on Rick's pelagic trip and got a few extra shorebirds. Seeing a red-billed tropicbird on that pelagic was the closest J.K. had come to a religious experience.

The Big Year quest was his love letter and his swan song to the birding he'd done in Southern California the last four years. Someone like him, with a reputation on both coasts, didn't take on a Big Year only to come in second place. Years ago, Pete had been with him in the car accident that killed J.K.'s sister. After that incident, J.K. had sensed that his father began to doubt him, maybe even thinking his son was worthless. But recently, when J.K. had described his Big Year quest to his father over the phone, he'd heard something different in his father's voice. It felt that after years, his father had finally *responded* to him. Jake didn't understand physics, but he loved competitive sports. Was Jake proud that his son was doing a Big Year?

Reputation is everything in the birding community, and there was no sharper eye or ear in the Alpena Bird Society than his. How J.K. had acquired these skills, no one in the A.B.S. quite knew. When Blake pressed him, J.K. had said, "I had a hillbilly upbringing. I was raised by wolves somewhere in New Jersey."

J.K. was aware of the burden he carried today. His flock depended on him, and he must deliver.

The piercing August sun was making it difficult for Karen to stand outside for long. The sun had stripped the ponds of all color, and the sandy dirt the birders stood on had been baking long enough now to give off its own heat, transforming the Air Force base into a giant sauna. Karen noticed, however, that the dry smothering heat didn't ruffle J.K., who looked as cool as a mint sprig, or Professor Kern, who stayed dead silent while birding, although he flashed a grin when he saw something nice. Paul Little, in tattered camouflage gear and tanned crisp brown, was also annoyingly heat-resistant. Spotting a redheaded duck, his scowl softened, and his wide gray teeth were exposed in a sickly smile.

Karen rarely joined the other birders. Instead, she stayed close to Blake, wielding her "mini air-conditioner"—a battery-operated water-spray fan. When Rick wandered by looking for owls, Karen offered to spray him. Although his cheeks were flushed pink, he declined being sprayed for fear that being cooled down might affect his tenacity.

"Come on, Rick," she teased. "Give yourself a break!"

"Okay, one spray."

As she sprayed him, Karen forgot the heat for a few precious moments. His nose wrinkled as the beads of water met his skin. He thanked her with a boyish grin. "Boy, is it hot!" he said. Karen's face broke into a smile. She liked that Rick trusted her; he even told her his Big Year count, though he kept it a secret from everyone else. He had asked her not to tell anyone, and she didn't, except for Blake, with whom she shared most everything.

At noon, it was impossible for Karen to endure the sun. She was being roasted. The diehards were still out there, and no one had once mentioned the word "lunch." Even the shade inside the jeep no longer offered comfort. She struggled to keep an open mind and be a good sport for her son's sake.

As everyone piled back into their cars, Karen took the sandwiches out of the cooler. When Blake said that they had better wait until they got to the lunch spot, she hoped they weren't planning to eat at their next destination—a sewage pond. The vehicles made a U-turn on a narrow sandy strip to get out of Piute Ponds. As Karen negotiated the turn, Professor Kern cut in front and speeded ahead, spraying slush over her newly washed jeep.

"Thanks a lot!" Karen said.

Paul Little pounded at Karen's window. "Is that your scope?"

Seeing their expensive scope on the tripod, abandoned in the dirt, Karen gasped.
"Oops!" Blake said.

"You better be more careful next time," she said. With ninety-nine percent of his mind fixated on the Baird's sandpiper, all else was forgotten.

Paul Little ran to grab the scope and then planted himself with it in their jeep.

Karen could hardly refuse him a ride now. She had to open her window as soon as he got in because a vile moldy smell took over the jeep.

The caravan stopped just outside the sewage ponds, in a spot where a truck with "Bud" painted on the driver's door was discharging its cargo of fresh sewage. After all the vehicles had collected, several birders began to eat their lunch. Some were so giddy anticipating the "peeps"—the name birders use for sandpipers—that they forgot where they were and planted their picnic coolers right on top of the metal lid of the discharge pit. They were supposed to have had a quick stop next to a liquor/convenience store, but the search for the Baird's had grown too hectic to stop for more than a few minutes. Karen opened up her sandwich at the wheel.

J.K. phoned the sewage headquarters and the automatic gate began to move.

"Open Sesame," Blake coaxed, knowing that J.K. had picked the next location because it was an almost sure spot for the Baird's.

The caravan drove onto a concrete road that turned into a dirt path flanked by unnerving signs such as "SELF-CONTAINED BREATHING AREA." Karen was starved and devoured her homemade turkey sandwich as she drove.

The road led into a surreal landscape where sewage ponds surrounded the vehicles on all sides. Karen was overwhelmed by a pungent smell of chemicals attempting to mask a persistent rotting smell. Mosquitoes and tiny bugs, brown and green, flew into the jeep and descended on her bare legs. She took a hand off the steering wheel to swat them, but the dirt road grew so narrow that this minor error on her part landed the jeep directly into a sewage pond.

Paul Little began to shriek like a loony.

Blake was hyperventilating, able only to croak, "Mom! Mom!"

Rick swore, and his face flashed red and white.

Meanwhile the jeep settled in the shallow muck.

"Oh Lord, help us!" Karen said, trying to keep her head on straight. A couple of years ago, a series of nightmares plagued her in which she was lost in a landscape of filthy pools of water. It was around that time that she pulled the kids out of public school. It was incredible to her that she was now living out her nightmare.

*3*

*A* sewage department employee on a tractor, guided by J.K. in rubber boots knee-deep in brownish-green water, pushed the jeep out of the muck until Karen could inch it up to where one gaunt path crossed another. She parked on this pencil-thin stretch of terra firma. The rest of the caravan applauded. Then the birders hopped out of their vehicles, unconcerned about falling into the sewage. Karen was left to consider what a disgusting mess her jeep was. When she had joined the bird society, the older women thought *she* was weird.

Glued to his scope at the edge of the water, Blake was tilting towards a pond. Karen was worried that he would slip into the muck. "Blake, I won't take you back home if you fall in."

He giggled and ran over to a new edge, camera, binoculars, and scope bouncing against his chest and arms. Ten-year-olds have the feet of adults, but much smaller bodies, so they trip all over themselves, Karen thought. The last thing she wanted in this heat was to deal with a sewage-covered klutz. Blake zoomed up to her, his three mechanical pairs of eyes banging around him, and opened the passenger door to sip water and grab his bird guide.

"Mom, will you take me back even if I fall in?" he said, as a swarm of mosquitoes trailed him in.

"Very reluctantly. And you'll have to stay in the guest house until you're sterilized." She sat in the jeep, not wanting to contemplate the scum on the deathly blue-green water. But even here she couldn't escape the rotting smell and the infernal mosquitoes. The clamminess of her skin and the unrelenting heat grew evermore oppressive. Her body was burning in twelve different places, and she could no longer tell where it was suffering from prickly heat and where from insect bites. The jeep offered no relief, but to step out into the deadly sun was unthinkable. She felt about as relaxed as a cowbird in a trap. This was insane—really insane. They were out in some sewage ponds in a desert in August in the dead heat of the day. Her own private inferno. This had gone too far. She felt too faded to even use the mini air-conditioner. Maybe if they had been here at 7:30 in the morning. But this was insane.

Blake was waving his arms at her. Karen sat undecided for a moment. Then she realized that unless she wanted to crush his childish enthusiasm, she had no option but to step out of the jeep and witness his latest marvel.

There were dozens of shorebirds in the ponds. This was a sorry place to call home, but it was safe. During hunting season, ducks flew here to escape the bullets in more picturesque locations, like Piute Ponds. No duck hunter would send his beloved dog into this rot to retrieve a dead duck.

Blake had dragged her out of the jeep because a solitary sandpiper had been spotted. He had seen the bird on a trip to the San Gabriel River with his father, but this was a life bird for her.

"I wanted to make sure you didn't miss it," Blake said.

At any other time, Karen would have been pleased to see a life bird, but now she took a quick peek at the peep. "What d'you say? Should we head back home now?" she asked him.

"Mom, you said you'd let me do cool stuff."

"I know. I know." Karen retreated to the jeep. The problem was that Blake no longer had any school friends. He knew boys from choir, but his best friend dropped out, and Blake never saw the rest outside of church. He had to have some interaction with the outside world. She pulled him out of school two years ago because she could homeschool him in the time it took to shepherd him through schoolwork. She didn't like what schools do to kids these days. Their staple produce is teenagers with horrible attitudes.

J.K. was in a state of full alert, determined to locate the trip's priority bird. It was as important to him to find the Baird's as it was to a preacher to deliver a fine Sunday sermon. He had gotten his own Baird's in July, and now he needed a semipalmated or a stilt sandpiper for his Big Year count. The sewage ponds were yielding a decent number of peeps, but none of these counted for him.

Jarring noises blasted from Rick's portable sound system, complete with mini-speakers. J.K. looked on, pained.

Next to a pond, Rick played the song of a sora in order to attract that elusive bird. At the beginning of every taped call, the narrator barked, "Sora." As soon as the song was over, Rick re-wound the tape and replayed it. The tape supposedly tricked the bird into thinking that a friend was calling, and then it would fly to the scene, only to be confused.

"It's poor form to rely on electronic devices," J.K. told Blake. It was embarrassing that the president of A.B.S. wasn't particular about ethics. J.K. wanted to confront Rick, but he avoided open battles.

"Hey Rick, I need to get those Ecuador checks out today," J.K. said.

"How many spots left?" Rick said.

"Only one as far as I know."

"Damn! I'm in, right?"

"Not until I've got your check," J.K. said in a harsher tone than he liked to use.

Many in the flock, including Dana and Frank, had clustered around Rick, but J.K. and Blake stayed away from the commotion. "The tapes are confusing, especially for the chicks," J.K. said to the boy. And they took something away from the experience of birding. It was the purist in J.K. that rebelled against electronic tricks. As aggressive as he was about pursuing birds, he also had a paternal urge to protect them. He was keeping secret the location of a family of burrowing owls in Antelope Valley, knowing that the only space they had was one undeveloped lot, and a crowd of human visitors would scare them off the property.

Rick's style of birding, of disturbing the birds as much as needed to get them to appear, was the opposite of J.K.'s philosophy. It took serious skill and patience to see birds in the wild without resorting to tricks that wasted time and energy, and treated them like toys made for human pleasure. There were birders in the L.A. bird society who were attempting a Big Year, but Rick was the only person giving J.K. real competition. J.K. felt that he would be betraying his own principles if he didn't win the Big Year. He must defeat Rick. The problem was that Rick had all the time in the world to bird, whereas J.K. needed to get hired as a postdoctoral researcher before his graduate student stipend ran out next May.

The sora had not responded. Rick turned up the volume on the tape machine. "On a recent solo trip, I played tapes for owls," he said to the birders who had gathered around him. "And a male and female owl did show up. And they stared at each other as I stood in between, clutching my sound system!"

Rick's cell phone rang. It was his wife, Meg.

"Dad wasn't well," she said. "I left early." He listened, as if wondering why she had interrupted him. "That French class we were thinking about . . ."

"Yeah?"

"Wish we'd go today to the Berlitz academy in old town," she said, "and have lunch at Mia Piace after."

"Honey, not right now." a grating note entering his voice.

"How much longer will you be?"

"Oh, I don't know," he said. "An hour or so."

"I'm hungry, but I think I can hold out. I'll wait to have lunch."

Rick's attention was diverted. A deerfly had settled on his arm, unnoticed until it stung. "Owww," he cried, swatting the fly, a drop of red blood welling up on his skin. Blake rushed forward to identify the fly. He had bought a field guide to bugs with the gift certificate the bird society gave him for raising the most money in last year's Big Day. He looked at the fly now to determine whether it was a "life bug." In the commotion, Rick turned off his phone.

Karen stewed in her jeep. Although she would prefer that Blake be a birder than a video-game addict, she wondered what meaning there was in such marathon birding. She liked watching birds herself—for about an hour. Now *that* would be a civilized way to bird!

The rest of the group continued their search, undeterred by the putrid odor, the army of bugs, or the burning sun. The only other person who had retired to her car was old Jean Savant, who came with opera glasses instead of binoculars. Jean was frail and she didn't say much. Karen wondered why Jean had bothered to come. Only when Karen saw Paul Little, Rick, Professor Kern, and Wynn posing for photos next to sewage pipes did she feel that her ordeal was nearing an end. Her vision of heaven was being back at her kitchen table, feet up, chilling with a bottle of Heineken. If Rick weren't carpooling with them, she would have yanked Blake into the slimy jeep and driven straight home. But as her last drops of patience evaporated, Blake's enthusiasm peaked. Visions of the Baird's sandpiper danced in his head with the curlew, the stilts, the scooters, and all the other birds he was spotting.

"Look, what we have here," Rick would begin, and then Blake, camera, bins, and all, would turn and scramble in Rick's direction. "Is it the Baird's? Is it the Baird's?"

Instead, a flock of phalaropes spun around in the waters of one pond like little boats. Blake stared through his scope at the soft gray birds with needle-like bills spinning in circles. He couldn't resist saying "Cool!" Behind the phalaropes, a group of black-necked stilts sauntered across the water, their pink legs gleaming in the sun. The poetry of the landscape and the birds became all one song, but Blake was too worked up to appreciate the subtleties of this beauty. The Baird's sandpiper summers on the tundra and only migrates through California on its way south. Blake dreamed of the silhouette of a slender Baird's against the shimmering water, with its longish beak and wings sticking out past its tail.

"Betcha J.K. mis-ID'd the Baird's last week," Paul Little said.

"It can't be," Blake said.

Paul Little shook his head. "He's mis-ID'd before; he's not reliable."

Blake's face darkened. He wanted to defend J.K., but couldn't think what to say.

"Dude, you learn stuff." Paul Little's voice rose. "Who's for real and who's bluffing!"

Karen was deciding whether to shower before or after the beer when Blake returned to the jeep with a defeated look on his face. "No Baird's," he said.

"It's okay," Karen said, rubbing his neck. "We tried. Let's go home now."

Blake was not cheered.

When she'd packed him into the jeep and felt that the chilled beer was all but in her hand, word came down the line that the caravan intended to make "one more stop." Immediately, all the vehicles began to drive out. Karen followed the caravan only to ask J.K. if he would give Rick a ride back to Joss Canyon.

But J.K. was driving so damned fast that soon they were at a godforsaken place in the middle of the desert where people had abandoned their raggedy sofas, corroded dishwashers, strips of graying cloth, rusted car parts, and other decaying household goods. Blake overheard talk that there was going to be a final search for the Baird's. As soon as this new hope captured him, there was no turning around.

Blake's earlier forlorn look evaporated, and he set about equipping himself for the final quest.

Karen got out of the jeep in disbelief. It was even more sweltering here than at the sewage ponds, which she hadn't thought possible. Paul Little headed with a stern expression in the direction of the garbage heap. The rest made their way to a fence with an opening cut into it where they were expected to slip through to the other side.

"The last time I was here I got arrested," J.K. said.

"And now you're telling us?" Karen just wanted to collapse somewhere. Professor Kern poked his head through the slit and then miraculously squeezed the rest of his body through. All that remained was to disentangle himself from the barbed wire that had grabbed on to his khaki clothing.

The flock followed J.K. down a desolate dirt path to what looked like the remains of a pond. The sun was so fierce that the handful of peeps in the disappearing water looked faded. Despite yelps among the group about the possibility that the bird flying about was a Baird's sandpiper, Karen could hardly stand in such burning light, much less tilt her head and look up at it. A slender peep was indeed flying from one puddle to the next, and most of the flock was determined to get a better look.

"The call," Professor Kern said, "is drier, like it's supposed to be."

Karen felt as if she'd been in a sauna all day with a sadistic attendant cranking up the heat all the time. What were these people doing? The scene before her rippled in the scorching air, and the other birders looked to her like street children in some poor country scouring garbage dumps for food. Feeling dizzy, she decided to return to the jeep. She guessed that birding had triggered a chemical imbalance in her body—she was always either too hot or too cold.

"Yes it is a Baird's! We've found the peep!" Karen heard, as she was struggling through the hole in the fence. Among the triumphant voices was her son's. "Yes! Cake!"

She turned around to look and got tangled in the barbs. Finally emerging from the nasty shortcut, she examined the bloody scratches on her arm and felt like a martyr.

A few feet ahead, Rick stood talking on his cell. "Honey, can we not discuss that now?" he was saying, wiping his face and neck with a handkerchief. His cowboy hat could have been rescued from the wardrobe of a defunct theatre company. "If I said I'd be back in an hour or so, I wasn't thinking. I didn't mean for you to starve."

Karen understood that he was talking to his wife. All the Southern California sun had not caused him to lose his cool, but now his voice was strained. In the thick of the afternoon, it was so bright that Rick wavered like a mirage in her eyes. Although normally he might have said something goofy to her, he looked at the dirt as she passed by. "I'll see ya later," he muttered into the phone. "Yeah, *now* I'll be back in an hour, counting from this second."

Karen sensed some movement in the nearby brush. She moved closer, trying to make out what bird it was. But in a moment, she was aware again of the sun on her neck like a fiery octopus, grabbing her with its burning arms. Sweat oozed down her shirt, and the clammy, airless feeling that had oppressed her all day settled on her like a wet blanket.

She gave up her search. What did she care? Why would she forsake a Saturday with her husband and daughter and drive into the blazing desert with her son in the middle of August? Was it so bad with her that she'd grab at anything to get out of the house, to not feel trapped? Why was it those nasty cowbird traps weighed on her conscience? The cowbirds were being led to the executioner's block and A.B.S. hadn't lifted a finger to save them. That was shameful! Sure, it was unsavory that cowbirds lay their eggs and leave them in the nests of birds of other species to hatch and rear. But that was nature's plan or the

Lord's plan for them. Who was Billy Grimsby to decide that the birds should be killed for doing what they'd done for a million years? Why hadn't A.B.S. confronted Billy about the mismanagement of Joss Canyon?

In wondering why the cowbird traps disturbed no one else in A.B.S., the uneasiness Karen had felt for months about the bird society found an objective to latch on. The culture within A.B.S. needed to change or this would be the last birding trip she was bringing Blake on. A.B.S. members didn't seem to care about the wellbeing of birds; they only wanted to gawk at them and make bird lists to bolster their own egos. Having resolved to speak up at the next board meeting, Karen retreated into the shade of the boiling jeep. She opened the glove compartment, but the first-aid kit was missing.

"Hey there!" Rick said, coming up to her. "After the Baird's, I'm at 302. I've just handed in my Ecuador check. Meg doesn't know yet. Hope she won't be mad . . . " He stopped when he saw her pale, clammy face. "Are you okay?"

"No, I'm not okay. I'm totally fed up." It was all Karen could do to keep from sobbing. She extended her wounded arm and Rick examined the bloodied gashes in her skin. He dug out an old alcohol swab and bandage from his bag and applied it to her arm. They said nothing to each other. She buried her face in his shoulder, stifling she didn't know what. Rick held her, though there was a flicker of surprise in his eyes. They held each other until they saw the rest of the human flock moving up in single file toward the jagged hole in the fence.

# 4

*I*t was real now. J.K. was collaborating on a physics paper with his supervisor, Dave Wagner. This, if anything, would improve his chances of getting a postdoctoral job. But would the paper get written in time? What was the root of his insecurity, the anxiety that made his stomach hurt? If he knew, he'd have pulled it out like a weed. Maybe it had to do with his father. He'd rather not bring up the guilt he experienced when he thought about his father. Then he felt defiant. His father was the one who ought to feel guilty. Why did he act as if J.K. were somehow a second-class citizen? Anne Marie's fragrance, lavender in summer, plum in winter, drifted into his mind. She didn't like him to be anxious—she assumed he'd be successful and acted surprised when he didn't play by that assumption.

J.K.'s stomach was cramping. He bought a tea at the university cafeteria. It tasted like coffee. He decided to walk over to Leaves Café.

He was glad to see Luna working behind the counter. It was a quiet hour, so she came over to say hi. "Mo' tea, Mister Ph.D.?" A smile quivered past her animated face.

Luna knew how to make his usual, a lemony blend of spearmint tea, just the way he liked it. "I've given up coffee," J.K. had told Luna a month ago, "because I already have too much energy and the caffeine keeps me up at night."

"Why the long face?" she asked him now.

"Work," he said. It was the stress of his final year as a Ph.D. candidate. He was the first in his family to venture so far into higher education. J.K.'s father, a construction worker of tight-lipped Dutch descent, would never say whether he'd completed high school. His mother became the academic in her Italian family when she went into the education field as a kindergarten teacher. Today, J.K. could taste his anxiety. He lingered with Luna.

"My supervisor gets me to do all the grunt work—the tedious calculations," he told Luna.

"Maybe you should fight him more, you know," she said, with a mock karate-chop.

*31*

"Can't afford to," he said, smiling. Luna had a way of squeezing smiles out of him, even in stressful moments. "We need to get this paper out soon, in time for my postdoc applications."

In September there was a pressure-cooker atmosphere at work. In physics, as in birding, J.K. liked to be meticulous and in control. But lately, everyone's nerves were frayed, and he was in the thick of academic warfare when he managed to piss off Dave in a diplomatic coup d'état.

J.K. disliked formal lunches because they were hard to escape, but Dave had asked him to lunch at the Faculty Club, to the envy of the German graduate student, Maurice, who loved nothing more than to sip expensive wines served by men in bow ties. Maurice's only consolation was that Dave had written his letter of recommendation already. "I tormented his secretary until she told me," Maurice told J.K.

They were in the graduate-student office, a grayish hall cluttered with desks, fake RADIATION DANGER signs, and a ratty orange carpet. J.K. was impressed—Maurice sure had a way with people when his interests were at stake. The only information J.K. had gotten out of Dave's secretary lately was how she told physicists and mathematicians apart: the physicists wore mismatched socks, whereas the mathematicians were likely to have no socks at all!

"I should ask Dave soon," J.K. said. Deadlines were approaching, but he was waiting for the perfect moment. A cold, surly Dave would write a much different letter from a warm, enthusiastic Dave. Warming up Dave was the task that lay ahead.

"You still haven't asked?" Maurice said.

"I meant to ask right after Dave and I made some progress on our paper," J.K. said. "I know I'm running out of time. I'll ask today at lunch, if Dave's in a good mood."

"What Dave writes can land you a job, or force you out of the field," Maurice said. Having failed his driver's license test three times, Maurice's only lifeline was a postdoctoral job in a city with better public transportation than Alpena. To avoid his bug-infested apartment, Maurice lived in the office, waiting for news of a postdoc offer.

"Did you get the calculation done?" Maurice said.

"I'm getting there," J.K. told him. His week had been consumed by a serpentine calculation for a minor paper he was writing with Maurice.

"I can't move forward until you get this done," Maurice said. "I'm exponentially more worried than before that the guys at Riverside will scoop us," he sighed. "Nothing gets done around here. Does Dave know about your Big Year?"

"Keeping it secret so far," J.K. said. He had explained to Maurice that a Big Year is like "extreme birding." Since it had nothing to do with physics, Maurice thought a Big Year "odd to the nth degree," and for someone who needed to get a postdoc next year, it was "borderline suicidal."

J.K. knew that without a stellar recommendation from Dave, he would have no future in physics. It was devastating to consider that a lukewarm letter could end his career and everything he had worked towards in his academic life. Starting from his last year in high school, it had taken J.K. ten years of "killer work" in physics just to get to this point. Dave had seen J.K.'s potential five years ago when Dave accepted him as a Ph.D. candidate. Dave couldn't possibly let this potential go to waste now. A part of J.K.'s safety net was the belief that Dave would do everything in his power to help launch J.K.'s career.

Dave, a lean, middle-aged man, was known in the physics community for the masterful discipline with which he had worked his way to the top. His dense eyebrows and the shadows under his sharp eyes gave him the appearance of a peregrine falcon. Like a falcon, Dave was a powerhouse and a fast worker (when he chose to be). J.K. admired his supervisor's focus, but wished he were less volatile. He would have asked Dave to write him a letter already if Dave hadn't been in a surly mood all week.

A legendary physicist was visiting from the East Coast, and J.K. spent the morning at the blackboard showing him Feynman diagrams relating to the Hierarchy Problem.

"Kaminski hasn't submitted a title for his afternoon talk," Dave complained, as he walked with J.K. to collect the visitor for lunch.

At J.K.'s suggestion, the three of them ate in the open courtyard of the Faculty Club. The light was soft with intermittent bursts of sunlight, as though autumn would not arrive until she had her fill of hide-and-seek. While the older men studied the menu, J.K. picked up the calls of mo-does (mourning doves), mo-birds (mocking birds), peeks (parakeets), and other regulars around the courtyard. He waited for the right moment to ask Dave for the recommendation letter.

"What I don't understand," Kaminski said, turning his pork-chop face to J.K., "is what's the reason for the cancellation? Suppose I add in higher-dimension operators. At what level is a quadratic divergence introduced?"

J.K. began to tell the story Dave and he had come up with to explain the mass scales of particles, but Kaminski cut him short.

"I dealt with that in my '92 paper," Kaminski said.

Dave shut his falcon eyes at Kaminski's challenge. Now he put forward his theory for what protects the Higgs mass from gravitational corrections. "We've hedged our bets," he said.

The conversation shifted away from the Hierarchy Problem, and Dave vented about the Bush administration's callous attitude towards science. J.K. birded by ear without taking his eye off the older men. He picked out the buzzing call of a MacGillivray's warbler. While Kaminski condemned the recent cutbacks in science, J.K. guessed that the warbler was calling from the east, from among the rose bushes or near the sumac trees.

Later, when Dave asked for the bill, J.K. was eager to vanish. Dave was in an off-mood anyhow—no point asking him for the letter today. But pork-chop face chose that moment to speculate on whether their model was experimentally excluded. J.K. was obliged to give an intelligent response while Dave looked on appraisingly. Sandwiched between two giants in the field, J.K. spoke carefully to avoid tripping.

The men walked back to the Physics building listening to J.K. defend the cancellation of quadratic divergences. Dave let him do most of the talking, and J.K. fielded the rapid-fire questions as best he could. Kaminski argued about an obscure technicality, forcing Dave to step in. They got out of the elevator.

"Does your model produce jets?" Kaminski barked.

"Jets?" Dave said. He paused because he hadn't quite looked into the matter. Kaminski sensed his hesitation. "We've got jets coming out of our ears," Dave shrugged. "But the QCD background is too large. You'll never see a signal."

"I'll have a surprise for you boys in my talk," Kaminski said, winking.

The talk was at 4 p.m., and J.K. was relieved to see old pork-chop disappear into the visitor's office to print out transparencies.

As J.K. walked into the graduate student office, Maurice looked up from his computer and asked which wine they had ordered. When J.K. said he hadn't noticed, Maurice let out a dissatisfied snort. "By the way," he added, glancing down at a piece of scrap paper, "Ed called about a red-faced warbler in Baldwin Park, and he has a Least Bell's vireo."

"A Bell's? Dang!" If J.K. had seen the vireo, it would have brought his Big Year count up to 314. All weekend, he had roamed empty fields for a Least Bell's vireo, in between trips to beaches to look for shorebirds. But the Bell's vireo, an endangered species, had eluded him. He could normally find at least one Bell's at Joss Canyon, but this year, despite the cowbird-control program that was supposed to help the vireos breed, the birds seemed to have vanished.

J.K. flew to the phone to return Ed McCoy's call. He cursed himself for not being able to afford a cell phone, requiring his birding contacts to call the graduate student office. He knew the calls gave Maurice the impression that his birding was interfering with his physics. But other graduate students had their quirks. Tim came to the office at 10 p.m. to start his day. But Tim might not have a career in physics, whereas J.K. considered himself in a different league. Neil did physics at Leaves Café in the morning, came to work after lunch, and stayed until nine when no one else was around. Idiosyncrasies were to be expected from physicists. But a secondary passion for birds was time-consuming.

If J.K.'s friends called in the morning with an important bird sighting, he weighed the risks of leaving during lunch. Today, tragically, his lunch break was used up, and only an emergency bird like the Bell's vireo could cause him to sacrifice an afternoon's work. He calculated that if he raced out immediately to Ken Malloy Harbor State Park, where Ed had seen the bird, he could be back almost in time for Kaminski's talk. The MacGillivray's warbler on campus could wait and so could the red-faced warbler, even though they were also count birds for J.K's Big Year. Having combed the county for a Least Bell's vireo all weekend, he couldn't let it slip away when it was within reach. Ed had told him that landing excruciatingly difficult birds is what gives the edge to a Big Year winner, and without J.K.'s network of spotters, Rick might not be able to score such an elusive bird on his own.

"I have to take care of this," J.K. said. "The Bell's endangered . . ."

"So is our paper," Maurice said. "We need to make it appear . . . like, *before* I get rejected for postdocs."

J.K. promised to forgo sleep if need be to finish their calculation. But his colleague's spotted face remained grim.

J.K. realized Maurice might not forgive him this abandonment. But what could he do? Give up the Big Year? It was like asking him to tear out his soul (if such a thing existed) from his body. He would sooner die.

And yet to live, he had to land a job in physics.

As J.K. drove to Ken Malloy Harbor State Park, he was aware that even speeding, the round trip was nearly two hours. Adding in the time it might take to track down the vireo, it would take a miracle to get back in time for Kaminski's talk. Dave had a thing about punctuality, and it would be unforgivably bad form to be late today, because there seemed to be an overlap in the talk and the paper he and Dave were working on. J.K. had toyed with the idea of doing a Big Year since he entered graduate school, but physics always got in the way. He liked to keep his conscience clear about how much time he spent away from physics.

The 110 Freeway seemed too congested when J.K. considered what Dave might think if he found out that he was gone chasing after a bird. If only he could explain to Dave that last year's Big Year winner, Ed McCoy, *quit his job* to optimize his birding! If a friend called Ed with a bird sighting, Ed dropped everything to see it.

The low-fuel indicator came on and J.K. looked at it with dismay. Swerving to the right, he exited on to a pot-holed surface street in the barrio near downtown Los Angeles. He had no sooner filled the gas tank and was heading back to the freeway when a bad smell, like burnt rubber, wafted in. He swore and pulled over. The tires didn't look so bad, and there was no smoke coming from the engine. He realized the smell wasn't coming from his car, but from a nearby bakery. Jumping back into the old Honda, he sped on.

J.K. had led several bird walks in Ken Molloy Harbor State Park, and he knew exactly which thicket of bushes at the end of the second pond Ed must have been near when he saw the Bell's vireo. Hiking past the first pond, J.K. approached the second. An egret with a bristly white crest was clawing the edge of the water with one foot. The beauty of water and greenery was spoiled by a glaring Target storefront in the distance. He stood still, hoping to hear the bird. But the vireo did not oblige. All he needed was one glance. A grayish-white bird, the vireo is about the size of a warbler, but with a stouter bill and a long tail that flicks handsomely.

Just take wing and fly here, J.K. thought. He wished the vireo wouldn't tease him today. He needed to get back in time for Kaminski's talk. As J.K. scanned the surrounding foliage, he could imagine a vireo inspecting leaves, top and bottom, for insect larvae. The vireo might cock its head at any moment and grace him with a sighting.

But things rarely come easy in moments of desperation. The bird wasn't cooperating. J.K. circled the park once, and then again, and spotted practically every other bird he'd ever seen here, all but the vireo. September was prime birding season and he ought to be getting more birds for his Big Year count. In the last four weeks, he'd gotten seven birds. At 313, his count felt static. No one could fault him for being less than meticulous. He normally called the Bird-Box hotline from the closest payphone he came across. On weekends, he was usually in the middle of nowhere, in remote fields or beaches, or in a phone booth calling one of his friends to see if they had leads. Depending on the month, J.K. did a loop of five or more parks on both days of the weekend. In August and September, he was more likely to get rare shorebirds, so he hung around places like Piute Ponds unless he'd gotten a message on his home phone, in which case he bee-lined to wherever a target bird had been spotted. In October, he was more likely to find a rare warbler, so he planned to stick to park areas. He stayed away from places frequented by birders, because if Ed McCoy were leading a group somewhere, he'd alert J.K. if he saw something special. There was no point in having two pairs of eyes after the same quarry. At night, especially on weekends, J.K. spent an hour on the phone networking with birding friends. Each conversation started with "So, do you have anything for me?"

There was no sign of the Bell's vireo. Tonight Ed's voice would have a mocking lilt when he found out that J.K. hadn't spotted the vireo. Annoyed, J.K. looked at the time and considered leaving when a voice called, "J.K.!" startling him.

The man was squatting behind some bushes. A familiar figure to anyone who had birded in Los Angeles for a couple of years, Paul Little left long messages on the Bird Box that were of interest only to himself. Recently he had left an excited message about two banded-tail pigeons mating near Torrance Toyota, where he helped convert nonfunctioning cars into scrap metal. Apparently, he lived with his aging mother, and had self-published a book of eco-poetry.

"What you looking for?" Paul Little said, pulling up his pants as he emerged.

"Just looking . . . for anything good," J.K. told him.

"Maybe I can help?" he said, shuffling over.

J.K. shook his head in irritation, realizing that Paul Little used public lands as dumping grounds. This man was the nemesis of any trip leader because of the false calls he made. If he called out a rufous-crowned sparrow during a trip, it was invariably a juvenile white-crowned. Paul was like a cowbird—there was something ugly or clumsy about the shape of his head and body. He was considered a pest by many of the other birders who were generally upper middle-class. The way Paul was always on the lookout for a ride was almost parasitic, but he was also tenacious like a cowbird. He considered himself a vital part of the birding community, whether or not others shared his opinion.

"Ed was snooping round here earlier," Paul Little said. "I figured he got somethin' cool."

"Bell's vireo." J.K. knew that Paul Little wouldn't stop nagging until he found out.

"Muy bien." Taking hold of J.K.'s sleeve, Paul Little urged him deep into the forested area past the willows. He confided that because of his way of life, he saw birds most people missed.

"I would've got the vireo at Joss Canyon," J.K. said. "But it's changed.

After the fire . . ."

"It'll get better," Paul Little said. "The construction's stopped. That's the main thing!"

J.K. looked at him curiously. He'd heard speculation that Paul Little had a hand in the fire. Billy Grimsby had planned to replace the modest Nature Center, which also served as the home of the Alpena Bird Society, with a series of structures that some people feared would rob the canyon of its wild beauty. Billy's ambitious project was halted a year ago when a fire had burned through Joss Canyon.

Paul Little chattered on and walked so noisily that J.K. was sure he had frightened the poor vireo out of the park. "Ladder-back woodpecker!" Paul called out.

J.K. looked at the bird in a barren tree. "It's a Nuttall's."

"No, it's not," Paul Little insisted, hands on his boxy stomach. "They have ladder-backs in this area." The bird produced a long, lazy drumming sound.

"Can't get any more Nuttall's than that," J.K. said.

Disgusted, Paul Little said, "I'm gonna find that vireo."

A twenty-minute search yielded nothing, however, but a headache for J.K., a damn cowbird trap, and the conviction in J.K. that there was something strange about Paul Little. The latter was filing his nails using a tool in his Swiss army knife. Saying that he had to get back to work, J.K. began to move toward his car, but Paul Little followed him.

"Would you drop me off at one of the beaches?"

"I can't," J.K. told him. "I'm late already."

"I don't need to go to Malibu. Santa Monica is fine. I could show you this bridge that gets a lot of bats. Muy bien." J.K. declined the invitation, but Paul Little grew aggressive. "I'm only trying to help," he said, grabbing J.K.'s arm, the knife still in Paul's other hand.

"I'll get fired if I don't get back to work," J.K. said.

"I really have to get to Malibu. I'm stranded here."

"Sorry, man." J.K. wrenched himself free and hurried to his car, feeling that some hungry monster was devouring his hours, one after another.

Paul Little looked on sullenly. "Shit, man, you're just like the rest of them!" he spat out.

His count still at 313, J.K. walked in twenty minutes late to Dr. Kaminski's talk.

Maurice smirked when J.K. entered, then cleared his throat, which caused Dave to look up. Seeing J.K. hurry to the back and sink, exhausted, into a chair, a look of irritation came into Dave's eyes.

On the board, Kaminski was presenting an improved calculation of mono-jets—the surprise he had mentioned. J.K. winced. This meant that their model was predicting phenomenon that had already been excluded at the Tevatron collider. Here was one more thing he and Dave would have to worry about before they could start writing their paper. It might take a couple of weeks at the least to iron out this kink, and he would miss some important deadlines if he waited that long to ask Dave for a recommendation letter.

In his gray office surrounded by gray corridors, nary a window anywhere, J.K. felt his unshaven facial hair pricking him. Something like a goatee covered his chin. He thought of Luna that morning. The memory of her voice was refreshing, and resembled the light in Malibu at dawn.

Anne Marie had wanted them to become engaged because her father was conservative about such things, but J.K. wondered if that was a necessary step to take. What was engagement? Or marriage? Those things weren't real in today's world. She already had his commitment. Why did she need anything else? He was so busy right now, he was thinking of cancelling his September trip to New Brunswick. But last night, they'd had a disturbing conversation, which made him decide that he should visit her after all.

"How long have you known this Luna girl?" Anne Marie said over the phone.

"A few months, I guess."

"And you're like . . . friends?"

At first, J.K. was amused. "You don't have to worry," he said. "After I met you, every other girl just slides past my vision like oil over water."

"Her vision was zeroed in on you," she insisted. "The way you look at birds, that's how she was eyeing you!"

J.K. laughed, but then, feeling defensive, he spoke tensely. "That's just plain delusional," he said. "I've no idea what you're talking about."

In his office, J.K. checked his email every five minutes. He had emailed an early draft of the paper to Dave and was waiting to hear from him. His morning slipped by in this state of anxiety. If only he could have gone birding instead! But Dave might crash into his office at any second, and J.K. didn't want to miss him. The thought flashed through his mind that Dave looked like his own father. There was some resemblance in the severe triangular face and the stiff gray hair. And maybe in their stiff hearts. J.K.'s fruitless attempts to do the right thing for his father's approval somehow never measured up.

He allowed himself a quick walk to Leaves Café to pick up some tea. A glance at Luna got him thinking that she represented everything his parents lacked. She was warm, curvy, amorphous, ambiguous, open. He checked himself. He rarely thought so much about Anne Marie. For that matter, he didn't think about any other girl either. To J.K., Luna was more of a tomboy in an anime film than a girl.

When he returned to his office, there was still no email from Dave.

But there was a rejection from a teaching college he had applied to. He was furious that such a place, where he would never have gone, should reject him!

The office door burst open. Dave, at last! No, it was Maurice.

"Care for some pizza, dude?" Maurice said. "It's cold, but it's free."

After lunch, J.K. walked into Dave's office and popped the question.

He received a chilly response.

"Sure I'll write you a letter," Dave said without enthusiasm. Turning his wiry back to J.K., he added, "And now, if you'll excuse me, I can't be late for my class."

J.K. stiffened and nodded mechanically. Something was being lost in that moment. Something slid away. He must grasp it again, but how? Not with Dave's back to him.

In a forlorn mood, J.K. made his way to the graduate student office, but seeing Maurice at his desk, he turned around and instead walked on towards Leaves Café, hoping that Luna might still be there.

Had Dave been irritated only in the moment? After all the work they had done together, Dave would surely cover for him. Dave would write him a good letter. But doubt travelled through J.K.'s insides. He wondered about his obsession with birding. Was he using it as a distraction, chasing his own tail? Where did he expect this Big Year to get him? Were there signs even now that birding would compromise his physics work? And yet, J.K. couldn't stop. His father was bitter about how his life turned out. J.K. was determined not to go down that path. He had been among the best physics students, and he would keep that up. Anything short of that was being mediocre. The field was too competitive, on the razor's edge between discovery and futility. If you weren't among the best, you were nothing. The thought of being anything like his father constricted J.K.'s throat.

If Anne Marie were to begin doubting him too, that would hurt. She wanted him to tone down his birding, to focus on school. That was the rational thing to do, after all. But that was the problem—everything about his life was so rational. Physics could be counterintuitive. He liked that. But the pressure to publish and to give talks, and the job applications, he could do without. Anne Marie wanted him to sharpen up, to keep an eye on his career. Her father, an economist, had drilled into her the importance of such things.

Birding, however, was the one thing that connected him to whatever was mysterious inside him, to his curiosity about the natural world and what made it tick. As much as he was determined to escape the failure that was destroying his father, birding was the one thing J.K. was not willing to sacrifice.

# 5

$\mathcal{A}$nne Marie considered his goatee with some disapproval. "It's so not you," she said. In contrast to his unkempt look, she'd had her shoulder-length hair styled at a salon.

"I got lazy," J.K. said. "I'll shave it after Christmas." In the harsh industrial light of the Newark airport, his sweetheart now seemed somehow less familiar. Her dark eyes met his coolly. A month had passed since they'd last seen each other, and it was evident, even when she met him at the airport, that they had each changed by a few degrees.

In the windy September afternoon, they hurried to the parking lot. When they got into her dad's silver Lexus, she giggled and reached over from the driver's seat to kiss him. He pulled her close and didn't let go until she complained that she would pass out from carbon monoxide poisoning.

That night they snuggled in her living room, on the gray sofa with clean lines. The coffee table was metal, from a design store. On the walls were three paintings, in navy and gold, in which human and animal figures were rendered in sharp angles. J.K. filled her in on his significant sightings in the last month.

"What's the best bird you saw?" Anne Marie said.

"I don't know. I never think like that. I'm dying to get a Bell's vireo though."

"After Christmas, you'll be done with birds for a while?"

"Except this one," he said, pulling her into his lean arms. He then began to kiss her.

"This one's special," Anne Marie said in a coquettish voice. "Don't get her confused with the other birds you see."

"I won't."

Later, he curled up like a child in her bed. He felt more at home in her apartment than at his parents' place. He planned to relax here (and do physics) and hadn't told his parents about this trip. He'd see them for Christmas anyway. He guessed that Anne Marie had expectations for this weekend—the third anniversary of their relationship. He hadn't had a chance to buy a ring for her. He thought of it as a friendship ring, not an engagement ring. He felt that ideally, their affection should be a gift enough for both of them. He didn't see the point in accumulating doo-dads and such.

In bed that night, J.K. wondered if Anne Marie would bring up the subject of their engagement. This is where they had the majority of their discussions, in the dark. He flirted with the idea of bringing it up. It might soften her before he let her know he planned to do physics all weekend. But since all he had to offer her was a silvery trinket (which he hadn't bought yet), maybe he should avoid the subject. When even she didn't bring it up, he wondered if she had forgotten her whim of getting engaged on their third anniversary. This disinterest made him lose any inclination he might have had to buy her a campus-bazaar ring.

The next day, as he'd planned, he mainly did physics in her apartment. When she asked if there were any news about his job search, however, bitter thoughts seized him.

"I have no idea what's going on," he said, "and Dave's been kind of distant lately."

That evening, they attended a reception at her college for pre-veterinary students.

Anne Marie, in a short skirt and a blouse of blue Indian silk, sat at a bay window; there she held court with an eager group of male students. The heating system was broken in the bare, soulless hall, and the meager snacks consisted of crackers, celery, and an unlimited supply of cheap alcohol. Every time Anne Marie drained her glass of wine, she handed it to J.K. to refill. He was ill at ease in her crowd and, as the evening progressed, he became concerned that she was getting plastered.

The night grew late. At one point, he said, "Let's go."

"I'm not done yet," she said. "Why don't you get yourself a drink?"

After a long day of birding, he liked a chilled beer, but otherwise he wasn't much of a drinker. He'd lost his taste for alcohol after the car accident that killed his sister. He wandered out of the reception hall. Why didn't he think of her by name anymore? She didn't deserve to lose her individuality in his mind only because she had died. Truthfully, he avoided thinking about Emma; it kept his guilt under control. His shoes were getting wet from walking on a muddy lawn. A fresh shower drove him back to the reception hall. Then he sat alone in a corner and waited for Anne Marie to be "done."

Anne Marie was apologetic when she came to collect him for the drive home. "I was just hanging out with my class," she told him. "You didn't have to sulk."

Adjusting the leather seat, Anne Marie added, "I'd love to spend a few days in Manhattan around Christmas."

"Manhattan?" J.K. said, surprised. "It'll be a hassle to book rooms, not to mention expensive."

"They're doing War and Peace at the MET, which I'd like to check out."

"I haven't read the novel."

"I haven't either," she said, "but it doesn't matter. It's going to be a big production, with live horses. I also want to go to the Pure Food and Wine restaurant, which I keep hearing fabulous things about." Now she hinted that this could be his engagement present for her.

"What engagement?" he said, because he disliked the uncertainty that dinosauric question had caused him.

She looked hurt. "Okay, so you don't want to get engaged. I'm not going to push it. And you don't want to do anything special over the holidays either."

J.K. wasn't enthusiastic about her Manhattan idea and was feeling too distracted to plan an extravagance. "December's going to be crazy," he muttered. He hoped she would change her mind. He was, in fact, thinking that on New Year's Day, he'd finally be sure of his Big Year victory. Other than that, all he cared about was spending time with her, and it didn't matter if they were in New Brunswick or someplace else. He didn't see why they should throw money at hotel rooms when they could stay with his parents or at her apartment over the holidays.

"This isn't about birds," she said. Her voice shook as if she were going to cry. "I'm just going to stay with Dad over the holidays if you're not planning anything special for us." She unlocked her front door and gloomily led the way into her apartment.

J.K. followed, letting his jacket slip to the floor, while she carefully hung up her embroidered handbag.

"I'm just not in the right mood to plan a vacation right now, and I can't afford it. If I had the money . . ."

"You always bring up money! We never do anything because you can't afford it. And then you complain when my dad says that money is important."

"That's not fair. I invited you to travel with me this summer."

"I told you I'm working through the summer. And you don't want to travel with me—you want a birding trip. I'd rather go to Europe." Her face lost its color and she stared at him with blank, vacant eyes. She became unnaturally calm.

"Let's order some pizza," he said. "I'm hungry." It would be a mistake to fight hunger; he'd say something he'd later regret.

Later that night, as they lay in bed, she commented that he seemed to be in low spirits. "Why is it that we can't have fun even at a party?"

In his plain way, he confided to her that he *was* worried about his job prospects. "I've gotten a couple more early rejections," he said. "I hope Dave didn't write me a crappy letter—he's unpredictable." The blue nightlight gave the room a chilly glow, making the abstract gold motifs on the bedspread look neon. "I'm going to be in deep shit if a job doesn't pan out."

"I wish I could say something that would help," she said. "It seems like this problem has been going on forever. I really don't know what to say, except 'Never say never' . . . or some stupid cliché like that."

She was in no mood to talk any more about the subject, and he had enough pride not to bring it up again.

They hardly spoke at all the next morning. They were listless and miserable in her apartment. He tried to do more physics, but couldn't really focus.

"It's not working out," she said. "I'm really sorry." She was breaking up with him.

His poor gray eyes flinched. "Are you serious?" he said, feeling numb. If it weren't for the raw look on her face, he would have believed she was playing a cruel joke. A faint ringing in his ears and the redness on her face told him otherwise.

"Why now, out of the blue?" he said. "Because we didn't have fun at that party?"

"Because you don't have any energy for me."

"Energy? What? Are you doing this on a whim? You decelerate from a hundred to zero without any warning?"

"I can't even talk to you without feeling like some clock is ticking."

"What clock?"

"What clock? Your physics clock! Your birding clock! You walk around with a massive clock on your face. I feel like I'm in this time machine, and if I talk one second too many, you'll be late for something, and a chute will come down and slice me in two. You have this long look on your face, like I'm talking too much. I'm very familiar with that look."

"You know, this *is* an important year in my life. The Big Year is more important than anything I've ever done other than physics . . . and you. And there is a lot of pressure at work—any average person would break down under the strain."

"I know. I know." She was normally particular about her grooming, but now her hair looked wild from not having combed it; she must have been pondering the break-up all night. For a few moments, his ears went deaf. He saw only her lips, shiny with plum gloss, flapping up and down.

He wasn't sure he heard anything more, but she also said something about them not doing fun things together and it being really hard for her to adjust to the notion of her boyfriend being "weak." He had always been the strong one in their relationship, the one who knew his mind, their bedrock. But lately he'd been so unsure of himself, she saw him as becoming weak.

"Because I'm worried about my job prospects, I'm weak?" he said. "I thought girls like sensitive guys."

She let out a tired smile. "I've thought about this. It's not easy for me. I mean, you're really nice, probably the nicest guy I've ever gone out with—that's why our relationship lasted this long."

"You mean you were burnt out after dating Mr. Wharton Finance Student? But now you've found your stride again?"

"That's not fair. You cringe when I say the M-word. And even if you didn't, you're so not into living the sort of life that makes me feel comfortable. I've never liked roughing it, and I've been honest with you about that. There's no point in letting you suffer."

"But you *are* making me suffer." He clutched her arm, apparently too firmly, because she wrenched it away. Then she looked apologetic, as if admitting that she knew he was gentle and that she was the one who had momentarily incited this violence in him.

"Women want it both ways," he said. "They want their guy to be rock-solid strong, and they want this macho monster to treat them with delicacy and respect."

She laughed. "Now you're philosophizing! Haven't done that in a while!"

"Okay, I'll be specific. I've always treated you as an equal. To behave any differently would never occur to me."

"Nor should it."

"Yeah, but when I'm having a hard time, this economics professor's daughter can't stomach the future of a jobless boyfriend hanging out at her place."

"Don't bring my dad into this."

"Your dad has always been in the middle of this." He swallowed hard. "How would you feel if the circumstances were reversed and *you* were feeling uncertain about your future—and I chose that moment to break up with you?"

"Look at it like this," Anne Marie said. "You didn't lose a lot of money on me."

"What?"

"You only visited three times last year, and you got to see your parents one time, and you also birded the other two times. And when I visited, you hardly ever spent a dime."

"Why are you talking of our relationship in terms of money?"

"No, it's not like that. I'm just pointing this out to make you feel better."

"That doesn't make me feel better." Listening to her, J.K.'s very blood had turned sour.

They spoke so rationally that it was depressing. He wished he could rouse himself into anger, but he felt too dog-tired to fight. Maybe she was right and he had grown weak. He no longer felt as hopeful as he had a year ago, and now he was fool enough to confide that to Anne Marie.

"I sensed that," she said, his newest admission further validating her decision. "And there's also this undercurrent in you," she continued. "It's like there's always something eating at you, something that pulls you down, that pulls us both down, so that we can't have fun even though we try."

His heart was dissolving into the acid that had replaced his blood. How did Anne Marie know? In three years, he had never really told Anne Marie the whole story around his sister Emma. Anne Marie and he had created a relationship of weekend honeymoons—there hadn't been an occasion to talk about Emma. "I've tried to protect you from all that," he said, almost under his breath. "I guess it didn't work."

Ultimately, there was nothing else to do but to give up. Maybe she was right. He thought about it for awhile, and then said, "I'll miss you."

"Me, too."

She planned to join some college friends at a party and offered to drop him at the airport on the way, but he declined. She got into the shower and came out in a navy and gold dress that matched the paintings in the living room.

"I'll be gone in an hour," J.K. said. But she urged him to stay on in her apartment for as long as he needed.

After she left, he went downstairs for a cup of coffee. He hadn't had coffee in months and it made his stomach queasy. He wandered the streets feeling chilled to the marrow. His bird society sweater had holes in it and the vireo logo was nearly smudged out. Most of his clothes were worn and coming apart. He had stopped noticing these things.

He returned to Anne Marie's apartment and sank into the couch. He couldn't imagine why he'd felt at home in this apartment. Now it felt stiff and cool, like a hotel lobby. He took a shower and fled in a cab to the airport.

They had spent three-and-a-half years of their lives together. Even though she had been a continent away most of that time, she was woven into his every thought. As he drove, he wondered if she would change her mind. He would have taken her to Manhattan if he'd known it meant that much. He choked up, envisioning her saying, "I was wrong. I can't live without you. I want to be with you always." But he knew that something had snapped between them, and they could never go back to the fantasy they had shared.

# 6

*R*ick got no sleep that night. He woke up feeling miserable, as if he were drowning. At breakfast, he munched Total cereal splashed with milk. Meg wanted him to abandon his Big Year. Had he fought so hard for so long, just to back out at this late stage?

Despite J.K.'s obvious skill, Rick considered him overrated. J.K. was running this race on adrenalin and anchovies (a disgusting habit). Rick wondered if J.K. had the capacity for the prepared toil he was putting in. He doubted it.

For Rick, the prospect of celebrating his Big Year victory with the Ecuador trip was sacrosanct. He mulled over his responsibilities as President—the board meetings he chaired, the monthly speakers he drummed up, the communications with other Chapters, appeals for money, and the upcoming Centennial. It was an endless labor to keep A.B.S. from collapsing.

"It's tiring you out," Meg said.

The bad spells between his wife and him usually lasted no more than ten days, but this time the days dragged on like alligators with their jaws locked at his feet. After the Piute Ponds trip, Meg fought with him. She grew shrill as a jaybird when he confessed to having paid for the Ecuador trip without first conferring with her. All Rick had hoped was that she would be caught up in a good mystery book when he got home and would shrug off the necessity of his going to Ecuador. But it became the beginning of an especially bad spell.

He lamented that Meg was in an ugly mood. She was cramping his style. When he first brought up the Ecuador trip, she balked at the expense, and he thought it best to let the matter rest until she was in a more receptive mood. But a good opportunity had eluded him and he'd run out of time. He meant to win the Big Year and had scrimped to treat himself to the ten-day trip as a victory lap. On the last weekend to submit checks, he'd asked J.K. to take his word and reserve him a spot, but the bastard wouldn't agree. Rick had had no choice but to pull out his checkbook and write a check for $6,000. He'd signed the check with a nervous flourish. He might not hear the end of this. But he wanted his g-r-a-t-i-f-i-c-a-t-i-o-n, thank you very much.

Meg signed up for a French class; she was sorry Rick couldn't. The week-nights the class was offered didn't coincide with the nights on which Rick at-tended A.B.S. meetings or went owling, so now it was a rare weeknight when they crossed paths. He suspected that her mother had goaded Meg to make life difficult for him. He saw a look in Meg's eye that usually had to do with her mother. Now that Meg's parents were old, she had forgotten their mutually trou-bled past, treated them like angels, and even valued their advice.

"What's on your mind?" Rick asked her as they carpooled from work one September evening.

Meg gave a start, like a cowbird caught pushing an egg out of a nest. She mumbled that it was nothing. But he persisted, and after some hesitation, she spoke. "I was thinking about . . . when you asked for exclusive access to me."

"Oh yeah," Rick said. " 'It's time to catch fish or cut bait.' "

It was Meg's favorite story. She was dating three men, or sometimes it was "several men," when she met Rick. But after no more than three months of see-ing her, Rick demanded "exclusive access." She always told the story with a twinkle in her eye, but today she ended on a sour note. "If I'd known what you'd do with exclusive access . . ."

Worry sprung up inside Rick. Was she going to divorce him? It would be just like her to do something that impulsive. The worry took root and began to nag at him. Lately she had been sitting on emotional junk, not processing it, and then flaring up without warning. How could she forget their summer so fast? He had even left L.A. county for six days for a trip to Oregon in July. There he birded most mornings, and in the evenings he treated her to the Asheville Shakespeare festival. Then fall, a swell time for birders, crept in like fog be-tween them. Meg was burying something. He must deal with the situation now or Meg would whack him with a major flare up. Her parents had gotten along poorly when she was a kid, and she grew used to surviving her home life by denying it.

Rick signaled to get off the freeway and then he drove up to Alpena. "Seems like you've been kinda upset off and on," he said. "Don't take this the wrong way, but would it help you to see a psychiatrist?"

"Oh, great. Thanks a lot," Meg said. "I'm saying that *you* have a problem, that you're not *present* for us, and you throw it right back at me? Just 'cause you have a depression issue doesn't mean you get to diagnose the rest of the world, too."

Rick drove into the underground garage of their condo building. "You're not exactly the rest of the world," he said quietly.

As usual, they didn't turn on the stove. Instead, they ate a dinner of bread, cheese, and wine. Meg had adopted this French habit long before she began language lessons. On evenings when he'd rather have hot food, they walked to a soup-and-sandwich place or to a cheap, ethnic restaurant.

"I've always been real easy," Meg said, drinking her supermarket wine too fast. "And I resent that you're trying to make a psychotic case out of me. I think you have a real problem. You can't do a Big Year, *and* be the president of A.B.S., *and* have the kind of relationship your wife wants. You'll have to make some choices."

She said it in such a threatening tone that he dared not ask what would happen if he didn't. She watched him all the next morning, keen as an eagle, expecting a concession.

Rick understood that Meg had backed him into a corner and that he had no choice but to relent to her longstanding demand to either give up his Big Year or resign as president.

Three years ago, when A.B.S. was on the brink of folding, Zanne McDonald, the newsletter editor, and Frank Leeds, the treasurer, had recruited Rick to be President. Including him, there had been only three board members then. Rick first joined A.B.S. simply to find the best places to bird. There was no cheaper source of information than the best birders in town. He liked going to the monthly talks because they had good slide shows and, over brownies and coffee, he became part of the buddy system that existed among the most knowledgeable members. A few months after he joined, they needed organizational help. He gave them a hand, thinking that the best of the bargain was still his; the free birding trips were well worth the occasional volunteer work. But then one president had moved away and another died, and to his surprise, Rick had been called upon to fill the post. The more he accomplished, the more his responsibilities increased. But what else was he to do?

"In three more years, we'll be a hundred years old," Zanne had told him then.

Rick had worried that if he walked away and let A.B.S. fold, the ghosts of all the presidents going back ninety-seven years would haunt him. He'd given a few birding classes at first to encourage new members to join A.B.S. It pleased him to discover he had natural leadership skills and a way with people. Apart from his administrative duties, it was a tradition for the president to lead a monthly bird walk at the local nature center. He'd enjoyed the easy walk and came to know all the birds at Joss Canyon and their perches in his sleep. Of course, that was before the fire changed everything.

They had more board members now, but the survival of the society was still far from secure. There were continuing episodes of financial despair. Last June, at the end of their official season, he conferred with Frank Leeds, the treasurer, and learned that the A.B.S. bank account held the sum of $481.35. That much and more was owed to the printer of their newsletter, *The Vireo.*

Last year, their chief fundraiser had been cute, ten-year-old Blake Mercer. But his voice would crack one of these days, and then where would they be? The newsletter bills were rarely paid on time, and the printer was threatening to drop them from his client list. The bank account was practically zeroed-out every time a bill was paid, and A.B.S. was spiraling around the brink of collapse like a tetherball.

At the breakfast table, Meg finished her cranberry-almond cereal and wiped her mouth with a tissue. She waited for his decision.

"All right," Rick said, slurping the last of his milk. "I'm going to resign as president."

"Is that a promise?" she said.

He nodded and kissed her plump cheek.

"Oh, I'm glad," she said. "Glad you're done with all that. Now we'll have some time to go out to dinner . . . with friends." Her face flashed pink, then white. She choked something down, unable to speak.

Rick walked up the stone staircase to the towering wood doors of the Alpena Presbyterian Church. He had come early to the September board meeting. He ate his last bite of sandwich and looked up at the blue and purple sky with wistful eyes. It was nearly seven, but the day's last light lingered. He walked into the church with a bundle of mail under his arm. He had picked up the mail at the trailer outpost that replaced the Joss Canyon Nature Center after the fire. He knew from experience that the pile was full of advertisements and letters about planning committees he was invited to join. As president, he had to read it all and respond. He also kept abreast of conservation issues so as to not cut a sorry figure when talking to other chapters, or when he was asked to send letters to legislators. He didn't see the need to tell Meg that since he would no longer be president, now he would have more time to focus on his Big Year. Now he could choose to bird by himself when he pleased without worrying about to which inane letter he had not yet responded, and to what event he must send a proxy.

Rick had emailed Frank Leeds to alert him that he wanted a word in private before the others arrived. It was best to get the resignation over with right before the first board meeting of their fiscal year. But now that Rick was faced with doing it, he felt almost sorry.

Frank was in the church's boardroom, rearranging the mahogany chairs around the stately table, when Rick entered. Frank was a member of the church vestry, and after the Nature Center burned down, he had strong-armed the church into letting the displaced bird society use this grand room for their meetings.

"Hola there!" Rick said. His easy cheer felt awkward now.

Frank paused, and then muttered, "Hola." He was a pasty-looking man in his late sixties with a full shock of white hair.

Rick took off his blue Alpena Bird Society sweater and pulled the chair away from the head of the table. On the walls hung gilded-frame portraits of pastors with melancholy expressions. A man was nothing but a ten-year-old boy who no longer had his priorities straight. There was a history of depression in his family, and he tried his damned best not to succumb. He had suffered enough setbacks in life, and now at forty-three, he must acknowledge his priorities. Wasn't it better to be a ten-year-old at heart than a forty-plus man hurtling towards a numbing middle age?

"I thought we might have a little heart-to-heart," he said.

Frank grinned uneasily. "Okay," he said in his particular way, drawing out the syllables as far as he could. His lips moved little when he spoke, and his waxy skin glistened in the light of the spidery chandelier that loomed above.

"Actually, I should come to the point, before someone else walks in."

"Is it our accounts?" Frank said.

"Not really. It's more to do with me."

Frank looked at him, not understanding. "Is Meg okay?"

Rick contorted his tanned face. "Okay-ish. With all I've been doing the last few years to keep A.B.S. going, I guess we haven't had a lot of time together."

"Or so she says!" Frank quipped.

But Rick's face remained serious. "The truth is, I'm sort of burned out."

"Oh-oh."

"I don't think I can be president anymore," Rick said. "And this isn't about my Big Year." The old man stared at Rick with a clammy, surprised face. "I was thinking that you might like to take over," Rick added.

"Me?" Frank said in a bloodless way.

Rick nodded.

"You've got to be kidding."

"No, as a matter of fact."

"But you were elected president last May!"

Elected was hardly the word for it. Rick was appointed by default, and everyone said, "Aye."

"And I'm sorry," Rick said. "But I . . . Meg could really use the break. And I think you'd be the perfect replacement. You've been with A.B.S. long enough."

Frank stared into the mahogany surface of the long oval table. The muscles in his face tightened, and color patched his cheeks. His watery blue eyes flicked up nervously. "But Rick," he said, adjusting his glasses, "it's the year of the Centennial. I can't manage that. You know everyone's gonna make a big fuss. Dana was wondering the other day what size cake we should order, and from where. I don't know. You'll have to flush out a guest of honor—put on a national-level show. We're the oldest society in the country! That must mean something. I'm just a retired accountant, and I would be happier staying on as treasurer."

"I'll be around to give you a hand," Rick said, trying to keep up his casual manner. "Just one email click away. I'm not going to disappear."

"Besides, Dana and I will be in Egypt all of October, on the Smithsonian tour. And in June, we'll be in Alaska for three weeks. We were going to come back just in time for the Centennial. The money's been paid for both the trips. It's too late to back out."

Rick looked at the older man. His plan was crumbling. The old fool had gone out and booked himself two insanely long vacations. Damn these old retirees and their month-long extravaganzas!

The door opened and Zanne McDonald, the editor of *The Vireo*, walked in. "Look who's here early!" she said in her deep, husky voice as she unloaded a bundle of files onto the table. "Hell, let's start already." A large-boned, athletic woman of seventy, she was famous for the shock of white hair that stood up on her head and gave her the look of a fierce snowy egret.

"This is between us," Rick whispered.

"As long as we're clear on the decision," Frank said, barely moving his lips.

The board members trickled in. Karen Mercer, Hospitality Chair, came with Blake and a cookie platter. "Hey there!" she greeted Rick. She remembered every bit of torture she'd endured on the Piute Ponds trip, and she meant to have her revenge today. "I'm in my element now," her smile said, "and just try to pull one over on me in a church!"

Patty Cole, their secretary, came in wearing sandpiper earrings—a silent tribute to the Piute Ponds trip. Robert Kern, vice president, had come straight from his genetics lab, and he grabbed a few cookies. Kenny Takahashi, Conservation Chair, came late in a leather jacket with fake fur collars. Frank's wife Dana, Membership Chair, was home with the flu, so eight out of nine board members were present.

The meeting began. Frank confirmed the tragic news that was suspected last year: the National Bird Society would no longer share membership dues with the local chapters. "We're officially on our own now," Frank reported. "And they've decided they're not going to back-pay us for last year, either."

"I don't think I can deal with the printer's bill anymore," the Egret said. "Someone with fewer gray hairs than me needs to do it."

Rick felt that his own hair was graying at an alarming rate, though it still looked darkish.

"As of yesterday, our account has $461.35," Frank said. "We lost one member over the summer. Dana's upset about it. A person who's still coming to our birding trips has stopped paying her membership dues."

It was nearly 8:30 p.m. when Zanne ran her hand through her stiff egret hair and interrupted their proceedings. "Before we run out of time, I've noticed we're missing an important item on the agenda."

Rick's heart ricocheted and his brown eyes were tense. He grew aware that there were no windows in this room. It was all shaggy carpets and gray walls; the pictures of glum pastors were hung where there should have been windows.

"I've been thinking about it all summer," the Egret said, "and it's bugging the hell out of me. Now what's our plan for the Centennial?"

"Actually, I was going to get to that," Rick said, although he had deliberately avoided putting the word "Centennial" on the agenda. Frank threw a meaningful look in his direction, but Rick ignored him. "I was going to ask the board to come up with some modest ideas."

Karen looked at Rick, surprised by his tepid tone. "I think we should do something exciting, don't you?" She fingered her silk scarf.

"Yeah," Kenny Takahashi said in a low voice. "I . . . we need to think *big*."

"We could invite chapter and national members in our area," Karen said. "Get out publicity and do a grand celebration and a fundraiser maybe."

"That sounds great," the Egret said. "But who's gonna do all that?"

An awkward silence collected in the room. Patty, the secretary, pursed her lips and stopped writing.

"Which is exactly why I said *modest* ideas," Rick said. "I'm thinking more along the lines of . . . we'll have our usual great potluck, and A.B.S. will spring for a hell of a cake and maybe some beer. Whatcha y'all think?"

"We'll all do it together," Karen said. She looked around with shining eyes as though the meaning of her existence had just been revealed to her. "I mean, *I* don't really have the time. I have two kids. Every day is over before I can blink. But this is the *Centennial*! We need to do *something* to make sure we're not always hovering on the brink of extinction. I mean, forget the endangered species. We can't do anything about them until we save ourselves first. Think what the founding fathers and mothers . . ."

"Not the founding mothers again!" Rick said, leaning back from the table. "Gang, maybe we're going too far. I mean, this year was the ninety-ninth, next year it'll be the hundredth, and the year after the hundred and first. What's the big deal?"

Patty's eyes seemed ready to pop out of her face as she looked up from her steno pad for the first time that evening. "Should I write all that down?" she said.

"Skip that," Rick said, "but write that I suggest scaling down."

"That's just what bothers me," Karen said. She leaned back in her chair, and the fingers of one hand played the edge of the table as if it were a piano. "At my church, for a long time they thought they couldn't do much with the tiny income they had. They barely got by. Two years ago, they ran out of money, so they went out and started to fundraise in a big way. And now they have a modest endowment again, and membership is up, and things have never been so exciting." A blush washed over her cheeks and neck. Watching his mother give this speech, Blake felt the same blush coming on, too.

An image of desperate, trapped cowbirds flashed into Karen's mind, and she added, "If all we do is buy cake and do nothing to celebrate the hundredth anniversary of the oldest birding society in the U.S., I don't think I could live with that." She exhaled deeply, relieved of *that* burden of her conscience.

"Actually, just the way you put that, Karen," the Egret said, her angular face softening, "makes me wanna say you're right." Feeling a sneeze coming on, she turned away from the table and pulled a tissue from her pocket.

Kenny nodded. "I feel just the same way," he added.

The Egret let out a monstrous sneeze. "Could we do it at Joss Canyon?"

"I doubt they'll let us," Rick said. "It's a huge mess after the fire."

"Maybe this will motivate Billy Grimsby to clean it up," Karen said.

"And charge us a ridiculous fee?" Rick said. "No, thanks! I don't think it's our mission to pay for the Joss Canyon fire restoration."

"Yeah, but until it's restored, we don't have a home," Karen said. "The church took us in temporarily when we became homeless. What happens when they kick us out?"

Rick looked around the room. "In any case, ya'll know we've tried to fundraise before, but we didn't even cover operating expenses."

"Shall we take a vote?" Karen said. Meeting with no objection, she continued, "I move we plan a Centennial celebration that's worthy of the oldest birding institution in the country."

"I second the motion," Kenny whispered.

"All in favor?"

"Aye," many in the board said.

"All opposed?"

Rick looked about him uneasily. Robert Kern was not the sort to voluntarily waste time on Centennial celebrations, but he remained dead silent and abstained from voting. Frank had voted in favor. It was well enough to do that if you planned to be away and skip the work. As it seemed that no one else would support his voice of reason, Rick declined to go on the record as the sole opponent. "The motion passes," he said.

Patty noted down the result in the minutes and the meeting adjourned. Blake had brought his latest photographs of backyard birds. Some in the group gathered around, and the boy came to life, chirping on about how he took an exceptional mockingbird photo.

Rick continued to sit in his chair at the head of the table. The entire evening, from the first moment to the last, had been a failure. Now if he brought up the issue of resigning, it would be taken to mean that he was chickening out of the Centennial celebrations. How could he resign now, in the face of Karen's idealism? She knew only what she was lecturing about up there. How was he going to explain this to Meg?

He had better not bring up Karen. Meg had concocted a strange notion that he was attracted to Karen. That was a good one. Ha! Meg would accuse him of having made the promise just to humor her, but of having no intention of keeping it. He looked up at the spidery chandelier and felt his head spinning. Everyone but him seemed to be leaving in a lighthearted mood.

"You all right, Rick?" the Egret said as she blew her nose.

Rick nodded as a sickly, hapless feeling spread through his stomach.

After a fifteen-minute walk from the church in the moonless night, Rick entered his first-floor condominium on Moraine Street. The beagle, Keats, and cat, Peugeot, scuttled up to the door. Keats sunk his teeth into Rick's sneakers as he was putting away his sports jacket and cowboy hat. Peugeot, the Blonde, having discerned that it was Rick and not someone more exciting who had walked in, slunk back into Meg's lap and curled up into the shape of a Bundt cake. Meg was watching a cop show on television, her short figure curled on the sofa in a parrot-green dress.

Rick came up from behind and put an arm around her. "Bonjour!"

"Bonsoir, mon cher," she said, steadying her glass of gimlet. "I wish you *had* taken that French class with me."

"I wanted to. But it seems that you can't always do everything in life that you want to."

Rick helped himself to a gimlet, a concoction of gin and lime, also her favorite drink. The bar was next to two shelves that housed his bird books. Two lamps stood like cracked pillars on flea-market tables. He sank on the sofa beside her and sipped his gimlet in silence.

"How did it go, mon cher?" she asked when the commercials came on.

He let out a pained guttural sound. Peugeot the Blonde opened her eyes and, perceiving that it was Rick again, fell back asleep. "And . . . ?" Meg prodded.

"And nada."

"You told them, right?" Her eyes grew expectant.

"It was no use. Frank will have nothing to do with it."

Meg looked at him with disbelief. As a legal secretary, she wasn't surprised by how low people could go to get out of a contract, but when a promise made to her was broken, she didn't take the matter lightly.

"They're going on two insane vacations," Rick told her. "Frank and Dana just won't be around. The board members were killing themselves thinking of even bigger ways to celebrate the Centennial. I couldn't get a word in."

"Oh, God! How can you stand them walking all over you?" The warmth in her voice was gone, as if she'd resigned herself to having the damn birds and A.B.S. drama take over Rick's life. Her face puckered, and all the irritation wrinkled around her nose. "Did Karen put you up to this?" He made no reply. "She has her fingers in too many pies."

"You know that's unfair."

"But it's fun to watch you defend her. I bet Karen can run the whole show by herself. She doesn't need the hand-holding you give her."

"Oh, Meg!"

"Why don't you ask her to take over?"

"But she's a mother of two and she's always pressed for time. She said herself tonight that every day is over before she can blink." Somehow he could not repeat with Karen the pathetic talk he had with Frank. He felt that in her school-girlish way, Karen looked up to him, if only as a role model for Blake, and he couldn't denigrate himself in her eyes with a "my wife told me to step down" story.

"Why can't you at least ask? She has no problem asking things of you."

The show came back on, and Meg switched her attention. She stroked the cat, but the Blonde jumped out of her lap. "Ever since the Big Year, you are Mr. Super Busy," she said with a bitter tone. "And now it's the Centennial! What is it that keeps us together? What binds us, if it's not the time we spend together?"

He stared at her, surprised. What bound him to her was that she was a gem, despite her bad gene pool, and that she was at heart a kind woman and had supported him when he decided to go back to college for a degree in legal administration.

"You know, the board members are worked up about the Centennial," he said. "And the idea of service. That's what I do at A.B.S. That's why I chose to give up working for a corporation and signed on with a city health board where my twelve-hour days supposedly contribute to the community!"

Meg raised her eyebrows. She had heard this defense before, and as with no more patience for his phony idealism, she turned back to the television set.

Rick pondered her question, "What binds us?" In their thirteen years of marriage, he had felt loved and supported her in return, despite the fights, but that question, "What binds us . . ." delivered with the steely look in Meg's eye, as though her mother had put her up to it, shook him. He knew she was simmering inside, and rather than suffer more days of hell, he wanted to do something about it. But what? What fireman was equal to dousing her anger? He needed a shower. His head was throbbing.

Rick sank into an armchair facing away from the television set. He usually sat there at night when he was not watching television with Meg, and studied the bird books from the two adjoining shelves. He had accumulated the books over seven years. He didn't like to spend money, but book-by-book, he had amassed this collection, reasoning that life was short and he shouldn't deny himself small pleasures. He aimed for the big stuff in his youth, too—a music career and bicycle racing—until he had suffered a minor stroke that took away the nimbleness of his fingers that had allowed him to play his bass guitar. The doctors added that his heart couldn't take the rigors of bicycle racing anymore either. Being forced to give up his dreams made life's cruelty clear to him. The experience hardened him against people he assumed had easier lives and made him keenly protective of the interests he still had power to pursue. Now he suspected that fulfillment was overrated. There was a lot to be said for a steady paycheck and a little self-indulgence like birding. Ever since he began the Big Year, life seemed worthwhile again, and every birding trip was an event to look forward to with great anticipation.

After another drink, Rick's pain began to ease. However, he couldn't shake off the feeling that he wasn't really living—only checking-off the hours. He'd been using a complicated patchwork of vacation time he had saved over the last two years, plus unpaid personal days, to support his Big Year. When he'd return after just a couple of days off, his desk would be piled with files. It seemed that most of his time was spent asking people to account for their time or giving them accounts of his. In his younger days he could lose himself in the band or bicycle racing. Now he had only the Big Year. The damn race against J.K. was keeping him alive! He did not want to join so many of the walking dead who worked for the city. He relished the challenge and skill the race required, and the freedom to ramble all day. Each bird added to his count was unique. One day he'd be excited to spot a rarity. Another day he'd bird for hours without accomplishing anything beyond enjoying the simple pleasure of seeing an old favorite with fresh eyes. What was wrong with that? Why must Meg kick up a fuss over his last remaining passion?

He had made progress this month with shorebirds, and was up to 310. But J.K., that smart-ass college kid, was still three birds ahead. Little more than three months remained in the year, and Rick needed to sharpen his strategy to win. If Karen were president, it would free up his time. If only there were a way to ask her without humiliating himself.

He looked up from a bird book and discovered that Meg had gone to bed. He went in to check on her. The light was off, but he could see that she turned away to make room for him. Rick stripped off his clothes and got into bed. He tucked his hand under Meg's waist, but by then the pretense of sleep was believable. He rolled over onto his side. The only reason he was hanging on as president was that there was no one to replace him. If he stepped down, the whole operation would damn near fold. What would Karen think if he walked away? Why was it that he didn't like to disappoint her? But he couldn't go on as president much longer. He pushed around paper all day at work, and he'd be damned if he'd do the same thing in his spare time and devastate his finances, marriage, and vacation plans in the process. There was no other way out. He would have to ask Karen to take over or find himself in an all-out war with Meg.

*7*

*J.K.* had just pushed his count up to 319, aided by a MacGillivray's warbler on campus and a red-faced warbler in the mountains, but the vireo was still missing. Joss Canyon had failed him.

Late Friday afternoon, he shaved his face clean and walked over to Leaves café. While Luna was blending his spearmint tea, J.K. told her about his breakup with Anne Marie.

"You two weren't cut of the same cloth," Luna said, tucking an untidy curl behind her ear, and revealing a dangling silver earring.

"What d'you mean?"

"You're cotton, and she's silk." Luna smiled, pleased by the analogy.

"So she's better than me?"

"Nope. Cotton's easier. Like, more breathable. But silk—you gotta hand-wash it." She handed him his tea.

J.K. gave her a puzzled look. "What are you?" he asked.

"Hemp." Luna laughed. "I'm hemp, man!"

"I feel like hell," he confessed. "But I don't even have time to process the breakup. My Big Year is totally eating up any free time I have right now."

"You're doing a Big Year?" Luna said. "Wow!"

"And tomorrow, I'm leading a fall-migrant trip."

"It's my day off. I wouldn't mind going on this trip."

"You're saying that cause you feel sorry for me?"

"No, I have some thinking to do. I'm stuck, brooding over something. I desperately need to spend more time outdoors. That's my new mantra, actually—more time outdoors!"

J.K. should have warned her that his field trips were not for the uninitiated, but he decided to let her come anyway. If they were going to become more than acquaintances, he might as well take her birding and let her taste his favorite pastime in person.

She might have been reading his thoughts, for she added, "I'll bring a book in case I get bored." Then, after a pause, "Just to be clear—this isn't a date or anything sentimental like that."

"No, of course not," J.K. said.

Watching her, J.K. felt drawn to her, but he also felt keenly that Luna was a stranger. The memory of Anne Marie singed him with fresh pain. Sometimes on campus, he saw a girl with Anne Marie's straight, long hair, and for a brief moment he allowed himself to feel the happiness he would experience if she were to surprise him with a visit. He couldn't humiliate himself by begging her to return, yet his heart refused to let go. He wished he could hate Anne Marie. Then all the excruciating wrenching feelings in him would go away. He could barely bring himself to dislike her. Their breakup had been too civilized. It was depressing to think about that. He had been powerless, unable to speak up for himself, barely able to speak at all. It was all so strange. Why couldn't he train his mind to stop thinking about her? He thought about her more now than when they'd been in relationship.

Last night, he'd called up Anne Marie, not to plead his case, but to clarify that honesty cannot be equated with weakness. She glossed over his argument and told him about a trundle bed she was planning to buy. "Retail Therapy" is what she called it. Then she just chatted about her friends. He wished he could be a typical guy and hate her. But he spoke to her without bitterness. He missed loving her and could not imagine being with any other girl without feeling like he was betraying Anne Marie.

Saturday morning, the Birdmobile swung into view, swerved around, and squealed to a halt on a leafy residential lane outside Karen's brownstone house. J.K. looked as though he had just tumbled out of bed; he greeted his flock with groggy eyes. "This is Luna," he said. "She's trying to spend more time outdoors."

Luna, in a snug blouse and jeans, added, "It's my fault we're late."

"I hadn't noticed you were late," Karen said.

"J.K. told me he was going to be late," Luna said, contorting her face. "So I want everyone to know it's my fault."

J.K. looked embarrassed. Their arrangement was to pick Luna up at Leaves, but when he got there, she was nowhere in sight. "I don't know why it takes a person forty-five minutes to get ready," he said. "I get out of bed, fill a brown bag with pickled hard-boiled eggs, pull on jeans, and head out with bins and the scope."

Karen gave the young people a sympathetic smile. She could guess that Luna had broken her personal record for the time she spent getting dressed, faced with the prospect of an early-morning birding expedition. Karen herself had been dead-set against going on another J.K.-led trip, but the fall migration season was in full swing and her young Bedouin wanted to make his pilgrimage with the master. And then she didn't know which was worse—a birding trip with J.K., or a day with Oscar's self-glorifying brother and sister-in-law. Oscar was going to spend the Saturday with his wealthy, rancher brother, and since she declined to join him, he planned to take the jeep and their daughter instead. At a quarter past four in the morning, Karen had squinted at herself in the mirror. Some days she still looked good enough for the stage. Knowing that she was going to carpool with Rick, she had been to her hair stylist the day before.

Miraculously, at a quarter past five, she and Blake were waiting outside their house. She rubbed her hands, wondering what she was doing here shivering when she could be in a cozy bed with her husband.

Blake had set his heart on submitting a collection to the Young Birders Photo Contest. She had lent him her precious 75-300 mm zoom lens and was going on this trip to support him. That was her number one reason. But she wondered if this had something to do with her, too. Was she trying to compensate for the lack of adventure in her life? She was resistant to the thought because it implied that Oscar wasn't up to giving her the life she desired. But it was true—something was lacking. Nowadays, Oscar didn't even talk much at dinner. Karen had to initiate the conversations. Sometimes she brought up things that might bore him, like the cowbird traps, but even then he responded sympathetically.

Karen squeezed into the back seat of the Birdmobile. She glanced up and just then she saw Oscar at their bedroom window. He waved, but his features looked pinched, as if he were anguished. Her heart felt wrung out in that moment. Oscar also deserved a nice Saturday with his wife. She mustn't take him so much for granted. Then the car began to move. J.K. roared off toward Rick's condominium, a few blocks away.

In the darkness, a tan SUV was parked on the road with Rick waiting inside. J.K. parked, and the four of them climbed out of the Birdmobile. Rick looked at Karen as she walked toward him. "Hey gang," he said.

The gang loaded into the "new-ish, second-hand" SUV Rick had bought at a used car dealership. He remembered with nostalgia his feisty pickup, "Old Girl," but he needed dependable transportation for his Big Year. And he couldn't help being impressed with the luxuries offered by the new-ish SUV. The heating system actually worked for early morning trips, and the seats were smooth tan leather. It was a gas-guzzler, though. Karen had teased him about driving an "environmental sinkhole," so he was reducing his guilt by allowing others to carpool with him.

They drove into the darkness. "You must have responded to an ad for an SUV that fits three scopes in the back," J.K. said.

Rick laughed. "Actually, there are four scopes. I brought my old one—Luna can borrow it if she wants."

J.K. glanced at Luna.

Sitting in the back, she broke into a mischievous smile.

"But I guess I could have put in a want ad," Rick said. " 'Desperate birder seeks rugged vehicle with trunk space for several large scopes.' "

"And bins and cameras," Blake said.

"And lunch coolers," Karen added.

Looking at Karen's glowing face, Rick smiled. Behind that smile lay the discomfort of a man who would rather sit on a tough decision than make it. He was torn between violating his "no politics while birding" policy and postponing the matter of getting Karen to replace him as president until the Centennial Committee meeting. But then he remembered how much less painful life would be if this thorn of contention between Meg and him were plucked out and he could know for sure that Meg wouldn't divorce him. He stole another look at Karen. If he could buttonhole Karen today, what a load off it would be!

In Malibu, five silhouettes with binoculars and scopes got out of an SUV in the dark of morning. The beach gates were shut. Rick parked on a shoulder of the Pacific Coast Highway, and they hiked down to Leo Carrillo State Beach. Blake tore past the lizard-shaped cliff aster and sagebrush, camera thudding against his stomach, down the sandy cliff to the beach. By the time the others caught up with him, he was pointing at a steely gray thing moving in the water. It was the fin of a bottlenose dolphin bobbing in and out of the distant waves. Two sea lions played next to the dolphin.

The water turned milky blue and the sky blushed pink. Touched by the first rays of the sun, the ocean waves became luminescent gold. Karen watched this play of light and water. The tide was low, and mussel shells, in iridescent blues, exposed themselves on the black rocks.   Starfish—orange, purple, and pink—were stuck fast to the rocks. Karen walked up the mussel-coated, craggy rocks and discovered a tide pool with purple sea urchins floating along the edges, and sea anemones, like marinated pink flowers, resting in mud caves. On the sand, sea kelp lay like silken ropes.

J.K. stood at the ocean's edge, like a tenacious reed that never tires of the wind, looking for rare shorebirds. He called out three parasitic jaegers—dark, bulky birds with white under-tail coverts—as they chased a flock of terns. While the birders gawked through their scopes at the jaegers, J.K. glanced at Luna. She had spread out a blanket a safe distance away from the group, next to an abandoned truck, and was reading a Joseph Campbell book, *Oriental Mythology*.

Cars began to pull into the beach parking lot. Frank and his wife, Dana, were the first to walk up behind the group. A quizzical smile lit up the corners of Frank's mouth. "Were you guys camping at the beach last night?" he asked.

"We don't give away our secrets," Rick said, retraining his eye on the scope.

"I don't get it," Frank said, squinting. "We were the first car in a lineup of about ten to get into the beach. And the gates only opened at seven."

"Oh, yeah. We were camping in that truck over there," Rick said, pointing to the battered rusty truck painted a black-and-white checkerboard pattern a few hundred yards away.

From behind the battered truck, Paul Little spied on the birders. He watched as Frank's pasty face took on a baffled look; Blake giggled and hopped, and his zoom lens bounced up and down. The rest of the birders began to arrive, lining up their scopes parallel to the beach, and the morning calm was interrupted only when someone called out "snowy-egret" or "long-billed curlew and marbled godwits flying by."

Paul Little was combing the beach with a metal detector. What bothered him most was that these aging yuppies had no way of understanding the lives of birds, nor would they survive a day in the wild without their R.E.I. clothing and fancy SUVs. They were wandering in a meaningless universe of plastic cards and made-in-China stuff, unaware that before them stood a man who was a real birder, true blue. But they didn't have eyes with which to see him. He found a quarter and plunked it into his fanny pack.

J.K. especially provoked Paul Little's ire. That guy didn't have it in him to be a leader. He was soft inside and could use a dose of hardening. Paul Little doubted if J.K. had any real concern for the environment, which made him worse than the rest of them. J.K. ought to know better, he thought.

Paul Little watched the birders gasp as a tern dove into the water fifty feet away. He did feel sorry for them, and yet he couldn't help despising their pathetic yuppie ways that were ruining the planet more every day. Paul Little scratched his back with dirty, uneven nails and considered ways of jolting these people out of the toxic fantasy that had poisoned their brains.

When everyone in the party settled in, the hum of their voices doubled, with Zanne calling in her sharp voice, "What d'you got?" and someone else needing to borrow a scope. But there were moments of calm, as when a dozen American pelicans flew by in formation, skimming the water, and the party cooed in a united "Ooh!"

With his metal detector, Paul Little walked on toward Blake. It shook him to the core to watch the boy's enthusiasm for birds, and he wished that he could save the boy somehow from his fussing, unfriendly mother, who would undoubtedly have a nasty influence on him and turn him into a clean-shaven, planet-destroying yuppie.

A willet flew from rock to water, exposing its striped, butterfly-like wings and, as reward for this labor, found a crab on which to snack. Blake advanced, one hand on his camera, towards the willet. Semipalmated plovers with button-black eyes and brown neck rings darted about. He inched up to the willet, pressed the trigger, and tried to get a closer shot as the gray bird poked its beak in the water in search of food. But the bird outwitted him and moved farther into the water. Blake's attention turned to a California gull holding a young starfish in its bright orange beak. The gull tried to eat the hard orange star, but threw it out right away. The boy looked on. Paul Little found a dime.

"It'll die if it eats that big, tough thing," Blake said.

"Maybe not," Paul Little said. "Just you watch."

"I poked a starfish this morning," Blake said. "It was hard as rock."

The gull made a second attempt. This time it cocked its head back, but three starfish arms still stuck out of its mouth. There was a struggle, and just when it seemed the gull would choke, it managed to pull the starfish in entirely. An unnatural bulge appeared in its throat.

"It's gonna explode!" Blake said.

But the gull moved her neck from side to side and the booty was shoved down to her stomach.

"You wanna bird with me sometime?" Paul Little said. "I'll tell you about how they live and then some."

"Blake!" Karen yelled.

It was time to move on to their next location, and Blake was sorry to leave the shorebirds on the golden beach. He was so taken with the starfish-eating gull that he'd forgotten to take a photograph. "My brain's going crazy!" he said.

Paul Little flashed a graying smile at the boy and hurried to gather his bags.

Luna shook out her blue-checkered blanket and followed J.K. as he walked up the sandy cliff toward the SUV. From beyond the battered checkerboard truck, a voice called out to them. Paul Little.

"Great, that's just what I need," J.K. said. The shambling figure in a torn camouflage outfit hurried toward the line of vehicles to wheedle a ride.

J.K. had stayed at the beach longer than he meant to, but he hadn't spotted a shorebird not already in his count. Disappointed, he pinned his hopes now on land birds. Lately, he had felt each hour tick by like the hand of a cruel timer, as though an internal spring kept him in a state of constant motion. Any moment he wasn't doing slave labor on the Hierarchy Problem for Dave was spent looking for elusive birds, which he had mapped out according to their area and seasonal distribution in an elaborate chart to systematize his quest.

"The Spanish call those plants Our Lord's Candle," Karen said, pointing to a patch of tall white plants on the Santa Monica Mountains.

Rick, scoping for hawks while driving, scolded, "Gang, we're birding here, not planting!" The caravan was on Highway One, driving northwest along the coast toward Sycamore Canyon. At the fee entrance, the American flag fluttered over the flag of California's grizzly bear. On the flagpole, two cowbirds were chattering. The male cocked its glossy head and broke into a burbling song.

"I didn't know cowbirds sang so nicely," Karen murmured.

The caravan parked in the large paved lot. In the brilliant light, Rick adjusted his cowboy hat and sauntered to a bridge overlooking a stream that emptied into the ocean on the far side of the highway. A turtle sunned on a rock jutting out of the green water. Warblers flew back and forth across the stream to the trees along its banks. A disagreement broke out between Rick and J.K. on the bridge, about whether one of the camouflaged warblers below was a chat. They stopped arguing when J.K. spotted another brightly colored bird, a common yellow throat with a black eye mask and white headband, sipping water where a thicket of reeds grew at the stream's edge.

Luna leaned against the other end of the bridge, reading her mythology book. J.K. meant to go over and check on her. He sensed she felt awkward around these people and either spoke too little or too much, which made her feel worse, and he didn't want her to regret coming in the first place. But the moment he saw a count bird, Luna was forgotten. His heart gave such a flutter that he called out the bird only after a second look. It was a white-winged dove by the stream's edge, nearly obscured by the shrubs.

It was his 320th catch of the year.

The bird was normally found in the desert in the southeastern part of the state when it migrated to Baja or Mexico. The dove was not where it should have been at September's end, and J.K. loved the dove for being adventurous.

Rick, who was tailing him, also got a look, and then J.K.'s white-winged fairy disappeared.

The birders moved off the bridge, and their smaller group waited for Luna to join them.

"It's the second big birding trip she's come to," Dana was saying, "without paying her membership dues. I've sent her two notices."

"Jean's been awful quiet lately," Zanne said about her carpool companion. "I know I ought to nag her, but . . ."

Observing the light that came into Rick's face after the episode of the dove, Karen grew thoughtful. "What's the current record?" she asked Rick.

"Three hundred forty-six," he said. "Ed McCoy raised the bar pretty high."

"But things are looking good? You always seem to be getting a new bird."

"Not really." Rick noted the dove in his Big Year notebook. "J.K. is two birds ahead."

"Oh, you're being modest," Karen said.

"I'm twenty-eight birds away from breaking the record. And the last twenty-eight are impossible birds!"

"Well, you're an impossible birder." The statement was meant as a compliment. Rick accepted it as such and smiled.

Putting her hand on his shoulder, Karen said, "What if we made the new L.A. County record holder—the Big Year Winner—the attraction for the Centennial? We could have an award . . . to bring attention to the plight of cowbirds. How about a Cowbird Cup? It's an award for a person who'll wander anywhere to look for a bird, who likes nothing better than to roam in the roughest places, in the most inconvenient times, under the worst circumstances, just to find that one extra count bird."

"That's great!" Rick said. "There are a few other people going for the record from the L.A. society, but I don't think they're as good as us."

In the parking lot, J.K. and Luna joined them, and Karen repeated her Cowbird Cup idea.

"There's no saying how it'll turn out," J.K. said, his anxious face heightening the effect of his tapered chin. "I know that Rick's planning to beat me."

Rick grinned mischievously.

"But you think you'll break the record?" Luna asked J.K.

"It's all about rarities now," J.K. said. He was twenty-six birds away from the record. "It's unpredictable. There's only so much I can travel within L.A. County. And I'm slammed at work. If I don't write up this paper soon, I might not get a job next year."

"Job-Shmob!" Rick said. "A Big Year always gets priority."

"Think of the publicity we would get," Karen said. "The Centennial is our chance to turn back the clock to reclaim Joss Canyon."

"Okay, back to birding!" Rick said, irked by the blasphemous mixing of board matters with the ritual of birding.

"You guys are our last hope," Karen said. "The board has gotten trapped and we haven't been able to do much. Fifty years ago, A.B.S. was a major force in the community. If we can bring half that excitement back . . ."

"That was back then," Rick said, frustrated. It was a bad sign that the Centennial wouldn't let him alone, even on a birding trip. If no one else were around, he would offer Karen the presidency on the spot. But he couldn't bear to get rejected in front of J.K., Blake, and Luna.

"But don't you think, even if only to lift some weight off your shoulders," she said, "that we've got to get out of this humiliating position where we're hoping we'll scrape by just one more year before it all comes to a crashing end?"

Karen's words hit Rick too accurately for him to argue the point. "I need to talk to you about this," he started. "I was sort of stalling until the Committee meeting."

"You got it! I'm opening up my house. Next Thursday. Wine and cake are on me," she smiled triumphantly. "I expect everyone to be there, including two guys who are busy being our heroes."

Rick was unable to say anything that might crush Karen right now. He managed only to beam at her.

Looking at Luna, J.K. said, "You see what's at stake here!"

"And I thought *you* were nuts," Luna confessed.

*8*

*L*adder-back!' Paul Little said. "Muy bien."

Karen saw no need to correct this nitwit. A nuttall's woodpecker, not a ladder-back, drummed on the ash-brown bark of a giant sycamore over a hundred feet high. The tree's five-fingered leaves sashayed in tune to the insistent note of a nearby song sparrow. They were in leafy Sycamore Canyon. The trail ran parallel to a stream and led them to a spot where slate-colored wrentits flitted about in wild grasses and willow shrubs. Seeing these secretive birds out in the open, Blake grew excited. He aimed his camera at one, but she moved fast and was difficult to bring into focus.

"You go on," he said to his mother.

"Don't be long," Karen said, continuing with the rest. Brown sycamore leaves, September's harvest, crunched under her shoes. The trees' branches were like so many arms reaching out to her. A flock of parrots with dusky gray wings and green bodies flew by in a flash across the trail, as though they were in a jungle. They made cackling sounds just before they flew by in a whisper. Karen looked on in awe. Such was the poetry that quickened the life inside her. It was her half-English blood, perhaps, that craved these elusive moments of charm and shrank from the prospect of passing her days in the concrete-paved suburbia where so many mothers were trapped.

It was clear to Karen that Joss Canyon, the last remaining wild space in Alpena, must be saved. But even though the A.B.S. mission statement emphasized conservation, no one would touch the subject with a ten-foot pole. Thankfully, she might be getting somewhere at last with Rick and J.K. Even if it was with a bit of trickery, she could now focus their attention on the cowbird problem. The trapped birds at Joss Canyon had visited her in her dreams and blighted her sleep. And J.K. told her that there were several more such traps in parks around the county.

Looking at birds wasn't exactly how she wanted to spend her time, but there was more adventure in these outings as a whole than in most activities that soaked up her time. Loneliness and monotony accumulated in a life where neighbors never thought of inviting each other over, and friends lived too far away to visit. And her family probably did a better job of entertaining each other than most. In the time she'd spent as a young woman at her aunt's in England, she had experienced the thrill of being in a social circle, of moving about with the stimulating people who visited her aunt and invited her to their homes. The memory of her English summers cast a shadow over the plainness of her everyday life in America, which had so much choice, yet so little charm.

Was it surprising, then, that she had begun to savor Rick's friendship? Even though she was not a real birder, she found herself teased into his way of life and became less resistant to Blake's pleading to spend yet another Saturday on an expedition that began at an ungodly hour and finished with her so exhausted that it was a miracle she was able to drive them safely back home.

Karen's eyes stung as she walked past a smoking fire pit in a cluster of campsites. A couple was making a late breakfast of bacon and coffee, and she felt a strong desire for steaming coffee. Instead, she hopped over the persistent roots of the old walnut trees that ran across the trail and hiked down with the others into the wash.

"Good look at willows," J.K. called out. He was usually the first in the group to spot unlikely birds. Two willow flycatchers were angling for mid-morning snacks, and the group watched, entranced. The wash was flooded with light, and the flycatchers operated from a shadowed mud cliff in the canyon. In the rocky stream bed, an old beer bottle lay in a pool of stagnant water in which water striders danced without creating even a ripple to mark their passage.

Karen remembered that Blake was not with her.

"Did you see Blake?" she asked Rick, who was just coming down into the wash.

Rick hadn't seen the boy, but he said they would be heading back soon anyway, as there wasn't much more to the wash than the area they were in.

Karen scanned the group. Paul Little was missing, too. She hurried back up to look for her son.

How could she have been so careless? The birding trips were supposed to be her gift to Blake, and instead she had taken to dreamily enjoying them herself and forgetting all about him. One would think that she was trying to escape her family life. She wanted to give Blake the chance to love nature as she had as a girl, but she mustn't be so foolish about leaving him exposed to predators.

The high-pitched whistle of a squirrel made her jump. Envisioning scenes of the boy crying as he was being tortured by that maniac, she moaned. How could she have been so naive, leaving the boy out of her sight? There was a story in the news not long ago about a grandma who waited while her grandson used a public restroom. After a while she went in and discovered that a convict on the run had shot him.

From the wash, Rick was calling out to her.

When Karen turned around, she saw Zanne, Dana, and a few others beckoning. She ran back and looked up to where they were pointing. Through the streamside trees, a part of the cement bridge was visible. Blake stood there waving. Karen felt a cool wave of relief. Then she saw Paul Little on the bridge, and she hurried up toward Blake. In her mistrust of strangers, she was more American at heart than she had realized.

On seeing how relieved Karen was, J.K. noticed that he also had lost track of Luna. He was alarmed for a moment before it occurred to him where she'd probably gone. Sure enough, when the birders returned to the parking lot, Luna was waiting perched on a jagged rock, a scarf barely sheltering her face from the sun. Hiding under her arms the damp semi-circles on the sides of her shirt, she shot J.K. a queasy look. "I have so many hats, you'd think I'd have brought one!" she said.

"We're almost done here," he told her in a sympathetic voice, before rushing off again to chase after a Harlequin's sparrow.

On their way to the Southland Sod Farms, J.K. had Rick pull over onto a shoulder of the highway before the Port Hueneme Naval Base. The base was fenced up all the way to the gravel shoulder, and a sign warned, "U.S. GOVERNMENT PROPERTY. NO TRESPASSING." But a sign never deterred J.K., and he soon had the group pulling out their scopes to spot birds attracted to the field and lagoon left wild beyond the fence.

Terns flew above, and marbled godwits lazed in the lagoon, letting the avocets and stilts do all the strutting. The vague silhouette of the Channel Islands floated above the horizon to the west like a fairyland.

When they returned to the parked SUV, J.K. found Luna stewing inside with her mythology book. She shrugged when he asked how she was doing. After the others were settled in, he could not do more than try to make eye contact, which she avoided.

Rick drove past the offices of the Southland Sod Farms, where they entered acres of surreal suburban lawn growing under a network of sprinkler pipes. Hearing some calls, J.K. cried out, "Stop!"

J.K. jumped out and walked closer to the fields. The SUV was leading the caravan, and the others soon veered off the road and stopped behind them.

"I hear about fifty laplands," J.K. said, when Rick came up behind him, "and there's one chestnut-collared among them." Rick scanned the field with his binoculars. "Saw the dark breast band," J.K added.

The lapland longspurs were still about. Rick spotted their brownish yellow heads at the far end of the field. But their rare cousin, the chestnut-collared, was nowhere to be seen. Both of these were count birds for J.K., and though he was paralyzed with anxiety about missing the second one, he kept absolutely silent. Only when the chestnut-collared deigned to call out again, and Rick confirmed it, did he dare breathe.

J.K. celebrated by popping a boiled egg into his mouth. In the SUV, he offered an egg to Luna, but she declined.

As they drove deep into the farms, past abandoned shacks in the distance, Karen smelled a malodorous composting station. In the distance, two towers painted like candy canes chugged out black smoke from a coal-fired power plant. In her dream world, J.K. would have ended the trip after Sycamore Canyon, and they would have stopped at a nice café on the way home. But such was life that when it gave you half a good day, it never forgot to balance the scale. But then the two extra birds for Rick's count were well worth the sacrifice. Karen shook her head. She was beginning to think like a birder.

An Hispanic man drove past in a tractor and threw a curious glance at the caravan. When Karen waved, he was surprised and waved only haltingly. In the distance, next to a tool shack, Hispanic workers stood about holding trash bags. Standing on the other side of the sod farm, Karen thought about how the workers' situation was starkly different from that of the birders. The workers piled into a pickup, and as they drove to work, one group broke into song. A majestic red-shouldered hawk stood on a telephone pole above them.

On the south end of the field, at a preserve owned by the Duck and Gun Club, four white-tailed kites were "kiting." They drifted a couple of hundred feet off the ground, looking for small mammals in the vegetation below. Periodically, each stopped and hovered in the air with rapid wing beats, splaying a magnificent white tail.

"It's too sensational to miss," Rick said, coaxing Luna out of the SUV.

J.K. looked on.

Luna came out and looked at the kites, and then, being too uncomfortable here in the open with all these people and birds, she retreated to the safety of the SUV.

A swarm of swallows appeared. Two barn swallows were called out and one tree swallow before they were gone as quickly as they came. The dance of the

barn swallows shimmering against the sky completed the day's brilliant success—three new birds for J.K.'s count. J.K. felt invincible, as though the world
and all its birds lay spread out before him. Life would have been decent if
Luna's mood hadn't soured so quickly, but there was nothing he could do about
it. He'd had a duty to steer his flock through the day's itinerary. As they drove
out of the sod farms and toward a grove of tamarisk trees, he became talkative
to counter her silence. "You guys should check out the pelagic in October," he
said to Blake and Karen. "October is a good month for sea birds."

Blake looked at his mother, eyes fired up. He had never been on a pelagic trip.

And for good reason, Karen thought. Apart from her dread of seasickness,
she wasn't crazy about the price. "How much are they now?" she asked.

"About a hundred dollars a pop," J.K. said, "but they're really worth it."

"Mom . . ." began Blake, clasping his hands in prayer.

"I know what you want," Karen told him, laughing, "but it's not going
to happen."

"It would be a chance for you to meet Ed McCoy," J.K. said. "He's good at
that fundraising stuff."

"I'll be good," Blake pleaded. "Reeaally goood!"

"Maybe Ed can come to one of our meetings," Karen said, ignoring her son.

"He has no time." J.K. snacked on Cheezits and passed them around. "He's
expecting twins any minute now. And he's hoping they're born between the two
pelagics. He'd hate to miss October."

The gang speculated on names for the twins. "Lucy and Virginia," Karen
said, referring to the warblers. "Lesser and Greater," Blake said, preferring
sandpipers.

"Clark's Grebe and Western Grebe" was J.K.'s suggestion.

"No child of mine will ever be called Clark's Grebe or Western Grebe,"
Luna said.

"I'd like to name my first daughter 'Prothonotary,' " Rick said.

Karen gazed at him with sparkling eyes and giggled uncontrollably.


Warblers are the delight of the fall migration season, and it was just these
puffs of magic that J.K. was hoping to catch at the "tams." But when they arrived at the tamarisk grove, the sun was so fierce that Karen felt like she was
walking directly underneath it. They had been on their feet for seven hours already. Luna was now permanently fixed in the SUV, and everyone guessed that
it was futile to try to coax her out. Walking along the tamarisks, flanked by a
dirt field and a farmer's house, they were treated to the hostile barks of the

farmer's dog, who leapt at the fence like a panther.

It soon became clear that all the warblers here were the nondescript orange-crowned. The old ladies in the group were beginning to fade. Even the younger birders ducked into the tamarisks to snatch what little shade the trees offered.

"These tams are an orange-crown colony," J.K. noted with disappointment. He told the flock that he had a second tamarisk grove up his sleeve and began to give directions.

Zanne, her snowy hair glistening as much as her silk tank top, tried to drum up support for lunch. "Have you brought lunch?" she asked Frank, Karen, and some others. Noting their nods, she walked up to J.K.

"Are we planning to stop for lunch?"

"Lunch?" J.K. said, as though he'd never heard the word before. "I thought people had lunch on the fly."

The Egret explained that she had a cooler and needed to spread out its contents to fix her lunch before eating it. But J.K. was unmoved. In response to her outraged expression and the pleading look of old Jean Savant, with whom she was carpooling, he said, "This is as good as it's going to get. At the second tams, there's parking for only three cars at each end, and we're right on the road."

Seeing that the current spot was devilishly sun-baked and there were no seating arrangements, the Egret swore, grabbed Savant, and left. But when the rest of the group got to the second grove, the two ladies were already parked in one of the three spots, meekly eating sandwiches in their car. The second tamarisk grove stood like a thin wall between a busy road and a strawberry farm. They parked their vehicles on one shoulder and birded on the other.

"Be careful," J.K. said. "The cars drive by really fast here and there's a high probability of getting hit while birding."

"Save that excitement for somebody else's trip," Rick added.

The single file of tamarisks turned out to be such a warbler heaven and produced such wings of gold that even the wilted old ladies began to revive. The warblers were bountiful and could be seen well with the naked eye. Blake swung up his camera and clicked, creeping from tree to tree like an over-stimulated monkey. The friendliest of the birds, those he got the best shots of, were hermit warblers, an uncommon species, perched on branches and foliage as close as five feet away. There were roughly fifty to eighty birds in the line of trees, and a dozen could be seen all at once by even a careless, old-lady glance.

"We've hit the jackpot," Rick said.

J.K. grinned, satisfied that he had lived up to his reputation as a trip leader.

Even rare species, such as a female American redstart and a black-and-white warbler, were seen flitting about, both of which are found primarily on the East Coast. That the black-and-white warbler was found—a count bird—was cause for celebration for both J.K. and Rick. The warbler was easy to identify, as it was white with black stripes and behaved like a creeper, scuttling up and down a tree trunk, gleaning insects along the way. The redstart fanned its yellow and black tail to attract insects; it hopped down to a branch, cunningly fanned its tail, grabbed whatever insect might come, and then hopped to another branch to repeat the trick. The most numerous of the uncommon warblers were the black-throated grays. A few were even seen on the ground, foraging for food.

The warbler display went over with the group like an extravagant dessert at the end of a feast, and J.K. felt an irresistible urge to top it off by going to look for owls at a nearby haunt. But he restrained himself when he saw the toxic expression on the face of his guest.

*9*

*I*n the evening, J.K. took Luna to Café Santorini, his favorite old-town restaurant, where the tablecloths were impeccable, and the warm rosemary breads were to die for. He ordered more expensive fare than he could afford—it was highway robbery, but he accepted it. He had only to look at the downward tilt of her face and the uncertain expression in her eyes to realize that she was in a fragile state and would need pampering to counter her unfortunate experience on the birding trip. They ate out on the patio.

"I thought it might be interesting . . ." Luna said, dipping rosemary bread into a plate of olive oil, ". . . but it felt weird. It's like the birders weren't human; they were glued to their bins like machines."

"I should've warned you. We get pretty focused on the birding trips. We have to be, or else we'll miss the birds. But I don't think I act like a machine."

"No, not you!" Her blueberry eyes flickered.

With a pita bread, J.K. swiped up the spicy hummus from his Mediterranean plate.

Luna warmed up to the wine and the expertly spiced food as she listened to the stories J.K. recalled about his early birding mishaps in New Jersey. Each faint smile that flitted across her face renewed his hope that the exhausting day would blur in her memory. She had a mix of fragility and courage that had drawn him to her ever since they met a few months ago at Leaves. After they had spoken a few times, it was interesting to discover how her brain orbited. He had gotten so used to the detached, understated way his parents showed affection that, when confronted with Luna's feisty nature, he sensed that she experienced life far more intensely. J.K.'s only regret was that his breakup with Anne Marie still made him feel too god-awful to be in any way present for Luna.

As they walked back to her car, J.K. said, "Actually, there's another place I'd like to take you, that is, if you're serious about wanting to spend more time outdoors."

"And this isn't a birding scheme?"

"Nope. It's a hiking scheme."

Luna groaned. "My body is not as conditioned as yours. So I get hot and bothered easy. But my spirit knows that fresh air is just what I need right now."

A few days later, J.K. got Luna to pack up some stuff, and deposit it into the trunk of the Birdmobile. Earlier in the afternoon, he had thrown two sleeping bags under the back seat.

The Mojave Desert was one of J.K.'s favorite trips, but the Big Year had prevented him from going there. He drove Luna into the desert just as the sun was being swallowed by the horizon, which was perfect, because he had come equipped with his black light. Luna looked confused, but his gleaming eyes told her to wait for an explanation.

J.K. walked her into the thick of the desert and shined the light in the like-liest places. The trick worked. In the dark, the scorpions glowed fluorescent green in its glare.

"Look how fast they go!" he cried. It was fun to see them scurry about. "They hear the sound of our shoes and they want to get out of here. They could get squished like any other bug."

"You're crazy!" she said good-naturedly.

They drove to Clark Mountain in the black of night. Armed with heavy-duty flashlights, they hiked along the dirt road and eventually up the steep in-cline that rose out of the desert like a phantom. They got cut up pretty badly getting there because of the thorns, but Luna kept up the best she could, as some part of her wanted to please J.K.

Luna wasn't a bad hiker, but J.K.'s brisk pace tired her. She stopped and leaned against a gnarled Joshua tree. "I'm getting a million scratches on my legs."

"The view in the morning will be worth the trouble," J.K. said.

"I'll be too wasted to enjoy it."

Luna kept on climbing, but she grew quiet.

The final, steep minutes to the top of Clark Mountain were terrifying for her. Their flashlights did nothing to relieve the stony darkness. He hiked on, feeling exhilarated, trying to encourage her. There were few things he enjoyed more than camping overnight on top of this mountain in a sleeping bag with only the sky above.

"We're sleeping without a tent?" Luna said when they got to the top.

He nodded. "We're here. Let's just enjoy it."

"We should knock out our shoes before putting them on in the morning," she said, "in case there are scorpions inside."

"Oh, yeah, I've heard that. Also that a reptile might crawl over my face at night if I sleep without a tent. But I've never run across anyone who said, 'The other day I woke up to find a dozen scorpions in my shoes!' Or, 'I opened my eyes, and there he was—a rattlesnake on my chest!'"

She groaned. "I hope you'll call for a helicopter instead of racing me down the mountain, in case an animal attacks me at night."

After they brushed their teeth using the water in her Aquafina bottle, they lay in their sleeping bags staring at the stars above.

"I have something for you."

"Uh-huh?"

J.K. pulled out the ring from his pocket, and showed it to her. It was a silver ring, with a pretty turquoise bead. He'd bought it at a campus bazaar.

Luna looked at him, bewildered.

He found it was hard to explain (even to himself) what he was doing. "It's a friendship ring," he said. "Nothing sentimental. I happened to pick it up without even thinking about it. Toss it down the mountain if you like. It's not expensive."

"If you were gonna give it to me, why not at Café Santorini? Right now I close my eyes and I see green scorpions and I'm half frightened to death!"

He looked away, and spoke with hesitation. "It might have confused you if I gave it to you then, and I'm my most courageous out in the open."

She looked at him, touched by how insecure he sounded.

Unzipping her sleeping bag, she reached over to him. "This is a surprise. The only thing is, are you this crazy all the time?"

He laughed. "I don't think of myself as being crazy."

"You're easy to talk to," she said, "unlike someone else I know."

"Who?"

She shrugged. "It doesn't matter. I'll tell you later."

They smiled sympathetically at each other. She put on the ring and kissed it.

"Quiero un beso," she said.

"Come again?"

She leaned over and kissed him.

This was joy. On top of his favorite mountain!

The rush of this moment was beyond what he might have anticipated. Surprisingly, he started to feel that everything that he wanted was no longer out of his reach. Knowing that Anne Marie would not be his companion for life was still a blow. It was Anne Marie's nature to expect him to divine her needs. Had she punished him because he'd hesitated to get engaged? Would this ring, if he'd remembered to purchase it in time, have changed the course of events?

He'd felt his safety net sagging after the breakup. He so wanted to stop feeling like a spider she'd swatted casually with her fancy handbag. Tonight, for the first time since that horrible afternoon in New Brunswick, things felt all right.

Reaching across sleeping bags, they kissed each other until they'd exhausted all possibilities from this position. Then he pulled her, gently, into his sleeping bag. When she didn't resist, he spread out his bag to make enough space for two, and pulled her sleeping bag over them as a blanket. Thus situated, they embraced, and for so long that the lingering embrace mingled with the night air, and the trees barely swaying above them also became part of it. Having already broken their promise to "not get sentimental," it was impossible now, in the scheme of things, to move backwards; so they moved in the only direction that still lay open—toward each other.

"So this is how you stay warm? Luna teased, her cheek resting momentarily in the curve of his neck.

"I'm usually here alone," J.K. said shyly. And yet, Anne Marie's shadow was with him—he couldn't shake it off. His lips brushed against Luna's collarbone, then played on it as though it were a flute. Luna giggled. He felt sorry he wasn't fully there for Luna, although he tried to be. He got lost in the softness of her and then—oh so fast—the moment of urgency, of release, was over. The tiredness from the hike blanketed them, and he drifted off. Only the embrace remained—and it was the embrace of two children lost in the forest.

A moment came when they were soundly asleep with only the night sky gazing at them.

On Monday morning, he woke her to watch the sun rise. Their campsite lacked even the most basic amenities; she told him she'd never had such a rough time getting ready. She had a noon shift at the café, so she needed to look "half-decent."

"I feel like a cave girl," she said.

Strangely though, through her looks, or in anything she said, there was only the slightest reference to what had happened between them the previous night.

They hiked hurriedly down the mountain, avoiding the thorn bushes, now that they could see where they were going. They jumped into the Honda, and he sped her straight toward town. If they were lucky, they'd get to Leaves almost in time.

There were too many billboards on this highway. He didn't like how they jarred his view.

"Remember I told you there was something I was brooding about?" Luna said in the car. J.K. glanced at her. She looked as unsure of herself as he'd ever seen.

"Uh-huh."

"That was about my first boyfriend, who right now happens to also be my boyfriend, and I'd probably prefer it if he were no longer my boyfriend. That's Luke—he's in my band."

"That's confusing," J.K. said, feeling let down. "Actually, that makes my head spin. Why didn't you say anything last night?"

"Cause I'm still mixed-up in *my* head—still thinking about it," she said, stiffening. "That's why I need to spend time outdoors. When my head clears up, one of these days, I'll check in with you and let you know."

"Okay, that's cool," he said. He became aware that his hands had uncomfortably gripped the steering wheel, and when he tried to relax, his chest tightened with a vague sense of betrayal. Everything she'd just said, it was so *not cool*.

Just before he dropped her off at Leaves, he couldn't resist saying, "How come this never came up earlier, that you have a boyfriend?" They had made it in time, mainly because he'd neglected the speed limit.

"Don't talk to me in that accusing tone," Luna said sharply, her eyes flashing. "I don't like that."

Later, after he'd returned to his cubbyhole and showered, J.K. felt almost disgusted with breakups and heartbreaks, and lies and betrayals. She'd used him, after all, to cheat on some poor guy. Luke? Was that his name? This was depressing. And now Luna was contemplating breaking up with this poor loser, probably as heartlessly as Anne Marie had broken up with him.

As J.K. walked over to the physics building, he decided he'd go "girl-free" for a while.

# 10

*A* Chinese elm guarded the front yard of the Mercer house. Karen had been meaning to get the tree uprooted and plant a native oak instead, but she never found the time. On a warm October evening, the patio was cluttered with old birdhouses and the remains of science projects. Rick walked up the creaking front steps and heard Blake practicing the piano. The boy was working on a Hayden sonata. Nine-year-old Crystal scurried to open the front door. She wore her hair in long, sinuous plaits and she greeted Rick with a serious expression, wondering what he was doing here. Her face, the color of wheat bread, reflected her father's soft, mixed, ethnic features, whereas Blake favored his mother and looked British.

"Come on in," Karen's voice called from inside. "I'm just getting the wine out. And I promise it's not Corona!"

"Good," Rick said. "Your house smells wonderful."

"That's the cake, not the wine," Crystal cut in.

"I always get my wine and cake mixed up."

The girl pierced him with another look. Of all the oldies in the bird society, she found Rick the most dangerous, with his sharply sculpted features and resonant, masculine voice. Feeling her legs go pins-and-needles in his presence, she fled and hid behind her father's trousers. Oscar responded by giving her a comforting, affectionate hug.

On his way out to teach a class at the community college where he was a professor, Oscar was stuffing papers into a briefcase. A dark balding man, mildly rotund, with a gentle smile, he rarely had anything to say to Rick. The men greeted each other, exchanged a word about the performance of the newish SUV, and said goodbye.

It was a sunny evening in October, and Rick kept his cowboy hat on. Karen had set up a table overlooking the pond in the backyard. A black phoebe was fly-catching from a stubby orange tree. On the olive tablecloth was a spread of freshly-baked, double-chocolate cake and gingerbread.

To ready herself for the evening, Karen had gone to Joss Canyon, where she'd had a frustrating talk with Billy Grimsby. Hummingbird earrings danced beside her face as she moved about adding touches to the table, while Rick settled in. "See the trouble I go through to get you to come?" In a blouse with a painted Matilija poppy, she was as animated as her husband was subdued.

Rick grinned, feeling his stress melting under the canopy of her warmth. Meg's suggestion—that if Karen were so enthusiastic about organizing a Centennial celebration, then she should take over as president—had caused him endless anxiety. Even at this late hour, he was debating how to bring up the subject. Karen had her own considerable load as Hospitality Chair. Even though he regarded Karen as a threat to his tranquility after the last board meeting, he knew she meant well. Her problem was in the overzealousness department. She was too idealistic, not practical enough. And yet her caring made up for these defects.

They heard Zanne's sharp voice inside, teasing Blake about jumbling up the climax of the Hayden sonata. "Blake is going to provide the musical accompaniment this evening," Karen said, glowing in her role as hostess, when Zanne came to the table. "You don't have to tip him, but he might benefit from a word of encouragement on the way out."

Crystal helped her mother set up the wine glasses and quail motif napkins. Then she grabbed the tween novel she was reading, ran into the living room, and flopped on the sofa next to the piano. She whispered something in her brother's ear, after which his playing grew unsure.

The adults speculated on who else might come.

"I'm expecting ten more people to show," Karen said. "There's enough goodies for double that in case we have a windfall." There had been an open invitation to the board, and Karen had posted notices on their listserv inviting members to help shape the Centennial. She had sweetened the offer with the promise of evening refreshments.

"I thought Kenny sounded pretty enthusiastic," Zanne said. "He ought to come."

Rick was skeptical, knowing better than to expect Kenny here. "I'd like to see our vice-president show up," he muttered.

"Fat chance!" Karen said. "Herr Professor only has time for turkeys." They laughed, having heard year after year that Robert Kern was still decoding the turkey genome. "Honestly, does he have no shame? It's on his resume that he's our V.P., but he makes not one contribution!"

As the minutes ticked by, the glow on Karen's face dimmed and turned to unease. The possibility presented itself that the cake and wine might be all theirs.

"I wouldn't want to share anyway," Rick said. "It's good wine."

Karen's lips settled into a thin line that drained the charm from her face. She stared at the beautiful cake she had baked, loaded with chocolate and large enough to serve twelve.

"I'll start by digging into the cake," Rick said, "and get that off your hands."

"Go right ahead," Karen said. "But don't worry about the cake. The kids will take care of that. They'll finish it or it'll finish them. It's my fault—I got carried away."

"Where should we start?" Rick said, discomfited by her pained expression.

"I think it's clear as daylight," the Egret said, pouring more wine. "No one's interested."

"That's pessimistic, don't you think?" Rick said, surprised that he wasn't agreeing with her. But he could tell that Karen was crushed. If she were blooming like a Matilija poppy at the start of the evening, the poppy seemed to have withered suddenly. He thought guiltily about his plan to resign.

"I don't know why we talked ourselves into this," the Egret said, "but if we're nuts enough, we'll have to do something about the Centennial ourselves." She stopped to straighten out a persistent cough. "Excuse me! If Frank and Dana pitch in when they can, we'll take all the help we can get. But it's clear that we three are the poles on which this tent is hanging."

"That still sounds pessimistic," Rick said. He looked at Karen. "That was a good idea you had the other day. Whoever breaks the record would get us publicity."

"If you can break the record, bless your heart!" the Egret said. "Did you squeeze out enough shorebirds in September?"

"Not really," Rick said. "It's too bad I have a life beyond birding." He doodled his score on a quail napkin, which he moved slightly in Karen's direction. She glanced at it—325.

"I'm beginning to wonder if we can pull this thing off," Karen said. "I mean if the members aren't interested, maybe we're barking up the wrong tree." It chafed her that her soiree had failed. She recalled her days as an actress, when nothing crushed her as much as rejection. Back then she'd been accepted into an elite actors' program, but she grew tired of egomaniacal wannabe actors and gave up the theater for a stable family life. Now, between her family and part-time work as an English lecturer, she had no time to breathe, and yet she felt like an underachiever.

Karen's thoughts fluttered as she tried to pinpoint the moment when she'd lost control over her life. In her twenties, she'd been full of those juices that cause young people to be so embarrassingly ambitious. But in her thirties she became a mother, and gave up her stressful job as a drama teacher. Life had a way of molding one's intellect into a fixed thing, no longer vital or filled with wonder. Was she becoming solid and square? Where was that enigmatic beauty she'd been? "The world's your oyster," Karen's mother had told her then, and her mom was not known for saying nice things to Karen. Maybe if she hadn't been so talented in the first place, the dissipation of her potential would cause her less pain. But she refused to accept that she'd already had her peak experiences and that she must live out the rest of her days feeding on their memory. She loved her family, every inch of them, but her life was an anticlimax.

That she was fighting tears was clear when she looked up at Rick with pinkish eyes.

Rick was unable to articulate his discomfort at seeing her pain, but Karen knew from the concern on his face that he cared.

"I'm sorry," Karen said. She felt that people must be going numb inside. It was astonishing that they didn't care about a hundred-year-old society, about traditions, or anything that didn't involve their personal interests. "They love going on birding trips, but they don't realize that if there's no A.B.S., there aren't going to be any trips. And unless they care about the environment, one day there aren't going to be all those pretty birds to see!"

Blake and Crystal approached the table, each goading the other to go first. Blake's eyes zeroed-in on the score doodled on Rick's napkin. Three hundred and twenty-five! Rick must have gotten a lot of shorebirds. J.K. was one bird behind—the first time he'd trailed Rick in the Big Year race.

"Mom, can we eat the cake now?" Crystal said.

"Sure, there's plenty to go around," Karen said.

To the adults, she said, "I don't know why the others can't see it, but I think A.B.S. is in danger of collapsing. We have no money. No plan. No membership. And we've forgotten about conservation. I think we should take the word "conservation" out of our mission statement and come clean that we're nothing but a birding club. You know, just be done with the Alpena Bird Society!"

Blake stopped chewing his cake. "Is A.B.S. going to die?" he said, looking at Rick as if it were his fault.

"Not while I'm alive, I don't think," the Egret said.

Sandwiched between the passions of two fierce women, Rick felt too cowardly to retreat. "Your mom was describing a hypothetical," he said to the boy. "The reason we're here tonight is to make sure that A.B.S. never has to collapse."

Blake gobbled up his cake, still deciding whether or not to believe Rick.

Light returned to Karen's face. "If that's how you two feel," she said, "I'll try to keep my chin up."

"There you go!" Rick said. But he despaired at having encouraged them too much. He kicked himself for drinking too much wine. Things were going in a direction that would land him in worse trouble with Meg. Unless he turned this around, she would never swallow the Ecuador trip. Instead, they would have the mother of all fights.

"Actually," he added, attempting to keep to his agreement with his wife, "I was going to suggest that if you want to take over the Centennial, I won't stand in the way. One of these days we'll have to look for a new president anyway."

"Oh, Rick!" Karen cried. "No, no, no! You misunderstood me completely. I don't know why you thought that I could have been so mean as to have suggested that you don't care. Oh, no! Far from it. It's because of you that Blake and I joined A.B.S. in the first place."

Rick looked on embarrassed, as Karen serenaded his abilities and the Egret joined in the chorus until he felt at best, a savior, and at worst, a hero, grossly misunderstood by his own wife. He shone under the sunbeams of their approval. As much as he disliked Karen's speechmaking, there was something to what she said. And then he would hate to see A.B.S. go back to the atrophied state from which he had rescued it. Not knowing how else to respond, he turned to practical matters. "We need a venue for the Centennial," he said.

"I wish we could do it at Joss Canyon," Karen said, putting her hand on his, relieved that things were straightened out between them.

"I've been wondering about it for months," the Egret said. "Are they ever going to rebuild that Nature Center?"

"It makes me mad," Karen said, savoring a cake crumb. "They've had that pathetic trailer for months. Grimsby mans it part-time. He says they're not rebuilding because a vagrant caused the fire and there are still vagrants in the area. I'm sorry, but that's lame. And the excuses he made—for trapping cowbirds by the dozen and murdering them—makes me wonder if he has something to hide!"

"Hopefully there's some science behind what Grimsby is doing," Rick said. "I've heard rumors that a developer wants to buy the property for a condo complex."

"God knows we don't have enough of those, right?" Karen grew thoughtful. Her grandmother had told her that at one time a river of poppies ran down from Alpena to the ocean. And now Joss Canyon was Alpena's last remaining wild land, where birds were being murdered and the land itself was now under threat. Although cowbirds were supposedly being euthanized because of their habit of parasitizing the nests of vireos, vireo populations were declining anyway, for some other mysterious reason.

"It's just a rumor, I hope," Karen said.

"I've heard the developer has applied for permits," Rick said.

"D.W.P. manages the land," the Egret said. "J.K. told me they're pretty harsh to trespassing birders. They threatened to arrest him once."

"I wish they had. We would have gotten some publicity out of that!" Karen said. "I think we've got to celebrate the Centennial in Joss Canyon and reclaim the place or else we'll lose it."

Rick liked the idea of keeping Joss Canyon wild as much as any birder, but he said that it was too ambitious a project for A.B.S. to take on unless they had a large grant. And even then he wouldn't know where to begin. The canyon was burnt in places and weedy or overgrown in others. While stubborn birders still scoped out the area, it wasn't practical for the average person to go trampling over hidden rattlesnakes while fighting off out-of-control poison oak.

"We could put up big, fat educational signs about cowbirds in the canyon," Karen said, "to shame Grimsby into restoring the area, and not turn it into a concentration camp."

"This is a terrific idea, but we don't have the money for any of it. You have very expensive ideas," Rick said. "Honestly, I don't know how you and Oscar get along!"

Karen laughed. "I get him to think it was his idea in the first place. Just think, if we could do the Centennial dinner and inaugurate the signs in a restored canyon!"

Rick sighed. The Centennial loomed before him like a monstrous hydra; each time he cut off one head, several others took its place. Desperate to extricate himself from the monster's clutches, he thought of Ed McCoy, last year's Big Year winner, who was also a fundraising consultant.

"Wouldn't it be great to have Ed on our side?" he said.

Karen looked on, unsure. "I've heard he's not the easiest person to deal with."

"Ed's planning to move," Rick said. "Maybe he could be lured to Alpena. People do want to get involved. Sometimes all they need is to be asked. I think you should take Blake on his first pelagic. Ed is helping me with the October one, and then we could invite him to join our Centennial Committee."

"Would you do that, maybe?" Karen said.

"I'll be too busy leading the pelagic to woo Ed," Rick said. "You're better at wooing, anyway."

Karen could not resist and, for a moment, their faces were joined in smiles. Rick secretly hoped that Ed would talk some sense into Karen. A.B.S. wasn't even able to raise its operating expenses each year, and to contemplate raising thousands of dollars for the signs, and the dinner, and restoring the canyon, was maniacal.

"That'll be expensive soliciting," Karen said, thinking about the hundred-dollar tickets for the pelagic trips.

"If anyone can help us, it's Ed," Rick said. "He does consultations for companies at a steep price. I wish I could tell you that a phone call would cut it. But Ed will slip away faster than an eel. He knows more than he lets on. You really have to sit him down and squeeze him dry. He doesn't like to talk."

Zanne's daughter was coming home from Boston the weekend of the pelagic. "She has some big news for me. I'm dying to hear if it's anything to do with the M-word. She's just over forty and beautiful. I don't know what takes these kids so long. Anyway, I can't drag her to a pelagic, though that's what J.K. would do!" They laughed. "But I'd like to put fifty bucks towards *your* trip."

"Oh, that's too much." Karen began.

"But you're going for us, and we ought to do something!"

"I'll put in twenty for Blake," Rick said, feeling there was no other way out, although it was not his habit to throw money away.

"All right. I'll talk to Ed," Karen said. She sensed from Rick's anxious look how much he was depending on her to win Ed over to their side.

When Blake got the news that he would be going on his first pelagic, he was so overjoyed that he was able to play the Hayden sonata straight through without messing it up. That night, he cleaned up his zoom lens and prayed that the irksome in-between days would hurry along and just let the day of the pelagic arrive.

# 11

$K$aren had been raised to be polite. The British side of her family had instilled this habit in her. Maybe this is why she couldn't go through with show business. That world was too rude for her. But something in her was rebelling now against all that civility. She picked up a bumper sticker and stuck it on her jeep: "Well-behaved women seldom make history." Her husband was amused by this.

Rain smashed on the jeep as Karen and Blake drove to Ventura County, where the October pelagic trip group was to meet at an Oxnard marina. On the side of the highway, a car had spun out of control and hit the guardrail, and was now surrounded by police cars. Karen drove nervously, hoping the rain would subside. Occasionally, it did let up, only to return with evangelical fervor. It took an hour longer than usual to get to the marina.

At the dock, an old woman was handing out nametags. It had stopped raining, but the skies were bleak. Blake's smile spread across his face as he chewed ginger candy. Their local vitamin-store lady swore that ginger controls motion sickness. "It's not toxic like the patch," she said, referring to the pharmaceutical patch many birders use.

They boarded the white, hundred-foot boat, *The Seagull*. Seeing Ed McCoy, a balding, chunky man about her age, Karen walked up and introduced herself as the Hospitality Chair of the Alpena Bird Society. Ed gave her no more than a nod. His thick, almond-shaped face looked strained, resembling the face you might expect after a bad day at work. With a bullhorn in hand, he was coaxing the thirty passengers to collect in one spot while he went through procedures.

"Rick will be on a speaker system for the duration of the trip," he announced. "He'll call out the birds as they fly by. If a passenger becomes motion-sick at any point, they are to avoid the upper deck, where the motion of the boat is magnified."

As they waited for Rick to arrive, another downpour began. Everyone scrambled into the cabin. "No wet ones allowed in here," muttered an old man.

Blake had lingered too long outside, and water was dripping from his nose and hair. Karen held onto his camera so it wouldn't get soaked. After the rain let up, the passengers dispersed, and Karen and Blake headed to the bow, as Rick had recommended. Blake had studied sea birds at length before coming and, knowing that he would begin seeing them within minutes, felt about ready to burst.

Kenny Takahashi stood at the bow in clothes that hung loosely from his lanky frame. Karen greeted him coolly, but that didn't prevent him from divulging that he got seasick on boat trips.

"I wish someone were torturing me instead," he said, straightening out the fake fur collar on his jacket, "so I can just give out the information they need and be done with it."

Karen hinted darkly at the poor attendance at the Centennial meeting.

Kenny grinned. "Ahhhh, that day." His face grew serious and his voice dropped. "My son had a doctor's appointment late in the day, and my wife had a muscle sprain. It was a bad day."

"I'm sorry," Karen said. Kenny's family went to the same church as hers, and she knew that his son had a medical condition.

"I'm on the patch today," he said, indicating the arm on which he had taped the drug to counter motion sickness. "But the expiration date was smudged out. So we'll see what happens."

Karen nodded. She could not make Kenny out. At first she thought that as Conservation Chair, he would be her ally in getting A.B.S. members to move beyond merely compiling their individual life lists of birds to the next and more important step of thinking about the pressures that were causing bird populations to dwindle across the country. Last year Kenny went to a weekend conference on cleaning up the Los Angeles River and reported on the event to their board. Since then he'd done nothing.

The captain came on the speaker system to give his sermon on the three life rings and vests in the boat for anyone who fell overboard. On motion sickness, he advised, "Come to the lower deck and get fresh air. And please do not throw up in the bathrooms!"

The boat began to move. All at once, Karen felt like the boat was rocking and rolling on six-foot waves. She struggled to hold onto the railing and felt lightheaded, as though she were being launched into space and becoming weightless, about to float at any moment. There was no option but to sit down on one of the two benches in the bow. She sat next to Patty Cole, the A.B.S. secretary with an inscrutable baby face and dangling gull earrings. Patty said that she wanted to retire from the snooty jewelry store where she worked so she could spend more time birding. But the stock market had gone down, and her non-birder husband said they couldn't retire just yet.

"I'm steeling myself to go to the upper deck," Karen told her. "I'm here to get Ed involved in our Centennial,"

"That would be great," Patty said. "We have too many octogenarians in A.B.S."

"And they won't be around forever."

"I do a birding class at the arboretum," Patty said, "and the last time, all eight oldies, including Jean Savant, showed up with opera glasses!"

"Oh, God! Jean should know better by now. By the way, we could really use you on our Centennial Committee."

Patty said she would do what she could to help on the day of the Centennial, but that she had too little free time to be involved with planning it.

Karen wondered why people were so reluctant to volunteer a few measly hours. Patty had no kids and no responsibilities other than her job and her husband, and surely she was efficient at handling both by now.

Karen's thoughts were interrupted by a wave of motion sickness. She bit on raw ginger and controlled the urge. Somehow, even though she hadn't willed it, the thread of her life was getting entangled with A.B.S. When she'd been a little girl, her mother took her on a driving trip one summer and they'd camped in the Grand Canyon and in Bryce and Zion. Other than the summers she spent with her aunt in England, socializing with her circle, that summer of camping was the most memorable in her life. A.B.S. was giving her a chance to recreate those experiences for her son. Her husband and daughter weren't into camping vacations, so she had to take Blake on these weekend trips herself.

She heard Rick on the speaker. "Parasitic jaeger at four o'clock."

But there was something terribly wrong in only watching the birds, in extracting pleasure from their cuteness, but not giving a damn if they didn't have places to live after suburban sprawl took away their habitats. Karen couldn't take Blake on the trips and simply stop there. She had to strengthen their doddering society and hold them to their original mission. If she didn't, what sort of example would she be setting for her child? Moreover, she and Rick were the two most vigorous members on the board, and he had come to depend on her. She appreciated Rick not only for the vitality he infused into their meetings, but also because his presence made the birding trips endurable, and even fun.

"Sooty shearwater near the horizon at twelve o'clock," Ed said.

Still seated on the bench, Karen tried to look for the flying bird.

Patty said that they would slow the boat for anything really good, so they needn't worry. "I'm not going to get up for anything that's not a life bird," she said.

Karen walked up to the railing and looked across the sea. She hadn't eaten all morning, except for the ginger and some tea. There was something pleasant about standing at the bow and watching the boat plow forward through the ocean.

"If I'm going to suffer," she said, putting an arm around Blake, "I might as well enjoy the view."

Blake was queasy, but planned on hiding it. He was still too much in awe over the novelty of the trip. The sooty shearwater was a life bird for him, but it flew by too fast. He prayed that the rare, red-billed tropicbird, which had been spotted during the September pelagic, would fly by. A photo of the tropicbird would be unbeatable in the contest. He could hear the drum-roll as he walked up to collect the Young Birders Award. A tossing motion interrupted his day-dream, and he lurched and grabbed the railing with both hands, simultaneously twisting his torso at a painful angle to keep his camera from crashing against the railing.

Karen had to sit down. This time the nausea was real. She spewed out watery ginger over the side. Luckily, no one saw her, but she felt uneasy.

Rick was on the speaker system. He was on the upper deck, where he could share a better view of the birds, along with two-thirds of the bravest passengers, who were either genetically protected from motion sickness or wore steely pharmaceutical armor. Kenny, chewing through a bag of Sun Chips, advised Karen to keep eating anytime she felt queasy. But he was on the patch, and she decided that this advice was not for her.

The sun began shining on the bow and Karen hoped it would do her good. As the rays hit the water parted by the bow, the droplets turned into crystals, flew high into the air and flung themselves back into the sea. The boat veered to the right to avoid a school of dolphins, about 300 strong. They leapt into the air in groups of three, swirls of grey milk and white chocolate, like little girls skipping rope.

Karen and Blake, both nauseous, sat on the bench nibbling raw ginger. Just as Karen closed her eyes to rest, a shower of seawater came flying into their faces. A storm was passing through. Five-foot swells regularly hit the boat. Karen wished she could speak to Ed before she got too sick, but she didn't dare go to the upper deck in these choppy conditions. She was tempted to send Blake up to ask if Ed would come down, but how could she risk letting the boy get sick? She cursed Rick for his wretched idea. There was quite a roll and pitch as the bow tossed with the waves. When the boat slowed for passengers to look at a small dark brown bird, a Leach's storm petrel, the tossing motion was magnified, and she felt like she was being tortured in slow motion. She prayed that sleep would come and rescue her from this sordid misadventure.

"Maybe we should get some water," she said.

Blake walked ahead of her on the way to the cabin and was searching his knapsack for his water bottle when she walked in. Immediately, she knew that the stuffy cabin made her feel worse, so she scooted out. Kenny walked by with a look of suffering in his eyes, and dispensed no more advice. Blake followed her out and got her to drink water, but she had barely gotten to the rail before she threw up in full view of Ed and Rick and the rest of the passengers on the upper deck. Unsure if she were suffering more from seasickness or embarrassment, she staggered back to her bench. Now she was in great shape to woo Ed!

They reached the open Pacific, and the water got rougher. It became hard for Karen to sit on the bench without being utterly sick. Blake came and sat next to her and urged her to suck on raw ginger. She tried to, but now the taste of ginger was too biting and hateful to endure. If only she could sleep through this!

Seeing Karen in such miserable condition, Patty offered to go into the cabin for some medicine. When she returned, Karen put the tiny pink tablet into her mouth and tried to not look at Patty's dangling gull earrings, which were moving annoyingly like pendulums. Karen followed Patty's advice and moved to the rear deck, which was supposed to be more stable.

In the square and larger rear deck, the waves were smaller and less choppy than in the small triangle of the bow. Karen had a view of the Channel Islands and the multitudes of sea gulls hovering over the rear of the boat, waiting to gobble the greasy popcorn one of the old women threw out from an oversized bag.

"A flock of hovering seagulls often attracts other birds who wonder if there's any food to be had," Rick explained over the speaker system.

"Sitting in the rear is great for seeing juvenile seagulls," Patty said.

There was a large, loud splash. Karen and Patty swung around and saw, to their astonishment, that Kenny Takahashi had dived into the water.

There were confused exclamations all around.

"What in hell . . . ?"

"You've got to be kidding!"

Ed and a few others came running down from the upper deck, and the boat turned about with such a violent tossing motion that half a dozen people became deathly sick at once.

Kenny was tadpoling in the open sea. The portly captain ran to get a life ring and vest, which he tossed out to Kenny.

"It's all right. Everything will be fine," cried the captain, who assumed that

Kenny was suicidal. "You're in good hands."

But the grim faces were all on the boat.

Kenny grinned. "It's better out here," he shouted. "I couldn't take it anymore."

"Ken, don't do this to us," Rick yelled, his face purple. "We don't carry insurance on these trips."

"You go on," Kenny said. "I'll follow you."

"We wouldn't want a shark to sniff you out," the captain said, despairing at the possibility of losing a passenger on his watch.

The rest of the birders chimed in and wheedled and bullied Kenny into grabbing onto the life ring. Finally, he was unable to resist their pleas. They yanked him aboard, stripped him, and wrapped his quivering body in blankets.

"A friend of mine at the pharmacy gave me a mega dose of the patch," Kenny said, his words punctuated with shivers. Feeling confident about his armor, he had eaten a greasy shark sandwich last night at a harbor restaurant and washed it down with beer. He never felt as sick in his life as he did on this boat ride, and had jumped into the water for relief.

"I just couldn't take it anymore," he confessed. "The patch must have expired a year ago. I always suspected this pharmacist was a bastard."

Kenny was given a cocktail of pills and "put to sleep" by the captain, who was unwilling to risk having an awake suicidal character on board.

Seeing her chance, Karen grabbed Ed's arm. It was an awkward moment, but she would have howled if necessary just to get his attention.

"I've decided to hit on you," she told him. "Rick says you're planning to move soon, and we're scheming to lure you to Alpena and get you involved with A.B.S."

Ed let out a tinny laugh.

"No, really!" Karen said. "I'd love to get your thoughts on fundraising . . . ummm . . . for our Centennial."

Ed blinked and rubbed his hand over his balding scalp as though waking up a dormant section of his brain. "You already know the best advice I can give you—and it's worked for the L.A. chapter—get all your hard core birders together and do a Big Day Birdathon."

Karen nodded, but she wanted more than vague advice. She told him about her plan to put up signs about cowbirds in Joss Canyon in time for the Centennial.

"You better get on it before they scare off all the birds," Ed said. "Anyhow, Joss Canyon will get sold one of these days."

"Not on my watch, it won't," Karen said.

Ed shrugged and moved toward the stairs.

Karen hollered that she would come talk to him after they docked.

Seeing Kenny lying down on a broad, blue-carpeted seat in the rear deck, Karen decided to do the same. The thin, blue, indoor-outdoor fabric was damp from the morning's rain, but sleep would be welcome at any cost. She put a hat over her face and closed her eyes. When she woke, it was only quarter past two and she tried to go back to sleep. She heard, over the speaker system, and with Blake's shouts repeating the news, that bottle-nosed dolphins were about. The next time she woke up, it was three p.m. She was glad that by then the boat was heading back. The sea was still gray, but it seemed calmer. Blake sat next to her, munching almonds. Refreshed after her sleep, and imagining that the pink tablet Patty had given her was working, Karen accepted some almonds and washed them down with water.

Half an hour later, she was wrenchingly sick. Patty, sitting behind her, and a few others, witnessed the spectacle of her heaving over the rail. Lying down didn't help this time. Blake sat with her all this while, comforting her. Karen wondered if she was going insane. What was she doing on this boat, throwing up like an out-of-control teenager? What compelled her to pay a hundred dollars to get tortured?

In the last year, Karen had noticed that she tired easily and her body wasn't what it used to be. It came as a shock that at forty-three, she had begun to contemplate old age. She hadn't expected to tackle such issues before fifty. She hadn't been to a doctor yet, but she felt that her energy was slipping away. She didn't want to be pessimistic. She knew she had a good many years before her, but she wanted to accomplish *something* while there was still a spark in her. Her job was all right, but her heart wasn't in it like in the old days.

Teaching was a thankless job, and even more so with the sort of students she taught, who would never really meet her expectations. She'd had a few gems over the years, and one had invited her recently to his wedding, but except for the delight of seeing him after so many years, the wedding only made her realize how old she was getting. There was so much potential in her. What a waste if she didn't put herself to use! If her life was to be about giving, then she wanted to give something commensurate with her talents. It frightened her to find herself wondering if she'd made a mistake by abandoning her theatre training for family life. She sensed a wave of bitterness heading in her direction and wanted to do something before she got drenched.

"The B.P.M. of this trip was kinda low," Patty said, referring to the birds-per-mile ratio. She, too, was feeling queasy now, and her baby face looked haggard.

Karen nodded.

Within an hour of port, the boat slowed beside the craggy Anacapa Island where more than five thousand brown pelicans roosted, looking like chopped walnuts on a rich cake. In one groove along the shoreline was a colony of mustard-brown seals. Everything seemed to slow down—the boat, the seals staring back at the humans, the pelicans minding their households, Kenny sleeping in the rear deck, and the turquoise water skimming the island.

Over the speaker, Rick announced from the upper deck that he had been on some 100-plus pelagics, and this was the fewest number of birds he had ever encountered. "So don't judge all pelagics by this one!" he laughed.

When they docked, land became a sacred treasure to Karen, and she wanted to get down on her knees and kiss it, but she had to go to the upper deck and speak to Ed before he slipped away. "I'd love to know more about the Big Day idea," she told him. Rick needed to rush back for dinner with his in-laws and had waved her a quick goodbye. "Maybe we can talk over coffee?"

Ed looked at her, distracted. "Sorry about the trip. But these things happen." He seemed ready to leave, but Karen fixed him with a sharp look. She had suffered far too much for it to be in vain.

"Yeah, the Big Day," he said. "Okay. Get your co-workers, and relatives, and your manicurist to sponsor you for fifty cents or a dollar-a-bird, just like any Birdathon. But instead of going at it piecemeal, really plan it out. J.K. knows how to do it. Four people can carpool and count off the same birds. But if you're all sponsored by different people, you can each pull in one or two grand. That's six or seven grand right there."

The captain came up to Ed and waited to speak to him.

"The signs are going to cost $10,000," Karen said. She knew a printer who had agreed to do permanent illustrated signs for that price. "And then there's the dinner . . ."

"Make it pay for itself, maybe more. Charge as much as you can."

"But we want to subsidize the tickets to encourage the community to come."

"Good luck with *that*!" He looked at her as if she were a clueless tot.

She wanted to punch him in the face, but instead she gave him her most appealing smile. "You're so good at this. We'd love to have you on our Centennial Committee."

Ed looked at her, exasperated. "I don't know how to sugarcoat this for you," he said. "The fact is that A.B.S. has been coming apart for a while. I feel sorry for you guys, and I'd be sorry to hear that your chapter had to fold. You need a miracle to bail you out."

Karen looked on, stunned at his rudeness.

"There's nothing I can do. I mean, Skua is going to be in town, and I don't even have time to take him birding," he said, referring to the president of the National Bird Society. "I haven't slept for a week."

"I'm going to need something extra for the clean-up staff," the captain broke in. "You should take a look at the restrooms." And Ed McCoy and the captain busied themselves with the grim details of wrapping up a pelagic trip.

As they walked back to the parking lot, Blake looked at his mother's wan face and sensed that she was suffering from something more than the disappointment of spotting too few birds. There was a melancholic determination about her. He felt confused, not knowing which mattered the most to her—his interest in shorebirds or the resolve forming in her mind.

"How dare he speak of us as though we're a ragtag bunch of beggars?" Karen said. "We're the oldest birding society in the U.S., and we won't go down easy."

The image of Ed's condescending smile returned to her, invisibly mocking her even now. That smug S.O.B. "I'm going to prove Ed wrong," she said. He said he hadn't slept for a week. The twins! She should have congratulated him, not that it would have made a difference.

Blake looked at his mother's eyes and ashen face, and he felt that whatever she was doing must be all right and he should back her up. He couldn't say why, but after her enduring the pelagic, she went up a notch in his estimation.

They got back to the jeep, and Karen found herself staring at the bumper sticker, "Well-behaved women seldom make history."

"If the president of National is coming to town," she said to Blake, "maybe J.K. can ask him to be the guest of honor at our Centennial. That, if anything, will spur Rick and the old fogies into action!"

Blake giggled. He was relieved to see the color returning to his mother's face.

But his excitement vanished when his pelagic photos came back from the camera store. They came out gray and blurry; there were only white smudges where there should have been birds. The only good shot was of Kenny floundering in the water, his mustache hanging like a shrimp. But how could he submit this curiosity to a Bird Photo contest?

# 12

The Saturday afternoon was bright and supple, and J.K. wished it would go on forever. Light shone on his bronzed face and cropped hair as he sauntered past the "NO TRESSPASSING" signs towards the dried-out Joss Canyon wash. There was nothing he liked better than to be out in the field with good birders, and Ed and Jim were that and more. Jim Skua, the president of the National Bird Society, was in L.A. for a couple of days, and Ed, who had political ambitions, wanted to treat him to an impromptu birding trip with their local boy wonder.

J.K. was torn about the invitation. He was saddled with the paper he and Dave were working on and trying to swerve around Kaminski's objections. Then he got a call from Karen. She wanted him to organize a Big Day to raise money for A.B.S. He made a vague promise to do one next spring. And then she said, "I need you to see Skua and invite him to be the guest of honor at the Centennial."

What really tempted J.K. to put aside his paper in favor of the trip was that Ed was up for taking Skua to the forbidden part of Joss Canyon, a premier birding spot for rare birds. The area was potential Bell's vireo habitat, and J.K. was intent on adding that bird to his Big Year count.

When he mentioned the plan to Karen, she said darkly, "Glad to hear that Ed has free time on his hands. I hope you can get Skua to accept in his presence, so that Ed knows not to commission a requiem for us just yet."

A mild wind ruffled the blue-eyed grass, setting its delicate blades trembling. Ed McCoy, in a creamy summer jacket worn over loose jeans, wandered about the grassy wash in the hopes of seeing a variant like the northern parula J.K. had spotted here in June, or the indigo bunting in July.

It was a delicious day for J.K. and there was just one thing spoiling it. At the other end of the wash, county men operated droning motorized mowers. The aroma of fresh cut grass gave J.K. no pleasure here. The long wild grass clumped into thickets preferred by secretive birds like the Bell's vireo. J.K. came often to the wash on the sly at odd hours to look for birds and had seen an array of local and migrant rarities here. But the county authorities were fanatical about cutting the grass down, slashing the habitat available to the birds. In the summer, J.K. had been harassed and kicked off this flood basin more than once. The last time, as he was being chewed out, he asked the county workers if they would give him a ride out. They flat-out refused. One county man threatened to call the cops on him.

The county men stopped their work and moved toward the three birders.

"Bastards," J.K. whispered.

Ed and Jim looked on as two D.W.P men in uniforms with glinting silver belt buckles walked up to them. "Y'all shouldn't be here," the older man barked.

"We're showing Mr. Skua around," Ed began. "He's the pres . . ."

"You aren't supposed to be here. Now get off the property!"

Ed's face twitched with anger. The baby fat on his face softened his features, and in private he was an easygoing, jovial man. But now he looked tense. J.K. worried that Ed's infamous temper would flare up.

"You people need a permit to cut this grass. Can I see it?" Ed said.

"I think I've made it clear what you ought to do," the D.W.P. man said. "Did you read the signs when you came in?" His partner looked on sullenly.

"I'd like to see your permit," Ed persisted.

"The signs are in big black letters," said the other. "Can't you read?"

Ed pulled a cell phone out of his jacket. "I know all your supervisors by name. I'm going to call Billy Grimsby and ask what's going on and complain about this."

The partner threw a nervous glance at the older man as he stood there, figuring out how to respond to these pesky trespassers. The older county man frowned and pierced the trespassers with cold green eyes.

The birders stood their ground.

The D.W.P. man signaled to his partner and they turned around. "Can't read . . ." he muttered as he left.

This unexpected victory amused J.K. He had warned Ed about possible trouble at this location. Karen was having a hard time getting a response from the D.W.P. about whether A.B.S. could put up signs in Joss Canyon. "I can't even get Grimsby to return my calls," she complained. "I don't know why he'd shut us out."

J.K. thought it important to test Karen's theory. That the county men were shaken by Ed's challenge suggested that their underhanded management of the wash would not bear scrutiny. The Least Bell's vireo was on the federal Endangered Species list; any potential habitat was a sensitive area. If the bird were actually seen breeding here, the wash would become a protected area. Armed with their report of this encounter, Karen might be able to pursue Grimsby more aggressively about putting up signs here.

They came upon a large, box-shaped object covered with muddy canvas, and a peek under the tarp revealed that it was a cowbird trap from last spring.

"For every cowbird, seven other birds get caught for no reason," J.K. told them. "They set up these traps during breeding season. By the time the wrong bird's released, it has spent far too much time away from its nest and may have no choice but to abandon it."

"All this supposedly to protect any Bell's that might breed here," Ed said. "But they don't stop mowing down the place! So the Bell's can't breed."

"The Bell's have disappeared," J.K. said. "So their program isn't exactly working—not for the birds anyhow."

"It's incredible," Skua said, shaking his head. A tall, athletic man, his expertly moisturized face defied age. "They get government money for these traps. I was in Texas recently, and they have a pretty much free-for-all cowbird policy there. They encourage boy scouts to shoot them. Their attitude is that the only good cowbird is a dead cowbird."

"It's a crime," J.K. said.

"The D.W.P. men have been killing cowbirds in the area for years," Ed said.

J.K. nodded. But he didn't expect the Bell's vireos to make a comeback. He saw one here last year, but it didn't stick around. He had killed too much time already looking for one for his Big Year. The Bell's vireo had become as elusive as the completion of his physics paper. If the D.W.P. men cared even one iota about the Bell's, they wouldn't be so decoupled from the bird's needs and would stop cutting the grass (as if this were an ordinary park!) and destroying the dense habitats this shy bird preferred.

"Maybe they're worried about flash floods? In Southern California, in the middle of a drought year?" Ed kidded.

"They're a bunch of idiots." J.K. paused, and then decided to not let loose his thoughts in the presence of the president of the National Bird Society. He wished they'd just let the wash grow into the willow forest it was aching to be. Three years of no cutting was all it needed, and the fourth spring he'd bet his life that breeding Bell's vireos would set up housekeeping here.

"I suspect they're afraid this area will become protected," Skua told them. "And they don't want to deal with that."

"Rick's been hearing rumors that the city wants to sell the land," J.K. said.

"Are you guys planning a counter-offensive?" Skua said.

"That's why Karen wants to put up informational signs here, about cowbirds and vireos, so people get to know what's at stake and have a say in how the area's managed. After the fire, it's really gone downhill." He explained Karen's theory—that the D.W.P. was being encouraged by the city to treat the wash as a wasteland so that the city could get public approval to sell the land at a premium price to developers.

"By the way, how's your count going?" Skua said, with the perfect ease of a birder who thinks briefly about conservation when the subject comes up, but is eager to get down to real business. "Rick's told me about your competition."

"Three hundred and thirty," J.K. said. "There used to be a time when birding was still fun."

Skua smiled. "Those days of innocence are long gone. By the way, Rick is at 329, just one bird behind you."

"Thanks." J.K. realized it had been wise to disclose his count to Skua, against his instincts. Now that they were entering the most challenging phase of the probability game, he preferred to keep his count quiet except from buddies like Ed, who fed him tips. He hadn't started a Big Year to set himself up for public humiliation. But being open with Skua had paid off with an authoritative report of Rick's count. J.K. wondered if his own count would be reported to Rick, in the spirit of fair competition.

"And you're also doing a Ph.D.?" Skua asked.

"Yeah, in physics."

"I'm amazed you find the time."

J.K. was amazed, too. He told Skua that though his Big Year had started by accident, he was determined to see it through.

Skua nodded. He admitted he'd done several Big Days, but had never found the time or inclination to commit to a Big Year. "I bet your chapter is proud of you," he said.

A thin smile played on J.K.'s lips. "Right now, they're stressing about putting on a show for the Centennial," he said.

Skua nodded, indicating he was aware of the upcoming Centennial. "You guys are first up in line," he said, "so all eyes are on you."

"Our Centennial Chair wants me to invite you as our guest of honor."

"Oh, that's great, but I don't know if I can get out here in June."

"My orders are to use force if necessary."

Skua grinned.

"Karen wants you to inaugurate the signs we'll put up here," J.K. persisted.

Ed looked down at his feet. "You're having money troubles, I hear," he said.

"We're broke!" J.K. said. "Especially since National no longer shares dues with the chapters."

"It's no longer economically viable for us," Skua said.

Not with the six-figure salary they pay you. But J.K. kept the thought to himself, because Ed was glaring at him for being undiplomatic enough to bring up politics on a birding trip. Ed belonged to the Los Angeles chapter, A.B.S.'s richer cousin, and was angling for a position on the board of the National Society.

"If we're going to survive, we need you on our side," J.K. said.

"Oh, I'm on your side," Skua said. "And so is Ed, I'm sure."

Ed smiled and ran his hand over his scalp.

It was Thursday afternoon at cookies-and-tea, and Dave Wagner was chatting with a senior professor. "The field is littered with the bones of young people," Dave said. The professor nodded heartily at his assessment.

J.K., overhearing this conversation, felt like he had been stabbed.

As one of the leaders in the field, Dave was in the know. He got calls from universities asking him to rank prospective postdoctoral candidates. The cream of the graduating class was snatched up in December, although offers for also-rans trickled in through the end of January.

J.K.'s fears had been heightened by another remark Dave made at lunch. They'd been eating the greasy Barcelona red pizza that passed for food in the student cafeteria when J.K. mentioned that he had applied to fifteen of the strongest universities that had positions available.

Dave seemed irritated by this information. His dense eyebrows came together, and his falcon eyes focused on J.K. "Apply to as many places as you can," Dave advised, chewing the rubbery crust. "Might increase your probability of getting in."

Taking his advice, J.K. applied to ten more universities, but he smarted at Dave's tone. J.K. had heard of losers shot-gunning applications for a hundred postdoc positions, but he'd always thought he was above such tactics. Dave must no longer have confidence in him, or else why would he advise him to apply to second-rate departments where there were no strong people with whom to collaborate? J.K. began brooding over the real possibility of being jobless and penniless next fall.

"I guess he thinks I won't make it," J.K. told his father over the phone.

"You're being paranoid," Jake said in a gruff, dismissive voice.

"Maybe not," J.K. said. "Dave and I have hit a wall. If we could get our paper out the same time as my applications, things would be different. Even if we could kick this baby out by the end of the month . . ."

"So why don't you?"

"We're not even close to being done. Dave thinks the project is going nowhere. I've published only one minor paper with Maurice in the last year, and he's pumped out two more without me."

Jake said nothing.

"What is it?" J.K. asked.

"You sound defeated."

Defeated? After he—the son of a construction worker—had enrolled in a world-class Ivy League institution to do his Ph.D.? His mother, Antonia, had been so proud that she only wanted a gift if it bore the logo of his university. Though his father didn't express it in so many words, J.K. knew he expected him to get a job after all this fuss and prove he was able to support himself. In Antonia's expectations, J.K. was to do much more than just support himself. When he received his degree, he would be launched on a brilliant career as a physicist. It was difficult for either of his parents to accept his pessimism or to understand why he went on birding feverishly despite it.

"Can't you somehow get money for breaking the record?" Antonia asked him.

"There is no money," J.K. said irritably.

"You're doing it for fame?"

"I don't care about that."

"Then why? You could be putting that time into physics!"

"I don't know. I must be crazy." His head was throbbing. "You know, I need a break now and then. It's not like I don't put time into physics!"

Their conversations became variations on this single theme, like a tune being covered by different pop groups over and over. But then his despair directed the theme into such jarring disharmony that they quarreled over the same words they had laughed at just weeks before.

Fighting a persistent headache, J.K. sank into paperwork as he cobbled together additional applications for postdoc jobs and exchanged emails with professors and secretaries to make sure his recommendation letters were arriving before the deadlines. After he had mailed out the last package, the headache gave way to a throbbing anxiety that aspirin didn't relieve. Even Luna's blended spearmint tea didn't help much. In fact, he hadn't exactly been a frequent customer at Leaves lately.

During his undergraduate years at Rutgers, he had been among the top students in physics, and was used to embarrassing mentions of a Nobel Prize when the subject of his future came up. But his current supervisor seemed as optimistic about his prospects as he was about his own soaring cholesterol levels.

J.K. couldn't bear Dave's gloomy mood whenever the subject of postdocs came up. Dave must have a rough approximation of what J.K.'s chances were. As J.K.'s confidence ebbed, so did his desire to slave over their paper. It pained him to think that Dave put such little stock in his potential, and J.K. wondered if Dave had indeed written him a lukewarm recommendation.

Any attempt to discuss his fears with his parents led only to tension at their end of the line. So J.K. let the matter drop. He decided not to tell his mother that he was losing his appetite for food. Despite his efforts to sound upbeat, Antonia said that he sounded different, and no longer seemed interested when she shared her anxieties. "Anne Marie dumped me," he told her, a month late. Ever since Antonia got that news, she had claimed her son as her own. There was a time when Antonia had considered her son the rock of her life, and now she wanted him back again. Being Antonia, she began this process by worrying out loud about him, and by sounding like a martyr.

J.K. knew his mother was juggling long hours at the primary school with his father's recent retirement. Maybe that's why she was so cranky these days.

In response, J.K. tried not to brood over his problems on the phone, but he couldn't disguise his low spirits. Something was changing inside him. He felt despondent, dreading a blow he sensed was coming his way.

Walking back to the Physics building after lunch one afternoon, J.K. found the quad particularly quiet. Students usually played Frisbee or touch football here at this hour. J.K. spotted a meadowlark in the distance and stood transfixed. The bird seemed impatient, and J.K. worried it would fly away. But it flew off in a boomerang trajectory and landed on the grass beneath a tree near J.K., where it displayed the bright yellow throat on which was drawn a pretty black bib.

Delighted, J.K. inched away, not wanting to flush the bird. J.K. had seen a small flock of meadowlarks in this field last October and was glad that one of them had thought to stop by again on its way south. J.K. felt an inexplicable sense of joy watching the bird poke its beak in the grass.

During this painful period of uncertainty about his future, the only thing that kept J.K.'s spirits up was the Big Year. He had 330 birds. The goal was seventeen birds away, and he had come too far now to give in to Antonia's pleas to give it all up for a week and visit her at home. He planned to stay in L.A. until at least December 24th, and he would have booked a flight for even later if it weren't for the fact that his mother was devoutly Catholic, and it would be cruel to put her through a lonely Christmas day.

His mother urged him to come east sooner, no later than the twenty-first. She wanted to throw a party, before her relatives left to spend Christmas in Florida. She even toyed with the idea of visiting him in California, but she was leery of spending so much money. As much as J.K. would have liked to see her, he didn't encourage her to come. Between physics and the Big Year, he didn't have a spare minute. And he was reluctant to book a ticket home as early as she wanted.

"The difference between the twenty-first and the twenty-fourth is not just three days," he told her, "but three *winter-break days*. If I bird 'round the clock, that could mean three extra birds for my record."

His calculations meant nothing to Antonia. She hated the idea of forgoing the family party—because if he weren't going to be there, she wouldn't throw it at all. It would be too embarrassing to explain his absence. "I only get to see you a handful days between Christmas and New Year's," she said. "And it's the holidays, for chrissake!"

J.K. caved, sacrificing three more birding days to family. He booked a ticket leaving December 21st. But until then he was determined to tough it out in Southern California.

Toward the end of the month, his physics project took flight like a kite that finally found the wind. There was a noticeable change in Dave's enthusiasm, and J.K. worked as hard as he ever had to exploit the unexpected momentum.

One afternoon, though, Dave and J.K. were eating lunch in the cafeteria when Maurice, who had joined them, thought of a constraint that, if it were relevant, would probably kill their project.

"Doesn't your model have a broken global symmetry?" Maurice had said.

"No, there aren't any," J.K. said, chewing a dry pizza crust.

Undeterred, Maurice scribbled down the Lagrangian for Dave and J.K.'s model on a series of greasy napkins, pointing out why there was a symmetry and how it got broken.

Realizing the implications of what Maurice was saying, J.K. pushed away his half-eaten pizza. It meant that they had a massless particle in their model according to Goldstone's theorem. And since this would be adding another massless particle to nature, something was terribly wrong.

Later that night, J.K. pondered the problem and realized that the so-called massless particle wasn't massless at all. Its mass was tiny, smaller than the Upsilon. But this was potentially dangerous. Looking into the experimental bound, however, he found that the limit was close. His model wasn't dead, but it *would* require a more careful computation.

The next day, J.K. showed Maurice that his refutation hadn't been strictly correct.

"The symmetry is only approximate, so this particle isn't truly massless," J.K. concluded.

Dave sat in on the impromptu blackboard-talk and nodded approvingly at J.K.'s conclusions. They continued to be hopeful about the probability of writing up a paper soon.

*13*

There wasn't a board member who didn't dread Zanne's reminder every two months about *The Vireo* deadline. The chairs of various committees were expected to drum up newsy pieces, and Zanne was irritated as hell if these did not arrive at her desk on time. She counted on a report from Blake for the "Chick Corner." He wrote these with more diligence than any essay for school, knowing the wrath that would fall upon him if he forgot, as had once happened. Even Robert Kern, whose work in genetics had reportedly been considered for a Nobel Prize, was made more anxious by a call from the Egret than rumors from Sweden. Kenny made it a policy not to pick up the phone at the end of every other month, fearing that it was the Egret soliciting his services. He had failed her at least as many times as he had come through, and he avoided her with more zeal than a debtor dodging a collector.

As the deadline approached, it wasn't unusual for puzzled families of board members to field irate calls from Zanne. "Listen, when you see him, can you tell him that I've read his article on endangered species six times now," the Egret berated Robert Kern's wife in late November, "and what's bugging the hell out of me is this line that says 'the young mussels take six to one-hundred-twenty days to become a juvenile.' "

"Oh?" Kathy Morton said.

"Now, did he mean *sixty* to one-hundred-twenty days, because it seems to me it would take at least that much?" Despite the nasal drawl, there was a blunt force to her voice that warned listeners to ignore her at their peril.

"You know, you're probably right," Kathy Morton said, "but Robert left for the airport an hour ago."

"Oh, God! That poor guy travels as much as my daughter."

Kathy Morton agreed that her husband traveled too much and offered to talk to him that night about the life cycle of mussels. "Would that be too late for you?"

"As long as you *do* get back to me tonight," the Egret said, satisfied with the seriousness with which Kern's wife was applying herself. "I usually go to bed around ten. Sometimes I fall asleep in a chair and wake up at midnight," she laughed. "And then I go to bed."

Karen encouraged Blake to write his first draft in pencil, which he wielded with such a heavy hand that it tore through the paper. After breaking many pencil tips, Blake typed out his report and had it corrected by his mother. Not until she was satisfied did he submit an electronic copy to Zanne.

After taking one look at the submission, a list-heavy piece about his first pelagic trip, Zanne picked up the phone. "This is all, 'We saw this bird, and we saw that bird, and we saw another bird,'" she scolded. "There's no description of the day or the boat or the people."

"I have trouble writing that stuff," the boy admitted. He giggled. "If you want a good story, call up Kenny."

"Oh, bless you! I knew I was forgetting something."

Since November was basically over and the Egret's summons hadn't arrived, Kenny was enjoying his stroke of luck and had reverted to picking up the phone on the second ring. It was a habit from his boyhood days. It pained him physically to let a phone ring unanswered, and today this cost him dearly.

"I want you to write something juicy about that pelagic," Zanne said.

"Oh, don't ask that!" he said, unwilling to remind readers about his now infamous jumping-off-the-boat incident. To his horror, the story had been circulating on the birding circuit in exaggerated forms. There was one nasty version claiming he'd had a nervous breakdown.

"Too late. I'm already asking," came the stern reply. "And what's more, I have my eye on you as the next editor. It would be good to get some young blood behind *The Vireo*."

"I'm not as young as you think," Kenny protested. "My kids are both teenagers."

"Oh, you're a lot younger than I am!" she told him. "Now if you'd only let me start training you, you'd be ready to take over the paper before the summer's out."

Kenny sighed, sensing he hadn't heard the last of the matter. He knew that the Egret liked to claw at him, but he consoled himself that it was done more out of habit than malice. Trapped as he was now in her talons, he decided he might as well tell his own light-hearted version of the pelagic fiasco, and once and for all put an end to the rumor that he was suicidal.

Meg was convinced that Rick wasn't being straight about why he stayed on as president. If only Meg would stop tormenting him! They had a quiet dinner at their usual Mediterranean eatery. The food had been especially fresh, but they had eaten in strained silence. Then word came that the kitchen was out of baklavas. After dinner, they took their dog, Keats, on his nightly walk. Rick tried to explain that it was too complicated for him to resign right now. "For all I know, A.B.S. won't make it through next year, and you won't have to worry about this anymore."

"Oh, come on. Don't give me that guilt trip." There was a tremor in her voice. "You're making a habit of this—you say one thing and do another. Is that pathological or something?"

Her reaction worried him. Ever since he'd gone back on his promise to re-sign, something had changed between them. The last time they spoke about A.B.S. was weeks ago. Since then they were barely speaking to each other at all. Why was it that change always targeted the man who liked things to stay as they were? Instead of a major flare-up, Meg had taken a different route. She had gone silent. Did Meg have a condition? Some kind of a bipolar disorder? But she got so defensive whenever he tried to broach the subject. The only con-dition he knew anything about was depression—the pervasive danger he was forever trying to steer away from, and which was now settling over him.

For Rick, always being viewed as the most capable person in the group was everything, and Meg's silent treatment made him feel like a failure—as a husband and as a man. Just now he needed to be psyched for his Big Year final push and not have her aggravate his deep, nagging suspicion that he was des-tined to fall short. If he gave in to that attitude, it would be a self-fulfilling prophecy.

"You want a drink?" Rick said, as they neared Leaves Café. While Meg decided, he got the beagle to practice his "play dead" trick, and avoided look-ing at her.

"I'd rather have gelato," Meg said.

Rick agreed, even though he was nervous about her on-again, off-again cold symptoms. He wondered if her silence was a sign of exhaustion or if she had given up on reforming him, but he was too chicken-hearted to ask. It was a cool Friday night, and Meg wore a thin silk blouse she'd bought on a trip to a boutique with her French class. Despite the bright color of the blouse, her face looked faded. She had been listless for days. Maybe it was nothing. It was winter. Everyone looked pale.

But Rick suspected that driving herself to master French on top of the strain of her full-time job was wearing her down. She had no energy left over to even quarrel! He had attended one of her French receptions and was irked by a red-haired man who sipped wine and chatted her up in a ridiculous French accent. Rick suspected this dandy had joined the class for reasons other than merely to learn French.

They walked past the Cold Stone Creamery, a recent addition to their neighborhood, and walked another block to Leaves Café. They had switched their repertoire from ice cream to gelato. In their earlier days, they could get away with eating anything, but now it seemed that every scoop showed. On their ice cream walks back in the early eighties, when ice cream chains opened stores on every block, it wasn't unusual for them to hit three stores in one walk and buy double-scoop cones at each. But back then they'd also gone bicycling all the time, along forested trails and even up to Mount Baldy. Last September they went to Big Bear, hoping to bike again, but the altitude—6,000 feet—got to Meg, so they settled for strolling to restaurants and back to the motel. She had suffered two episodes of pneumonia in the last few years, and her lungs were scarred as a result. Another episode, the doctor said, could cause her lungs to collapse. She was to avoid strain. Under the circumstances, her zeal to change careers and become a French translator seemed foolhardy to him.

"Don't push yourself," Rick wanted to tell her, "or you'll trigger another episode." But he hesitated. Though it was his responsibility to remind her to look after herself, he knew where it would lead if she thought he was nagging her. The accusation would be hurled back at him, in some grotesque form, that he allowed his Big Year outings to jeopardize his own health.

After Meg had stopped talking to him, he'd begun to notice that his every-day life had grown silent. There was no longer a melody in it. He managed legal affairs at the city's health board, and a new law that was to take effect next year regulating senior care required him to put in thirteen-hour days, surrounded by a whirlwind of paperwork and bureaucracy. At home, there was barely enough time to complete the checklist of chores: feed the cat, clean the litter box, walk the dog, get groceries. He was so tense from this stifling routine that daytrips from Alpena for his Big Year no longer brought relief. Only the dream of tropical, exotic Ecuador eased his muscles and restored some anticipation of a better future. At night in bed, he closed his eyes and visions swam before him of colorful birds, dense foliage, green mountains, raging streams, and above all, the luxury of birding nonstop for ten days.

Leaves Café had planted itself judiciously in the vicinity of restaurants, and even on a late November evening there was a line inside. Rick got in line. He had to be careful to not set Meg off in any way. He hoped she wouldn't get into one of her moods before he left on the trip. He couldn't meddle with the precarious balance of their peace. He meant to win the Big Year in a month's time, and then he'd need her tacit approval for the Ecuador trip. He wondered if he were giving himself false assurances. It paralyzed him to consider how far he and Meg might drift apart in the two weeks he'd be in Ecuador without her. Worse, it might spoil his trip if the whole time he kept dreading the prospect of returning home to a stranger. January wasn't much more than a month away. When he'd bought a *Birds of Ecuador* book, he figured he could ease into the subject of the trip, but when she saw it, she chose not to comment.

"I can't believe this," Meg said. A man and three children were taking their time tasting flavors and were holding up the server.

"Oh, Jeez," Rick said. "Poor Luna." The girl behind the café counter was an aspiring musician. She had told him about her band. Was it *Leopard* or *Cheetah*?

Meg elbowed him. "Is that Jared?"

Rick considered the bulky outline of the man at last paying for his order. The essential lines of his body were unchanged, even though twelve years had filled him out considerably. The man turned; he was Rick's best friend from college.

"Jared?" Rick said, as the man began to leave the store with his boys.

The man turned around. "Rick!" he said. His jaw had always sprawled across his face, but now his torso was so much wider that the face looked almost narrow.

They exchanged hugs while the three children licked gelato with colorful spoons. After Jared got over his initial awkwardness, he was all smiles. "How are you guys?"

Even after Rick's marriage, Jared had spent many a night crashing on their sofa. "Do you remember Sunday afternoons when we'd go biking together?" Rick asked him.

"And you were both so skinny!" Meg said.

"Aren't I still?" Jared said. Something like the old smile returned to his face and he patted his considerable belly.

Rick shook his head. Just a couple of years after those bicycling days, Jared married an Evangelist and moved twenty minutes away. They never saw him again. Jared stood chatting as Meg picked a flavor—peach. Rick was glad she ordered a pint. So she wasn't trying to impress the dandy in her French class by slimming down!

"We gotta get together soon," Jared said, as he corralled his kids to leave.

Rick untied Keats from the post, and the trio began to walk back home. Meg wondered if Jared's cheeriness was simply an act, or if he really did want to reconnect with them.

"They never let us know where they moved to," she said.

"They did send us a change of address card," Rick told her.

"So they say."

"Marriages do change relationships," he said with quiet conviction.

In their thirteen years of marriage, many couples they'd known at work had gotten divorced. Jared had disappeared, and Meg never heard from her high-school friends after she stopped band practice. She went to college late and never acquired a close friend there. Her sisters had moved out of town. Even the pets died and had to be replaced. Other than Rick's birding friends—who were just that, Rick's friends—their only social contacts were two couples whom they'd gotten to know basically by accident and had dinner with every few months. Rick agreed to go only because one of the husbands could talk intelligently about both bicycle racing and jazz.

Tonight, the realization that the wider world was so far removed from them pulled him closer to Meg, and he was thankful that their marriage had survived.

"It's strange to think that we've been together so long," Meg said, confirming that she was thinking about the same thing.

"The best part is when you have common memories," he said with a tender smile.

Over the years, Rick had stopped thinking about Jared, but now he viewed this chance encounter as a parting gift from his friend because it freed the flow of conversation between him and Meg, which had become clogged in the past several weeks.

In bed that night he plucked up the courage to speak to her. He adjusted his elbow on the pillow. His other arm sprawled lazily against her waist. "Karen is working very hard for the Centennial, and without much help," he said, "and it would be a huge setback if I were to resign out of the blue."

She looked at him and didn't say anything for a while.

"So it is because of Karen that you won't resign?"

He turned over sulkily and lay on his back. "It's because of A.B.S. I feel this . . . this . . . obligation to see us through the Centennial. And then I guess it can go to hell! Isn't that what you want?"

She didn't respond. The air in the bedroom seemed to go still. She liked to keep all the windows in the condo closed, so there weren't any night sounds to distract them.

That was the end of their discussion for the night.

"We'll do something spectacular next summer," Rick said the next morning, although he had no notion of what that "something spectacular" might be.

"I might have plans."

"Oh, yeah?" he said in a hoarse whisper.

"To stay in the south of France. In a cottage somewhere."

Rick pictured the red-haired dandy—was he to go, too?

"Do they have birds in France?" he asked.

"I don't know. I've never looked into it."

A flock of bushtits descended on the eucalyptus tree outside their living room window, setting the air ringing with their distinctive twitter. The pale, honeyed flowers of the tree nodded as the bushtits hopped from branch to branch. Rick and Meg walked out to their balcony with mugs of coffee and watched the slate-gray birds hang upside down, topsy-turvy, and every which way to get at their morning meal. After the flock had its fill, only a faint twitter rang out occasionally. Then they were gone until the next day.

Rick stared at the slim, elongated eucalyptus leaves, lonely and dull after being abandoned by the bushtits. Maybe Meg felt the same way when he was preoccupied with his Big Year and A.B.S. business. Through the leaves he saw the faded pink and white walls of the building across the street. He felt guilty that he hadn't cautioned Meg about her health, but under the circumstances, it was best not to pressure her. It was enough for the moment that they were talking again. He slipped an arm around her and was comforted that she didn't pull away. He decided that if he stayed on as president a little bit longer, she probably wouldn't divorce him.

A week later, Rick got a phone call from Karen. She sounded devastated. The Department of Water and Power had rejected her request to put up informational signs in Joss Canyon.

"If they don't even let us put up the signs," she said, "forget about us having a place for the Centennial. And you can say goodbye to the Bell's vireo right now. They're certainly not going to stop mowing the place down. All those dead cowbirds are on *our* conscience!"

Rick was unable to respond. His brain refused to process anything that wasn't connected to his Big Year.

Karen added that their only hope was Billy Grimsby, who had communicated the D.W.P.'s decision to her, and had agreed to a meeting at her insistence.

"Great!" Rick said, hoping she had called him only for a psychological boost.

"I'm not going to face him alone," she said. "I need you to come."

Sometimes it all seemed like a cruel joke to Karen. The board apparently had so much confidence in her plan to launch the Centennial that no one bothered to failsafe it. No one asked, "What if we're not able to raise "x" amount of dollars during the Big Day?" J.K. refused to talk strategy until a week before the Big Day, which he said he would do "maybe in April." Rick agreed to participate, but right now he was too absorbed in his own Big Year to care about anything else. So, as usual, everything was left up to Karen.

At the December board meeting, there had been no surge in interest, despite Karen's plea for help with the signs. Only their owlish secretary, Patty Cole, offered to make a few drawings of native plants.

"I've heard J.K. draws well," Rick said. "Maybe he can help you with the birds?"

"Yeah, right," Karen said. "If I can get him to help me with the Big Day, that'll be quite an accomplishment."

There were snickers, but no more suggestions for volunteers.

She had to go on doing this, despite the board's apathy. It all depended on her now.

A hastily pulled together group of three—Rick, Frank, and Dana—arrived at Karen's house the next evening to look over and approve a sample sign about their state bird, the California quail. Karen's family had pitched in to make the sign on short notice, with Blake contributing the photo and Oscar doing the scanning and graphic arts work.

Even though Dana's compliments, true to her nature, were given grudgingly, Frank and Rick agreed that the handsome sign might cause Billy Grimsby to change his mind. Karen glowed. She had studied a few Forest Service signs and had phrased hers accordingly. She was proud of the text she had inserted about quail behavior, and the addition of subtle touches of color.

The next day the four board members walked into the trailer at Joss Canyon. Karen placed the sign on Billy Grimsby's desk to show him right away how serious their proposal was.

A plump, bearded man, Grimsby turned the sign around in his large hands. "Hmm . . ." His gorilla-like face darkened.

"Is there a problem?" Karen said.

"This doesn't meet our specifications."

She looked at him, baffled. "Why?"

"There are grammatical errors."

"I'm an English teacher," she said. "What exactly are you talking about?"

"You'll have to speak to our sign-interpreter about the technical stuff," Grimsby said. "We have very strict requirements for the signs we allow on city property. The text has to be worded a specific way. How many signs were you hoping to put up? A couple?"

"Ten," Karen said. "I told you in my email."

"We can't let this sort of thing become a habit."

"You don't have to worry about that," Karen said. "Our next Centennial isn't for another hundred years."

Seeing that her face was flushed, and sensing she was in danger of blowing up, Rick put a hand on Karen's shoulder. His intervention came at the right time; she felt too insulted to continue being civil to Grimsby. Retreating to a corner, she let Rick take over the fight.

Rick tried to persuade Billy, wielding his twin weapons of reason and reassurance. Karen couldn't help but admire the poise with which he dealt with the situation. Aware that she was savoring his presence, she looked guiltily at Rick as he talked. She seemed to be growing fond of Rick, and she hoped there was nothing horribly wrong going on inside her. Maybe the stress of the upcoming Centennial was distorting her judgment. On the evenings when Oscar was away teaching a class, she found herself replaying the moments she and Rick spent together on the last birding trip!

In the end, Grimsby yielded just enough to give them some hope. "You'll have to make templates with all the text and photos," he said, "and get them approved by our sign-interpreter before I can make any more decisions."

"I might be able to do that over Christmas, if I'm lucky," Karen said.

Later she confided to Rick that it would take her at least two months, realistically, to make the signs. "And I would have told him so," she said, "except I didn't want to give him one more excuse to say no."

"Maybe Grimsby will be persuaded with a few sample signs," Rick said.

But Karen wasn't sure if they had the time to wait for his answer. "I think we should put out an announcement in the December newsletter, so people can save the date and buy tickets."

"But we don't even know if we have Joss Canyon!" Rick said.

"And we should print five times our normal number of copies."

"What are we gonna do with all those copies of *Vireos*?"

"We'll distribute them in the community. I mean, this is a big deal. We may have Skua as our guest of honor!"

"You're kidding," Rick said.

"He told J.K. he might be able to come."

"It's funny. I don't remember discussing this invitation with you," Rick said.

"Because you didn't. I made up my mind when I was at the pelagic, throwing up like a teenager and getting snubbed by Ed."

"I'm sorry. I know that I encouraged you to go."

"Maybe you'd like to make up for it by putting out a plea for money in the newsletter?"

"But my normal plea month is April!" said Rick, who hated to write begging letters.

Karen insisted. Her hazel eyes, which had been sensuous in the days of her courtship with Oscar, now exuded all their can-do, girl-scout charm. Rick's mind was too clouded by his Big Year to put up stronger resistance.

With Rick's support, Karen was able to bring the board around to her way of thinking. Despite the Egret's violent opposition, a thousand copies of *The Vireo* were mailed out in December instead of the usual two hundred, carrying a plea for donations to A.B.S. and announcing a grand Centennial celebration in June. The result of the mailing was that A.B.S. went absolutely bankrupt. Even the old printer, who had let them stay on as a client for fear of confronting the Egret, grew disgusted with their partial payments and promises and gave notice that he'd do no more of their printing until his bill was paid in full.

*14*

$A$s the year drew to a close, Anissa Montez, a *Los Angeles Times* reporter who sometimes came on Alpena Bird Society trips, made contact with J.K and Rick to keep tabs on their Big Year counts.

Dave had recently discovered J.K.'s madness for birding, and the rest of the faculty soon knew what he was up to. J.K. became an object of curiosity in the physics department. There was even a rumor that the elusive Nobel laureate in their department had asked Dave to point out J.K.

The last pelagic trip of the year was over, and Rick had closed the gap to one bird in J.K.'s favor, forcing J.K. to bird frenetically to keep his lead. The pressure that Dave put on him to write up their paper, in addition to the silence from the universities he'd applied to, felt to J.K. like so many creeping vines tightening around his neck. The feeling unnerved him. Ordinarily, J.K. felt comfortable in his own skin. He'd learned the habit from his parents, who had put no academic pressure on him in his school years. It was only because he had progressed so far from his blue-collar origins that they, too, now had high expectations for him.

In the first two weeks of December, Maurice received offers from Princeton and Maryland, but not a single postdoctoral offer made its way to J.K. And to think that he had his heart set on Princeton! J.K.'s best chance at improving his attractiveness as a candidate would only come if he and Dave posted their paper on the arXiv website before Christmas. This meant he could no longer bird as intensely as he needed to, but he planned to make up for it in the few days between pumping out the paper and leaving for Christmas.

J.K. stayed up late every night in his cubbyhole, doing the grunt labor of running complex calculations on Mathematica to verify an important result in their paper. The stress was even too much even for the computer, which froze at the most inconvenient times. "Either I'll kill you or you'll kill me!" he shouted at the machine, exasperated.

A flurry of leads helped J.K. widen the gap to two birds in his favor. He spent the first two weekends in December chasing a scoter and a longspur, both of which he got. But his mad scrambles up the San Gabriel Mountains on week-day mornings did not yield a winter wren as he had hoped. He drove his Bird-mobile so hard that he nearly wrecked the poor thing, which only added to his worries, knowing that he couldn't afford another car. His father was sympathetic to the idea of competitive birding, like any sport, but he would never understand sacrificing a car to it.

Working at his computer overnight as he fought off sleep, J.K. longed for a moment's peace in an open field somewhere with no barbed wire and no Target store on the horizon. But he dared not give in to the thought or sleep would overcome him. He rubbed his eyes and discovered he'd been staring at the computer so long that it hurt to blink. He drank yet another cup of stale tea and prepared to wrestle another bout with the machine. An untidy goatee again claimed his face.

Last spring, a spider had spun a fresh web outside his apartment every evening to catch insects and flies. Each night when J.K. got home from work, a new web glistened in the porch light. During the day, the spider dismantled the web. That's how J.K. used to feel while birding, as though the web was disman-tled and he could relax in those hours. But now, even birding was no longer free of pressure. Time suffocated him no matter where he turned. He yearned for open spaces to roam in freely. He now understood his father's decision to move to a remote mountain community.

There was no time to cook. J.K. pickled his birding medicine—boiled eggs—in jars of vinegar, to have them handy. To mix things up, he kept a bag of canned anchovies as a weekend treat. He even gave in to buying Ramen noo-dles, which had been a staple before he'd taught himself to cook Chinese. Some-times, to give his eyes a rest from the computer monitor, J.K. went to the Wild Oats store next to Leaves Café and bought a bowl of stir-fried noodles. He'd sit in the open courtyard eating his dinner, and if Luna were on her shift, she'd wave hello.

"Mister Ph.D.!" Luna said one day, not even expecting a response. "You like noodles, huh?"

"I like Chinese, though this isn't the real thing."

"I love Chinese!" she said. "My best friend lives in San Francisco—she's a milliner. I wanna visit her and pig out."

"Milliner?"

"Makes hats."

"I need to figure out a gig like that."

"Liar. You like to exaggerate."

J.K. laughed. And this bit of human interaction returned a spark to his weary face.

A few days before he was to fly home for Christmas break, J.K. found a minor error in a calculation that undermined the result he and Dave thought they had. A minus sign hadn't been transferred over, which meant the positive result they were excited about was in fact negative. The error had been made initially by J.K., but Dave hadn't caught it when he looked over the calculation. J.K. only noticed it when he checked their results one last time while they were writing up the paper. Once the error was factored in, their effect was mildly interesting, but essentially trivial. J.K. tried as best he could to patch up the torn kite, and Dave looked on, offering encouragement, but the way out was by no means obvious.

Soon it seemed that Dave no longer thought it worth his time to even write up the paper. Or maybe he thought it was no longer worthy of bearing his name. He hadn't taken a vacation in nearly a decade and was leaving for a family reunion in Florida. J.K. knew he couldn't write the paper without Dave's help, and tried to persuade him to not give up.

"I know it's a minor paper," J.K. said, staring at the shaggy orange carpet in the graduate student office, "but it'd be good for me anyway."

"Most committees have met already," Dave said, "if that's what you had in mind."

"Yeah, but . . ." His mouth trembled. He knew that offers were still being made. He might be on a waiting list. A tally of three published papers instead of two would help his case.

"Anyway, you should get into the habit of abandoning things that don't work out," Dave said, and then he casually left the room.

Didn't Dave understand what was at stake? J.K. had to sit down. It was fine for Dave to abandon the paper when his name was already on hundreds. But a new paper might cause a small institution that was on the fence about J.K. to make up their mind in his favor. It was pathetic to be desperate about being hired by a third-rate school, but he might no longer have a choice.

J.K. continued to tinker with the project, and wrote up a couple more pages. In the end, he knew it would be dumb to defy Dave and send out a half-baked paper without his consent. Crushed that his paper was dead, J.K.'s anxiety level soared as he waited to hear about a postdoc offer. He administered the only therapy he knew—he plunged headlong into the rush of Big Year birding.

J.K. was just one bird short of Ed McCoy's Big Year record when a lead passed on by Blake took him to the parking lot of the community college where Karen taught, and straight into the arms of a broad-tailed hummingbird. A fine mist aspired to become rain, and the heroic gingko trees that did their best to bring color to California autumns were shedding gold leaves. The hummer hovered over a flowering bush, its tail spread out like a Japanese fan.

J.K. watched, transfixed. It was his 346th bird. He had equaled Ed McCoy's record. He was pleased with himself, a feeling he hadn't had in a long, long time.

Rain drizzled on fiery Japanese maples, and J.K. smiled as the cool bluish air swirled yellow-red leaves across the parking lot. As he drove out of the college, the world seemed calm and good, until the first storefront blaring holiday music, and then the next, jarred his mood. The commercialization of "the spirit of giving" nauseated him. His mind retreated back to the watercolor image of gilded trees lining the misty path to his hummer.

J.K. kept mum about his success, and urged Blake to do the same, in order to not set Rick off. Other than Blake, he confided only in Ed, the current holder of the record.

Ed congratulated him, but didn't sound surprised. "Between heavyweights like you and Rick," he said, "I figured my record would get blasted one way or the other." Having accepted this, he had preferred to feed leads to J.K.

"Thanks, man," J.K. told him.

Rick had been suspiciously silent for the last couple of weeks. But Ed had moles in the birding community, and he assured J.K. that, as far as anyone had heard, Rick was close but hadn't yet equaled the record.

Even so, J.K. was uneasy about his plan to leave town for Christmas. He first had to build a firewall of safety birds between himself and Rick. It was conceivable that Rick could get two or three more birds in the next ten days between now and New Year's Day and demolish J.K.'s hard-won victory. J.K. wanted to postpone his flight a few days, but that was expensive. His father said it was his decision, but his mother got upset when she heard he was considering changing his travel plans.

There was tension in her voice, revealing that something important was troubling her, but she wouldn't admit it over the phone. She hadn't brought up that family party in a few weeks, and he didn't ask why. Sometimes he thought she was too needy. But since she hadn't seen him for nearly a year, he felt more sorry for her than he liked to admit.

The day before he flew back to New Jersey, J.K. got an urgent call from Paul Little that a bald eagle had been seen north of a park in the Chatsworth area. Paul Little could be unreliable, but J.K. figured that an eagle would be easy to confirm or dismiss. After work, he sped west on the 210 Freeway to Chatsworth. The traffic was horrendous, but this was the last night of J.K.'s Big Year.

I'll be damned if I'll spend tonight sulking in the cubbyhole, he told himself.

J.K. turned onto Devonshire Street, which shot straight into the park. Two police cars were parked outside the gate. Daylight was fading, and he asked a police officer if the park closed at dusk. Earlier in the year, a ranger had fined him sixty dollars for leaving his car in the parking lot of a state park past dusk, and he could ill afford such drains on his savings now.

"Park's open till eight," the officer said. "And they've probably even stopped locking it up now."

J.K. saw a sign for the Old Stage Coach Equestrian Trail, a historic wagon route that connected Los Angeles and San Francisco in the nineteenth century. He walked along the flat mud path until he came upon a recently posted sign that warned of mountain lions in the area. He understood now why a tall fence ran along this part of the path, separating it from the wilderness beyond. The trail was flanked on one side by a manicured park and on the other by the fenced-out wilderness, before it meandered into the hills. Further along, in the last of the day's light, he made out a second sign warning of mountain lions and rattlesnakes.

If there were a mountain lion around, this was the time he'd wake up and get active for the night. This was cause for concern, but adding the eagle to his count would be worth it. He had a desire to see a mountain lion, which he thought was one of the coolest creatures on the planet. On previous hikes, he'd seen marks left behind by a lion—paw prints, a recent kill stashed away—but he'd never actually seen the solitary creature. The world took the lion's power for granted. J.K. wanted to be like that. He never cared to exhibit himself. But he knew he was one of the sharper young physicists around. If only he'd published more lately! Walking here at dusk, with an easy stride, thinking about his possible closeness to a lion caused an electric thrill to surge through him.

J.K. came to a junction where two trails forked-off into the hills. It was even darker up there than where he stood. Paul Little had warned him that the hike up to the top was unmarked and it was easy to get lost. But J.K. thought that if he went far enough up, he might at least hear the eagle. Technically, hearing a bird was enough to count it. Normally, he preferred not to use that fallback option, but he couldn't afford to be a purist. As he stood there feeling uneasy about the mountain lion signs, a familiar figure came stumbling down the farthest of the two trails—Paul Little, sporting an old L.A. Marathon t-shirt instead of his usual military garb.

"Hey!" Paul Little said, pleased that J.K. had taken his tip seriously. "You take Old Coach here all the way up to the top. Haven't seen her in a few hours, but she was floating up there this morning and should be back around now."

"So I go up the way you just came?" J.K. said.

Paul Little began to give elaborate directions, but then stopped in mid-sentence. "Let me get you started," he offered.

Without waiting for a response, Paul Little was climbing back up the trail. J.K. hurried to keep pace as his guide scrambled up steep unmarked shortcuts. The moon had taken charge of the evening. J.K. lamented that he had gotten a late start and probably couldn't hike all the way to the top. But Paul Little continued to scuttle up the steep, muddy slope, and J.K. followed, grabbing rocks and saplings to steady his climb.

"It's called Devil's Slide," his guide called out in the darkness.

"No kidding!"

J.K. was questioning his own sanity as well as that of his guide when Paul finally stopped at the top of a hill. J.K. clambered up behind him and, straightening his back, took in a sweeping view of the desert landscape. Paul Little dismissed his question about mountain lions, saying that there might have been an incident long ago, but the signs were still up because of lazy authorities. Though the signs had looked brand-new to J.K., he decided not to make it an issue.

Towering sandy boulders, jutting out against the mountains, stood out in the moonlight. To the far northeast, in contrast, streams of red and yellow lights pointed out suburban Simi Valley.

"I come from Four Waters," Paul Little volunteered. He pointed to the red and yellow lights. "Ten years ago there was nothing out there. I could take trails from there all the way up here." Now the trails were choked off by endless rows of housing developments. "Last year, after the rains, there was flooding everywhere, even on the streets."

"That's erosion for you," J.K. said. "They chop down all the trees, and then they wonder why it floods."

Paul Little stared at the lights, hypnotized.

J.K. watched him.

"Is that why you set fire to Joss Canyon?" J.K. said. It was something he had always wondered about, but never had the courage to ask.

"I didn't do it on purpose," Paul Little told him. "I was stoking a campfire to make soup. And I had to leave to get some potatoes. When I got back, things had gotten kinda out of control. I just didn't care about stopping it, man. I thought it was for the best, the way that jerk Grimsby was gonna ruin the canyon anyhow, so I just walked away."

J.K. nodded. Paul Little's confession was too much to process right now. Night was upon them, and J.K. didn't want to lose what chance he had to hear the eagle.

"I'll be fine now," J.K. said.

Sensing that he was being dismissed, Paul Little walked an irritated circle in the dust, but then he left.

J.K. followed the zigzag trail that led along the ridge, his eyes carefully tracing his steps in the moonlight. After a while, he could no longer see the white rock at the peak of the mountain to the south, marking the topmost point of the trail. The moon shone from the deep blue sky. Along a sandy boulder the size of an elephant, grew a spindly tree silhouetted against the night. All around was silence, but J.K. felt caution in the air, a warning that only boulders and trees understood was being murmured.

J.K. noticed an anomaly in the mud and pointed his flashlight down at it. It was a fresh paw print with no claw marks. He felt numb looking at it. He had come upon this kind of paw print only once before, as abruptly as this, one dawn when he was up in Switzer Canyon in the San Gabriel Mountains. He knew what it meant. A mountain lion had passed through here no more than a day ago.

In the silence, a sudden jangling rang out and a flash of light lit the hills. J.K. turned around to see a passenger train, sleek and luminous, streaming along a track midway down the dark westerly mountain. Looking at the dramatic streak of light whizzing by, with the suggestion of commuters in the glow of the windows, J.K. felt as though he and the train were two characters in an Arabian fairytale, divorced from the rest of the world. The glowing snake disappeared into the mountains and an oppressive darkness reasserted itself. J.K. trudged back toward the white marker at an even pace for a few minutes, then he trotted to Devil's Slide and rock-slid his way down like a frightened child.

On December 21st, two hours before his flight was scheduled to depart for New Jersey, J.K. still needed one more bird to solidify his record. The night before, Ed had called to alert him about a prairie warbler.

"That's awesome," J.K. had said. He told Ed about his sighting of mountain lion paw prints.

Ed marveled at the risks he was willing to take. "If you could stay put a few more days," Ed said, "you'd be in beautiful shape."

"I'd like nothing better than a firewall," J.K. said, "but my mom will kill me."

J.K. reached the construction site Ed had told him about at 5 a.m., but found a high fence between himself and the supposed location of the warbler. Ed had warned that entry to this area wasn't guaranteed. J.K. walked along the tall fence looking for a break or a weakness where he could hop over, but it was uniformly maintained all around. There was a gate, but that was double-pad-locked. Signs warned of trespassing fines and citations. J.K. scanned past the fence as best he could and saw the usual birds. A pair of mo-does (mourning doves) flitted about. A mocker (mockingbird) called out shrilly. There was some junkage (junckos) on the ground. But he didn't see or hear a warbler.

At 5:30 a.m., J.K. heard the arrival of a construction crew and spotted workers on the other side of the fence. They must have come in via a separate entrance. Ed had seen the warbler in a brushy area past the northeast side of the fence where J.K. stood.

J.K. shouted at the construction workers and, after a few yells, they heard him. A bulky man walked up to the fence and looked him over suspiciously.

"I have a flight out to New Jersey in an hour and a half," J.K. told him, try-ing not to sound like an asylum escapee, "and there's a bird on the other side of this fence I need to see before I leave."

The worker stared at him, puzzled. "A bird?" he repeated.

"Please unlock the gate," J.K. said. "I'll try to find the bird quickly and then leave right away. I promise."

Taking in J.K.'s desperate look, the man walked back to his crew and re-turned with a key to open the gate.

"Thanks man. This is great!" J.K. said.

As soon as he was in, J.K. set about his work. He saw a brushy area and headed straight for it, eager to escape the curious looks of the construction workers. He felt his way through the brush and walked instinctively into the spots he thought the warbler might choose. Hearing a shrill note behind him, he turned around. But it was only a spotted towhee, orange and black, darting from a tree into the bush.

Many of the trees had lost their foliage. A scrawny oak stood a few feet away, and a kinglet danced among its branches, calling out like a poet on a typewriter.

Then J.K. heard another call with an exaggerated *zzzzz* note that he didn't immediately recognize. He was drawn like a magnet in the direction of the call. In a bush, camouflaged by twigs and leaves, was a small warbler with a gray top and a yellow underside. With his binoculars, J.K. pinpointed two dark bands along its flanks. As the bird turned its head, J.K. picked out the shadow under its eye and the up-and-down bobbing tail. The bird was a prairie warbler.

A sense of triumph swept over him, along with relief that the year-long ordeal was over. He had broken the record. It had taken him all of five minutes to locate the warbler once he'd passed through the gate, but it was a year's toil to accrue the significance of this moment for him. As always, he wrote down the distinguishing features and the exact location of the warbler in his notebook. His count was 347; he circled the number in his notebook. He calculated that at the rate of one new bird a week—and more was hardly possible in the December of this Big Year—Rick would still be one behind him come New Year's Day.

J.K. wanted to collapse on the spot and relive the year's triumphs, allowing them to course through him all at once. He felt a ray of sunlight penetrate him through what he supposed people refer to as a "soul," and the memories of his most dearly earned birds came alive within him. He felt the rare sensation of being in the *center* of life, rather than standing at the periphery and looking in.

The warbler called again, and then the bird noticed him and flew away.

From the deepest part of his heart, J.K. wished the bird good fortune on its journey south. He wished he could physically express his gratitude somehow, to this bird. He wished he could bottle up the light in him at this moment and open it up any day he felt forsaken, because he knew the feeling was as fleeting as the bird, and he would live a long, sometimes dispirited life.

But right now he needed to get to the airport.

*15*

Rick was counting ducks at the Santa Fe Dam when Karen called on his cell phone, and he continued to count birds while half-listening.

"If you can get $10,000 out of Gina for the signs," Karen said, "it'll free us up to use the money we make on the Big Day for the dinner."

"One more," Rick muttered to himself, as he spotted a cinnamon teal floating by.

"You've known Gina for a while," she said, "so I really hope you can make something happen."

"We'll give it a shot," Rick said absently.

"Great!" Feeling reassured, Karen hung up.

For the Christmas Bird Count, A.B.S. members had fanned out into all the significant birding spots in the Alpena area to record not just individual species, but also the *number* of each species seen. They planned to regroup at a Mexican restaurant for dinner and tallying. Karen and Blake had been assigned Joss Canyon, and Karen was determined to attend the evening's dinner, especially since Gina Hernandez from the California Bird Society was in town and was going to join them. Karen had been pestering Robert Kern for months to look into grants, but to no avail. It was now too late to apply for grant money, but Kern had told her recently that C.B.S. had a small grant program for local chapters. Karen felt that, if appealed to personally, Gina might get C.B.S. to sponsor the Joss Canyon signs. But a phone call to her husband caused Karen to change her plans abruptly. She needed to head home immediately to talk some sense into Oscar.

"We'll send our results in writing," she told Blake, as they walked back to the Joss Canyon parking lot.

"I wanna find out what birds the others got," Blake said. "And I like Mexican food! Can't you just drop me off there, mom?"

"Nope," Karen said. "Then I'll have to drive across town to pick you up."

Blake saw that it was no use arguing with his mother. His only consolation was that he had gotten a close-up shot of a red-crowned parrot. He had spent the day counting in Joss Canyon with his mother and ducking Paul Little's attempts to help them. Paul Little had lately established residence under the bridge there, and now claimed to have an unparalleled expertise in birds of the area.

"We're not being mean," Karen told Blake about her refusal to allow Paul Little—with his metal detector—to trail them all day. "The important thing about a bird count is accuracy. And that isn't exactly his strong point."

"That's true," Blake conceded. But he felt confused. He thought Paul Little was all right, and he respected his enthusiasm for birds. Blake wasn't sure why the man got on his mother's nerves. He guessed it was because Paul didn't shower, ever.

That Paul Little had taken to living in Joss Canyon was a sure sign to Karen that the place was going to seed. Before the fire, she'd brought her family, even her husband and daughter, to spend a pleasant hour hiking the canyon on Saturday mornings on their way to a pancake brunch. But that was no longer possible. Give it another year, and this might become Alpena's homeless colony. Then the city would have no trouble convincing voters that we should have condos here instead.

Karen drove home in a hurry, hoping that she could still change Oscar's mind. He had been diagnosed with a hernia condition, and although he'd initially agreed to an operation, he was having second thoughts now about its timing.

"How will we do Christmas?" he said when she got home.

"We'll do it," Karen told him.

But Oscar was anxious. There was the issue of visiting his family, and hers, and figuring out something special to do for the kids. Where family matters were concerned, he was willing to make any sacrifice. "I'll live with the discomfort," he told his wife. "I've lived with worse before. It's manageable."

Karen shook her head. "Everyone in the extended family knows you love them," she said. "You don't have to kill yourself to prove it."

He grinned. "I know. But this is what I want to do."

There was a two-week break from teaching in the spring, and he planned to have the operation then, even though it meant sleeping on the living room sofa if his pain prevented him from climbing the stairs to their bedroom. He was eager to end the discussion. Crystal needed to be taken to church for a play rehearsal, and Oscar volunteered to take her.

He doesn't want to miss Crystal's Christmas performance, Karen thought with a pang. She felt as though someone had kicked her. How could she have not seen this before? Crystal had been chosen to play "slave-girl" in a musical about Moses, and had been floating on clouds ever since. Of course, Crystal would be disappointed if darling Papa couldn't make it, and he, naturally, couldn't bear to disappoint his daughter.

Was it strange, Karen wondered, that Oscar and their daughter had such a tight bond, and that she spent most of her free time with Blake? How had it come to be? She and her husband still loved each other, but their children had taken precedence in their lives. Oscar needed to make a major medical decision, and he thought automatically of Crystal's needs first. And Karen turned to Blake whether she was compiling a grocery list or deciding how to spend her weekend. Her life for the last months had revolved compulsively around Blake's needs.

Christmas, Karen hoped, would be a time for balance. She had long wanted to simplify her life so she would have more personal time than just two weeks of vacation after working a hectic eleven-and-a-half months. There was something less than human about such a system. But then she remembered that unless she worked on the Joss Canyon signs through the holiday season, they would never get done. The signs were essential. Without them the whole Centennial would lack meaning. She thought of how Rick was depending on her, and how Grimsby would gloat over her incompetence if the signs weren't produced. The county men would keep killing cowbirds and mowing down vireo habitat, and the city's homeless would set up a permanent colony among the picnic benches. She shuddered as she pictured the ruin of Joss Canyon, and her determination to do the goddamn signs over Christmas grew stronger.

Rick leaned back with a supremely relaxed air at the Mexican restaurant, Guadalupe. The guacamole, prepared fresh at the table, was moist and spicy, just right with the warm chips. The tequila burned softly inside him and he glowed with something like heavenly contentment. "At 4500 feet, you were in purple-finch-ish area," he declared.

"I *said* it was a purple finch!" Frank said. "But Dana kept shooting me down."

Having returned last month from the Egypt trip, Frank chatted in good spirits at the Christmas Count dinner. The effect of the vacation was that he had lost the timid look of a mouse who gets swatted constantly by a temperamental cat.

"It was great," he said about their first vacation in Egypt, "except for a bomb scare on the bus. But the police were very organized. They evacuated everyone and cleared out the streets."

"Is terrorism a big problem there?" Robert Kern asked from the end of the table.

Frank shrugged. "We only had to wait twenty minutes for another bus."

"I can't wait to go to Alaska," Dana said, leaning her girth against the table.

"You guys are going to love it," Zanne told them. "Lorna, my future son-in-law's mother, went to the South Gerogia Island last spring. They had an historian onboard the ship who took them to Shackleton's grave. He died of a heart attack, at forty-seven, in the middle of a voyage."

"I think I read about that," Rick said. "That's too bad,"

"Lorna didn't think it was such a bad thing, because all he wanted was to explore the sea. 'I am not cut out to do anything else but to be an explorer,' he wrote to his wife, meaning he wasn't cut out to be a husband or a father."

"Bye, Bye, Meg," Rick said, with a look on his face that Zanne could not resist putting into words.

"I'm not cut out to be anything but a birder?" she said.

Rick chuckled agreeably. He had found a winter wren in the Santa Ana canyon this morning and thus had broken Ed McCoy's Big Year record. Rick had only two birds to go now in order to upset J.K.'s lead. He wished he could confide in Karen about this. He had begun to see her as his cheerleader-in-chief. She was the one person sincerely rooting for him to win the Big Year. But he would have to wait to tell her. It was best not to spread the word until his victory was secure. And then he could look forward to his well-deserved Ecuador trip in January. He now saw the possibilities of a thrilling life as a globetrotting adventurer, in search of exquisite rare species. Upon his return, he planned to buy sophisticated birding software that compiled not only a North American life list, but also an *international* list.

While everyone drank margaritas, Rick passed around the table a scrapbook of his Big Year photos, including numerous shots of shimmering hummingbirds. The guest of honor at the dinner was Gina Hernandez, an officer of the California Bird Society. Meg hadn't felt well enough to come, so Rick sat next to Gina. He regaled her with tales about their biggest fundraiser, Blake.

"He's single-handedly kept A.B.S. solvent for the last three years," Rick told her. "Even the crabbiest heart can't refuse fifty cents a bird to a cute ten-year-old."

"Why don't you bring him to Ecuador?" said Gina, who was also going on the trip.

Rick's response was a mild frown that signaled disinterest. "Karen won't be able to take ten days off," he said, as a steaming plate of tamales was put in front of him. "That means *I'd* have to take him. And I can only have a ten-year-old boy with me for so long." He mouthed, *Four hours.* Then he changed his mind. *No, two hours.*

"Is he still ten?" Zanne said. "I thought he was ten two years ago."

"Blake is growing up," Rick said gloomily. "He's lankier at every board meeting. Pretty soon he'll have facial hair, and our fundraising flow will dry out."

Zanne clucked. "Now, now, it's Christmas time. Let's not get too apocalyptic." But beneath the laughter, they gave each other a tragic look, reflecting the society's bankrupt condition.

Sandwiched between Patty and Dana, Robert Kern considered the schoolgirl bangs on Patty's forehead and the way her eyes and mouth screwed into her face when she mouthed, "Okay." In keeping with her quiet manner, the secretary did not utter a word at the dinner except for the "Ayes" when Rick ran through a list of local birds and asked if each one had been seen. Even though Kern met the A.B.S. members regularly, he could not, even by a stretch, call them friends. Nor could it be said that they knew much about him.

Sitting on his other side was Frank's wife, Dana, the Membership Coordinator, with dyed blonde curls. Kern had come to know little about her over the years other than that she was active in her church and was an excellent "birder by ear." And when they were once voting on whether to pay $100 or $300 for one or three school buses to take kindergarten children to the Joss Canyon Nature Center, Dana obstinately voted for one.

Kern had researched the C.B.S. grant and brought it to Karen's attention, and she had asked him to put in a word with Gina. However, he was seated inconveniently at the opposite end of the table. Seeing that Rick had Gina cornered, he figured the lobbying was being handled. Kern had long ago drawn a red line in his life between his research and political activities. He'd crossed the line once in his younger days, and it had resulted in a mess that cost his lab a major source of funding. He did care about some issues that were an outgrowth of his research, but he didn't have the time to get involved.

Kern was chairing the A.B.S. outreach effort. He was doing his bit anyway. Beyond that, he had no desire to entangle himself in so-called "action." He was tempted to tell Karen about his latest research, given her interest in helping cowbirds. But he sensed that she could be militant by nature, and he dreaded that she would latch onto him for support and he'd never hear the end of it. Just after the count was done, he left the restaurant, citing a cold as the reason.

Gina tried to shake hands with him, but Kern backed away.

"Sorry. I don't want my microorganisms to spill out on you," Kern said, sniffing faintly as he scooted out.

"Where is Karen?" someone asked.

"Busy making signs."

There was genial laughter all around.

"That reminds me," said Rick, who was enjoying trading stories with Gina so much that he had forgotten about the signs. "Karen wants me to ask you if we can get a grant from headquarters for our nature signs. We hope to unveil them at the Centennial."

"Our grant process is pretty involved," Gina told him. "To have a decent shot, you guys should have started prepping your application a month ago."

Dessert was being served when Rick got a call on his cell.

Meg was feeling uneasy and was breathing with difficulty.

There was something about her voice that caused Rick to abandon the enticing chocolate cake that had been put in front of him and rush back home.

Rick arrived at the condo with barely enough time to get into the ambulance before it sped away. It was a glum December night, and the sirens jarred his insides.

He hovered over Meg, trying not to get in the way of the paramedics who had put her on a respirator. It was nightmarish to see his wife hooked up to these tubes, as though she had been vacuumed into one of the TV shows she loved to watch, and he wished that he could somehow shut off this depressing show and deposit them back in the safety of their living room.

Meg was taken into E.R., and after the first set of tests, the doctors confirmed that she was suffering from a fresh episode of pneumonia.

Rick berated himself for not having urged her to be more cautious.

"There can be many factors," the doctor said, responding to Rick's inquiry. "Genetics, diet, stress . . ."

Meg's family had a history of lung trouble. But both her parents were nearing seventy, and were still in reasonably good health. Meg was only in her forties! This was completely abnormal. Rick repeated to himself that stress couldn't cause pneumonia.

Life was too much sometimes. He had built, hour by hour, the tower of his freedom, and that cherished structure had been struck down all over again. His hand grazed her soft cheek and she smiled, although her eyes were closed. He could barely sit by her hospital bed for five minutes at a time. Her breathing grew shallower.

The Big Year! What was he to do about that now? His count was up to 344, just three birds short of smashing an impossibly high record.

Although she'd had two bouts of pneumonia before, this time her lungs were taking a beating. After another set of tests, the doctor confirmed to Rick that she was having a close call. Her lungs were being put through considerable stress. The doctor refused to talk about the future while she was still fighting for her life.

Despondent, Rick couldn't shake off the feeling that some of the tension between them had weakened her health.

The French class must go, he decided. But he didn't have the heart to tell her now.

Meg stayed in the hospital over the weekend and was scheduled to leave on Sunday. Her parents showed up Sunday morning to help bring her back home, but Meg's condition continued to worsen. She was given blood transfusions and still there was no improvement.

In a moment of weakness, Rick confessed to Meg's mother what the doctor told him—that Meg had come close—and her mother shuddered.

"This doesn't bode well," her mother said, and then she looked at Rick as if she held him personally responsible for Meg's condition.

During the stressful week that followed, Rick grew even more distant from Meg's parents. He slipped out of the hospital shortly after they came in, claiming that he had errands to run. He stared out windows, and images from his Big Year choked him up. Maybe he had been selfish and insensitive. He couldn't understand why every time he regressed into being a kid and allowed himself a bit of fun for a change, life responded by kicking him in the teeth. He had long avoided making a choice between Meg and birding, and now he'd almost lost her because of his own indecision.

The next weekend, Meg was stable enough to be released. Rick would have to nurse her carefully to see that she didn't suffer a relapse. The doctor advised that she do nothing for the next couple of months except stay at home to recuperate.

Rick knew of a birder in the L.A. society who was a gun for hire. Rick hated to waste money, but he'd have to pay this man to scope out the last few birds he needed to beat J.K.

Then there was the trip. Rick gulped. The Ecuador trip would have to be cancelled.

# 16

$\mathcal{T}$heirs was an old-fashioned, three-bedroom house, which his construction-worker father had built—a fact he liked to brag about. Jake had moved his family to the mountains because he was furious. Jake grew up when much of New Jersey was farm country. "Everything is paved over now!" he complained. "I'll die a slow death in this damn suburb." When J.K. was nine, his father sold his side business and relocated the family, though his wife wasn't exactly pleased that they were moving to "the middle of nowhere."

When J.K. spilled out the news that he had smashed the L.A. County Big Year record, his folks grew unusually festive; he felt glad he was here, though he soon realized his mother had used the party as an excuse to get him home early.

"Now I wish I *were* throwing a party!" Antonia said. "I wasn't able to, because my relatives ran away to Florida so fast." She wore a velvety chocolate jumpsuit; her face, once graceful, but now haggard, was a testament to how she had never gotten over her daughter's death.

After the first day, the days passed a minute at a time. Every afternoon, continued silence from the physics world spun a fresh web of fear and ate at J.K.'s hopes of getting a postdoc offer. To distract himself, and to let the fear slacken, he let a grotesque idea take shape in his mind. His brain needed to see a way out or it would burst with the strain. If all else failed, maybe he could move back to New Jersey to be with his parents. Only until he'd figured things out. It seemed to him that his mother was getting frustrated with seeing her son so infrequently. His father wouldn't say so, but he, too, would be pleased to have him closer. It pained J.K. to think of giving up physics, though, and it felt like slinking away. In his glorious undergraduate days, he'd have scorned anyone who quit physics. But physics was turning away from him, not the other way around. Then again, what other option did he have? Once he'd moved in with his parents, he'd have to try his luck getting a job with an environmental organization.

"I have a surprise," J.K. said to his mother one afternoon. Hurt by how her face lit up, he added, "It's not what you have in mind."

"That's interesting," she said when he told her his idea.

He gave her a searching look, puzzled by her lukewarm response.

"Of course I want you here," she told him. "But it makes me nervous that the one environmental organization you've applied to just ignored your application."

Did his mother no longer believe in him? Why else would she have doubts about him moving back home? His spirit deflated. They were interrupted by a phone call from one of her relatives. She was busy finishing some housework, so he decided to leave her alone for a few hours. He drove endlessly on the curving roads around his parents' remote mountainside home.

When he got back, Antonia wondered aloud if he would come with her to Florida for a few days to see "the rest of the gang." She would only go if he did. But J.K. was reluctant. She didn't press him, knowing there weren't many days left in his trip anyhow.

Another day went by without news of a postdoc offer. The elation of his Big Year triumph began to fade, and the looming threat of joblessness resurfaced. He'd given up all hope of being accepted at a first-tier institution, but he felt sure that second-tier places would still be interested, and that he'd hear from one any day now. He wondered how it would feel, being exiled to a Podunk college for the next three years.

On Christmas morning, J.K. realized that his parents were excited by the notion that he had a brilliant future ahead of him.

"It's your last Christmas as a student," his mother mused. "Who knows what wonderful job you'll have this time next year!" For the moment, Antonia seemed incapable of seeing her one remaining child as anything but perfect.

They tried to give him the best Christmas the family had had since his sister's death, no doubt spurred on by the awareness that next year he would be a man of the world. His mother was deeply moved that their years of toil were bearing fruit. "Remember that?" she said, speaking of the time when they opened a mom-and-pop café and little J.K. and Emma followed her around as she served.

"It was all low-lifes that came to that place." J.K. laughed. "But it was all right."

They gave him an expensive gray suit as a gift, made by a celebrated Italian tailor with whom his mother had family connections. She had taken his measurements, claiming she was knitting him a sweater. The suit accentuated his height, which he had inherited from his mother, and the liquid gray eyes of his father. He thought he had never looked so ridiculous in his life.

Although J.K. normally wished his parents weren't so characteristically solemn, now he felt uneasy about their cheerfulness. He had been checking his emails and phone messages obsessively, but there was no news of an offer. Instead he learned from Ed McCoy that Rick had hired someone in the Los Angeles Bird Society to scope out land birds for him and, as a result, had picked up not just the winter wren but also the prairie warbler that up until now had eluded Rick.

Rick's count was now up to 347—the same as J.K.'s.

"It's kinda shameful," Ed wrote. "Some guys will do anything to win."

"Rick's neck-and-neck with me," J.K. told his father over a pancake breakfast—a Christmas tradition. "If he keeps this up, he'll get ahead. He's still got a week."

J.K. had a wild hope, inarticulate inside him, that knowing how much the Big Year meant to him, his father would encourage him to fly to California and offer to pay for his flight. His father, after all, was into competitive sports. But Jake swallowed the news as easily as his third cup of coffee. They sat around a wooden table with a flowery plastic cover that Anne Marie would probably find embarrassing. A scrawny pinched man of Dutch descent who didn't put on an extra ounce no matter what he ate, Jake requested one more pancake from his wife. J.K.'s Big Year was the last thing on his mind, though he thought it was a cool idea. A blue-collar worker who once wondered why his son needed to get a Ph.D., he now marveled how, at this rate, his son might someday win a Nobel Prize, and this prospect had done wonders for his appetite.

"Takes the edge off how my life didn't work out," Jake said.

Used to that sort of statement, J.K. ignored it. "If I could fly back tomorrow to California," he persisted, "I might be able to catch a couple more birds."

"Don't do that!" Antonia said. She had been preparing a feast for every meal. "You come home for three days, and then you want to leave. And for what?"

Every muscle inside J.K. ached to return to California to counter Rick's challenge, but he rationalized that for the sake of his parents, he had to stay. Their feelings would be really hurt, he was sure, if he got on the next plane. Instead, he tried to prepare them for bad news.

"The best candidates get multiple offers," he said, "but I haven't gotten a single one yet. I guess something might still turn up, but if it doesn't, I'll have to move back to New Jersey and look for a job, or maybe a volunteer position with an environmental organization."

"But with your physics degree," his mother said, "don't you want to be a Dr. so and so, on your way up to becoming a professor?"

"Usually, if you're second on the list and they expect the first one to decline the offer, they'll at least get in touch with you. But . . ." He turned away, struggling to stay composed. "Anyhow, Dave hasn't been encouraging," he said in a cracked voice.

His mother guffawed, mocking her son's words. She thought he put too much stock in Dave's encouragement. "Your future is your own doing," she said. "A lot of good Dave has done you! Look at your father. Who's helped him? Look at the sacrifices he's had to make."

"Mom," J.K. interrupted. "Don't start on that."

"Whenever I talk sense, you cut me off."

Jake had left the breakfast table and was loading plates in the dishwasher. "You gotta think bigger now, son," he said. "You gotta be serious . . . and make up somehow for the fact that we lost our Emma."

J.K. shuddered. He looked at his father. "So you still think it was my fault?"

"I didn't say anything of the sort." He rounded up the cups on the table in silence.

"Yeah, but you treat me as though it *was* my fault."

His mother began to cry; the tears came hot and fast.

"Antonia . . ." Jake consoled in a pained voice.

"Oh, he'll understand some day. When he has kids, he'll get it." Her face grew scrunched, and she looked ten years older. "We've done our best," she gasped, breathless, unable to speak. "Never good enough for him."

J.K.'s heart was pounding; his parents had cornered him. "*I'm* doing my best. But you're saying I've got to be doubly successful to make up for the fact that I wasn't driving that night? Because I let Emma drive? Because I'd had too much to drink?" He would have broken down, but instead he held himself together with superhuman effort. He stood trembling in the kitchen, and watched his father turn on the dishwasher. They hadn't had a scene like this in awhile. Is that why they had stopped talking—because it might lead to a scene? His father was soaping his large, rough hands; he hated this kind of messy drama, but he must have really wanted to say Emma's name out loud, poor man, to risk this situation.

Jake wiped his hands on a red-checkered towel. Then he absently patted his son's back and walked out of the kitchen.

Antonia wiped her tears, but she looked on with those pink, inflamed eyes that J.K. couldn't quite face. "Is that goatee for keeps?" she muttered, to cool things off.

"Nah. I don't like it either. I'll keep it until the year's over."

At Christmas dinner, all three kept up the pretense, at first, that the morning's conversation hadn't occurred. They ate in the more formal dining room, but even here the oak table was covered with a milky sheet of plastic. The centerpiece was a cylindrical glass vase with plastic roses. J.K. was astonished when his parents steered the conversation back to physics, and suggested it would be best if he got a post-doctoral position somewhere on the East Coast.

"Can't you fix it up like that?" Jake said, swallowing his herbed mashed potatoes.

J.K. shook his head and hoped that the bleak look on his face would give the old man an inkling of bad news to come. That didn't work. Tracing a finger over the plastic cover, he tried to joke about the situation. "Now that I know I can't come crawling back home if I don't get an offer, I'll have to think of some other alternative!"

His parents didn't see how he could take the matter so lightly.

Now it occurred to J.K. that his parents viewed his success or failure as a commentary on their lives as well. They were desperate to see him succeed not only for his sake, but also for their own sakes. He had already tried to communicate his fears to them, but that hadn't worked. Their level of comprehension hadn't advanced much beyond his high school days. Every year when he came home, he had to remind them that they were interacting with an adult, not with the sixteen-year-old boy who used to live with them. Now the boy felt more like a burnt-out old has-been. The string beans were limp and cool. He wished his mother would cook them crispy, with soy sauce and pepper flakes.

Over the next few days, J.K. grew sure that he was no university's first choice, and if something were offered to him in January, it would be only because the person they really wanted had turned down their offer.

But it seemed his parents were unwilling or unable to absorb this bad news.

Antonia loved holidays like New Year's Day, and daydreamed about how they would spend even the most insignificant of special occasions (even though she rarely seemed to carry out her plans). Maybe, because she had spent so much time away from her son, she wanted their time together to be magical, a concentrated elixir of all the good times they could have had if he lived close by. She was wondering if she should now invite her relatives—who had just returned from Florida—to dinner.

"There is nothing to celebrate anyway," J.K. told her. "It looks like Rick beat me. I found out this morning. Is it okay if I borrow your car for a few days to drive to Cape May? I'd like to hang out there for awhile and sort a few things out."

"Okay. I won't throw my dinner party, then." She looked disappointed and fussed with a stain on her lemony jumpsuit. Then she added sarcastically, "I'll wait until you've had better luck looking for a job."

J.K. birded the rest of the day in Cape May. He wasn't motivated enough to find a motel room, and instead drove to an old haunt where he and his high-school pal, Pete, had camped during their undergraduate days, which he now realized were the best years of his life. It grew crazy windy like in the old days, and he remembered the countless hours he and Pete had spent watching warblers blow about in the wind like leaves.

Walking past the bums settling in for the night, he tried to recall the warm, glorious morning when he'd seen the prairie warbler, but it vanished from his grasp like a cruel mirage.

He slept in his mother's car. He'd never felt so alone, so maddeningly alone in the world. The previous New Year's Day had been so different. That's when he and Pete began to "bird their asses off" for the Big Year. He considered calling Pete, but he was in such miserable shape that he felt sure he'd be terrible company. Falling apart in front of Pete would sour their old smart-alecky friendship. He preferred to hang onto the memory of their brotherhood—it was the one story in his life that didn't have a bad ending. Pete was the one who'd talked him into joining their high-school academic wilderness team. Their coach took them into the nearby forest and expected them to identify trees by looking at the bark. Because of his upbringing in the remote southern part of the state, to which his stubborn father had retreated, J.K. was a natural at outdoorsy stuff. The high school teacher who led the wilderness team was a birding enthusiast, and soon he had the entire team interested in bird watching. After high school, J.K. and Pete were roommates at Rutgers, and on weekends they escaped to the funnel-shaped island of Cape May, a natural resting spot—or as birders call it, "a trap"—for fall migrants. Here they'd seen thirty-two species of warblers in one day. In the fall, the birds numbered in the thousands.

The next day, J.K. wandered absently through familiar locations like the old lighthouse and the trails crisscrossing around it. He mechanically checked off the birds he saw over the next couple of days. He ate at a mom-and-pop store, since the beachside sandwich places he was used to were closed for the season. He spoke to no one, except for the grandma who took his order.

One afternoon, after he was done birding, J.K. ran into some old acquaintances who invited him to a condo party. He got so drunk that someone took pity and let him crash on the couch for the night.

The next morning, J.K. drove to his parents' place to drop off the car. He needed to get to the airport later that afternoon. He told them that he wouldn't be moving back to New Jersey after all. They looked at him with sympathy, but otherwise took the news stoically. Tired of admitting that he was a loser, he didn't bother to give them an update on his job situation.

"You never did shave your goatee," his mother said.

*17*

*B*lake had scanned December's *Vireo* the moment it arrived, and memorized the trip schedule for the first third of the year. The first big birding trip was at the end of January. Denied its share of rain, which is normally spread over three or four months beginning in November, January took a furiously hot turn. When Blake begged to be taken on the weekend trip to the sweltering Salton Sea, over two hours southeast of Alpena, Karen said a firm "No."

The boy sulked for a while and then came up with an urgent reason why he *had* to go on the trip. "The deadline for the Young Birders Contest is in two weeks," he said, his cheeks growing pink, "and I have nothing to submit." He swore that he had learned from his photography mishaps, from the spots and smudges instead of birds, and that he now felt ready now to shoot a masterpiece.

Karen peered into *The Vireo* and saw that Rick was listed as the leader of the Salton Sea trip. He had been quiet during the holidays, and she heard of his Big Year victory only through their listserv. Rick had ignored her congratulatory emails and also the emails she sent him about the cowbird signs. She wondered if he felt guilty that he hadn't been able to coax a grant out of the California Bird Society.

"I have a pile of term papers on Shakespeare to correct," she told Blake. "But let me think about it."

Infused with fresh hope, Blake began to hop about, and even though Karen ignored him, he ran such circles in the backyard garden that Crystal complained he was making her dizzy. The brother and sister, confined close together (they also shared a room), grew testy and fought for no reason. Oscar suggested that they put the kids back in the school system.

"At school, he'll be forced to widen his interests," Oscar told her.

"Yeah, in video games . . . and maybe drugs," Karen said.

Now she had to take responsibility for homeschooling Blake and making sure he got enough outings. The next day, she got an email from Rick. She was disappointed to find out that he couldn't lead the trip. This was the first she heard of Meg's illness, and she was stunned that it took him so long to tell her about something this serious in his life.

"The doctors weren't sure if Meg was going to make it," he wrote in the email, which was also addressed to Zanne and Frank. "But luckily she's back home for a two-month rest. I need extra time to take care of her. Because this is also a busy time of transition for me at work, I'll have to resign as the president of A.B.S. I propose that Frank take over as interim president until elections in June."

Frank and Dana were reluctant to take on the responsibility being thrust upon them, but there wasn't a respectable way out under the circumstances. The change was so sudden and yet so casually made that Karen grew even more nervous about the society's future. Frank was the best treasurer any society could have, but presidential material he was not. He lacked Rick's charisma and the ability to draw people into A.B.S. or get them excited about working together. A retired accountant, Frank was an introverted man and, despite good intentions, his personality was about as exciting as cooked squash.

But the change was made. And the Salton Sea trip, which Rick normally led at the end of January, was delegated to Frank and Dana. As the day to sign up for the trip approached, Blake grew feverish. He paced the house, reciting a soliloquy with Shakespearian poise: "Does thou knowest of a more scenic place to take photos than the dazzling blue Salton Sea, with its bizarre colony of pink flamingoes?" he intoned, "and with a million shorebirds begging to be recorded for posterity! And doth my own blood mother deny me the chance?"

The boy's imaginative version of nagging melted Karen's resolve, and despite the heat and the pile of term papers waiting to be corrected, she caved. The Mercers were buying a new computer, and she figured that Oscar would be busy all weekend doing research. Since it wasn't her idea of fun to listen to him extol the virtues of hard drives, she might as well take a forced vacation. The computer was supposed to be a Christmas present for the kids, but such was the insane busy-ness of the Mercer holidays that they had postponed the purchase until January.

"The computer was my idea," Karen said to Dana, as the birders stopped en route to the Salton Sea to observe a peregrine falcon on a telephone pole. "But I made it seem like it was his idea. That's how our marriage has lasted so long!"

Dana shook with laughter. Alerted, the falcon spread out his wings, revealing bluish-gray trouser legs before flying away.

"Did you call Rick?" Dana said, her eyes narrowing.

"Oh, yeah. Right away. I told him, 'If there's anything I can do, let me know.' He said he would," Karen shrugged, "and I never heard from him again."

As though trying to convince herself, she added, "I guess it's good he's getting some time off. We don't want to burn him out."

Dana nodded. "Frank tried to contact J.K. to see if he'd be interested in leading this trip, but he never returned our calls."

"He has a habit of not returning emails either," Karen added, as they walked back to their vehicles. "He's probably crushed that he lost the Big Year."

"If he'd stuck it out in L.A. instead of rushing back to New Jersey, he wouldn't have fallen behind," Blake said authoritatively.

Karen shrugged. There was an article in the *L.A. Times* glorifying Rick, and it annoyed her that the Alpena Bird Society, which could have used the publicity, was barely mentioned. There was no formal trophy for winning the Big Year, but Rick's reputation had soared since then, and he was now famous in the Southern California birding community. Even Jim Skua, President of the National Bird Society, had called to congratulate him.

Dana ran a hand through her mop of curly blonde hair. "Men!" she said, rolling her eyes. The women gave each other knowing smiles.

Near the Salton Sea, the caravan stopped on a road hugging a state prison facility to witness Sandhill cranes in their unearthly beauty cavorting on the sunny field between the road and the prison. Blake tried to get a good photograph, but the cranes clustered so tightly that he could not get "clean corners."

"Dumb cranes," Blake muttered.

"Seventeen," Kenny counted with a satisfied look. In the sunlight, his face looked rugged with deep lines vanishing in multiple directions.

As they approached the final turnoff, Blake, sitting in the passenger seat, tried to make out the garbled talk on walkie-talkie station 1122. "I just saw a police car," Kenny's voice came in. "We might get busted," added the schoolteacher, Wynn.

"I'm losing you!" Blake said. "Trip-leader, roger?"

"Frank's too old to figure out this walkie-talkie stuff," Dana piped in.

The caravan, six vehicles strong, slowed to let the police car pass. Ignoring the "No Trespassing" and "Security Police" signs, they drove to the end of the road where fruit fields necked with the sea. Jumping out of their vehicles after the long drive, the birders looked about, but they found nothing better than the ubiquitous yellow-rumped warblers in the bushes. On the dirt path, they discovered the remains of a quail shot by hunters.

Blake was reduced to taking photographs of the dead bird and its feathers strewn about next to shotgun shells and broken glass.

"Is it a California or a Gambel's?" Frank said. The dead quail's head was pressed firmly into the ground with one eye looking up.

"Oh, stop it now!" Dana said in a disgusted tone.

"I'm surprised there are no cigarette butts," Karen said. "Usually the three go together—dead birds, bullets, and cigarette butts." The bleak location increased her feeling of desolation. There was no denying that the trip seemed barren because Rick wasn't here. Whether consciously or not, she had grown used to soaking up the attention he gave her. Maybe it was a vestige of her desire to be a theatre actress—that she couldn't resist having someone special for whom she could perform. As a college student, she judged her fellow actors severely for the reckless choices they made in their personal lives. Their vanity and self-importance left her with a bad taste. She quit acting because what she wanted ultimately was a family life, and she wasn't going to give that up for the company of egomaniacs. And so she walked away from the career of her dreams.

Teaching had been an afterthought, and it was clear now that it didn't fulfill her, nor did her perfect family life. She needed something more. She was restless and had fallen into the trap of enjoying, and even seeking out Rick's attention. And now that Rick was suffering, could she help it if her heart went out to him? Surely that wasn't inappropriate. She wished he would allow her into his life somehow in a way that was acceptable, and let her to do something for him. But since Meg had fallen ill, he had created a wall around himself, and the emails she wrote him went unanswered. She lamented that the era of neighborliness was a thing of the past.

Just when they had given up the spot as a bust, an unfamiliar call rang out from the saltbush. There was a hush among the birders, and hope enlivened their whispers. A small bushtit-like bird emerged, with a yellow forehead and red marks on the wing.

"It's a verdin!" Blake sang out.

After a steak dinner—a tradition Rick had instituted and that Blake supported wholeheartedly—and an overnight stay at a musty motel, the birders woke up early Sunday morning. At their first location, as they all stood bickering over a gull, J.K., looking gaunt, made a surprise appearance.

It was 7:30 a.m., and they were congregated on a cliff overlooking a pond near the Mexican border. Swallows and gulls flew over the pond, and rails called from the mysterious depths of the reeds. In the distance, an unidentified whitish bird hovered. At first Blake thought it was a tern. The bird attracted everyone's attention because of the irregularities in its markings. There was a black spot behind the eye, causing a few to conclude that it was a Bonaparte's gull. But others thought the spot looked more like a smudge, so this party began to shout "Franklin's," basing their conclusion on the color of the bird's leg. Meanwhile, the bird flew about unconcerned, turning away from them and disappearing occasionally into a ditch. Blake ran around like a circus acrobat trying to photograph it.

"I think it's a laughing gull," Karen said, disagreeing with both factions. "The white spots from the primaries are too small for a Franklin's."

The schoolteacher, Wynn, pointed out that the smudging on the head behind the eyes also seemed too faint to be a Franklin's. When the disagreements were the thickest and violence seemed imminent, J.K. arrived on the scene to everyone's relief, because he could be counted on to deliver a reliable verdict. He was inclined to call out a laughing gull from the start, but the bird was foraging on the ground and he waited to be sure. When it took flight, the solid black wingtips were visible.

"Laughing gull!" he called out with confidence.

Everyone else demurred. "Of course!"

They hovered as their expert, tailed by Blake, pointed out a few more gulls. They thought that J.K. looked pale and were careful not to mention Rick or the Big Year. Blake was in heaven, enjoying both being near J.K. and the feeling that he had taken a successful shot of the laughing gull.

The schoolteacher, Wynn, a stocky, red-haired guy, began to tell J.K. about his summers in Alaska. "I camp in remote areas so I don't have to pay a fee," Wynn said. "I love it when I can snag a freebie—fruits off a roadside tree or such. I live on, like, a few dollars a day, max."

"I could use some economy," J.K. said. "Anchovies aren't cheap."

A flock of geese flew by, and Kenny called out "Three" and "Seven," nodding after each such count. "Are you aware of the largest prime number ever calculated?" he asked J.K.

J.K. looked up from his scope. "I usually don't follow those things," he said.

"This guy I knew devoted ten years to the work," Kenny said.

"I once wrote a program to generate prime numbers," J.K. said, "but that's only because I was a dork."

At this revelation, Kenny's face lit up. To Blake's dismay, he cornered J.K. and explained to him a theory he'd been nursing for several years—that birds appear in prime numbers. He had fresh data from the Sandhill cranes yesterday to support this.

J.K. nodded, suppressing a smile, and when Kenny tried to coax agreement out of him, J.K. said, "Well, I'm not an expert on those things."

He kept mostly to himself after that and had left quietly by the time the party made the weekend's last stop to look for the master of camouflage—the nighthawk.

After examining the on-screen images of a few signs and insisting on a series of corrections, Grimsby was willing to let A.B.S. use Joss Canyon for its Centennial dinner, but only if they paid a hefty fee. No amount of protest on Karen's part, that the fee would eat up their fundraising, would change Grimsby's mind. He thought it fair that they should pay a location fee for the dinner, since they were charging to let people in, and that they also pay to put up the controversial cowbird signs, as these might lead to his next budget being cut.

So now Karen had to fundraise for the signs *and* the dinner *and* Grimsby's fees. Naturally, she was left to handle the planning alone. An urgent appeal for funds went out to all the members by phone and was posted on the A.B.S.'s website, but the appeal barely brought in enough money to cover the cost of printing invitations. Since Rick had withdrawn from active participation on the board, the Centennial Committee had lost its legs. After haggling like a woman in a Turkish bazaar, Karen negotiated an agreement with a new printer to make the cowbird signs. Zanne's daughter had narrowed her wedding date to late spring, and ever since she'd received the news, Zanne's attention had been so diverted that Karen simply lost touch with her.

There was never any trouble getting people to attend a board meeting; they seemed to treat it as a nice evening's entertainment. But ask them to actually give A.B.S. a minute's thought before or after the meeting and everyone suddenly had insanely busy schedules. They expected things to run like clockwork, but were shocked when asked to help stage an event they absolutely planned to attend. The cowbird signs were progressing at a glacial pace because nobody besides Blake and Patty had cared to contribute labor. The board members were hopeless when it came to vision, still Karen was almost fond of them, the way one tolerates a batty aunt. More often than not, if a crisis were impending, as was the case now, the membership would grudgingly pitch in.

At the February board meeting, they all sat around the table, solemnly licking envelopes. Invitations were going out to all their local members, plus notables in the California Bird Society. Now it was left up to Karen to pull the Centennial out of a hat. Nobody inquired very deeply into the arrangements, maybe out of guilt, or because they feared that one of these days Karen might "go postal" if someone said the wrong thing. And she might have given up, if she didn't suspect that A.B.S. was in danger of dissolving altogether and would get no better chance than the Centennial to resurrect itself. Besides, the fact that she was taking on the burden of Rick's role appealed to both her romantic and generous impulses.

A soprano in her church choir fell sick, and their conductor asked Karen to sing the opening duet in Bach's *Mass in B minor*. At any other time she'd have jumped at the chance, but how could she pack extra rehearsals into her impossible schedule? She still needed to finish correcting the term papers, which she had neglected for the Salton Sea trip. And then there were the many incomplete signs that had only received scattered attention from her over Christmas. It was a wonder she wasn't sick with worry, because practically nothing had been done yet about the Centennial. But then Oscar reminded her of her long-unfulfilled dream to sing a duet with the choir.

"You're damn right," she said, still wondering how in the world she would find the time. But in the end she said yes to the conductor. "You know what?" she said to Oscar. "I'm doing all I can for A.B.S., but I'm going to leave the Centennial up to God. Only He can save it now."

Karen went to a stylist the morning before the performance and had her hair colored autumn brown. Two small diamond studs shone in her earlobes. It was her first duet ever, and she sang it with a plump woman whose hair was colored blonde and fell down to her cheeks like the wings of a golden warbler. Before they began, the two looked at each other, and their faces melted into smiles; the warblers broke out into joyful song. The sunlight outside was transformed into white sparkles by the stained-glass windows. As she sang, Karen felt both joy and loss, like a butterfly that had at last unfurled her wings. She looked up from the pearly light dancing on the hardwood stage to the audience assembled in front of her, and she felt herself soaring on the wings of her song, soaring above the silver cross and swaths of dried purple flowers.

Karen swayed, trance-like, surrounded by the voices of angels and being transported into Bach's heavenly dream. This was the state her soul aspired to—to be on stage, a golden bird, singing her heart out to the world. If only she could hold onto this feeling and glaze it over the span of her life! But that was as unthinkable as scraping the color off butterfly wings.

The success of the performance made Karen think about what she could do with A.B.S. if only she had Rick's active support. She lamented the time that had been lost already. It would be March soon, and during spring break there would be the added stress of Oscar's hernia surgery, and then within three months, the Centennial would be upon them. She tortured herself imagining that the Centennial would be a disaster due to her carelessness, and then there would be the dissolution of A.B.S. at one final summer board meeting, during which Blake would cry his heart out. He would lose the one passion that meant the world to him, and Karen would be bawling too, because she'd made a fool of herself, and had failed to save her son's beloved bird society while she still had the chance.

At times when Karen felt unequal to the task of putting together the Centennial, she retreated into her kitchen and sat at the table with a bottle of beer. As she drank, she stared at a black-and-white photograph taken by her grandmother, which she'd recently had enlarged and framed. It hung on the best wall in her kitchen, next to the window, and it showed Joss Canyon as it was in 1920—totally wild—a lake, silvery-gray, with a wildflower meadow and a lone, sunlit cow in the foreground. On the freshly-grazed grass stood a cowbird, digging out insects. The fact that she was lending a hand to save the canyon her grandmother had loved tethered Karen to Alpena's past and to the reality that this, not England, was her true home. She could be fatalistic when there was no other option. When she got too tired or exasperated with the responsibility, she decided that it was meant to be. No one could pull this off but her. On afternoons like this, she drank two bottles of beer instead of one. By God, I'm going to do this! she vowed.

Karen's fiscal plan was geared around the Big Day. She and Blake hit up anyone they could think of for sponsorships, especially the members of her church choir. Those who could afford it were asked to pledge a dollar a bird, after full disclosure that a birder of Blake's skill might find over 250 species on a spectacular Big Day. Other donors were offered the opportunity to put up fifty cents a bird.

The Big Day was, by tradition, scheduled for early April, but Blake was already mapping out draft plans a few days before Valentine's Day.

They talked every day about the upcoming event, and Crystal—who had come along on two Big Days in years past and swore the last time that she'd never be part of another "Crazy Day"—guessed accurately that she'd be Shanghaied into contributing her eyes and ears again to assist her brother. There was no use arguing with her mother about something that meant so much to her. Crystal wasn't interested in birds, but she had a sharp eye, and her "Did you see that one?" or "What about the one over there?" had been helpful during previous Big Days. After dinner some nights, she and Blake argued over which of them had the most sponsors so far, and for how much per bird, and when they totaled up the money they'd be owed based on how many birds Blake expected to spot, Crystal's reluctance melted into determination.

It became clear even to Oscar that he would be roped in as chauffeur for the birding marathon, which was to start at an ungodly 3 a.m. and return him to his recliner and glass of Scotch a shattered man, body and soul, well after midnight. He would have liked to have squeezed in an afternoon nap, but his wife made arrangements with a neighbor to feed the dog so they wouldn't have any excuse to return home early.

Karen emailed J.K. about her Big Day plans, but didn't hear back. Assuming he was busy with work, she forwarded him the email once more, but again there was no response. She wrote a third time, wondering if he was all right. He finally wrote back, apologetic about the delay. "I have no idea what my crazy schedule is like in April," he wrote, "but I'll try to help."

"That's not too encouraging," Karen muttered to her husband, who sat nearby reading a scholarly work on Victorian mores. "And J.K. was my last hope!"

One of Oscar's virtues was that he never deprived her of a shoulder to sob on, and Karen took full advantage of his comforting arms now.

*18*

*Y*ou're way behind!" Rick said, when he realized that she hadn't been told.

Karen had phoned him to find out how things were when he gave her the news. Old Jean Savant, who'd trudged faithfully on many A.B.S. trips, didn't make it through the holiday season.

Jean Savant's death saddened Karen, but she wanted to discuss J.K. with him. She recalled that when J.K. materialized at the Salton Sea trip, he looked forlorn and lost, despite trying to keep up appearances. Blake had complained that J.K. was becoming harder to spot than a nighthawk.

"From my understanding, his girlfriend, Anne Marie, broke up with him a few months ago," Rick said. "It hit him out of the blue. He still hasn't gotten over it. He spent New Year's Day sleeping in a car in Cape May."

"Poor guy!"

"Before that he was trying to reorganize his life around being there to support her."

Karen shook her head. "That just makes me mad."

"From what I can tell, he's avoiding everyone right now."

"He's probably lost faith in the human race," Karen said.

"I guess I should feel sorry that he didn't win the Big Year, but I won it fair and square," Rick said, forgetting that in desperation he had hired a birder from the L.A. Bird Society at the last minute to scope two rare birds for him. Anyhow, J.K. had enough decency to congratulate him, though in a lukewarm way.

Blake wanted nothing more than to pester J.K. about the Big Day routes he had mapped out, but Karen advised him to wait another couple of weeks.

Turning on the rice cooker, she thought J.K. was a pretty nice guy. Other than being handsome, he was considerate to others most of the time. The same twenty-five-year-old girl who had dumped him might find herself a few years down the road without a mate and wonder why. She was used to hearing about the romantic misadventures of her cousin, who was still single at thirty-four. Maybe girls nowadays were misled by notions of the woman-who-can-have-everything to the extent that they couldn't see the difference between big problems and small ones. They let go of relationships over trivialities, and then despaired in their thirties when confronted with the horror of being alone in a world that was full of loneliness. Karen wondered if her half-English blood accounted for her own common sense. She was aware it might be old-fashioned and conventional to appreciate being married, but sometimes giving in to convention made sense to her.

And what was wrong with Oscar? He was a nice guy, nicer actually than J.K. To hurt Oscar was the last thing she would want, but her temperament wasn't suited to the quiet, sedentary life with which Oscar was content. And yet she loved him enough to want her attraction to Rick to fade away. The trouble was that she loved her family, but was tired of her life. There was nothing she could do about the fact that her heart raced when Rick called. But if she could focus on the Centennial and make it a success, if she could invigorate her life through the work she did for A.B.S., her restlessness might be satisfied.

Anyhow, it was clear to her now that she needed to bring Rick back into A.B.S. His abrupt exit had left such a vacuum that her struggle to use the Centennial to revitalize A.B.S. had lost all focus. Without Rick, she had lost her compass.

J.K. avoided going to lunch with colleagues because their self-satisfied faces only aggravated his sense of failure. Today he sat at a table under a Japanese cherry tree and was struck by its fragrance. Why the blasted tree had picked Valentine's Day to flower, he didn't know, but the cruel irony made him ache. Anne Marie's perception of him as a weakling still haunted him. He thought that was unfair. He had been honest with her about his feelings, but she clearly preferred insincerity.

Because the paper with Dave had fizzled, J.K. needed to write another paper to meet his department's requirements for a Ph.D. He tried to come up with something. He needed only one original idea that would be robust enough to not collapse in its development. But it was as if his brain was drained of its power, and he knew of no cables that could jump-start it. It performed mechanical calculations tolerably enough, but in its current hybrid state of depressed tension or tense depression (he wasn't sure which), an original idea was beyond him. Occasionally, just when he thought he had the ghost of an idea, it gave him the slip. He used to do his best thinking in the mornings, when his mind was fresh. But today, while he ate his oatmeal, his mind wandered to his misadventure with Luna (another ghost), and even though he knew that dwelling on his humiliation was pointless, he couldn't control it.

Outside his apartment, a bauhinia tree's pink flowers had overwhelmed its heart-shaped leaves, and from his window he had a rare view of a pair of "modoes"—mourning doves—building a nest in the tree. For days, the male brought back twigs, two at a time, until one day the female was satisfied enough to sit in the nest. J.K. began to observe them over long stretches of his mornings. He'd named the male "Amoeba" and the female "Hiba." A stream of sunshine fell on Hiba as she sat in her camouflaged bower. She pecked at twigs occasionally, but some mornings she was so still that it took close scrutiny to confirm she was still there. J.K. relied on that tree for his ordinary bird-watching, and he was fascinated by the domestic life of the doves. It became a morning ritual to watch the "changing of the guard," when Amoeba gingerly slid off the egg and Hiba took over.

Then, as though no thing of beauty could be left in peace, three workers showed up one Saturday at the lot next door and sawed down a towering bay tree.

J.K. dashed to his computer and scoured a city website to find out if the bauhinia tree was a protected species. When he learnt that a permit was needed to cut down the *bauhinia variegata*, he was relieved, but still he kept an eye on the workers. To his horror, he saw them moving toward the bauhinia with a chain saw.

J.K. rushed out to confront them. "Do you have a permit to cut down this tree?" he asked, as the male dove hovered around.

One of the workers nodded.

"Can I see it?"

The man went to his rusty pickup and returned with a folded piece of paper.

"This is for the bay tree," J.K. said, reading the permit. "The bauhinia right here is a protected tree. You can't cut it down."

The men, day laborers who spoke little English, looked puzzled and a little frightened, and they disappeared soon after. J.K. couldn't shake off his suspicion that some suit in an office would send them back another day. But it felt good to have protected his modoes, at least for the time being. He wished the chick would hurry up and hatch already.

He wanted to wring Luna out of his mind somehow, because he had more serious problems to worry about. He was living month-to-month on his graduate student stipend, and had no clue how he would support himself once May arrived and the checks stopped coming. But lately, his mind, like a mechanical toy, spun again and again toward thoughts of Luna. He longed for the few moments of peace he sometimes experienced sitting at the Leaves Café.

Recent rains had cleared the visibility, and on sunny afternoons he sat outside the café and looked at the San Gabriel Mountains in all their glory. The air was crisp. If he were lucky, on some afternoons the snow-tipped peak of Mt. Baldy came into view. Now and then he noticed Luna throwing a glance in his direction from the counter. Or maybe he imagined it.

There were hardly any openings in environmental organizations except for entry-level jobs, for which J.K. was overqualified with an impending Ph.D. He had two interviews for better positions. One involved identifying California's "important bird areas" for biological study, and the other was a seasonal position to band hummingbirds. He could not imagine a better candidate for either job than himself. Even though he had no course work or research qualifications for these jobs, his reputation as a birder preceded him to both interviews. He thought the interviews went well enough, and that these people had been impressed with his knowledge of the status and distribution of birds.

As a fallback position, he asked Dave if he could get a year's extension at the university, which would allow him to try his luck again at postdoctoral positions. He asked with a sick heart, knowing that this meant going through the stress of applying for postdocs all over again next year and possibly being rejected again. But what alternative did he have? There wasn't going to be any financial assistance from his parents, he was sure, because his father believed in the principal that "a man ought to be able to support himself through hard work, without anybody's charity."

"I'll find out in a month or so," Dave told him. "In the beginning of April—that's when the committee meets."

A month was a torturous amount of time to wait, but the modoe chick hatched, mercifully, and provided some distraction. "Gulliver" was an ugly little thing, a dirty gray mass that squeaked in a high-pitched voice, but its parents fussed over it, astonished by its charm. During this time, J.K. experienced the feeling that there was no one he could turn to for relief. In the past he had assumed, as young people do, that not only would his future be satisfying to him, but that it would be of consequence to others. But now he was forced to check off the names of the very people to whom he thought his future mattered—his supervisor, his ex-girlfriend, his parents (caring about how he would make money didn't count), and the people at A.B.S.

The bauhinia tree was better protected than he was. He realized that his perception of his connection to others was false. Human bonds were weaker and more inconsequential than he had believed. He was essentially alone. This was the only truth.

Anne Marie used to say that his smile was the cutest thing about his face. Smiling now seemed to him a colossal waste of energy. He felt distaste for human relationships and the falsities they entailed. The times spent in nature were his only unsullied experiences. He didn't regret doing the Big Year; he only wished he hadn't told anyone about it.

One day, as he walked back to his apartment after work, the walls of the complex seemed sunnier than before. He saw with disbelief that the entire bauhinia tree had vanished, and in its place was a sorry stump. He found Gulliver, the modoe chick, in the middle of the road, while Hiba and Amoeba hovered over it, screeching.

Gulliver had miraculously avoided being hit by a car.

Dodging traffic, J.K. scooped the chick into his hands. Amoeba pecked angrily at his head, assuming he was a predator. Ignoring the attack, J.K. planted the chick on the dirt around the tree stump and hurried away. He hoped his human scent on the chick wouldn't disgust the doves enough to abandon it.

Having decided that Rick would have to be pulled back into the fold after Meg's illness, Karen had called only to nudge him in the right direction. As she saw it, it was critical to get him on his feet and back into the presidential chair. The changing of the guard had occurred two months ago, in January, and Frank now presided at their board meetings. But Karen could no longer bear to attend the meetings or plan the Centennial without Rick there. They couldn't afford to lose him. He must stay on at least as Program Chair. The charm would go out of A.B.S. if Rick left. And, knowing that the way to his heart was through a birding trip, she called to consult him about their semi-annual March trip to Piute Ponds. "We seem to be missing a trip leader," she said. "Usually J.K. would handle this."

"I have a feeling he's still in a lousy mood," Rick said.

"Have you talked to him?" Karen said.

"Not really."

"Is there any chance we can get you to lead it?"

"Do I have a choice?" he said cryptically. "As things stand, I don't see why not."

Delighted, though not entirely sure what to make of his response, Karen added, "Should we have a bad weather cancellation policy?"

"The weather be damned!" he said.

The worse the weather got, the better Rick felt. It snowed in the second week of March, and the Forest Service closed some roads up in the San Gabriel Mountains. When he heard predictions of a storm, Rick's spirits rose for the first time in weeks. And that was just when Karen called to ask if he would lead the trip to Piute Ponds.

After Meg came home from the hospital, Rick shooed away his family—especially his mother. She was never altogether fond of Meg and blamed her for their decision not to have children, when in fact it was mostly Rick's suggestion. His sister saw Meg's close call as an opportunity to work Jewish tradition back into his life, but he was determined to resist her. His sister was married to an orthodox Jew, which was fine, but personally he liked to spend his free time birding. He even shooed away his guilt over his Big Year being the possible cause of Meg's collapse. Fearing that such thinking would gray his hair completely, he plunged instead into the twin tasks of reducing the mound of paperwork in his office and warming up assorted instant soups for Meg at home.

Meg's parents had offered to spend a Saturday with her, and Rick happily took them up on it. Though he had given the job of caregiver a solid try, he wasn't a nurse by instinct, and felt that he needed to get his own strength back before he could warm up any more soups. He was emerging from a wintry, claustrophobic episode in his life, and he felt a strong urge to break free or he wouldn't be able to go on.

The forecasts warned that the higher elevations were in for highway closures, winter storms, and rain and snow, but when Rick had promised Karen and Blake a ride, he simply told them to wear clothes that were "warm inside and waterproof outside."

He picked them up at 5:50 in the morning at their house. There was already another passenger in Rick's SUV. A study in the color purple, Kenny was wearing purple stockings, a cap under a sun hat, dark purple hiking pants, and a purple windbreaker over multiple layers of clothing. The front pockets of the windbreaker were stuffed with gloves and other items, which gave his belly such a pregnant look that they could just as easily be rushing him to a delivery room.

"It's cold out there," Blake complained, getting into the SUV.

"There's no such thing as cold," Kenny said, "just inadequate clothing." His wide, long face was clean-shaven today. "I'm having problems with my teenagers," he admitted as they drove toward the freeway. "My staying at home really doesn't do anything," he said with a grimace that began on his forehead and traveled to his lips. "It only aggravates them."

"Oscar said we were going to get killed," Karen said, "when he found out we were planning to go despite the weather warnings. 'Even if you can get there,' he said, 'the weather will be so bad that no one will have a good time.'" Karen thought that Oscar, not exactly a risk taker, had developed an even more nervous disposition as he prepared to face hernia surgery.

Rick shrugged, as if to dismiss Oscar's concerns.

Soon the San Gabriel Mountains came into sight, dusted liberally with snow. The birders gasped. Normally, one had to look as far east as Mount Baldy for snow, and even then smog usually hid the snow-capped peak. "Meteorologists in Southern California are having a great time," Rick told them. "How often do they get to say there's a snowstorm coming?"

They drove along Highway 14, which led up into the Antelope Valley. Rick adjusted the temperature control, but it was still cool in the SUV, though it was obviously much colder outside. "I should get one of those temperature gauge things," he said.

The snowstorm had left a distinct mark on the hills along the highway. The modest cliffs, normally sandy brown, were streaked with the purest white. The chaparral scrubs dotting the hills and the distant mountains were powdered all over with snow. The valley below glistened solid white, as did the flat roofs of the few houses they passed.

"Wow! It's real snow!" Rick said. Born and bred in Alpena, he could count on one hand the times he had seen real snow. He felt more awed than a child at Christmas. "It's like a winter wonderland," he said without irony. He felt as if the happiness of his Big Year victory, buried inside him for two months, was suddenly swirling around him.

"It's a good thing I got you to come," Karen said, nudging his collar.

Blake noticed how friendly his mother really was to Rick, and he blushed, though he didn't know why.

So thrilled was Karen by Rick's sooner-than-expected return to A.B.S. that she decided not to risk scaring him off by bugging him about the Centennial. She had just made up her mind to thoroughly enjoy herself for once when her cell phone rang. In the habit of shutting everything else out when she was with Rick, she let the call go to voicemail. She let Blake listen to message—his dad was saying that there was snow on Henniger Flats, at 1500 ft., whereas the snowline for their area was normally 6000 ft. Blake relayed this news to his fellow birders, and Karen didn't call Oscar back.

As they drove, triangular mountains with few dark green spots left untouched by snow surrounded them. "Isn't it wonderful?" Rick said. "Isn't it gorgeous? Have I said that already?"

Karen's face melted into a smile.

"It's amazing what's happening to us," he said.

Karen looked at him curiously, but a glimpse of her expression in the rear view mirror put him on guard and he retreated from whatever it was he was going to say. What did he mean? What's happening to us? Karen felt her blood go warm. An oversized snowman stood in a valley park with his carroty nose pointed at the road. Even the road signs were blasted with snow.

"I went to Duluth last winter to look for great grays," Kenny said. "It was so cold that the owls had migrated down from Canada. The temperature gauge read minus forty degrees. Even the Minnesotans in the group were impressed."

"I bet you were dressed warmly," Karen said.

"Actually, I was so bundled up all day that when I met the group at a restaurant for dinner, I had to reintroduce myself to everyone."

"Weather shmeather!" Rick said. "You see, people worry too much."

At Piute Ponds, Kenny put on two more layers of clothing. Robert Kern's SUV was waiting for them. "Kathy Morton just saw a rare species of sage," announced Kern, in a khaki jacket that matched his safari clothes.

Kathy Morton, Kern's wife, with graying hair spilling out from under a cowgirl hat, began to point out the difference between purple, white, and California sage.

To Rick's annoyance, the gang crowded around Kathy, and he had to issue strict "No planting!" orders to disperse everyone to search for shorebirds. Blake was soon rewarded with a family of sanderlings who slid on a narrow beach as though entertaining themselves on an ice rink. Cormorants posed on rocks in the middle of a pond, spreading their wings out to dry after fishing. After a prolific morning spotting smartly colored avocets and stilts, and treats such as long-billed curlews and a glowering barn owl, the gang felt encouraged enough to head to Apollo Park in search of ducks and warblers.

The suburban park looked eerily empty without the usual crowds of picnickers and dudes playing frisbee golf. The wind picked up, and the tops of trees swayed, threatening to fly off.

Trying to point out an orange-crowned warbler to Kenny, Rick said, "You see that part of the tree that's quiet?"

"What part?" Kenny said. All the branches of the tree were fluttering like ribbons.

"Right there!" Rick said. "About eight o'clock."

"My birding is rusty," Kenny said, still unable to locate the bird.

Rick looked on, frustrated at being held up by an amateur.

Just then the warbler was blown to a distant tree by a gust of wind. Kenny walked off in disgust.

They ate lunch at the picnic tables, deserted but for a few ducks and geese who came up to introduce themselves. From here, the park looked desolate. Kathy Morton backed her SUV up next to the picnic tables. She opened the trunk and brought out, one by one, big jars of peanut butter, jelly, cut avocadoes, and mayonnaise, then set about assembling these items into sandwiches. Between reminders from his wife to eat up his canned peaches, Robert Kern said, "Kathy Morton has a knack for coming up with good fillings for our sandwiches."

Karen noted that although the trunk of Kern's jeep was loaded with more goodies than would be needed for the Queen's picnic, he didn't think to offer anything to the other birders in the party who were making do with more modest fare on this cold, windy day. "Do you like dates?" she said to Rick, trying to make up for Kern's lack of hospitality.

"For eating," Rick said, "or for going on?"

She laughed and handed him a couple of dark, moist Mejdool dates.

"These are great," he said, chewing slowly and with pleasure. As she watched him enjoying the treat, she knew somehow that she had succeeded in luring him back to A.B.S.

There was an argument about whether one goose someone spotted was a white-fronted or not. Another bird was a Canada goose. "This one is a cross between them," said Robert Kern, who was a knowledgeable old goat on the subject of hybrids.

"You're so pretty," Rick said to the Canada goose. "Come talk to me."

He threw a crumb of his sandwich to the goose. She tasted it eagerly at first, but spit it out. The hybrid goose began to consider the crumb.

"She didn't like it," Rick laughed. "You don't like mayo? C'mon, mayo is good." The sun shone cheerily through the clouds, and he chuckled as he held out another crumb for her.

The hybrid goose moved toward him. He bent over to get a closer look, but she hissed, and then, to Karen's horror, she struck out and bit his nose.

"Oh, Mom, look!" Blake cried, as he ran to shoo away the goose.

"The cut isn't too deep," she said, cleaning off the blood with an alcohol swab. "She just wanted a little taste of you." Karen rummaged through her purse, unnerved by Rick's pained cries, and dug out ointment from the first-aid supplies, which she slathered on his nose. Rick looked into her face and smiled mournfully. "That'll teach me to flirt," he muttered.

It was decided to cut the trip short due to the poor weather and the trip leader's incapacitated state. Karen was far from disappointed. Rick's goose bite was a small price to pay for his return. She led her patient back to the SUV and, with her not inconsiderable charm, kept him entertained as they waited for Kenny. He had asked to be excused so he could go "defrock" before getting back into the warmth of the SUV.

*19*

$B$lake was feeling on edge because the results of the Young Birders Contest would be announced the next day. His father had promised a special treat if there were good news. Blake hoped he would win; it would lift his father's spirits. Oscar was convalescing from hernia surgery with instructions not to climb stairs or take a shower for five days. Instead, he spent his hours hobbling the length of the house in a despondent mood. After many tortured decisions, Blake had submitted a scrapbook and a photo of the laughing gull for the contest. He cared less about the prizes, which would likely be books and doo-dads he already owned, than about the title.

He was crushed that J.K. hadn't won the Big Year competition and thought his hero ought to at least get some other award. He had bugged his mother about this injustice all the way to the March board meeting.

There was something unusual in the air that night, alluded to by certain looks between Rick and Zanne, but Karen couldn't make out what was going on. Frank walked in late, opening his A.B.S. mail as he entered the church boardroom. He puzzled over a package from the National Bird Society, addressed to a deceased president of A.B.S.

"Let me get this right," Zanne said. "You open your mail right before the board meeting?"

Frank laughed. "You got that exactly right."

The Egret opened her mouth to protest. It was a tradition for the A.B.S. president to open the mail on his own time and incorporate its contents into the meeting's agenda. "You know what?" she started, and then after a pause, "Never mind." Remembering that Frank had ascended to the presidency unwillingly, she decided to go easy on him.

Robert Kern announced that somewhere downtown there was going to be a free screening of *Winged Migration*.

Kenny squinted and opened his jaw halfway. "What's that?" he said. "A musical?"

Frank tore open the mystery letter addressed to the dead president, saying, "It's strange. There seems to be a pattern of letters to and from dead people."

Karen looked at him, not understanding what he meant.

"I don't think his wife is alive either," Frank added. He found a note inside. "Now here's the president of the National Bird Society, Jim Skua, accepting our invitation to the Centennial Dinner."

Karen swooned. Rick, a band-aid over his nose, wondered if he should have his arms ready to catch her in case she fell. She grinned, barely able to believe the good news. The clock could not be turned back now; the Centennial must be celebrated. And she gave J.K. full credit for this "get," even though he had nagged Skua only at her urging.

Ignoring the general confusion and murmurs, Karen proposed that J.K. be awarded the first Cowbird Award for his contribution to A.B.S.

Rick frowned, knowing that the award had originally been proposed, in J.K.'s presence, to go to the winner of the Big Year. "It sounds like a cop-out," he said. "He's a scientist. Maybe he'd be embarrassed with an award."

"When it comes to awards," said Robert Kern with a wink, "scientists prefer to win."

"I think we need to thank J.K. for all he's done for A.B.S. and all the trips he's led," Karen said. "And to encourage him to continue to be active with us."

"I agree!" chimed in Blake, who rarely spoke during board meetings. He was pleased when his mother made it a formal motion.

After some sluggish resistance, most of the board voted "Aye." And so it was that J.K. was picked as the first recipient of the Cowbird Award.

Despite this victory, Karen didn't dare gloat. It was mid-March already. She was more worried now than ever. They hadn't even begun the groundwork for the June Centennial, and now they had a high-falutin' guest of honor. Her brain was compiling Centennial chores that she needed to delegate. "We need money fast," she said. "Rick, are you willing to take prospective donors on a night owling trip? It might be an exciting novelty for some donors."

"An owling trip in general is a great idea," Rick said. Looks were exchanged between Frank, Rick, and the Egret. "But I don't think that it would serve the purpose you have in mind."

Again, Karen wondered if something were happening without her knowledge. "I need people to donate and I need more volunteers," she continued. "I don't know where to begin." She enticed them with tidbits she had learned about Joss Canyon. In a part of the canyon relatively unscathed by the fire, a native black walnut tree was growing. The Tonquin tribe once used these trees for medicinal purposes. She had asked Grimsby why, when the canyon contained such treasures, the D.W.P. insisted on mowing down the natural vegetation. "And I was told that if the reedy plants are allowed to grow unchecked, they could become a fire hazard!"

"Unbelievable," Robert Kern muttered. A black look came over his face, as though he were going to reveal something, but then he stopped himself.

Karen sighed. "This is not going to stop, folks, unless we do something. I'm hoping we can pressure them with the signs. Patty has given me some excellent bird drawings, but I still have no cowbirds or vireos."

"I can't draw a straight line," Kern said.

"C'mon people, send me some bird photos if you can't draw, or I'll be forced to credit Blake for every single sign."

"I don't own a camera," Kern said.

"Can you get someone to talk to us about cowbirds?" she said. "It's an important subject that we're not informed enough about. Maybe you can do the talk?"

"I can't," Kern said.

*Or won't*, Karen thought. In the past they used to have informative talks on birds, but that tradition was fading after A.B.S. lost its home in Joss Canyon.

"I may be able to get someone else interested," Kern told her. "There's a guy, David Lin, at U.C. Santa Cruz, who studies cowbirds."

"Oh, good!"

Rick mentioned that J.K. was good at sketching birds.

"Can you get in touch with him and ask him to make some sketches?" Karen said. "He's not responding to my emails."

"Okay, . . . moving on." Frank said.

"Um, I have a couple of questions," Kenny interrupted. He squinted before continuing. "The tree that you mentioned, the walnut tree, does it have a water source nearby?"

After Karen had explained that yes, there was a stream nearby, he said, "Ah, . . . the tribe . . . I think you said the Tonquin tribe . . ." He adjusted his glasses and thought carefully before he let his comment escape. "I've never heard of it before."

Karen's face wilted. "I'm never going to get anything done," she said. She felt trapped in a time loop. The board met diligently every month, but it seemed that nothing ever got accomplished, except for noting how their bank account crept ever downwards. She could no longer trust herself to contain her mounting frustration.

The board looked at her sympathetically. Knowing that she had everyone's attention for about one second, she said, "I'm going to put together a list of everything that needs to be done. I'm busy doing what I can—buying table-cloths from Target, arranging for someone to manage the bar. . . ."

"It'd be great to have a guitarist," Rick said. "I know a gal who'd be really good."

Karen groaned. Rick seemed strangely carefree and no longer worried about the society's perilous finances. And the one person she had counted on to look over all the catering details, Zanne, continued to be wrapped up in wedding planning. Karen resolved to confront Zanne about her negligence, because she needed at least one other solid person to work with.

When the meeting was over, Karen walked up to Rick. It was a miracle she hadn't exploded already. "I know you're in over your head with things, . . ." she began. But a strange glint in his eye stopped her.

"All right. What is it?" she demanded. "What's with the schoolboy looks you've been exchanging with everyone but me?"

Cornered, Rick stammered and hinted that a matter of great importance to A.B.S. was brewing behind the scenes.

Karen was flustered and irritated that she should be the last to find out.

"It's not a done deal yet. I don't want to get people's hopes up."

"Wait! Start from the beginning."

"I found out sometime in February," he said.

Karen was forced to interrupt him. Before Zanne could escape the meeting, she grabbed her. "I need to talk to you."

"I'm seventy-six," Zanne said, "and as much as I love being editor of *The Vireo*, I would like to show someone else how to take over within the year. I have gray hair, and I'd like to turn it over to those who don't."

"Oh, God!" Karen said. "I don't want to hear about this right now." She knew she should give Zanne up as a loss, but couldn't resist adding, "All I want to know is that you'll pick a caterer before the end of the month."

"I can try," Zanne said.

Feeling hopeless, Karen turned back to Rick. "All right! Just don't give me bad news."

"Someone's mentioned A.B.S. in her bequest," he said.

"What?" she cried.

Rick proceeded to tell her about Jean B. Savant, who had died in December without much in her bank account, but with title to a prime condominium. According to her bequest, the proceeds of the sale of this property were to be divided equally among her two children, the Humane Society, and the Alpena Bird Society. Savant's A.B.S. membership had expired a year ago; for some reason she had ignored Dana's reminders and hadn't bothered to renew it. Their newsletter was mailed out to members only, but due to some clerical error, Savant had still been getting it. After her death, the relatives found a copy of the December issue of *The Vireo*, with its urgent appeal for donations, on her desk.

"Thank God you put that appeal in when I asked you to! Good old Jean! Who'd have thought? So why's it not a done deal? What's stopping us from getting that money? I'm hyperventilating. I can't breathe!"

"There could be several factors," Rick said. Being in the legal field, he knew well enough what the possible hurdles might be.

"Oh, come on!"

"I've heard that her kids might contest the bequest. Try to prove that she was batty when she made it—which she probably was."

"Oh, Rick!"

"Or there might be something wrong with her condo and it may not sell at market value. Anything could go wrong. All that's happened so far is that a lawyer acting as executor has notified us of the bequest, as he's supposed to do. But that's not a guarantee we'll get the money."

"What's the market value of the condo?"

"Anywhere between six to eight hundred thousand," Rick said, rubbing his nose. "Maybe a little bit more. And there might be taxes to be paid. And we'll get only a quarter of the proceeds, if there ever are any."

"What a sweet woman!" Karen said, ignoring his lawyerly concerns. "I wish I'd looked past the opera glasses and taken the time to talk to her."

"Her kids will portray her as a lunatic."

"Oh, Rick! Let's be optimistic, okay? Just this once?"

"With these things, you never know," he said darkly.

"Oh God! I can stop worrying about how little the Big Day might bring in!"

"No way. Absolutely not. Even if we get the money, which is a big if, we won't be able to touch it for at least a year."

Despite Rick's cautionary tone, the news of the bequest buoyed Karen's spirits. She marveled at what she had been able to do so far. She had fought with Rick to put out his plea letter four months early, and now her instinct had been rewarded with this unexpected windfall. She wondered if the Lord was somehow working through her to save A.B.S. Not to mention that she had accomplished the delicate task of pulling Rick back into the fold. She felt exhilarated.

And the streak of good fortune continued. The next day, Blake was notified that his scrapbook of sketches and photographs won Third Prize in the Young

Birders Contest. His photo of the laughing gull won an Honorable Mention.

Karen forwarded the news to Rick, who passed it on to Anissa Montez at the *L.A. Times*. Anissa had done his Big Year interview, which hung now in a gilded frame in Rick's downtown office. Within a week, a reporter from the *Alpena Star News* was at the Mercer house to interview Blake and his mother and take photos.

To celebrate the triumph, Blake's father, a meat-and-potatoes man, dispatched him with his rancher uncle on his first hunting trip. To Karen's dismay, they shot a rabbit, the boy being incapable of pointing a gun at birds. Blake did have some misgivings about shooting the rabbit. It had been a jackrabbit, sitting next to a flowering bush, looking so innocent, pretending it had no intention of eating the yellow flowers. Blake could still feel the trembling of the rabbit's curved, upright ears. After Oscar skinned the animal for a stew, he showed the boy how to dry the rabbit's foot, which they hung on the front porch next to abandoned birdhouses.

The article appeared on a Saturday morning, and it conferred on Blake a title beyond his wildest dreams. He rubbed the rabbit's foot in his pocket, unable to believe that he was finally getting the respect he deserved. The photograph the reporter took of him was captioned "Master Birder."

The family clustered around the newspaper at the kitchen table, under the photograph of Joss Canyon taken by Blake's great-grandmother. His mother began to make his favorite breakfast: eggs and bacon. When Blake saw her proud smile, he threw his head back, dazed.

"My brain's going crazy!" he declared.

## 20

*J.K.* knew that he must get out of his cubbyhole, out of the two-square-mile area around the university, and most of all, out of the dark, hopeless state he'd been in since Christmas. He still avoided Leaves Café, though he didn't stop going there altogether. A few times, in his loneliness, he took comfort in Luna's familiar face, though he reminded himself that she was essentially a stranger (and not a trustworthy one either). One day, she got talky and bright, and his reticence faded; he told her how he'd lost the Big Year competition by one bird. They spoke "over the counter" while she took his cash and made tea.

"But you broke the old record, you said? That's amazing."

"Yeah, but I didn't win. And at the same time, my thesis project fell through. I'm really bottom-of-the-barrel stuff now."

"Hmm. 'Oh, I used to be disgusted, and now I try to be amused.' Elvis Costello."

J.K. let out a thin smile. "I still haven't found a job."

"Hey, I know all about that. Try becoming a musician and watch how the world tries to swat you down. But you're a smart guy. You'll figure it out."

Even if J.K. didn't need the exercise, he began to make regular treks to a neighborhood gym. Rock climbing there was the only time when his head wasn't buzzing with thoughts of where he did or didn't go wrong in the last year, or how he could have handled his job search better. How had it come to be that the whole world lay in front of him just months ago, and now no one as much as glanced at him? He knew it made no sense to brood over these things, but who was to say what did or didn't make sense anymore?

When he allowed himself a visit to Leaves Café, he preferred that Luna were serving a line of customers, so she wouldn't have time to talk to him. Strangely, only in Leaves did he feel light enough to be able to read without slipping into a morass of self-pity. He lapped up Hemingway's *Old Man and the Sea*, and it amused him to imagine himself as the old man, wrestling with a big, unwieldy marlin. He thought the symbolism described perfectly how he felt.

Paul Little was trying to convince Luna to let him open her performance at a local art gallery. "I was playing the song in the middle of the night," he said, "with the cat right by my side. And I said, 'Damn! That's good!' "

J.K. normally was careful not to sit near Paul Little, who was becoming a regular at the café and was always on the lookout for conversation.

Luna had been practicing new songs for some months now, and she finally gave into her band's itch to perform in public. Handing J.K. a flyer about the concert by her band, Leopard, Luna said, "I don't know if you like this sort of music." Her cheeks were flushed. It was the first time she'd walked up to him since that old Clark Mountain episode. She wore black slacks under a faded summer dress that emphasized the roundness of her figure.

J.K. smiled shyly. "You must have already guessed that I'm a nerd," he said. His clear gray eyes met hers and neither looked away.

The girl, wearing a café apron, considered his tousled hair, faded jeans and a lumberjack shirt, which suited his nearly six-foot height. She thought he was being modest in labeling himself a nerd.

"It'll be fun if you come," Luna said.

It was late March and purple wisterias were in bloom, their grapelike vines and flowers hanging in conical bunches from the Roman arches on campus. In cherry trees, hummingbirds were abuzz communing with flowery pink clouds. A drizzling rain occasionally exploded into a shower, and then it was clear for two whole days. Just when J.K. expected it would be sunny through the summer, a cloudy afternoon and cool evening brought a fresh drizzle the next morning.

Not one interview for the environmental jobs yielded callbacks. The positions eventually went to lesser birders than him, but they had administrative experience working for non-profit organizations. His job search fell to a low point when he heard that a native plant nursery was looking to hire a handyman, and he drove there the same afternoon.

At the nursery, a rufous hummingbird hovered in the air and opened its beak to grab a swarm of tiny black flies. After swallowing a mouthful, she sat on the fence to rest before hovering back up to the swarm. Sunlight glinted off her metallic, rust-colored feathers. The ceonathus "dark star" was in bloom. Potted plants were cluttered under tin canopies, and it was depressing to see so many cultivars around.

J.K. liked nature just as it was, not potted up and confined. He introduced himself to the owner, who said they needed someone to start full time right away. The salary was minimum wage. Disheartened, he returned to his overly warm car, actually considering this absurd offer.

In April, J.K. waited for a chance to go to the San Gabriel Mountains, but the roads were still closed. It was an unusually rough weather year for the area. Some people wondered if climate change had anything to do with it. The rain continued into the beginning of the month. Jasmine flowers peeked out, nodding their white heads and scenting the evening breeze. Cherry blossoms, which were in the height of their bloom in March, were now drooping. Looking at the delicate pink trees, J.K. wished that the rain would stop assaulting them.

In the mornings, he ate hot oatmeal and stared at the steady showers outside. It was not the kind of weather to go birding. Instead, he nagged at himself to sketch some birds for Karen's signs, using memory and his collection of photographs as aids. At the end of the week, just when he thought the rain couldn't possibly go on longer—this was Los Angeles County after all—he woke up to the sound of it coming down in sheets.

J.K. drove to Joss Canyon one morning to see how it was faring, and discovered a scene of chaos. The wash was clogged with fallen branches and muddy debris, and his jeans became coated thick with mud as he trampled about. The canyon was so weakened by poor land management that the season of heavy rains nearly ruined it.

Karen drove with Blake to Joss Canyon one day to survey the damage done by the rains. The downpour had uprooted many of the trees, including the rare walnut.

"Oh, no. Look at that!" the boy said.

Karen looked on, dismayed. The D.W.P.'s policy of mowing the upland had undoubtedly worsened the flooding. Much of Joss Canyon was now a wasteland of dirt and boulders. Where there once stood rows of eucalyptus trees, and even a bunting deigned to fly about, there was now only a flat, mud-caked plain. The remaining wild areas in the canyon had responded to the rain by growing even wilder. Before, the trails were overgrown and hard to find; now they were smudged out altogether. Would the A.B.S. ever be able to return home?

Karen needed to summon up strength before she could speak to the man in the trailer. Not wanting to leave Blake alone, she took him along.

Billy Grimsby had a bewildered look, not knowing where he would start, had he been asked to bring some semblance of order to his canyon. It was unusual to find him at his desk these days. "I'm in meetings all day," he said. "I've been using an office in City Hall. It gets lonely in the trailer."

To Karen, this admission meant only that Grimsby was becoming tight with city officials.

"Where should we set up the tents?" Karen said, impatient to get to the point. "The wild part, I think, would be nicer."

"Yeah," Grimsby said. Looking at Blake, he added, "But if you're gonna have kids about, I would worry about poison ivy and rattlesnakes."

They both knew what this warning meant. The tents would have to be set up in the wasteland. "It's not what I had hoped for," she said. "Have you heard D.W.P. say anything about the signs?"

Grimsby shrugged. "I never find out about things until the last minute," he said. His face looked overly wrinkled for a man not yet sixty. "And they still need to approve the use of this location for the Centennial banquet."

Karen groaned. When she got home, she called up J.K. She was surprised to find him unusually responsive.

"I know the canyon is a mess," J.K. said. "It's good Grimsby wasn't around when I was there, or I'd have punched his lights out. Anyway, I'm working on the sketches you wanted."

"And the Big Day?" Karen said.

"Oh, yeah. I'll do what I can to help."

This time J.K. was as good as his word. He prepared a tentative route for the Big Day and began to discuss it with Blake. It was decided that the best strategy would be for J.K., Karen, Blake, and Rick to travel together in Rick's SUV. Karen felt a renewed sense of hope, but no one was happier than her husband and daughter when they learned that they were excused from the "Crazy Day" arrangements.

It had been a long time since J.K. was invited to a party, and he took the precaution of looking cool. His arms, buffed from rock climbing, showed through a faded t-shirt. Jeans hung loosely from his hips. When he arrived at the Hatch Gallery on Friday evening, it was still light out and Luna was pacing on the grassy lawn just outside the gallery.

"I'm glad you could make it," Luna said, when she saw him. A sweet smile passed over her face. She wore a sheer hat with bold curves. "My friend, the milliner, sent it," she told him.

"The one in San Francisco?"

Luna nodded. She looked like a girlish tomboy in a gauzy, white summer dress. When she bent over to check something in her guitar case, J.K. had a good view of her smooth thighs.

The front wall of the gallery was glass, and they stood on the lawn listening through the open door. Paul Little was playing a guitar solo. The lyrics were an incomprehensible jumble, and didn't get any better after J.K. paid the ten-dollar cover and found a seat inside, while Luna went to find her band. Paul Little strummed a rough tune and mumbled away with his eyes closed and a face as bloodless as a slab of Muenster cheese. A shabby ponytail hung from under his scuffed-up black hat. His guitar banged against an unused microphone, and as if to magnify the mistake, he banged the guitar again. At well over forty, in an old Spiderman t-shirt and tight black jeans, he was too old for this act.

Luna smiled from the back of the room, a certain smile meant to reassure J.K. that the music would get better. The next band, Killsonic Deux was a powerhouse. The Cuban drummer mixed frenzied bursts with long stretches of a slow, hypnotic beat. His partner, a stocky man with intense green eyes, played the bass as though he were embracing a cow who responded by mooing soulfully.

As J.K. walked back from the makeshift bar with a cheap beer and salted peanuts, he found Luna looking anxious. "We're on next," she said, putting an arm around him. Drawn to her apprehensive eyes and plump red mouth, he drew in to kiss her. "You'll be fine," he told her. She smelled strongly of alcohol. They kissed again. He slipped an arm around her, feeling the rough texture of her boyish hair, her supple neck, and the way her back curved down to her waist. A band member, Luke, came looking for her, and she abruptly broke away from the embrace. Feeling embarrassed, J.K. hurried with his beer to his seat.

As the emcee introduced Luke and Luna, a gaggle of twenty-something girls slipped in through the front door, doubling the size of the audience. J.K. was amused to see two Luna look-alikes among them, but he decided they didn't have her spark.

In an area that an imaginary line marked off as the stage, Luna sat on a milk carton and Luke sat on a stool beside her, both playing woodsy acoustic guitars. Paul Little pranced like a drunk monkey in a bandana and sunglasses, his belly showing under the Spiderman t-shirt. The microphone wasn't working. Luna sang something nonsensical over the house music so the soundman could adjust the levels. While Luke and the soundman investigated the trouble, Luna's enthusiasm ebbed and she retreated into herself, slouching on the milk crate.

When the problem was fixed, Luna began to croon in a singsong, Sinead O'Connor voice, her mouth pressed so close to the microphone that she could have been swallowing it. She kicked out the milk crate from beneath her, stood up, and began to move on the little stage like she owned it.

*My lover . . .*
*Sweetest skin I've ever tasted,*
*Lips so thick, I feel wasted.*

Her voice shook sometimes, but what she lacked in steadiness, she made up for in talent. Her bond with Luke was evident in how their guitars harmonized. The folksy tune ran counter to her urgent plaintive voice. She knocked down her water bottle and the soundman mopped up the liquid with a dirty rag.

After three songs, Luke left the stage. Luna switched guitars and began a solo; it was sung with feeling, but she seemed dissatisfied, even frustrated with it. Luke watched anxiously from the back of the room. When the song was over, Luna signaled to him to return to the stage, and for the rest of the time, they performed together.

J.K. sensed that Luna was aiming for perfection, and because she wasn't quite there tonight, the artist in her had rebelled and wanted to erase the imperfect solo. Although he couldn't put it into words, he felt that Luna's quest to do something perfect was not dissimilar to his own attempt at a Big Year.

Some of the audience had migrated to the lawn, but those who were left gave Luna a whooping ovation. J.K. grinned at her; she noticed and grinned back, but then she slunk away.

After Luna, the acts plummeted. When a one-person band began to perform attired only in a diaper, J.K. got up find Luna. He heard the gallery man urging the people gathered on the lawn with beer bottles to come inside, as the police had just called and said they would be arrested.

J.K. found Luna alone backstage, her head buried in a guitar.

"You did fine out there," he said.

"You think so?"

"Oh, yeah. Absolutely! Let's get out of here."

He drove Luna in the Birdmobile to her apartment in Silver Lake. Luke had driven her to the concert. "He was my boyfriend—the one I told you about—but now he's like my brother," she told J.K. "We broke up three months ago."

They didn't talk much in the car, instead taking in the silent April night.

J.K. parked outside her building, and opened the trunk so she could retrieve her guitar. Luna plunked the guitar on the pavement, and peeped in through the passenger door.

"I wonder if I should tell," Luna said. She perched her knee against the seat and smiled.

"Tell what?" J.K. said.

"I had a dream about you last night," she said, and was nearly out of the car again. Some impulse got him to reach out, take her arm, and pull her back in.

"What happened in this dream?"

She laughed. "I'm cold. I've gotta pee. Come in for a sec, then."

He followed her into her second-floor apartment. It was a large studio, decorated with quirky stuff from thrift shops. Luna took off her hat and hung it on a well-stocked stand. From an open drawer spilled out a waterfall of sheer scarves. There was an Asian-inspired chest—red, with dragon-like birds painted on it. On top of this chest lay the "friendship ring" he'd given her.

Luna came out of the bathroom and saw him staring at the silver ring with the turquoise bead. He hadn't been able to look away fast enough.

"Want a drive in my ratty Ford?" she said.

J.K. nodded. "Sure."

Luna drove them to the reservoir—Silver Lake's version of the Central Park Reservoir.

"Three months ago, I started jogging here," Luna said. "I come almost every morning. Helps to clear my mind." She showed him where she began her daily jog, and then they continued walking along the path.

J.K. thought he might hear some interesting birds. A few minutes later, he heard the honks of Canada geese. He was trying to listen closely when, to his surprise, Luna tore off her white summer dress. Her panties and bra still on, she jumped into the water.

There was nothing else to do but to strip and follow her. The water was metallic black, but less cold than he had imagined.

Luna swam over to him.

"Are you okay?" J.K. said.

"Sometimes I feel like I don't know who I am," she said. "Just a ghost occupying a body, doing a job. But when I sing a song, however badly, . . ."

"You don't sing badly," he said. He was shivering.

"Anyhow, when I sing a song, or right now, with you, I feel alive."

They embraced in the water, and they kissed. And then her tongue flicked him playfully. "Hiss," she whispered.

J.K. laughed. He felt her thigh slither against his. What followed was the most delicious kissing embrace he'd ever experienced. Before they could do anything more, she swam away. They swam together for a few minutes. She was a strong swimmer, and he hadn't swum in a while. Then she got out of the water and put on her white dress as rapidly as she'd taken it off.

Unwillingly, he got out of the soft, pliable water, back onto the concrete path, and put his clothes back on.

She jogged back to her car, and he jogged behind her. They didn't discuss what had happened.

Luna dropped him off at his car, and she didn't invite him back to her apartment, although she was politely friendly.

"See you at Leaves?" she said.

"Leaves," J.K. affirmed.

It was too late by the time he realized that she had not told him about her dream.


On the following Tuesday afternoon, J.K. saw Luna for the first time since the weekend.

"Your usual?" she said.

He nodded.

Luna rang up his order of spearmint tea and gave him an embarrassed smile. This was his chance. If he said the right thing now, things could move forward. It would be nice to go eat Chinese food with her. She had told him she loved Chinese. She had broken up with her so-called boyfriend and was available now. Why couldn't he ask her out? Did he not trust her?

Then there was the other matter—he admired her as an artist. He wanted to reassure her, tell her she'd given a fine concert. Why had she acted so strangely at the reservoir? And yet, that experience had touched something inside him; he'd felt his core for a split-second, and then the feeling had vanished. He swallowed something back; he wanted to taste her lips again. But he couldn't find any words. It was as though Anne Marie had taken all his confidence with her when she left him. Even a nighthawk, that slumbering bird, must have more initiative than J.K. He wished he could stop feeling so bruised.

Luna had slunk through the plastic curtain into the employees' room. His opportunity was lost.

Less than an hour later, when he left the café, he found her sleeping on the cement stairs outdoors. At first he didn't recognize her, mistaking the jeans-clad legs for a guy's. But there she lay, asleep in the stark sunlight, in an all-black outfit of strapless shirt, jeans, and canvas shoes. Her face was upturned to the still-bright sun, to recharge herself. She lay on the steps, as mysterious and unknowable as a cat.

## 21

*T*he outcome of the Savant endowment was still in doubt, and the success of the Centennial depended on how many birds could be spotted, and therefore how much money could be raised, during the Big Day itself. On the morning of the event, Rick woke up at 3:30 a.m. Half an hour later, he loaded three passengers, who stood waiting in the dark outside Karen's brownstone, into his SUV. Anxious not to waste a second, he had taken the precaution of filling the tank the evening before.

"All right, gang. It's going to be a long day," Rick said sleepily, as they sped toward the freeway.

Blake felt nervous. He grabbed the map from J.K.'s hands and they began to discuss the sequence of locations. In the end, Blake deferred to J.K.'s judgment. He had the strategic advantage of having done a preliminary scout of the key locations the week before. Blake wondered out loud if they should round up all the regulars at Joss Canyon before moving on to challenging locations in the mountains, but J.K. vetoed this idea. "The regulars are going to come to us throughout the day," he said. "We don't need to chase them."

"Don't anyone bring up Joss Canyon right now," Karen added. "It gets me depressed just thinking about it."

"Mom, no politics while birding!"

Rick chuckled. "That should be our motto for the trip!"

Because of J.K.'s meticulous planning, they were able to drive up to specific locations in the San Gabriel Mountains, stop for a few moments, listen for the call of a grosbeak or some other bird, cross it off their list, and move on without even getting out of the SUV.

This pattern of stopping only to hear and cross off and then speeding to the next location continued throughout the day.

During the long drive to Piute Ponds, there was time to talk.

"If only we knew for sure about the endowment," Karen said, to the immediate groans of everyone around her. "It would be such a load off!"

"Hmmm . . ." Rick mused. "True." As he drove, he was getting Blake to look up in his Sibley Guide the distribution of sage thrashers in California at this time of the year.

"What's holding it up?" Karen said. "I guess it's her kids. We should have heard by now."

"Did you tell J.K. he's getting the Cowbird Award?" Rick said, to change the subject.

"Oh, Rick!" Karen said. "It was supposed to be a surprise."

"Oops. Sorry!" Rick said.

J.K. smiled. In the midst of his worries, it had taken a Herculean effort to concentrate on the Big Day. "I'll pretend I didn't hear," he said, as Blake giggled.

At Piute Ponds, they split into two groups. J.K. and Rick counted all the species of shorebirds in the long series of ponds, while Blake and Karen bagged the marsh birds. It was a clear April morning and the men made solid progress, ticking off the many shorebirds they spotted. As they waited for the others to join them at the last pond, J.K., who normally wouldn't bring up personal matters during such an important birding trip, felt distracted enough to confide in Rick, half-hoping for some advice.

"My job prospects aren't looking good. I may still be in California next year."

Rick, who was noting down the last of the shorebirds, looked up at him. "That's great!" he said.

"Actually, it's pretty clear I'm going to be unemployed. My only hope is that they might let me stay on at the university an extra year. But I don't know yet."

"Good luck!" Rick's attention was diverted by a call. "Is that an oriole?"

"Where?" Blake said, walking up to them.

"There's our baby!" Rick said, propping up his cowboy hat and pointing to a laurel sumac tree. "And a good clean view. Look at that!"

The afternoon sun shone at just the right angle to show off the oriole's tropical colors. Blake couldn't help gawking at the bird. J.K. gave up trying to talk to Rick. It was difficult to get Rick's attention when it didn't involve his self-interest.

"Blake, we're not birding," Rick reminded the boy.

"What are we doing then?" Blake asked dreamily. It was hard to tear away from such an otherworldly sight.

"Counting."

Blake was forced to look away when he realized that his mother had grabbed the edge of his shirt and was dragging him toward the SUV.

At Sycamore canyon, Blake saw a flash of yellow in a dense willow shrub and spotted a female Wilson's warbler at its nest.

"Look, Mom!" he said.

The petite songbird was feeding a chick almost double its size.

"That's a cowbird chick," Rick told them.

The puffed-up, grayish chick was whining to be fed almost continuously. Karen looked on, fascinated. When the mother left the nest in search of more food, the chick did not turn in the direction the mother had flown, but sat unmoving and continued to bark out commands.

"It's probably tiring out its host mother," J.K. said. "The warbler might neglect its own chicks in favor of this robust baby."

"To see this is amazing," Karen said. "My heart goes out to that poor warbler. It really does. So we kill cowbirds because of this mean trick they play? We get to decide? Aye, aye! Kern's rounded up a speaker to talk about cowbirds—boy, do we need a good lecture on this!"

Late at night, on the way back home, the foursome did the math and figured out that they had made around $10,000 for the Centennial.

"Thanks, you guys!" Karen said. "This is unbelievable." All her anxiety and work was not for nothing. Now they had to collect the money and put it to good use. "It's my birthday on the day of the cowbird talk," she added. "I want a party, okay?"

Karen thought there was an odd look in J.K.'s eyes, almost like a lost chick who can't stop wandering. She would have shared this thought with Rick after they dropped J.K. off, but she was too exhausted even to speak.

J.K. was the only member of the gang who had volunteered to go back up to the San Gabriel Mountains later to look for a family of nightjars rumored to be hanging out in the back parking lot of a restaurant.

Rick got home at one in the morning, twenty-one hours after he had left, his notepad filled with the names of the 165 species he had seen or heard that day. "I'm getting too old for this," he mumbled, getting under the covers beside Meg. Wasted as he was, he hadn't felt this exhilarated in months, and he slept like a ten-year-old boy.

Frank had taken on the A.B.S. presidency grudgingly, and Dana was not amused when Rick drove over one day and dumped boxes of A.B.S. paraphernalia, including last year's unsold "bucket-style" hats in her garage. Frank's attitude changed after the possibility of the Jean B. Savant endowment was rumored. The robust feeling that came to him while overseeing large chunks of money returned. This time, he wouldn't have to deal with the additional stresses of traveling, as he had in his old job. Seven years of retirement had robbed him of his sense of purpose, and Dana took unfair advantage by swatting him down at every turn. Frank had yielded to her attacks, regarding them as essentially harmless, whereas he would have fought back more forcefully in his office-going days. Slowly, his feeling of worth corroded, and he didn't realize to what extent until he imagined the check for $200,000 resting in his plump hands.

Frank had started a dull career as an accountant, and had worked his way up to being auditor. Now he couldn't help that his face glistened when he considered the importance the stewardship of this endowment would confer on him. When he spoke of the possibility of this happening and how he would handle it, he fancied that Dana looked at him with new respect. He made some calls and set about creating an Investment Committee for when the time came. He would head the committee, and he recruited Rick and Zanne as members.

"Karen is too crazed with the Centennial, and I don't know if I'm going to ask her," Frank said.

Dana smiled her peculiar half-smile and tucked a curl behind her ear. "That would be about as stupid a thing as anyone could do—to involve Karen in this business," she said. "The first thing we need to do when the money comes is to rent a storage unit. Half our garage is taken over with A.B.S. junk. It's ridiculous!"

Frank nodded. Then he prayed for patience, for even an astute man can't guess when a lawyer might call. There still loomed the question of whether Savant's children would make a legal challenge to her bequest, and the wheels had in no way started to move in favor of A.B.S. But he was prepared all right. He paced alone in the backyard, surveying the straggly plants. A smugness came over his face, now that he finally knew what he was put on this earth to do.

Two weeks later, the church let a grief-management group take over the boardroom, while relocating the Alpena Bird Society to an upstairs kindergarten room. At any other time, Frank would have been upset and thrown his weight around as a member of the church vestry. But nothing could detract from the sensational news he'd received that A.B.S. would indeed get the endowment money. He was too relieved to be disappointed by the stipulations that the money couldn't be used to pay off debts, nor could it be accessed for another year. In keeping with his guarded instincts towards money in general, Frank kept the news to himself and took pains to not mention it to the membership-at-large. He didn't even show any signs of pleasure to his fellow board members.

Taking their cue from the president, the board members also avoided the subject of the money, and their meetings were noticeably more solemn. There was a persistent feeling that a two-humped camel was buried under the rug, but that it mustn't be discussed. That the money could not be put to use right away and that the board pretended to not even care were sore spots for Karen, who would have loved to put some of the money toward the Centennial.

But she couldn't complain. This was the most amazing thing that had happened to them in a long while. It felt like they had been set free. She knew now that the immediate future of A.B.S. was secure and she no longer needed to keep her nose to the grindstone once the Centennial was over. For starters, they could create a Cowbird Fund to stop the killing of cowbirds. They could set up another fund to preserve native plants in Joss Canyon, and muscle the county into managing the place better.

Yet why did she feel uneasy? Maybe it was because of the secrecy with which everything was being handled. She didn't doubt Frank's honesty for a second. However, it seemed odd that the money hadn't yet come into their hands and the Investment Committee was already making a decision on where to invest it. Karen had to complain when she found out, almost by accident, the intentions of the Investment Committee. She wrote emails to Frank touting green funds, because she felt strongly that, in keeping with the A.B.S. mission, the money shouldn't be invested in companies that were polluting the environment.

Frank ignored her long emails. As a former chartered accountant, he felt sure that the money should not be trusted to some new-age firm, but should be put in the hands of a reputable investment fund.

Karen then made a formal recommendation to the Investment Committee that they invest in socially responsible mutual funds, in keeping with the environmental agenda of A.B.S. When she met with resistance from Frank and the Egret, she called up Rick and made a plea to him to see to it the money was invested in bird-friendly funds. "These other companies that conventional funds invest in, many of the big ones, they slash and burn habitat for birds."

"I don't know what to say," Rick told her. "I really don't know the first thing about green funds."

"Allow me to correct that situation," she said.

She threw herself into research and sent Rick all the information she could find on socially responsible investments, including the one in which her own tiny retirement plan was invested. She did this research in lieu of planning a treasure hunt in their garden for Easter.

"The kids are getting too old for a treasure hunt anyhow," she told Oscar that night. "It's sad, but true."

Oscar put his glasses on their bedside table. "I'll swing by Rite-aid tomorrow," he said. "I'll set something up for them. You don't have to worry."

In the April board meeting, a decision was to be made about the money. Since Karen had not gotten any negative feedback on her recommendations, she felt assured that they had listened to her. She tried to shrug off even their demotion by the church to the kindergarten room. When she was unable to squeeze into one of the kiddie chairs, she sat without complaint on a play table, although she couldn't help thinking it was high time the Joss Canyon Nature Center was rebuilt. The church was clearly getting tired of hosting A.B.S.

"These are *good*," Kenny said, munching her cowbird-shaped cookies.

"I had to research online to find the molds," Karen told him.

"You should bring these to the cowbird talk next month. That's May 18th, right?"

"It's my birthday that day. I'll let y'all bring refreshments and throw me a party instead."

Frank announced, in his understated way, that the Investment Committee had conferred over email and decided that the money should be put in the hands of the Entrust Mutual Funds Company. One additional benefit of picking this company was that it had a branch in Alpena's business district.

As Karen listened, her face reddened one minute and went cold the next. Entrust was just one of the big, conventional firms. The person she would have lashed out at—Rick—wasn't at the meeting. She sat speechless, noting that no mention was made whatsoever of her eco-friendly recommendations. She looked to Kenny, but no support was forthcoming from the A.B.S. Conservation Chair.

"If we can get a ten percent return from Entrust," Frank said, "that should cover the operating costs of A.B.S. year after year."

Frank suggested they put the matter to vote and settle the affair, but Karen interrupted. "I've spoken to a few others, including Kenny, who think it would be hypocritical to put the money into a conventional fund," she said.

The Egret eyed her with disbelief. Her tuft of snowy hair stood up on ends.

Sensing Karen's despair, Kenny tried to help. "Um . . . I was wondering . . . are we reinventing the wheel here?" he said. "Are there other organizations that have invested in some sort of green funds?"

"Not that we know of," Dana snapped.

As Frank and the Egret were of the same mind, Kenny's theoretical objections were clamped down. Even so, Kenny suggested that they split the money between a traditional mutual fund and an S.R.I., but Frank said that Entrust took on only large accounts, and it would be unwieldy and impractical to split the small amount they had. Kenny didn't see fit to resist further. "I think as we go on we can explore these other options," he said. "I have no problem with continuing where we are for now."

To add to Karen's frustration, Kenny left the meeting abruptly before the vote was taken. Maybe he disliked that she had brought his name up and put him on the spot, and that he had failed completely in shifting the board's opinion.

Karen now looked to Robert Kern for support. He had sat quietly throughout the meeting, speaking up only once in a detached tone. He met her look, but remained silent. Not exactly a fighter, he had a habit of swallowing his bitterness and letting it disappear somewhere within.

"How about special projects?" Karen said. "I was hoping we would create a Cowbird Fund and fight the killing going on at Joss Canyon."

"I think that's a good idea, actually," Robert Kern said. "The trapping isn't supported by the latest research."

"The cowbirds are doing very well for themselves, thank you very much," Dana said. "They're about as aggressive a bird . . . Next thing we'll want to create a Crow Fund."

"I don't think we should touch the capital anyhow," Frank said. "It's not a financially sound idea."

There was tense silence in the room. Karen looked at each board member in turn, but they seemed to consciously avoid looking back at her.

"What does Rick think about all this?" she asked.

"Oh, he's in agreement with us," Frank chimed in.

"Really?" she said, steaming.

Frank proposed the motion, the Egret seconded it, and the rest of the team voted aye, except Karen and Blake, who voted nay, and Robert Kern who abstained. Karen felt sick to think that not only was her proposal not accepted, but it wasn't even seriously considered. She was being treated as a meddlesome outsider, not the one member who was struggling to keep afloat an organization that had been sinking before this unexpected good fortune came along. And why did Rick not bother to come here and defend her? What could be more important than a meeting that would decide the future course of A.B.S.?

When Karen was upset, a severity came into her face that nothing short of total capitulation would erase. She looked on, bitter and stone-faced, as the motion passed, and it was settled that the bequest money would be put into the Entrust Mutual Funds Company.

Frank said he would go down to the business district the next day and sign the papers. He intended to go over to Karen and calm her down after the meeting. Clearly, she didn't understand the concept of fiscal responsibility. However, he was delayed when he and Robert Kern started chatting about a fight they had witnessed between a hummingbird and a kestrel. A grin appeared on Kern's face and his eyes lit up.

Karen was in such a bad way that as soon as the meeting was over, she intended to leave with Blake without exchanging a word with anyone.

Frank came up to her just as she was leaving. "You know that we have to put a minimum of a hundred thousand to be in this firm . . ." he started.

"I know that," she shot back, her eyes flaring up. "I'm not stupid. But I was idealistic enough to hope that we'd use some of this money to stop the killing of birds, instead of giving it away to companies that couldn't care less about the environment!"

She couldn't bear to look at him right now and fled the room. She had nearly reached the staircase when she felt a hand on her shoulder. It was Robert Kern.

"Don't worry," he said. "We'll get it reversed."

# 22

*J. K.* drove up a winding road that seemed to be taking him to the end of the world. Mist blanketed the mountains in San Louis Obispo County, a two-hour drive north of Los Angeles. Clouds foretold that it would rain again. It was so remote here that it was surprising there was a road at all. They had probably used unemployed soldiers to build it after World War II. It must take real precision to dynamite perfectly level slices into a mountain. All was moist and green, like the gently rolling hills of Northern California, but he wasn't even north of the Central Valley. There were fences along some hills, and he figured that this land was part of a cattle ranch.

Usually J.K. came to the Carrizo Plain National monument in December to look for migrating raptors. But this December being what it was, he hadn't made the trip. He missed the place—it was one of the largest remaining open lands in California. After he received the bad news from Dave, there had been nothing else to do but drive away, somewhere far. His stomach ached when he thought of the look on Dave's face as he gave J.K. the news. The old man, Kaminski, had told him that in his peak, Dave was a sight to behold, performing marvels at the blackboard and cracking wicked jokes all at the same time. All these years, J.K. had harbored a secret admiration for his supervisor, for his ability to juggle multiple projects at once. And now J.K. lamented that he had measured so short of his mentor.

As was his habit, J.K. had brought no tent and planned to sleep in the open wilderness. He normally entered the Carrizo monument from the south, but having heard that the longer route to the north entrance was worthwhile, he was testing it out. It was mid-April, and patches of goldfields had sprung up throughout the hills and rolling meadows. In an instant, he came upon a massive hill to his right that was covered with gold. Something melted inside him, and he wanted to utter a cry, but he couldn't find his voice. Three hills, all gilded, curved around a glorious meadow, where at one end stood a simple old shack.

It consoled J.K. that such beauty existed. He wondered if witnessing it could pull his spirits out of the dark spiral that was already consuming him.

He had never given wildflowers much thought, but now he wished he could live out the rest of his life in this broken shack nestled in the gilded mountains. Tears blurred his eyes. This was the most emotion he had felt in a long time, maybe since that day on the fall migration trip to the sod farm when he felt young, the sky was full of swallows, and it seemed the whole world lay open to him. He was twenty-six and had lived through the detached love of his parents, the premature death of his sister, and the unexpected heartbreak of losing his true love. He now felt ready to retire to a shack made of corrugated tin.

Maybe nature would take him in when everyone else had turned him away.

"The committee denied your request," Dave told him last week. "There's not enough funds to keep you here an extra year. I'm sorry."

J.K. was stunned that even his fallback plan, the option he would have taken only grudgingly, was denied him. There was nothing to do now but to stop hoping or planning. All the structure in his life was going slack. Girlfriend gone. Academic career gone. He'd get his last paycheck in three weeks, in early May—and then what? How fragile the strings that had tied him to the world! Now that they had snapped, he wondered if he'd simply been a puppet animated by those strings. He felt free-floating, weightless, like a hot-air balloon losing steam.

He had heard that the manager of the Carrizo Plain National Monument committed suicide last summer. The news shocked him then. How was it possible to live in the midst of such beauty and still feel forlorn enough to kill oneself? But he understood now. Some days he was able to go about his routines as though nothing out of the ordinary had happened. But then he would suddenly be confronted with the chilling thought that he had wasted the last nine years of his life. His college years seemed futile in retrospect, and his love had abandoned him. He wondered if there were anything about this fickle life that made it worth living. All the promise of love, and of learning and endeavor, had soured before his eyes.

Suicide might shatter his parents, who had already lost one child and now were left with only a feckless son.

Some of his fellow graduate students who weren't considered quite as bright as him five years ago were going on to postdoctoral positions at Ivy League universities. They had played the system in a way that wasn't natural to him. They went religiously to conferences and gave talks, even if they were working on mundane problems on which he would have been ashamed to lecture. They promoted themselves, publishing each talk as a paper, and wrangling invitations up and down the conference circuit, where they flogged the same presentation over and over. It was true, he had gotten sidetracked by birding. That damage was self-inflicted, but he'd had no choice—a force had propelled him, one that he couldn't put into words. But he had never stinted from working equally hard in physics. He simply hadn't bothered—or had too much dignity—to promote himself. He did the Big Year for personal satisfaction, not for recognition. But now that he had lost his job prospects and his girlfriend, it irked him that he had lost the Big Year challenge, too.

Completing his Ph.D. now seemed a bitter prospect. J.K. met with Dave and asked what he needed to do to get the degree. He might as well get the damn piece of paper and cut his losses. The answer was obvious, Dave told him. He needed to get out at least one more paper to qualify for a thesis defense. He had since made a disciplined effort to scan all the new physics papers, but it had not yet generated a decent idea on which he could bear to work. That was part of his problem—he couldn't do anything half-heartedly. If he were going to write a final paper, it had to be something worthwhile. If he were going to give up the field he had shown such talent for in his undergraduate days, he would go out with dignity, publishing a paper that would reflect what he could have accomplished had he been given the chance.

J.K. got out of his car and walked into a meadow. The goldfields were gleaming wet and among them were purple owl's clover and blue lupines. The nodding grass swayed from side to side in the cool morning wind, and his lumberjack shirt flapped about him. A meadowlark flew by, and he wished he could call the bird to him and stroke it against his chest, but then he was afraid he would crush the bird, so powerful was his feeling. Why must it come now? Why must there be this blinding need when there was no one to love? The scene aroused a ravenous longing in him, and he climbed back into the car and continued to drive up the mountain, half hoping that he would shoot through the clouds and into the vast open sky.

In the Carrizo Plain there were wildflowers, too, although it was not a good year and only a couple of fields were fully carpeted with goldfields or coreopsis. J.K. drove on the unpaved sections of Soda Lake Road, stopping occasionally to look at a tri-colored blackbird perched high on the grass, or a prairie falcon shooting by overhead. The morning swallowed his pain and turned into afternoon. An antelope squirrel poked its head out of a roadside burrow and gazed at him before disappearing into the mind-boggling network of tunnels it had constructed with its friends.

Kingbirds, meadowlarks, horned larks, and lark sparrows were everywhere, hopping from one fence post to the next. The bumpy dirt roads and lack of potable water suited J.K. fine as long as they kept the crowds away. A Lawrence's goldfinch sat boldly on the fence, and J.K. greeted the handsome fellow. It was a quiet, lazy day, and the sun peeked out from the clouds just long enough to keep him from feeling cold. Later it became so windy that he had to pull on his jacket whenever he got out of the car. Two cowbirds glanced down at him from the fluttering branch of a rare willow tree.

He had meant to wander into a milk vetch thicket when a cream-colored object on the side of the road caught his eye. It was partially hidden by the wild mustard, which he parted with his foot. A rattlesnake lay belly-up and was being devoured by ants. There was the triangular head with a fang half out, like a dead man's lolling tongue, and the rattle was visible at the end of the tail. The snake was not alive, but was still whole, though with the ants and other scavengers about, it wouldn't be so for long. On the custard-colored underside of its coiled body were bloodied marks—perhaps a roadrunner had pierced it with its talons and then, for some reason, abandoned it to undignified death and decay.

J.K. felt sympathy for the snake. He had also been wounded. Life had pierced something inside him—he didn't know what, for he was unsure if there were such a thing as a soul. And the wound had left him half-dead, which might explain why he wasn't even able to get a job at an environmental non-profit. Maybe people could see that he was only half alive.

He didn't know how to rouse himself from this despondency. He could no longer fight off the feeling of helplessness, like a man sinking in a marsh who flails about at first, but then realizes that some great powerful force beyond his control has him in its grip. J.K. had succumbed to that acceptance of defeat. There was nothing he could do for the snake; nature must take its course. He walked back to his car, having lost his taste for a hike, and drove dispiritedly towards his campground while the afternoon was still young.

## 23

*B*lake hovered in the doorway of the church kitchen, searching the crowd that milled about in the meeting room, nibbling cowbird-shaped cookies as they waited for the evening's program to begin. A well-known professor from Santa Cruz was to give the talk on cowbirds.

J.K. got out of his car, and a few roses swayed as he walked up the path to the church. Frustrated that he was making no progress on his new physics paper, he'd decided that his evening would be better spent learning about an issue that had long troubled him—why it was considered necessary to euthanize multitudes of cowbirds across the nation's parks. The practice of killing cowbirds was intended to protect other species, but he didn't see that it was helping. When he walked into the hall full of people, something recoiled inside him and he wanted to slink into a corner. To socialize in his depressed state was distasteful to him. He peeked into the kitchen and saw Karen standing there alone. "Do you need help setting things out?" he asked, going in.

"Everything's out already." Karen continued to stare into space with her arms folded across her chest. Her lips were compressed into a thin line, and her face was as colorless as if the life had been drained out of it.

"Oh, I forgot to bring my drawings," J.K. said, wondering if she were upset at him because he hadn't yet produced the cowbird drawings for her signs.

Karen didn't seem to know what he was talking about, though she had been pestering him about the drawings for two months.

"I guess I can bring them over to your house," he added.

"Yeah, whatever." She stared straight ahead, not even looking at him.

"It's her birthday," Blake whispered to J.K., explaining his mother's strange behavior.

"Happy Birthday!" J.K. said to her, remembering that Karen had told them during the Big Day that on the date of the cowbird talk, she wanted a party.

"I am really angry," Karen said, looking up at him with pinkish eyes.

He felt sorry that they hadn't acknowledged her birthday, when she went out of her way each month to make their events special with her bird-shaped baked treats.

"They've gone ahead and put the money into the hands of a conventional mutual fund," she said, "without even considering an S.R.I. And they snubbed my plan to earmark a small amount for the protection of cowbirds in Joss Canyon.

"I can't tell you how angry I am," she went on. "It spoiled my Easter. It's nearly spoiled my birthday. I prayed during Easter. I prayed and prayed." She closed her eyes.

"'Forgive them, Lord, for they know not what they do.'" Her hands were clasped and her eyes closed as if in prayer, but when she opened them, they were still pink and angry.

J.K. looked on, feeling bewildered.

"We have no control over what we're supporting with A.B.S. funds," she said. "We're giving money to *Walmart*." She shook her head in disbelief that her beloved A.B.S. would have anything to do with Walmart. "Here, take this!" she said, as if thrusting the money at someone. "Do with it as you like!" Her face turned away from the imagined transaction. "They're a cause of habitat destruction," she moaned.

"They'll probably invest in McDonald's," J.K. said, "and they're making people fat." Ed McCoy insisted on feeding his amorphous body at McDonald's whenever he got the chance, and even slipped fries into the mouths of his twins when his wife wasn't looking.

"Oh, yeah," Karen said. "Not only that . . . the meat comes from South America. And . . ." She went on to explain why McDonald's policies were reprehensible. She couldn't believe that she had been trampled over and her voice ignored. "I'm livid," she confessed, returning to the subject of the investment. "Then I found out later from Robert Kern that they could have set aside a small amount to temporarily stop the killing of cowbirds if they had wanted to. But now it's too late. Frank came up to me this evening and said that what 'we' did makes good financial sense. So I told him I'm too angry about this right now and I don't think you should be talking to me about it."

"So what did he say?"

She shook her head. "'Oh, okay,' he said," imitating Frank's wide-eyed expression. "And then he walked out."

"And you know what I wanted to say?" She mouthed the profanity and then whispered it out to J.K. She saw too late that Blake was looking straight at her.

J.K. glanced at the boy, and then at her, feeling uncomfortable.

There was a moment of silence. "And I've never used that expression in front of my son before."

"Oh, yes you have," Blake said without hesitation. "Plenty of times."

J.K. laughed and Blake joined in. "Usually when you're drunk," Blake added.

Karen smiled. Unable to counter Blake's claim, she returned to the question of what values A.B.S. stood for. "At the board meeting, Kenny brought it up and they all shut him down. It didn't take long to see where their hearts lie. I wanted to say, 'Has anyone seen *The Treasure of the Sierra Madre*? Has anyone learned anything from that film?' " Her arms shot into the air.

"It is a good film," J.K. admitted.

"They're prostitutes," Karen said. "When people do things they wouldn't otherwise do, just for money. They didn't think twice about it. They're *worse* than prostitutes. They're sluts."

"Mom, you're forgetting we're in a church," Blake said.

J.K. looked on, startled by this outburst. He didn't expect this kind of talk from Karen, and it made him realize how upset she was.

"I'm sorry. Actually, we're not in the church; we're in a kitchen," she told Blake. "After all the information I put together and sent them! I sent them all the links," she said, about her research on S.R.I.'s. 'This is not our money,' Rick says. 'That's not the way to think about it,' " she added, imitating Rick.

"It's someone else's legacy," J.K. said, "and it's been put into our hands."

"And you know all the other organizations she gave to—they all help animals." Leaning over, Karen put a hand on his shoulder. "And will we lift a finger to help birds? Oh, no! We'd rather put our money into Walmart, who takes away their habitats."

One of the society's members walked into the kitchen. Abe was a dignified-looking man, an insurance agent, who came to all the talks, but never to the board meetings. "Is there any milk in here?" he said, holding a cup of coffee.

"I have enough on my hands, thank you very much," Karen said.

Abe looked at her, confused. Karen was irritated with this man; he'd been trying to scare board members into getting an expensive insurance policy—*before* anyone fell deliberately during one of their talks and sued them for a chunk of endowment money.

"There's no milk," Blake said. "Just the packets out there."

"If you really want milk, you can bring some to the next meeting," Karen added, "or ask your lovely wife. Please, feel free."

"Thank you," Abe muttered, trying to reclaim his dignity. "I'll do that."

The lecture was about to start, and the trio edged to the kitchen doorway, from where they could keep an eye on the proceedings.

"I think we need a change of board," Karen whispered to J.K. "*That's* what we need." A smug expression came over her face, as though she knew what she was talking about. "And they're having elections on the night of the Centennial."

The A.B.S. elections, conducted every June, were a tame affair, where the names of the officers during the past year were read out, someone asserted that they were doing a fine job, and did anyone have any objections to them continuing in their posts? There were never objections, so the elections concluded and everyone adjourned for coffee.

"Are you going to run for president?" J.K. said, fearing for the first time that his sympathy might involve him in an embarrassing situation.

"You know, they say when your heart's racing and it throbs in your throat, you have the Holy Spirit. The Lord wants you to do something and you should speak up. So I'll wait to see if that happens." She finished in a lighter tone. Although it seemed that she wasn't going to do something about this today, the look in her eyes said, *Stay tuned, and don't be surprised if things are different in a year's time.*

"Robert Kern came up to me after the board meeting and he said . . ." She put a hand on J.K.'s shoulder to demonstrate how he said it. " 'Don't worry. We'll get it shifted.' "

"That's good," J.K. said, feeling heartened that he wouldn't be singled-out as a sole conspirator in Karen's coup. "I'm glad he said that."

Karen left to refill the hot water for tea. Just before the lecture began, J.K. went up to her. "Have you talked to Rick about this?" he whispered.

"He's part of the Investment Committee," she said. "He was part of this decision." J.K. nodded. "But you and I are among the two youngest people in the group," Karen said.

J.K. smiled, wondering if Karen thought he was older than he was.

Frank was on the podium making the first announcement, and the crowd had settled into their seats.

"I mean, Rick's not *much* older," Karen said, as if she were catching J.K.'s thought, "but in many ways he's *old*." She gave J.K. a meaningful look. "He works in the court system!" she said, hoping to prove her point.

"Our originally chosen speaker had to cancel," Frank was announcing, "and so Robert Kern, who I just found out today is his collaborator, will speak to us about cowbirds."

"I'll be darned," Karen whispered. "Robert Kern and cowbirds?"

"That's strange," J.K. said, "and he never once said a word!"

Robert Kern, dressed in khakis and a red-checkered shirt, had come reluctantly to take the place of his colleague, David Lin, from Santa Cruz. He had arranged for the talk to relieve his uneasiness about the situation and to give Karen some ammunition to help cowbirds, while keeping himself out of the picture. He told Lin not to disclose to A.B.S. that they were collaborators. But Lin had cancelled on him at the last minute, and now Kern had no choice but to give the talk. After Frank's tepid introduction, he came up to the lectern and began describing the fruits of their many years of research.

He dropped a bomb, as far as J.K. was concerned.

"Cowbird control is practiced by many land managers, disregarding research that it might not be necessary," Kern said. "Traps are created with decoy cowbirds in them. Since cowbirds are very social birds, they come on over to say hello and get themselves trapped."

J.K. remembered Skua saying that in Texas there's a "wild west" policy regarding cowbirds. Now Kern elaborated on the problem.

"On top of this," he told the audience, "there's essentially no oversight for these programs, and no data is collected, so people may be trapping or shooting all sorts of other birds, not knowing how to distinguish cowbirds from similar-looking birds, and no one is the wiser. No one is accountable."

Abe raised his hand. "Does Grimsby know about this?" he said. "Because I'd think if he knew, he'd take down the traps in Joss Canyon."

"Oh, yeah. Grimsby knows." Kern smiled drily. "The scientific results are out there for people to look at. But what land managers choose to guide policy is another matter."

Kenny began to speak in a low voice; Kern inched closer to catch the question. "Ah, . . . I'm wondering, just how much money is involved here? I mean . . . what's the cost?

"In California alone, a million dollars is used up every year for cowbird control," Kern said. "I'm by no means an activist. I've been involved in cowbird control as a land management policy in the past, and I've been researching cowbirds for a number of years. But this is taxpayers' money being wasted, and it could be used for better purposes."

J.K. and Karen glanced at each other, both wanting to ask follow-up questions.

"The Endangered Species act has a 'mitigation' policy," Kern continued, "whereby any developer, who, for example, goes out and constructs a shopping mall on riparian habitat—of which we have destroyed approximately 95% in California—they have to then go out and 'mitigate' that damage by planting, for example, habitat somewhere else. Unfortunately, however, cowbird control is allowed as one of the mitigation methods. So again, this allows developers to put a bit of money into something that's not going to be helpful, and ignore entirely the real problem of habitat loss."

Feeling thoroughly confused, J.K. raised his hand. Just then Dana butted in with a maddeningly irrelevant question about cowbird song patterns. Kern looked at her with gleaming eyes and launched into a long-winded answer, and then he wrapped up the talk.

After the talk, J.K. went up to Kern to find out what sort of public awareness existed about this mass euthanizing of cowbirds.

"Animal rights groups don't know about cowbird control programs," Kern admitted. "It's not on their radar. They don't know what's going on or that it's practiced when it may not be necessary or effective." He smiled, his face still pink from the talk. "If they found out, they could raise a big hue and cry. There would be a lot of trouble. That would probably also complicate other cases of animal control that may be necessary."

"So you've tried to show your research to land managers?" J.K. said, puzzled that Kern had never bothered to bring up the matter with A.B.S. until now.

"Oh, yeah," Kern said. "But even when they're confronted with the research, they're reluctant to take it off their management plan, because they don't want to lose the budget associated with it. So the outdated plan continues, the managers continue to 'manage,' and the science comes second."

In his talk, Kern had said that cowbird control may be effective to protect four to six severely endangered species, such as the Bell's vireo. But now he admitted privately to J.K. that, even in these cases, the main threat is habitat loss.

"That's something I'd guessed all along," J.K. said. It was unconscionable to him that the county men were mowing down the dense undergrowth in Joss Canyon that the Bell's vireo needed, and at the same time killing countless cowbirds in the name of the vireo. He was shocked to find out that this went on year after year to justify a line item in Grimsby's budget so he'd continue to have a secure job.

Karen's daughter, Crystal, came up to them with a plate of leftover brownies, and Kern used the opportunity to stuff a big one in his mouth and bid J.K. goodbye. "My mother is visiting from out of town," he mumbled, savoring the brownie, and then he left.

That night J.K. wrote up a summary of the talk and emailed it to Rick, suggesting that they plant an article in the *L.A. Times* about this outrage.

"This is interesting," Rick wrote back.

And that was the last J.K. ever heard from him about the issue.

Irritated by Rick's lack of concern, J.K. did some research on his own. He looked up Kern's website and found to his surprise that Kern was one of the top genetics researchers in the country. After additional internet sleuthing, he learned that Kern had been researching cowbird speciation and vocalizations for ten years. He couldn't understand why Kern hadn't disclosed to anyone in A.B.S. that he was doing research on cowbirds. Karen often said during A.B.S. trips that she found cowbird traps appalling, and surely Kern must have heard her climb onto her soapbox more than once. On the internet, there was no way to get any insight into Kern's motives. But some major eyestrain later, J.K. discovered rumors that Kern was being considered for a Nobel Prize for his work on the turkey genome.

*24*

*D*uring Meg's illness, Rick promised her that he would take a break from birding. But on weekend evenings, after she was asleep, he drove up into the mountains. There was something thrilling about being out there alone at night. He had encountered a pygmy owl a couple of years ago when he'd stopped his pickup abruptly at a forested roadside in Ojai, on instinct that this would be a good place to look for birds. He scanned the brush and, seeing nothing, was about to return to the car, when he felt someone was looking at him. Turning his head, he came face-to-face with the pygmy. The stunning owl stood less than seven inches tall, with the body of a Russian nesting doll—a Matryoshka—and a tail sticking out sideways. It was on a low tree branch, no more than twenty feet away. To gaze into its yellow glassy eyes, fixed piercingly on Rick's own eyes, was startling. The owl rotated its head 180 degrees, and Rick saw its second pair of eyes—the false eyes—that keep predators at bay while it searches for insects. He stood mesmerized. The owl rotated its real face back at him again, just to let him know he hadn't forgotten Rick was there.

Rick's mother had sent him a package recently with a note saying, "I thought you might like to have these." It was a salt-and-pepper shaker set in the shape of owls. As a kid, he had loved these, along with a jigsaw puzzle of an owl, which he discovered she'd also included in the package. The puzzle was missing several pieces, and he tried to locate another on the Internet, but was unsuccessful. Instead, he ended up buying a few other owl puzzles online and found that working on them made hanging out at home with Meg less irritating.

Ed McCoy had gone to Minnesota on a birding trip, and on his return, he regaled Rick with stories that whet Rick's appetite even more. In Minnesota, Ed had seen a great gray owl descend talons-first on a snowy field and snap up a vole. These large owls need the equivalent of five to seven voles a day in order to survive, and as the habitat for these smaller mammals was shrinking, many great grays had been found dead in recent winters. They were dying of starvation.

Rick had heard that in some cultures an owl is a symbol of death, and for others, a symbol of good luck; all he knew was that he'd had extraordinary experiences encountering these birds. The acknowledged king of local birding, he now needed a little something different to get juiced up. His Big Year victory had been sweet, and he couldn't have enjoyed the newspaper article more, but without the Ecuador trip, it lacked a punch. Maybe, to make up for that lost adventure, he found himself becoming obsessed with owling. J.K. had been bugging him about some new research on cowbird control, but that was no more than noise to him. Looking for owls, especially at night, was where the excitement was. Owling, as far as Rick was concerned, was the new frontier of birding.

Zanne's daughter's lavish wedding took place in May on the flowery grounds of a historic Alpena house. Despite their differences, Karen waited patiently for an invitation. She and Zanne had worked so closely on last year's annual potluck—even meeting at each other's homes—that Karen felt she might get some acknowledgement of their friendship and maybe an apology, or at least some sign that she hadn't been crossed off Zanne's list. But the invitation never came, and Karen's feeling that A.B.S. members were a family of sorts, who shared their joys and setbacks with each other, received another blow.

"She didn't even find us a caterer," Karen complained to her son. "She promised to take me on a taste test. We were going to try out that new Italian place." Lately it seemed that A.B.S. had ceased to exist for Zanne.

"Mom, can we just pick Danny's Steak House?" Blake asked.

"No. We've got some vegetarians coming. I doubt Danny's can cater to them."

Though she was stressed about Zanne's flightiness, Karen controlled her emotions and didn't call to confront her, not wanting to cast a shadow over what was probably one of the happiest occasions in Zanne's life. Meanwhile, any task she tried to delegate to Frank and Dana was deflected back at her with the comment, "Sorry, we'll be in Alaska then."

The board members, Karen decided, were no less parasitic than the cowbird, who places its egg in the nest of another bird for it to raise. The board depended on her to organize the Centennial, and felt no guilt about not participating in its evolution. Now they would no longer bother to fundraise for A.B.S. because they had an endowment, nor would they put the money to any use, pleading fiscal responsibility. Although she had long been faced with the grim reality that she would have to do everything herself, Karen became so sick of excuses about vacations and weddings that she decided to postpone the Centennial work until after she got back from her own vacation.

In the beginning of May, the Mercers left for Arizona. They needed a change of air to lift Oscar's spirits. Though he could now climb the stairs to his bedroom, he hadn't psychologically recovered from the surgery and complained that he was beginning to feel like an old man. Karen picked Arizona because for a long time, Blake had wanted to look for trogons, but she talked up the state's historic charm to get her husband and daughter to go there. They got a nice surprise before they left. The article that had appeared in the local Alpena paper about Blake's third place position in the Young Birder's Photo Competition, along with excerpts from the interview, was showcased on the *Alpena Star News* website, and Blake was getting email congratulations from many of their acquaintances. During the vacation, every chance they got, the family referred to Blake by his new title, Master Birder. The boy pretended to be annoyed, but his heart swelled with pride.

A few days after the Mercers returned from Arizona, J.K. was walking back from Leaves Café late one afternoon, thinking that there was awkwardness now between him and Luna. They no longer chatted as easily as acquaintances do, but their leap to becoming closer hadn't exactly been smooth. Some additional barrier would have to be broken before they could even talk things over. They had gotten intimate too fast, and then they each retreated into their respective shells. Going to Leaves was no longer relaxing as it used to be. Today, J.K. had overheard a conversation between Luna and Paul Little that confounded him. He hoped Luna was not using him in some random thought experiment.

"I'm interested in missed opportunities," Luna said, "in what doesn't happen, as much as what happens." She was sealing a bag of used coffee grounds, for composting.

"My whole life's been missed opportunities," Paul Little said.

"The coolest moments can be silent," Luna said. "Blank periods have a way of shaping us, like wind shaping rock."

J.K. stood there awkwardly, unable to participate. He wished he could say something intelligent. Maybe he wasn't the most introspective guy. Luna seemed articulate enough about her thoughts. It was about time they talked and made some sense of their misadventure camping on top of Clark Mountain and this new strange incident in the reservoir—or at least stop pretending those things hadn't happened. That he even wanted to deal with these things told him that this was turning out to be a formative year in his life. His expectations hadn't been met, certainly, and his hopes were crushed. Yet, he was beginning to reevaluate his priorities in a way he'd never done before.

Ahead of him, J.K. spotted the two Mercer children walking on the street.

"Hey there!" he called after them. "Where are you off to?"

Blake turned around at the sound of the familiar voice and grinned wide. "We're going to our music lesson," he said, pointing to an apartment building. "Our teacher lives right here."

J.K. inquired about their vacation, and Blake said they were gone one week and it was all birding. Crystal stood quietly next to Blake.

"You didn't do anything else?" J.K. asked the girl.

"The non-birding event we were gonna do," Blake interjected, "a reenactment of a shootout at the O.K. Corral, was packed at one place and closed at the other."

"So what did you do?" J.K. asked Crystal.

"Oh, mostly watched TV," she said, shrugging. After a searching pause, she remembered something and her eyes lit up. "Mom and I went out to buy jewelry one day," she added.

He asked Crystal if she spent any time reading during the vacation, and she began to answer, "Ah, . . ." but Blake cut her off again. "We looked long and hard for trogons. But we didn't see any. I was pretty bummed out." Then he began to reminisce about the Big Day. Crystal's chin drooped to the base of her neck, and a small frown appeared on her soft brown face.

When Blake continually cut off his sister, it wasn't in a mean-spirited way, but with a natural confidence that what he had to say was more important than his sister's mumblings. Blake began to expound on trivia about birds they had seen during the Arizona trip.

"You don't like birding?" J.K. said, turning to Crystal.

She frowned again and shook her head.

"She gets bored," Blake explained. "I want to go to the Grand Canyon next."

"It's nice," J.K. told him. "I've been there."

"Did you see any good birds there?"

J.K. began to talk about the hawk-watch he came upon while in the canyon. Two Sierra Club volunteers were counting the number and species of hawks flying by.

"What other species did you see?" Blake interrupted.

J.K. mumbled out the names of a few species and ended by saying, "Oh, and I also saw bats."

"Cool!" Blake said.

There was only one exciting thing that Crystal had to tell J.K., and she volunteered this information with shy eagerness. "My violin group is putting together a tape tonight to send to Disneyland, so we can be in a contest to play there."

"That's great," J.K. said. He felt himself becoming irritated that Karen was directing her kids' potential into lightweight hobbies that wouldn't equip them for the job market. The boy's hobby had more career potential than the girl's, but even that wasn't being mined in a substantial way. The useless title of Master Birder in a local newspaper and a few days of fleeting glory weren't going to make something out of him. Ever since the newspaper article, Blake's interest in birds had become focused exclusively on counting, and every conversation devolved into the question, "Which species?" The boy's personality seemed narrower and less interesting than before.

J.K. asked Blake if he ever thought about which college he wanted to go to, and the boy said he would probably go to the community college, where his parents taught, because he would get free tuition there.

J.K. thought to himself how sad that was, because the community college would hardly be a strong launching pad for a scientific career. If the boy had a passion for birds, J.K. didn't see why he shouldn't become an ornithologist. However, because Blake was being home-schooled, it was unlikely he would be confronted with ambitious peers who could cause him to reexamine his plan.

"We should get going," Blake said. "Our teacher will worry."

J.K. nodded. He thought it ironic that he was worrying about Blake's future when his own life had turned out so badly. He still hadn't come up with an idea for a third paper and was thus unable to set up a thesis defense with his department. In a moment of frustration, he told Dave that he was quitting physics.

"Okay. Have a great life," was all Dave said.

J.K. had waited to speak with Dave, figuring that they would have a long talk, that Dave would try to convince him to stick to physics, help him figure out how to make things work. In the weak lamplight of his studio, J.K. stared at a spider moving about on the walls. Nine years of round-the-clock work in physics—was that really all for nothing? Dave didn't care that he wouldn't get his Ph.D., despite all the slave labor J.K. had put in on Dave's projects. He didn't offer J.K. any guidance, nor did he show any interest in staying in touch with him. Dave simply accepted his decision and turned away. Would Dave even care if J.K. fell off the face of the earth?

That night, J.K. lay on his futon with a fever. He didn't bother using a thermometer; it felt like he was burning up from the inside out. J.K. woke up around noon and crawled to the fridge, which he could access from the futon, for a boiled egg and a Coke. He felt blindsided, the way he had when Anne Marie broke up with him. Anne Marie and Dave were two people whose opinions J.K. had cared about; he would have done most anything to look good in their eyes. But those two had so easily walked away from him. They had both treated the parting as though it were an ordinary, everyday occurrence.

J.K.'s peers at the department were caught up in graduation fever and didn't even know how poorly things were going for him. He felt like he wasn't even a human being, but rather a leaf drifting to the ground that no one thought to give a second glance.

His father's reaction—"Well, now you ought to get out there and get yourself a real job"—gave him no consolation. The people at A.B.S. didn't even care enough to ask if he had found a job. Rick, to whom he had confided his anxieties, gave him no more than a moment's thought.

J.K. wondered if this was truly the end of his career as a scientist. Was there anyone left who might be willing to help him? Robert Kern had been a biology professor a long time. He studied the genetics of birds, and probably also worked with ornithologists. J.K. didn't know much about the formal structure of those fields. Could his expertise in bird watching and solid math skills get him a position at a biology lab? He emailed Kern, asking to meet with him.

J.K. felt better. Why hadn't he done this earlier? Kern might be able to point him in the right direction.

Kern agreed to meet him for tea at the Faculty Club. He worked downtown at the University of Southern California, but came up to J.K.'s campus once a week to meet with collaborators. They sat in the same courtyard where J.K. had eaten lunch with Dave Wagner and Dr. Kaminski a few months ago. In a striped red tie and gray blazer, Kern was as neatly dressed as ever. They ordered oolong tea and a plate of butter cookies.

"So tell me about your Big Year," Kern said with enthusiasm.

The Big Year was a sore subject for J.K., but he tried to satisfy Kern's curiosity. He described in detail the last big December moments—the broad-tailed hummingbird and the prairie warbler.

"I wasn't able to finish my thesis," J.K. told him later. "And they didn't have funds for an extra year, so I kinda got kicked out of the physics department."

Kern ate a butter cookie while he swallowed the news. "In academics, there are always setbacks," he said.

"I'd like to make the switch somehow from physics to biology."

Kern smiled, not necessarily taking this seriously. "Tell me what you do in physics."

"You've heard of the Standard Model?"

Kern nodded.

"I basically study why particles have mass."

Kern spent the next half hour questioning J.K. about physics. Then Kern looked at his watch and asked for the check. "I have to attend a genetics talk

I came up here for," he said.

They paid up and walked out of the Faculty Club. J.K. wanted to bring the subject back to whether it might be possible for him to switch to biology. But he sensed Kern's lack of interest in his problem and didn't say anything more. Why should Kern's indifference surprise him when Dave Wagner had given him such a brusque goodbye? Dave hadn't even left the door open to having another talk. Having a talk with Kern hadn't been very helpful either.

Tired of people, J.K. considered living in the mountains for a while. The schoolteacher, Wynn, had told him more than once about how he roughed it out in Alaska during the summers. Maybe J.K. could do something like that, right here in the San Gabriel Mountains.

## 25

*A*t the May board meeting, Karen exploded. She hadn't planned on it, but everything that had been festering inside of her was growing so poisonous that she had no choice but to let it all out. The Egret's car was being towed for being illegally parked, and she had called Frank to let him know that she couldn't make the meeting. It helped that the Egret wasn't there, so Karen had one less adversary with whom she had to contend.

"I can't believe my bird society is doing this," Karen said, looking around at the board members sitting in the kindergarten room. "I can't believe that when the time came to put our money where our mouth is, we weren't willing to do it."

Dana stopped short of rolling her eyes, and the suggestion of a sneer that was always present on her face erupted into the real thing.

Frank, who was made nervous by outbursts, explained to Karen that no one he had spoken to had heard of "green or blue funds."

"I'm a teacher, and my retirement nest egg, what little is there, is tied into S.R.I.'s," she shot back. "And so are the retirement savings of many teachers. I sent Rick all this information." Rick was absent again from the board meeting. It seemed that he only cared to go on birding trips now.

"We just can't take risks with this kind of money," Frank countered.

"What about Goldman Sachs? They have conventional funds, but the chairman is a birder, and he's not going to invest in companies that are bad for birds!"

The board members felt either too awkward or surprised to make any rebuttal, but they were disinclined to agree with Karen anyway. Robert Kern looked on, flustered. He wanted to speak out in support of Karen, but after years of silent neutrality on conservation issues, he was unable to break his inertia and defend her.

"Unless the Board plans to revisit this decision," Karen said, "I plan to leave A.B.S. And I'll be taking Blake with me." She delivered her ultimatum in a steely voice.

It was clear now that a battle had begun, and that it would not be resolved without bloodletting. Those who were used to treating the board meetings as

relaxing evenings with friends considered Karen's insistence rude and shock-
ing, and could never understand why she couldn't simply "let things be."

Being asked to give a talk on "My Big Year" was the best thing that happened to Rick in awhile, because it allowed him to relive his wonderful quest,
which belonged to a time before his life took another dark turn. At the end of
May, Leeks Park, a nature center in Los Angeles, was hosting the annual joint
Alpena-L.A. Bird Society lecture. Rick spent two days scanning his Big Year
photos into the computer and put together a Powerpoint presentation that was
list-heavy and touristy in tone.

J.K. arrived at the center not to attend the talk, but to have a word with
Karen. He found her tending the hospitality table in the outdoor walkway between the kitchen and the lecture hall.

"There you are," he said, walking up to her. "I was looking for you."

"I was in the kitchen," she said, and then she mouthed sarcastically,
"Where I always am." She was in a black mood. People were making their way
into the lecture hall. "But when there was still a beeline for the refreshment
table," she said, "I noticed that Zanne has somehow found time to come. She's
avoiding me." At one point, when she happened to look over to where the Egret
stood, their eyes met, and then the Egret coolly averted her gaze.

"So now Dana has company!" Karen concluded. "Do they hate that I spoke
for what I believe in? Or do they simply despise what I believe in?"

"I actually came here to give you my drawings," J.K. said.

Karen looked over the sketches. The best were those of a cowbird and a
Bell's vireo, but her response was tepid. "They're not in color," she said.

"I didn't realize you wanted color," J.K. said, disappointed. "So they can't
be used?"

"Maybe I can get my husband to colorize them on the computer."

"How are the rest of the signs going?"

"I don't know. Maybe I'm kidding myself that they'll be ready in time for
the Centennial." Unable to restrain herself, she added, "I mean, have you ever
seen anything that A.B.S. has actually accomplished, other than talk?"

J.K. saw that Karen's anger had transformed into something cooler, and
worse. When she'd been angry at the church before the cowbird talk, she still
had an earnest look about her. This was no longer the case. "Right now my attitude toward this organization is that I can feel my middle finger rising," she
told him. When J.K. smiled uneasily, she added, "And I don't feel that way
very often."

Karen went on to say that because Zanne wasn't at the last board meeting to witness her outburst, she looked now like she probably had a thing or two to say about that. "She's cut me off before. We've stopped talking to each other because of "things." Zanne is a Republican, and that's fine. My grandparents were Republicans, but in the spirit of Eisenhower who warned us that the thing we have to be most cautious of in this country is the military-industrial complex. And he was right!"

"I'm more a fan of Teddy Roosevelt."

Karen waved aside J.K.'s comment. "Sure, he's one of the most brilliant Presidents we've had. Do you know how much public land he set aside? He's largely responsible for the National Park System we have today. Anyway, I stopped talking to Zanne after I found out that she thinks Arnold Schwartznegger is the best thing to hit earth after life crawled up out of the ocean." She gave him a sly smile. "And I thought, 'How can you think that? You'd have to be a moron.'"

Karen's bitterness had drained the glow from her face and left in its place an unsettling pallor. Even when she smiled, she seemed to be stretching her mouth too far, and the contrast between her narrowed eyes and her broad smile was too obvious for the smile to have been genuine. This confirmed J.K.'s conviction that smiling was foolish and insincere.

Even Blake seemed to sense his mother's explosive mood and maintained a safe distance from her, wandering off down the colonnade with his camera, and focusing on flowers.

"There's something I should tell you," J.K. began. He hesitated, guessing that Karen wouldn't be happy with what he was about to say. "I appreciate your giving me the Cowbird Award and all, but I'm not going to be around in June."

"Oh?"

"I might take some time off and roam the mountains."

"Okay. That sounds nice," she said, her torso tightening with this jab.

"You could always give it to someone else," he said foolishly. "Robert Kern may be up for the Nobel Prize. It would be nice to have the Cowbird Award be a predictor of that."

"Thanks for the suggestion."

"Cool. I'll see you around."

"Yeah. See you."

"J.K.," she called after him. He turned around. "Nothing. Forget it."

"You know I was thinking," he added. "You might want to watch out how much time Blake spends birding."

"Excuse me?" Karen said.

"It's just that you wouldn't want him to end up like me."

"Are you saying I'm not bringing up my son right?"

J.K. walked away, looking embarrassed.

"I want to kill him," she muttered to Blake, "but I'm probably menopausal."

After an appropriate number of seconds had elapsed, Blake left his mother alone. He was upset to find out that J.K. was refusing the Cowbird Award, and he darted after his hero.

When the boy prodded him, J.K. said, "I'm going to try living like a hermit for a while. It's an experiment."

Blake looked at him, not sure whether to believe him.

J.K. continued. "You know, my parents aren't happy about this either. They were hoping I'd join them on a cruise with my mom's extended family. I was supposed to be taking a redeye tonight." J.K.'s eyes sparkled. "My parents were gonna pick me up at the airport and race me to where the cruise starts. But from now on, I refuse to do stuff that's just gonna torment me."

"You're not going to give up birding, are you?" Blake said.

"Maybe I should. It hasn't gotten me anywhere."

"You're kidding, right, 'cause you're so good, they should have a degree named after you. When I get to be as good, I'll call myself Blake Mercer, J.K."

J.K. looked at the boy, astonished, yet pleased.

"I lost the Big Year," he said. "In this world, it's winning or losing that counts."

"When I think like that, about all the people who're ahead of me, I feel awful," Blake said. "When I'm not thick-headed, when I don't want 'em so bad, that's when good birds fly to me. When I don't care so much about winning, that's when I have the best time."

"I used to be like you," J.K. said. He could have wept. "Thanks for reminding me."

The program was about to start. Karen went into the lecture hall stony-faced, but there was no seat for either her or Blake. He was content to stand, but it was too much for her that she should spend an afternoon baking, the evening driving goodies through rush-hour traffic, serving them, with no one caring enough to even save her a seat. She returned to the kitchen, sat down on a stool and cried.

Rick found her there after his slideshow. He had come to snag a cookie for the drive home. "Are you okay?" he asked with concern.

"You know, after the Centennial is over, I am going to resign as Hospitality Chair."

He looked at her, not understanding. "Is something wrong?"

"I may even leave A.B.S."

"You're kidding, right?"

"You bet I'm not. Zanne's not talking to me. She stared at me from a distance like a disgusted owl." Karen screwed up her eyes to demonstrate. "And she kept doing it all evening."

"So this wouldn't be a good time to tell you that Meg and I discovered we have a prior engagement to attend a wedding on the date of the Centennial."

Karen broke into fresh tears. All her emotions bubbled up and burst out. "Do you want me to scrap the plans for the Centennial?"

"Of course not. It's just that Meg and I have had a tough year. And she's insisting on going to this wedding."

Rick gave her a hug as an apology of sorts, and she melted into his embrace like butter on warm bread. When they looked into each other's eyes again, she said, "Why am I killing myself over this?"

"You know what, . . . let me talk to Meg."

"You *have* to come," she whispered. "It has something to do with an award."

"I thought J.K. was receiving the award," Rick said.

"Not anymore, he isn't."

Rick looked at her, intrigued, but decided it was safest to change the subject. "And there's something else I've been meaning to tell you."

Karen perked up. She wiped her tears and was aware that her cheeks were flushed.

"You remember you asked me a while ago to put together an owling trip?"

"I may have. I can't think why."

"Anyway, I'm putting one together. I want the members to have a little celebration of our own. I know you're into big Centennial events, but I'd like to treat you and Blake to a little one—a night out owling. We'll keep it intimate. Not more than eight people, tops. How about it?"

"That's nice. But I don't think that's the answer to the questions I've been asking."

"And here's the part you'll like—I plan to drag Billy Grimsby along. I thought if we take him on a really cool trip and reintroduce him to the pleasures of nature . . . who knows? It might help smooth out the Centennial arrangements. I mentioned this to Blake and he thinks it's a great idea."

Karen groaned. "Oh, no! Blake knows about this?"

But her mind had already moved on from the hopeless subject of the owling trip. Her heart was racing in a particular way, and she wondered if the Lord was urging her to do something radical. "You know, part of me thinks that I should either quit A.B.S. or run for president," she said. "Unless you plan to be president again. I have only those two choices left at this point."

"I don't think you should quit A.B.S.," Rick said uneasily. "And I don't think that I can come back and be president anytime soon."

"Well, I care too much to stand by and watch as it completely changes course from what it's supposed to be."

Rick wondered how he'd gotten caught in this quagmire. Life might have been simpler if he'd skipped the cookie and driven straight back home.

"Do you want me to run for president?" Karen asked him.

"You know, if you want, I can talk Frank out of running."

"No," she said. "I want there to be a fair election. If A.B.S. doesn't want me, I'm not going to force myself on them."

Rick nodded, wondering if anyone could talk Frank out of being president, now that he was getting such a rush from managing the endowment.

"Would you let Zanne know of my decision?" she said. "Because I think the deadline for candidates announcing their intention is this Friday."

Later that night, Rick called Karen at home.

"Meg says we can go to both events," he said. "And," he added, "I'm making arrangements for a guitarist for the Centennial."


J.K. loved conifers—the scaly needles of incense cedar, wiry junipers, and spruces in soft glorious blues. The tea he made from Douglas fir tasted like aromatic lake water. The snakeskin bark of the Ponderosa pine contrasted with that of the Jeffrey pines he couldn't resist sniffing, with their wonderful aroma of vanilla. When he was among his beloved conifers, with nuthatches and creepers and white-headed woodpeckers, he experienced a heady sensation of being far from the cares of the world, of being in a universe of his own. Water flowed clear in the streams, and at these higher elevations, the air was so crisp he could almost taste it. It was to this forested world he escaped when he felt that everyone who had been dear to him had forsaken him.

He packed up his apartment, the cubbyhole, feeling that he had no choice but to escape its atmosphere of curdled memories. The books that he couldn't part with yet, he shipped home. Keeping a single box of their son's things wasn't too much to ask. He threw away what he could, and hauled the rest to the Salvation Army a few blocks away. He kept a powder-blue suitcase his mother had given him and packed it with clothes. He put his papers and sleeping bag in a backpack, and kept an empty gym bag, which he planned to fill with dry food. Even this, he felt, wasn't a light enough load, but he couldn't see a way of further paring-down his belongings.

On Saturday afternoon, he loaded the Honda, left the apartment keys in the mailbox for his landlady, and drove to Wild Oats to buy enough dry goods to last him a month. His total savings were around $700, and he meant to stretch this out through the summer months, and hopefully, into the fall.

To his surprise, his mother was relieved that he'd decided not to go on the extended-family cruise. He assumed it was because she had touted his success so much to the relatives that his unemployment was embarrassing to her. J.K. wondered for the first time not *how much* his parents loved him, but if they loved him at all. Maybe he was being unfair, but his heart didn't sense their love. Whatever he chose to do was only a practical matter to them. As long as he had a title and drew a salary, they assumed all was well in his life. Closeness with their only son was of little value to them. They'd rather hold on to their materialistic views. He asked himself now if they would have been happier if it had been him, not his sister, who had died.

But why couldn't he either forgive Anne Marie or let her go? Their breakup had happened months ago! Maybe it was the terror of being utterly alone in the world. As much as he felt that she had forsaken him when he most needed her, he also found himself making excuses for her. How could I expect her to dig my lifestyle? What was I thinking, putting her through the torture—and it must have been torture for her—of being stuck in the cubbyhole the few weekends she flew here to see me?

He corrected himself. If hers were a true love, she shouldn't have minded the cubbyhole. Obviously, she preferred being pampered by some buffoon she didn't love. The next moment he thought he was being heartless. When had he ever given her an amazing weekend to remember him by?

But surely, true love doesn't require extravagant weekends. However bitterly he now viewed their relationship, his heart wouldn't let Anne Marie go. It refused to release her and risk abandonment. Things might have been easier if he knew where Luna stood. But that was impossible to know, since he'd been all but avoiding Luna.

At Wild Oats, J.K. bought only food that would not spoil—bulk oatmeal, couscous, raisins, dates, nuts, spices, apples enough for the first few days, and a few baguettes. He would buy some firewood on the way, and he had packed one pot to boil water for tea, to make oatmeal for breakfast and couscous for dinner.

He noticed Luna when he was walking back to the parking lot with his shopping bags.

"Hey, how's it going?" she called out.

"Hey!" he said.

He didn't have the heart to go over and talk to her, in case she might ask him questions or find out about his expedition. He couldn't risk a distraction at this late stage.

But she called out again. "Where have you been lately?"

"Oh, wandering."

"Do you have time to talk?"

"Can't right now. I'm sorry."

Luna looked disappointed. "Listen, I wanted to say I'm sorry, for that mess-up . . . at the mountain, when I didn't tell you about my boyfriend. Now, my ex . . . But there's been a lot of water under the bridge since then, don't you think? Anyhow, what I really wanted to say is that I have a little surprise for you."

"What's that?"

"You'll find out," she said.

"Oh, no. You'd better tell me now."

"Then it wouldn't be a surprise, would it?"

"That's true." He paused. "You told me once that you had a dream about me, but you never said what it was."

Luna smiled—a smile he remembered from Clark Mountain. "Actually, it wasn't one dream; there were a few. Don't get excited! I don't remember them well. But every few mornings, I'd wake up feeling like we'd been talking that night, even though I knew this was just in my head. I couldn't get these silly dreams to go away."

J.K. looked into her eyes, feeling moved for some reason, but said nothing.

Luna continued. "Look, I think there was something really special between us at that mountain, but we never talked about it. But it was real! And it meant something to me. I think I had the dreams because I wanted to tell you that, 'cause I hadn't done it in person."

What could he say? His paper bags were growing heavy. He paused, and then walked on to the Honda. After he'd unloaded the bags into the car, he was tempted to run back, but he did not feel motivated enough to act on that. Armed with his supplies, he refocused on his plan and drove toward the mountains.

He would start the evening with Rick's owling trip and then go his own way.

*26*

*J.K.* drove up into the San Gabriel Mountains along winding Highway 2 and stopped at mile marker 29.3 to begin what was to be his last birding trip with the Alpena Bird Society. It was mid-June, but he was dressed in a jacket with gloves tucked into his pockets. He had diligently packed the items on his checklist—flashlight, tea thermos, etc.—but somehow couldn't find his wool hat. For now, this was not a problem. It was still light out.

Two elderly couples and the schoolteacher, Wynn, greeted him, along with the honeyed smell of Spanish broom. It grew in clusters with flowers, deep yellow like the setting sun, entwined around tall stems. A few more cars pulled onto the side of the road. Dana got out of her Subaru and sprayed herself and Frank with mosquito repellent.

"The Spanish broom is pretty," Wynn remarked.

"I find the smell cloying. It makes me nauseous," Dana said, wrinkling her nose. "They're non-native," she added by way of explanation.

Rick, the trip leader, arrived in his SUV, accompanied by Billy Grimsby and Blake, who had insisted that his mother let him go with Rick, since she had no spare time for owling. For several nights, Rick had come to the mountains to plan out this trip and had eventually seen all five species of owl found here. In a burst of optimism, he promised all five to Blake, and the boy had reminded him of the promise many times during the drive up the mountain.

The first target bird of the trip was the pygmy owl. Last year J.K. had looked long and hard for a pygmy for his Big Year, but without luck. Rick assured the gang that just two weeks ago, he had found a pygmy two hundred yards from where they stood. The plan was that Rick would play a tape recording of the owl's call, and if one were around and co-operative, it might respond.

Two old ladies arrived and Paul Little spilled out of their back seat, holding a Target shopping bag. He wore a fanny pack around his waist under an army-surplus rain poncho, giving his belly a swollen look. He greeted J.K. with enthusiasm, but received an indifferent response. Paul Little spotted Blake dressed in a turtleneck over which he wore the bird society sweater.

"Scored a brand new poncho," he told the boy, high-fiving him.

Everyone gathered around Rick as he turned on his portable tape player. "Toot . . . toot . . . toot."

They waited for a response, looking around excitedly. J.K. still felt uneasy about Rick's use of electronic devices, but Rick was trip leader today and J.K. didn't like to tread on other people's territory.

"There's the pygmy!" Paul Little called out. There was so much confidence in his voice that everyone raised their binoculars at once. The bird atop a naked tree he was pointing to was a flicker. There were disappointed groans. Undeterred, Paul Little made another false call minutes later, frustrating his fellow birders. Rick was annoyed. He didn't want Grimsby to think they were a bunch of idiots. And he meant to get five out of five owls today, without distractions and false calls. Feeling guilty about neglecting the Centennial, he wanted to win Grimsby over to their side. Such were the burdens of being looked upon as a leader by others. For Karen's sake, Rick needed to cinch Joss Canyon as their Centennial banquet location. To make matters worse, Grimsby whispered in his ear, "That man in the camouflage outfit is squatting in Joss Canyon—a situation that's completely unacceptable."

Rick played the tape again. "Toot . . . toot . . ."

This time, they heard something. A muffled "Toot . . . toot . . ." came from the distance. The pygmy had responded. Rick replayed the recording in the hope that the owl would come closer to check who was calling. It didn't.

It was dusk, and the party of about fifteen people parted brush, hopped over mud and rocks, and made their way toward the call. A sea of yellow Spanish broom and pale orange, sticky-monkey flowers surrounded them. Past this magical burst loomed only pine trees and mountains. The owl seemed to be calling from a grove of pine trees.

"Anyone see it?" Rick asked, walking up to the trees and scanning them. Light was fading and the group looked about anxiously.

"There he is!" Dana yelled.

"In the most obvious spot," Rick added.

Grimsby clutched his binoculars with plump hands and gazed at the Matryoshka nesting doll shape on top of a tall pine tree, with its egg-like silhouette and tail sticking out sideways. The pygmy stayed until a songbird chased it off its perch and into the canyon.

"Not bad, huh?" Rick said.

Grimsby stroked his beard and let out a gruff murmur of appreciation. The group returned to their cars, amazed at how well the evening had started, and then they headed seven miles north to their next destination—Red Box.

"Would you like one?" Dana said, extending a plate of cookies towards Blake. They were at the Red Box parking lot, in dying light.

Blake looked at her, feeling puzzled. He knew that his mother and Dana were enemies, but chocolate chunk cookies were his favorite, so he guiltily accepted two.

Rick waited for everyone to stop chewing the various snacks being passed around before he announced, "At this stop, we'll be standing on concrete-ish grainy stuff that can be really noisy, so please try not to move around."

He waited for everyone to be positioned and told them how to listen for the great-horned, the largest of all owls.

A car door slammed shut and Paul Little walked up to them. "Is this poncho too rustly?" he asked Rick, the poncho rustling as he spoke.

Restraining his impulse to knock the man out cold, Rick said, "Yeah, it is. Can you try not to move?"

Paul Little looked to J.K. for sympathy, but getting none, he moved to the end of the line, where he tried to stand still, but his poncho rustled anyhow.

The great-horned owl did not come.

From Red Box onwards, they carpooled. J.K., Grimsby, and Blake piled into Rick's SUV. J.K. sat in front, as he was prone to getting dizzy on curvy roads when in the backseat. They drove up twenty-six miles to their next stop, Islip Saddle. In the darkness, trees swayed around them.

"The wind is our enemy," Rick warned. The wind made it difficult for the owls to hear the recordings and for the birders to hear them.

When they hopped out of the SUV at 6,500 feet, the first thing J.K. noticed was the wind. The second thing he noticed was how cold it was. He wished now that he had his wool hat. The flammulated owl would be a perfect antidote for the cold weather.

"The flammulated is named after the Latin word for 'flame-like,' " the schoolteacher, Wynn, told them. "I've been looking for one for about a month— for my life count."

Rick's method was to listen for the owl, and when nothing was heard, to play the tape of the flammulated's single note "Who . . . who . . . who."

But the flammulated didn't seem to want to know "who" just now and didn't return the call even though Rick played the recording three times. Next, he played the saw-whet owl's call, which sounded like a truck backing up: "Beep, beep, beep, beep."

J.K. wrapped his arms around his chest, trying not to shiver. He was quiet as Rick had warned them to be, but no saw-whet owl, with its distinctive light brown facial disc, materialized. Rick looked apologetically at Grimsby.

"Occasionally, a saw-whet will fly silently to a tree next to you without calling," Rick said. "Pointing a strong light, especially on the lower branches of a tree, might reveal it."

The night was black now and they strained to see in what little moonlight filtered through the trees. As a last resort, Rick allowed the gang to turn on their flashlights.

Flashlights roved everywhere, but the pine trees revealed nothing.

The gang made three more stops at the high elevation, looking primarily for the flammulated while also playing saw-whet recordings, but they had luck with neither. By the third stop, Dana, Frank, and Grimsby were shivering openly. Coke cans and tea mugs were being sipped from silently, and Paul Little even had the audacity to noisily open a bag of chips.

If they were to return to the Red Box parking lot at midnight as planned, they now had no choice but to descend to lower elevations and look for other owls. Rick reluctantly abandoned the search for the flammulated. At the next stop, he played recordings for three owls: the saw-whet (truck backing up), the western screech (bouncing ball), and the spotted (barking dog).

"I'll play the spotted last," Rick said. "This owl can be nearly three times the size of the first two and has been known to eat the smaller owls."

They stood silently, in anticipation, and only shifted positions to avoid the wind. Paul Little returned from the portable restroom in the parking lot, snapping twigs with his boots while a recording played, and received a scolding from Rick. The pine trees were silent again, however, and they had no choice but to move on.

Back in the SUV, Rick was disappointed. "Such are the perils of birding," he muttered.

Blake assured him that the pygmy owl they got earlier in the evening—a life bird for him—"counts as one hundred percent in my books," but Rick continued to brood about his failure.

"There are hardly any bugs out today," Rick said. "It's cold for a June night."

At the next stop, they stood at the edge of a stunning canyon. Only the moon illuminated the boundary between solid ground and sheer drop as they clustered in groups of two and threes. Rick played his recordings. The three-quarter moon allowed a view of sloping pine trees disappearing into blackness at the bottom of the canyon. Once, they heard a short, sharp noise.

"That was a dog barking," Rick said, before anyone got their hopes up.

When they returned to the SUV, Rick confided that the next and last stop before Red Box was a near-guaranteed saw-whet site. He had once brought Ed McCoy there, and they'd not only heard saw-whets, but had also seen them from no more than twenty feet away. To reassure the group that they were in good hands, Rick couldn't resist reminiscing about his past successes. A couple of months ago, he had fed some L.A. Bird Society people information on owl whereabouts. "And they got seven out of eight species," he said. "They feed me information in return. It's like we scratch each other's backs."

"Yeah, I like the free flow of information between birders," Blake said from the back seat. Without his mom there, Blake felt like he was one of the guys. While they were looking for the saw-whet owl, he found himself counting the years until he'd get his driver's license.

"When you travel," Rick said, "you can tell the birders apart right away. They're real friendly."

During the last couple of stops, the others in the party had begun to giggle at the end of each failed attempt when Rick announced which owl species they were going to look for next.

"Fools that we are, such as we are." Dana mumbled. Grimsby nodded ruefully. People were cold and sleepy; even the indefatigable Wynn was worn out, and for at least half the party—the over sixty-five set—it was well past their bedtime.

"Hope springs eternal in the human breast," Rick said, as they pulled into the "near-guaranteed" location. But once he surveyed the faces of the weary, giggling party, he reminded them—as if they didn't know already—that there are no guarantees in owling. First, he tried the saw-whet tape, this time playing it four times instead of three.

"The wind is our enemy," Rick said.

It was much too windy here to linger, and after a frenzied attempt, with flashlights and silent prayers that two owl eyes would reflect back, they were ordered back into their cars. Inside, Blake rubbed his gloved hands to thaw his fingers, but didn't lose hope they would see another owl.

As they drove back toward Red Box, where the trip was to end, Rick grew reflective. "There are times when I'm up here alone," he said. "And it's cold and windy out . . . and I wonder, 'What am I doing here?' "

J.K. laughed nervously. Blake had already made one too many attempts to assure Rick that the trip had not been a failure.

"But there are times when they come," Rick said, "and then you have cosmic experiences with these birds. They come and sit there, and you can study them all you want."

At Red Box, people got out of their heated cars reluctantly and walked over to Rick to thank him for the trip. They were in a hurry to get back, but Rick indicated that he had something to say. "For those who want to leave now, I can understand," he said. "But J.K. is going to drive up Mt. Wilson road, and he'll let us pile into his car."

Paul Little would have loved to come, but he had to leave because of his ride. "Unless you could drop me off later?" he said to J.K.

"Sorry man. I'm camping tonight."

"Cool. I could camp with you."

"I can't. My plans are too fluid right now."

Two old women waved goodbye to Rick, close to his face, lest their gesture be misunderstood, and hurried back to their car. "Shit, man!" Paul Little muttered, and then he scooted after them, unwilling to miss his one sure ride.

Everyone vanished in a moment.


Grimsby was there only because Rick was his ride. Now Rick turned to him. "Are you coming with us?"

There was a plaintive look in Rick's face as he asked this question. It was close to midnight. As tired and cold as Grimbsy was, he could not bear to directly refuse. "How much farther is it?" he asked disinterestedly.

"Not much."

"How long will it take?" he asked, ready to claim he had a big day ahead of him tomorrow.

"As long as you want." Seeing that Grimsby was cornered, Rick added, "Not more than half an hour." The plea never left his face, so Grimsby decided to be a good sport, though sleep was beckoning him home.

As the Honda turned onto the Mount Wilson road, J.K. mentioned that the road was swarmed with drag racers on weekends. They passed two souped-up cars before tucking into a dirt parking spot. It was a remote road. Because of the drag racers, and because there were few parking spots here, Rick hadn't included this detour in the official part of the trip. It was quiet, and as they stepped over to the edge of the canyon, they had an even wider south view. Rick played the saw-whet tape.

"It's a lovely call," Rick said. The wind was howling, but only in whispers.

"I heard something," J.K. said.

And then Rick seemed to hear it, too. "Did you hear it?" he asked Grimsby.

Grimsby shook his head. But a few seconds later, he heard it. In the distance, from what had to be the far-east end of the canyon, was heard the gentle, but unmistakable call, "Beep, beep, beep, beep."

They were giddy with success. There was a saw-whet owl somewhere in this vast dark canyon, and it was calling out to them. Rick played the recording a few more times to get the owl to come closer, but it seemed content where it was. They were content, too, that at last their persistence had paid off.

Their last stop of the night—the end of the Mt. Wilson road—overlooked the city of Alpena and the sister cities surrounding it. This spectacular view, a sea of golden lights, was framed by the two hills between which they stood. But the silver moon above the city outshone all its lights, and to its right, Jupiter pierced the sky. Rick played his recordings, and though no owls responded, bats flew over their heads. J.K. stood still, soaking up the fairyland view, as a racer occasionally droned by.

They were driving back toward Red Box, negotiating the winding road, when headlights approached them head-on. The turquoise car was driving much too fast for a road like this and had swung halfway into their lane on the curve, not anticipating oncoming traffic.

A silent scream went through J.K. as he saw they were headed for collision. He had joked earlier in the evening that the brakes on his Birdmobile were turning it into a boat that took a mile to stop, but he swerved to the right and brought the car to a halt in a spray of gravel, just short of the guardrail and, beyond that, the canyon below. The race car driver appeared to have lost control, climbing up his lane's shoulder before veering back onto the road at an angle, headed directly for them. It seemed inevitable that the other driver would broadside them, when at the last moment he jerked sharply to his right, bounced off the Birdmobile, and disappeared without slowing down around the next bend in the road. The front fender of the Honda was scrunched-in and mangled by the glancing impact.

Blake, huddled in a ball, had been thrown on top of Grimsby, who was laid out flat and groaning on the floor of the backseat. J.K. and Rick had been secured by their seatbelts, but the pain in Rick's neck caused him to howl like a coyote.

The race-car driver never returned, and J.K. drove the Honda gingerly back to Red Box. They were all shaken. J.K. began to jibber nonsense. The others sympathized with him.

"After all, I had a better view than you," he told them. "Dang! That punk could have killed us!" It happened so fast, a geyser inside him erupted; without knowing it, J.K. began to sob at the wheel.

They were at the Red Box parking lot. Rick patted J.K., and murmured something reassuring. Then, not knowing how else to respond, Rick tumbled out of the car.

Too much in shock to feel the cold, Rick felt glad to be alive.

"You okay?" Blake said, straightening himself out.

"Yeah," J.K. said, trying to regain control. "I remembered an accident I was in awhile back. I've been carrying that around with me all these years."

J.K. and Blake helped the still-groaning Grimsby into Rick's SUV while Rick staggered behind them, emitting low moans.

"You'll be fine, Billy," Rick assured him. "I think I got it worse."

Grimsby looked at him with pained, disbelieving eyes.

"This might be goodbye for a while," J.K. said. When Rick looked puzzled, he added, "I'm gonna spend the summer away from civilization. I've given up my apartment. I'll sleep somewhere in the mountains tonight."

"Wow!" Rick said.

J.K. considered the mangled front of the Honda. "Hopefully, it won't give out on me," he said, "or I'm in trouble."

"But you'll come to the Centennial?" Blake said.

"I can't really say."

"My mom needs your vote. She's running for president. She'll be really mad if you don't show up."

"I know. But I'd like to drop out for a while. I don't have a job or anything."

"You have to promise you'll come." Blake tugged nervously at the neck of his bird society sweater. "You have to *promise*!"

"Okay," J.K. relented. "If it means that much, I'll try."

Satisfied, Blake turned to Grimsby. "You'll let us do the Centennial at Joss Canyon, right? We can't afford the huge fees you're charging us."

Grimsby, lying in the back seat, let out a string of curses. "I've never tried to stop it," he added. "If you weren't obsessed with those blasted cowbird signs!"

Rick picked up a large sugar-pine cone as a souvenir of the trip; Blake followed his lead and grabbed an even more massive cone. It was becoming a sentimental habit with Rick to pick something up—a feather, a stone, or a pinecone—from his owling trips, though the Forest Service forbade it.

After confirming with Rick the location of a particular owling spot, J.K. got into the battered Honda, waved his goodbyes, and headed back up to higher elevations to find it. It was nearly 1 a.m.

"Drive safely," Rick called out after him, before he, too, disappeared into the night.

# 27

$\mathcal{M}$y whole life has been a preparation for this," Karen said.

Robert Kern sipped wine and looked on, puzzled.

Karen's face was aglow, a flame now burning within her. She had slaved for months to pull off the Centennial dinner, and this June day was the fruit of her efforts. Joss Canyon had never looked uglier, but such a well-decorated tent as this had never graced its mud-caked grounds either. She was having an "early bird" talk before the evening officially began. She had forgiven Kern after he let her use his research to reinforce the message of the cowbird signs. Karen's conscience felt lighter because she was educating people on the evils of cowbird control, and she'd added comment boxes so that people could have their say.

"We're having a little conflict within the board," Karen explained in a purposefully understated way to Kern's wife who sat across from her, "about money."

Kathy Morton put on as sympathetic a look as she could muster.

"But I can handle the board," Karen told her, waving her hand and leaning back. "This is not the first time we've had a problem in A.B.S." She described the speed bumps she'd encountered after Rick's withdrawal from the Centennial Committee, and Zanne's neglect, and the maturity with which she handled all of it. She stopped just short of endorsing herself as president, because canvassing wasn't allowed on election day. Instead she dwelt on the breakdown in communication between Grimsby and herself, and the genius with which Blake gained Grimsby's consent after the car accident.

"Grimsby was admitted with a ribcage fracture," Karen said.

"Did he waive the location fee?" Kern asked.

"Nope, but he gave us a discount. And he's letting us put up the bird signs only temporarily. When you're dealing with a tough cookie, you have to do it one bite at a time. He agreed to our demands, from the hospital, on the condition that . . ."

"On the condition that I'm no longer obliged to go on any birding trips with A.B.S.," Blake mimicked Grimsby's gruff voice.

Kern looked at Blake admiringly. "I need someone to count parakeets in South America," he said. "If you were old enough, I'd give you the job."

Blake felt so good, he blushed. "Mom . . ." he began.

"Nope," Karen said. "You'll go to college first."

Then Blake remembered something. "J.K. doesn't have a job. Can you give it to him?"

"He might be overqualified," Kern said.

Karen raised an eyebrow and fiddled with the animal motifs in her turquoise necklace. She couldn't wait to get into her velvet outfit. She stood up with a start, unsure where she'd left the vireo-embossed napkins. She'd been here since morning, finalizing the placement of the tables and the centerpieces which she had created, handpicking the succulent plants and Wrightwood stones that were showcased in Italian earthenware pots. She personally oversaw the arrangements with the Mexican food caterer. No detail escaped her. Blake and Crystal fluttered about the tent like moths, carrying out her instructions, as did her husband when he arrived.

Blake's brain was going crazy with the question, "Mom, do you think you'll get elected?" But he took care not to aggravate her, since he knew from experience she was prone to mood swings at harried times. He tried to relax his mind by sifting through facts. The western gull, he thought, is the only gull to use the California coast as a summer nesting ground. But is it a migrating gull? This he could not remember. Life was so much easier when J.K. had been around. He could answer any bird question. Blake wished he would grow up one day to be exactly like J.K. The accident and the battered Honda only served to glorify his idol and burnish his reputation as a die-hard birder.

The guitarist came at 6 p.m. Luna was radiant in her blue pillbox hat. Karen greeted her with an enthusiastic hug, acting very much like an opera impresario. She introduced her to Robert Kern and his wife as Rick's friends and joked that "Now I'll introduce you to thirty-one more people!"

Karen steered Luna to a corner of the tent, where she had decided the guitarist's presence would create the best effect. By quarter past six, all the set pieces had come together to Karen's satisfaction, and she felt that it was safe to drop everything for a moment to get dressed.

She had made prior arrangements with Grimsby to use his trailer. His desk was smothered with moldering papers and files; Karen swept them aside to make room for her floral bag. She pulled out her black velvet slacks and a sheer blouse. First, she put on earrings of aquamarine blue that she'd acquired on the Arizona vacation. Paired with the dangling, animal-motif necklace, she considered this the most beautiful set she owned.

A golden dusk lit up the landscape and softened its bare ugliness. The few meager poppies had closed their buttery orange petals for the day. Two bush sunflowers swayed in the wind as Paul Little, holding on to his stomach, clambered down from his under-the-graffiti-bridge dwelling. He walked through the little garden surrounding the Joss Canyon trailer. Grimsby had had this oasis planted as a buffer against the wasteland that was now Joss Canyon.

Paul Little knocked on the trailer door and began to open it. He thought Grimsby might have returned from his hospital stay in time for the Centennial. Instead, he saw a half-naked woman inside; she let out a shriek and ran to shut the door, all the while flapping her arms like a chicken.

Karen felt humiliated that Paul Little had seen her in shabby underwear. She hadn't had time to buy something nice. Damn that vagrant! He had a way of wrecking her mood. Her dignity had been completely violated.

Feeling confused, Paul Little walked away. He had planned to enter the Centennial tent with Grimsby and thus avoid the tricky matter of buying a ticket. A D.W.P. man had visited him a few days ago and warned that they would no longer tolerate him living on public land. He must vacate or he'd be arrested. Paul Little was still upset from his encounter with the D.W.P. When Grimsby returned, he might cut him some slack.

Paul Little walked along the narrow trail leading to the tent, ignoring the new mumbo-jumbo signs about cowbirds and Bell's vireos. A whiff of sage perfumed the air. He followed the scent and tore off some sagebrush, and rubbed it on his fingers—Cowboy cologne. He felt something scurry under his right shoe. Before he could step out of the way, he heard a watery crunching sound. Looking down, he discovered he'd stepped on a green Pacific tree frog and murdered it entirely.

After cleaning his hiking shoe as best he could on the grass, he turned his thoughts to the feast that lay ahead, and made his way to the canvas tent where the Centennial was being celebrated. He was glad to see the mousy Patty Cole manning the ticket booth. He figured he could talk her into letting him in. But at that moment Karen, fully dressed, walked up to the table, and his tongue was paralyzed. He had suspected for a while that she didn't like him, and the dirty look she gave him now did nothing to dispel that notion.

"You have a ticket?" Karen said.

Paul Little could have sworn. If it had been just Patty, he would have convinced her one way or the other that he ought to be let in.

"Well?" Karen said.

He shook his head. "I don't," he said. "But . . ."

"I'm sorry. We're not letting people in without tickets."

"How much is it?"

"We're all sold out." And it was evident from the way Karen's face flushed all over that she had lied.

Paul Little glowered. He'd like to show her. The gumption she had, kicking him out. Joss Canyon was his home! Blake came and stood by his mother, and Paul Little gave the boy a pleading look, but the boy stood dumb as a snail.

"Are you a member?" Patty said.

He shook his head. It was too damn expensive to become a member.

Patty pointed to a stack of application brochures. "Because, you know, members can come in for free to vote in the election. You just can't eat dinner."

Paul Little was fuming. People were always trying to get rid of him. He could smell dinner being warmed up inside, and the aroma of mashed potatoes and butter and a spicy chili stew infuriated him further. But he was unwilling to get into an argument with the formidable Karen, and he slunk away with the application brochure. As he was leaving, he heard an exchange that stuck with him.

"Is J.K. coming?" Patty asked. "He's not on the list."

"He's living in Chilao campground," Blake said. He giggled. "I wanna visit him."

"He's camping in the mountains or something crazy like that," Karen said. "I have no idea what he's up to. I'm not letting Blake anywhere near him after that car accident. It's terrifying. You let your kid out of sight for one night and he nearly gets killed! And J.K. hasn't called to apologize, either."

The women shook their heads at J.K.'s inexplicable behavior.

Paul Little had an idea. He knew what that brat, J.K., was up to. He would show him. He'd look for that bugger in Chilao, even if it took an hour to get there. He had an idea where that snot-nose was. That would teach him to refuse Paul Little as a camping companion. His name had been maligned in Alpena. People gave him real attitude here. They didn't treat him like a human being.

He needed a fresh start. He needed to get out. He'd always wanted to explore Northern California. He was hearing rumors that condors were making a comeback there, and he wanted to see one first-hand. But he'd need a car to drive there and get around. J.K. had a car. An idea began to take shape in his head. Paul Little walked over to a broken-down shed. After scaring off a lizard and three spiders, he brought out his old Stumpjumper mountain bike.

## 28

*P*aul Little took the city bus as far as he could into the San Gabriel Mountains, which wasn't far enough. In a rough jerk, the bus stopped to down-shift just when the serious incline began, and then it turned around to return to the city. Nasty. He got out of the bus and grabbed his bike off the rack. He hitched a ride to Red Box, but twenty minutes later he was riding his trusty Stumpjumper again. It was still light out, but the road up the mountains snaked dangerously, and the makeshift lamp on his bike might not protect him from being hit by tourists speeding home in fancy cars. He began to bike uphill. When he thought his legs could pedal no more, the vision of J.K.'s black Honda urged him on.

During a birding trip, when J.K. gave him a ride, Paul Little had discovered that J.K. kept a spare key under one of the floor mats. All he had to do was break in and the car was his. He had an old license plate in his bag that he'd rescued from a car he sold for scrap, and he aimed to use it to disguise the car if someone reported it stolen. He didn't mean to steal the car; maybe he'd ask J.K. if he could borrow it. If only Karen hadn't gotten him so riled! Feeling con-fused, he decided he'd figure things out when he got to the campground. He began to fantasize about driving to San Francisco and chasing after a condor.

Occasionally, a couple of motorcyclists drove by in the opposite direction and honked tauntingly at Paul Little. His temper rose with each incident. It was an excruciating ride up the switchback road, and he was out of shape. At one point, he was sure his heart would give out. He stopped and heaved. His stomach was in quadruple knots.

By the time he got to the Chilao campground at 5,300 feet, he was all sweat, slippery as a slug, and he collapsed on a picnic bench like a dead man.

J.K. had read in John Muir's book that holly berries make good rations in summertime, and he was out berry collecting with a ratty wicker basket. A scrub jay had squawked noisily at J.K.'s campsite all afternoon, which reminded him of Rick for some reason, and his headache had gotten worse. Recovering from a bad cold, J.K. was trying to add more vitamin C to his diet. He could have used more specific advice from Muir. Too bad Muir never really hung out in Southern California, but sequestered himself instead in Yosemite.

As J.K. walked back to his campsite, his stomach felt empty, despite his berry feast. He had been camping for three weeks and was low on supplies. It would take an hour to cook a more substantial dinner. His thoughts wandered to where he might camp next. A nuttall's woodpecker was drumming, and chickadees twittered about. He had given no serious thought to how long he would go on camping alone, because every time he dwelled on it, his heart seemed to break all over again.

He had wondered about going to the Centennial. He missed the company of others, but he couldn't spare thirty dollars for the dinner ticket; that was a week's worth of groceries. He didn't need to bankrupt himself just to see the same old people. He assumed they had forgotten him, like everyone else. It seemed to him that there was a stronger bond in A.B.S. between people and birds than between people and people. He smiled, remembering Karen's heartbreak when her eyes had been opened to the greed and lack of idealism in A.B.S. She was probably counting on his vote to bring about change, but he couldn't help that. The powers-that-be at A.B.S. were too old and entrenched for her to be able to take them on single-handedly. And he had lost his desire to engage in the world. A.B.S. was on its own as far as he was concerned.

Carrying berries in the wicker basket, J.K. returned to his campsite. He was surprised to see someone leaning studiously over his car door.

"Hey, what are you doing?"

Paul Little straightened up with a jerk.

"Paul?" J.K. said, surprised. He must be really lonely to be so glad to see any familiar face—even Paul Little's.

"You're back," Paul Little said in a hoarse whisper.

"Dang! You startled me! What are you doing here?"

"I need to borrow your car. You can keep my bike."

"What?"

"Just for a few days, man. If you'll front me some cash, I'll be back, week or two, tops, with supplies."

"Are you nuts?"

The words seemed to aggravate the man to the point of madness. He threw himself at J.K. and tried to wrest the keys out of his pocket.

J.K. resisted, and they began scuffling in the dirt. In the furious tangle of limbs, the wicker basket got kicked and the holly berries scattered in the dirt.

His afternoon's labor was spoiled. Annoyed, J.K. landed a hard punch on Paul Little's jaw.

Paul Little pulled a Swiss army knife out of his back pocket. "Don't be crazy," J.K. warned as he backed away, the stinging odor of sweat in his nostrils.

"Don't you call me crazy!" Paul Little threatened. The blade glinted dull silver.

"I don't believe this," J.K. said. "What d'you need the car for anyhow?" The Honda was practically the only possession he had and was still dear to him, even in its beat-up condition. "Hey, why don't you go rip off someone who's rich?"

Paul Little let out a dry laugh.

For a moment, J.K. thought it was all over, some kind of forgivable misunderstanding, but then the look on the other man's face became more intent. J.K. had an animalistic fear of being wounded; getting all cut up made survival in the wilderness much more complicated. There was no telling whether the man in front of him had gone loony or was just out to rob him. J.K. lunged to grab Paul Little's wrist and was able to flick the knife away. It landed on the dirt near the berries.

Paul Little clutched J.K.'s arm and twisted it behind his back. J.K. gasped. Some muscle had gotten pulled. The instant was over so fast, like a snakebite, that J.K. was stung with disbelief as much as pain. He staggered back, thinking Paul Little might hurt him more, but then his nerves screamed.

Paul Little broke into his car and found what he was after—the spare key under the foot mat. J.K. kept it there, in case he was scrambling in the mountains, chasing a bird, and he lost his keys. In remote areas, he kept a back door of the car unlocked so he'd have a way to get back in.

"Hey, wait!" J.K. said, trying to reason with Paul Little.

Plunging into the Birdmobile like a jackrabbit, Paul Little started the engine and drove away.

J.K. looked at the Stumpjumper mountain bike Paul had left him, but decided not to bike in the dark. He stared at the empty spot where his beloved Birdmobile had been parked. His eyes blurred and his face dissolved into weariness. He slung his knapsack over his shoulders, strapped on a headlamp, and began to hike along a trail lined with ponderosa pines that led down to the ranger station. He must report the theft of his Honda. The Visitor Center would be closed, and he'd have to hike up to the ranger's cottage from there. Even in his tired state, he started out with a light step, more like a deer than a young man.

Weak from a meager diet, a bad cold, and still in shock from the theft of his car, he was tired and made slow progress. All kinds of thoughts faded in and out of his mind—the events of last year, the Big Year of his downward slide, the year the safety nets gave way—they all spun around him. He could hardly blame Paul Little for taking what was left. Paul Little was a scavenger, a turkey vulture. It had been Dave, that falcon that had wheeled overhead, watching from on high as he, J.K., a small, vulnerable prey, got pounced on. It wasn't possible in this greedy, survival-of-the-fittest world for someone like J.K. to be anything other than prey. Anne Marie strutted in and out of his awareness like a cackling parrot. A.B.S. was a pecking order of foragers, each one fighting for minuscule crumbs and pushing everyone else out of the way. Karen was right. A.B.S. members only paid lip service to caring about birds. What they cared about most was their lists. He'd been guilty of that, too.

He tried to focus his mind on potential dangers. Falling off an unseen ledge. Hypothermia. It was too high up here for snakes, but this was bear country. There also loomed the threat of a mountain lion; there had been a sighting in this area just weeks ago. The possibility of encountering it had sounded exciting at the time, but now he wasn't so sure.

Just a year ago, anyone would have thought that J.K.'s future looked bright. He was on an enviable career path; now, he was on a dirt path heading downhill. Who could have guessed that a physicist working on a Ph.D. would be stumbling alone in the dark, praying (agnostically) for a ranger to find him before a lion did? His lips were parched. He flicked his tongue and tasted sweat and the berries he'd been picking. He wished he didn't feel this empty. He had begun to understand the quicksand nature of life in this past year. A guy assumes his life matters until failure and heartbreak suck him in, and the spot where he once stood fills up quickly, as though he hadn't existed at all. His own sister had vanished from his thoughts only a few years after her death, even though they'd been inseparable as children. That's when his parents became distant. He rationalized his parents' coldness: they *did* care about him, but didn't know how to deal with it.

Muffled barking echoed in the nearby canyon. Spotted owl, he decided. He looked at the stars above and remembered how Luna looked in that white summer dress. He liked her in that dress. In the last year, Luna, inexplicably, had been a comfort to him. They had felt mismatched, awkward. But when they swam together in the Silver Lake reservoir, things had felt deliciously right.

The path narrowed and abruptly disappeared into underbrush. J.K. had to backtrack. He was taking a shortcut to the Visitor Center; walking along the road or a wider trail would take too long. Even when he was reasonably sure he was on the trail, it twisted maddeningly, mostly tending down, and a sudden turn would lead up an incline. He looked up to check the position of the stars. How long had he been walking? Forty minutes?

Hiking on the cold forest trail, J.K. reached out for the memory of something warm. Last summer. August was hot. That had been a hopeful time. The Piute Ponds trip. For four years, he had luxuriated in the freedom of wandering the Air Force base in the summers, birding in Piute Ponds and dreaming of a Big Year. But last August was something else.

In the darkness, J.K. shivered. He thought he saw paw prints, faint and muddy, a few feet away. They were bigger than a cat's paw, much bigger. Maybe he was imagining them—his senses might be confused. He focused his headlamp, and there they were again, distinct in a muddy patch. His eyes followed the prints into the grass beyond the trail. J.K. bit his dry lips, using the pain to sharpen his awareness. In the same way that he could sense his parents' love, though they didn't show it, he could now sense a tawny animal, invisible in the dark, with powerful, sinuous lines. He hoped it was a bobcat; if so, it might hiss at him and leave him alone. More likely a bobcat would just run away. He held on to a sapling pine for support. Some instinct caused him to turn off his headlamp. He could see the dirt path in the moonlight.

The Piute Ponds trip flashed through his mind. He must hold on to the memory and keep moving. It would keep him from passing out. Everyone was after the Baird's Sandpiper that day. A rare bird. He'd seen one earlier in the summer and Rick expected him to serve it up magically. Rick was feverish about it. He had wanted that bird as bad as a man can want anything. But then Rick was the King of all listers. The Piute Ponds trip was the last carefree trip that he led for A.B.S. The occasional detour through sewage muck was nothing; it was the price you paid for real birding.

J.K. found it satisfying to consider that he was the only civilian in the greater L.A. area who was entrusted with the secret code for the gates to the Air Force base and Piute Ponds. The trip shone in his memory like the crescent moon in the sky above. The secret code was in his brain, never to be compromised. He doubted the Air Force folks would divulge it to any other person.

He heard movement in the nearby brush. His brain sifted through stock survival advice he'd read. Scare off a threatening animal by waving your arms to appear bigger than you are. Make noise. Don't run, for God's sake. When wolves come upon a herd of caribou, the wolves test them, looking for the weakest animal—the sick, the injured, the vulnerable.

The ground was freezing. The spotted owl let out a harsh bark, and the hair on J.K.'s neck bristled. He thought about his aunt's comment at Emma's funeral. She wondered what goes through a person's mind in the moment before sudden death. Do we review our entire lives in that instant?

Even if he were to fast-forward through the first twenty-five years of his life, he needed time to sort thought this last year, his twenty-sixth. The futility of it rankled him. He thought he belonged to the bird society and was connected to a community, but now he realized how alone he'd been. Whether they were any kind of real community was questionable. He had faced all the trials and the joys of this last year alone, and now he would face this predator alone. He wished he didn't feel cynical; he'd never been like this before last year. He was inclined to put up a fight, whether or not his body had the strength for it.

Drawing on the power of his mind to give him strength, J.K. visualized Luna. Now there was a fighter! What security did she have while pursuing her music career? She'd told him she'd only had erratic jobs. There was something almost spiritual in Luna's piercing eyes, her smile dancing at the corners of her ripe mouth.

Anne Marie's allure was in the whole. There was nothing plain about Anne Marie's face; in fact, it was attractive. But one's eye stopped not at her face, as it did with Luna, but rather drifted down her body to the small breasts and the teardrop hips.

Strange that he should think of Luna now, but it made him feel stronger to think of her. Who could ever make out what she was about? He'd avoided her lately because she, too, was unpredictable—like Anne Marie—and he didn't want to get hurt again. He wondered if Luna might understand him better because she was similarly pursuing an uncertain path. Like him, Luna was trying to figure herself out.

Beyond the brush was a narrow meadow. At the far north end of the meadow, past a cluster of pines, J.K. saw the outline of a deer—a young one, trotting a few paces behind its mother. The fawn stopped to munch on a bush. Berries, probably.

Having deer around increased the probability that a mountain lion might be nearby. J.K. adjusted his knapsack and began to walk briskly. No more shortcuts, no more quiet trails. He needed to get closer to the main road.

Getting away from the secluded trail was not easy, especially since he was in a hurry. Fighting a thicket of Spanish broom, his hands scratched and sore,

J.K. headed toward a stretch of gravel just beyond. Then he ran toward the main road.

At any other time, J.K. might have been thrilled to see a mountain lion. But now, J.K. could only remember the early morning hike in Switzer Canyon when he saw a deer leg poking out of the brush. A lion had not eaten its kill. Instead, it covered the deer carcass with a rough shamble of twigs and leaves. J.K. had heard this is how mountain lions cache fresh kills until they can return to feed. He'd felt sorry for that deer. He'd wondered if the deer had cried in agony when the lion's claws gripped its neck and broke its vertebra. What was it like the moment before it was all over? A ranger had told him that deer let out the most horrifying groan when they think they're going to die—it is otherworldly.

J.K.'s lungs were devoid of air, and he felt that nothing he did would matter now, so he tried his best to shout for help. Now he was running on the side of the road.

There was a glare of headlights. It hurt his eyes. How was this possible? Had the Birdmobile returned to rescue him? The car was parked on the shoulder of the road. J.K. wanted to laugh, but he couldn't. He was all frozen inside. He heard the clang of a metal tool. Paul Little was crouched over a tire, having jacked up the car.

J.K. wanted to say something biting, like telling Paul he was on his way to report him to a ranger. But J.K. didn't have air in him just now. He felt as flat as the tire Paul Little was trying to replace.

"Man!" Paul Little whined. "This is how all my ventures end."

Just then, the jack slipped. Paul Little groaned and began all over again.

At first, J.K. was amused by Paul's clumsiness. The instant of amusement was soon over. J.K. almost didn't see the lion, muscular and magnificent, backlit by the moonlight.

Paul Little, crouched down, must have looked like small and easy pickings to the lion.

"I almost got this beaut fixed," Paul Little said. He stopped dead, catching J.K.'s expression. "You alright, man?"

"Watch out!" J.K. yelled.

The attack came out of nowhere. The lion jumped on Paul Little unexpectedly, Paul's back painfully absorbing the lion's claws.

J.K. turned to stone. A horrific shadow play, a mingling of man and beast. Where was a ranger when you needed one?

There was no way for Paul to drag himself away. The sheer mass of the lion was overpowering.

J.K.'s legs dissolved like sugar in lemonade. He wanted to howl. Instead he charged at the two-body problem that was the lion and Paul Little. "Get up!" he yelled. "Stand up, you idiot!"

Paul Little tried to shake the lion off, but couldn't. The lion grabbed Paul Little's neck with his teeth.

J.K. picked up the tire iron and swung it, howling like a coyote—the most terrific din he'd ever made in his life.

J.K. clipped the lion's legs with the tire iron, first one hind leg, then the other. The lion looked up. J.K.'s adrenaline was at full force, and he hit the lion again, letting out another coyote-howl.

The lion hovered for a moment in shock and pain, then it abandoned Paul Little and limped into the dark forest, admitting defeat. In an instant, the lion had vanished. Did it sense that J.K. wasn't afraid?

Honks. A car, driving uphill, slowed down even more by the narrow switch-back, had stopped and the driver watched the scene. The sound of a window rolling down. The driver popped his head out and gaped. Another series of honks.

The car's driver spoke with a Texan accent. "You guys need some help or what?"

"You okay?" J.K. asked Paul Little.

Paul Little let out a series of whimpering cries.

With the Texan's help, J.K. picked up Paul Little. They tended to his bruises, cuts, claw marks—he had puncture marks from the canines on his neck.

Within minutes, they'd fixed the flat.

J.K. turned to the Texan. "Can you drive down to the ranger station and let him know about this? If he's not there, just post a note, would you?"

"You got it!" the Texan said, glad to leave, in case the mountain lion was still lurking.

"You saved my life, man!" Paul Little whispered. " I've seen a lot, but this . . ."

J.K. helped him into the passenger seat of the Birdmobile and quickly re-examined Paul's neck and back. J.K. secured the bandages on Paul's neck with a bandanna. The honks had come like the answer to a prayer that had remained unformed inside J.K. He was astonished that Paul Little had gotten out of this situation alive and, looking at his sorry face now, J.K. felt sure he didn't want to report him to the ranger. J.K. had gotten his car back anyhow.

Paul Little handed him the keys. "I thought I was a dead man for sure."

J.K. nodded. Paul Little had made it, unlike Emma, or that deer, he thought to himself. Emma didn't even get to become an adult. One moment, Emma had been alive, dancing for the first time, cheek to cheek, with a boy at a party. J.K. had teased her about it, and she'd pleaded with him not to tell Dad. Despite being the chaperone, J.K. had filled up on beer. Pete and he were shooting the breeze—how they might go birding in South America. They lost track of how much they drank, so they "designated" Emma as their driver. She'd just gotten her license, and Dad didn't like her to drive on mountain roads. Jake was protective about his daughter. Anyhow, one moment Emma was alive, in a white peasant blouse and cut-off jeans. J.K. told her not to mess with changing radio stations while driving—they got poor reception on mountain roads. The next moment, a pickup hit them, almost out of nowhere. Pete and he got away with a few smashed ribs and a couple of nights at the hospital. Poor Emma died on the spot; that was brutal.

"We gotta get outta here, man," Paul Little said.

J.K. nodded, turning on the ignition. He hadn't been able to save Emma. But now he'd been given the chance to make up for that. He'd saved someone else's life. How much guilt had he carried around all these years? He never realized just how much it had been weighing him down.

All these months, he'd been beating up on himself and how his life was turning out. But at least he was alive. *He* could have been the one on whom the lion had pounced. That was close! Now he was driving on a forest road, instead of being stashed in some brush with a leg poking out. His emotions were running everywhere, causing confusion.

If he continued to live in the wilderness, he was sure to run into this sort of thing again. This was the danger of regressing into his loner self and camping in remote areas for weeks at a time. Surely, he didn't want to go the way of Paul Little.

How could he be part of the world again? It wasn't clear. He had tried. Things hadn't worked out. But strangely, he felt a certain heaviness that he had been carrying most of his life beginning to lift, beginning to free him.

J.K. forced himself to stop thinking and continued driving.

Paul Little looked over at J.K. "Would you do me a favor, man? Would you not say anything about this to Luna?"

"Why's that?"

"She'd be upset that I left you stranded, though I meant to return the car at some point. I didn't mean to piss you off. Needed the car real quick. Anyhow, Luna digs you, man."

"Digs me? I don't have any friends."

Paul Little considered this. "That's horseshit, man. I'm the dude that's got no friends. Luna's gotta be the only person that's nice to me. She gave me a chance—to open for her concert." He blew his nose. "She's gigging at the Centennial tonight."

J.K. whistled. Was that Luna's surprise?

"I owe you mucho," Paul Little said.

"Don't sweat it," J.K. said.

"No, I'd like to make it up to you. I'm going to San Francisco to look for a condor, and I bet you'd like to see one, too. We could see condors together; might even see other really good stuff, who knows, make a reputation for ourselves, get a fresh start in Northern Cal."

J.K. blinked. "I don't think there are any condors in San Francisco."

"No, north of there. I have my sources . . . real condor sources. It'll be a fine time. You gotta come. Let's leave tonight. Right now!"

The car-theft episode had happened without warning, startling J.K. more than terrifying him, so he realized it was crazy to believe anything Paul Little said. Even though he might have to risk Paul Little's volatility, J.K. now felt compelled to go to the Centennial. He must not disappoint Blake. That's what he said to himself. Blake's voice was calling out to him, to help Karen with her cause. But in his heart, J.K. felt something else.

The occasional car whizzed by, mostly going downhill.

J.K. felt how sore his legs were. In the darkness, he heard a clear "Toot . . . toot . . . toot." A pygmy owl, nearby. He relived the sensation he felt when he saw the lion go for Paul Little's neck. There was horror in that moment, definitely, but something inside him also recognized the event as life in its raw form—animals and people *did* get eaten alive, one way or another.

Something had happened to him. Had he absorbed something? Mountain-lion spirit? It was as though, in the moments while the lion pawed heavily at Paul Little, all fear had been drained out of him. Anyhow, wasn't it too early in life for him to become a victim? Nor did he care to be some kind of passive loser. His head felt like it was on fire. He probably had a mean fever.

"I have another buddy, who, I mean, if we can find him, we'll pick him up, and it'll be a party," Paul Little said. "The three of us, looking for a condor. We can hang out at his digs for a while. He's found this real cool private beach, and the owners are like never there."

J.K. did not respond.

Paul Little looked at him with that stare of his, wondering what J.K. was waiting for.

"I'll go on one condition," J.K. said. "We make a stop before we leave."

"Shit, man!"

J.K. considered him. "We're short on time?"

"A stop at a cop house, dude?"

"Nope." J.K. laughed, although he did give it brief consideration. "I need to check out this Centennial Karen made such a fuss about. I have a promise to keep." The promise was made to the youngest member of his flock, and J.K. felt that even if his life were now going to slide down the straight road to perdition, he might face the journey more easily if he did right by Blake. Of anybody, he supposed Blake was the one who *had* stood by him. Blake was a hardcore birder, and J.K. must not disappoint one of his own kind. But that wasn't the real reason he must to go to the Centennial.

J.K. swallowed, swearing he could taste his heart. "You said Luna is gigging there. She's wanted to go to S.F. for a while. Maybe she'll wanna come." He must check in with Luna. It might clear his head. If Paul Little was going to take him on some crazy-ass trip, J.K. wanted to see Luna first.

"That's cool, man," Paul Little said. "Luna could play us some nice songs on the way."

J.K. hit the pedal, and the Birdmobile sped out of the dark forest.

The winding freeway churned Paul Little's stomach, and he opened his window to throw up some clear liquid. Closing the window, he turned to the driver.

"I'm starving," Paul Little said. "I need un poco chow in me."

"We'll eat at Joss Canyon, I guess."

"I don't know, man. Those folks already gave me shit." As they drove toward Alpena, Paul Little told J.K. how he'd been refused dinner at the Centennial, how the women had treated him like a tapeworm, and how he was being kicked out of Joss Canyon, which had been his home for the last little while.

## 29

*F*rom 6:30 p.m. onwards, a stream of guests began congregating outside the tent. It was a pleasant June evening, highlighted by the liquid call of a mockingbird and a thrasher's cry mingled with the chatter of birders around long tables. Karen was no less worried about the election than Blake, but after the enormous amount of work she had done in the last year, she wasn't going to let election anxiety interfere with her role as hostess of the Centennial. Just before 7:00, she interrupted the chatter to ask people how they were enjoying the appetizers. There were murmurs of appreciation.

Karen gestured to the Mexican chef and his female assistant, whom she had called forward to receive the applause. "You guys did a great job," she told them.

To the guests, she announced, "Dinner will be served at 7:30." She left to tend to the buffet table, but noticing that a silence was left in her wake, she turned back with a flourish and commanded, "As you were . . ." signaling them to continue their chatter.

When Jim Skua, President of the National Bird Society, arrived, followed closely by a photographer from the *Alpena Star News*, it was all Karen could do to contain her tears. Expecting Rick to arrive any second, she corralled everyone for a Centennial photograph. But a quarter of an hour later, Rick had still not shown up.

"He said he'd be here by 7:30!" she whispered to Blake.

Blake pointed out that it was only 7:35.

Karen looked out in the direction of the parking lot, uneasy about having the photo taken without Rick. Such a crowd had gathered. There were at least two dozen octogenarians; all eight board members, except Rick, some with grandchildren; die-hards like the schoolteacher, Wynn, and younger couples, many from the L.A. bird society, who came mostly to the birding trips; Grimsby's teenage son on his father's complimentary ticket, along with a clique of three; several floaters; middle-aged people like the insurance man, Abe, and his wife, who came only to the talks. Where were all these people when she was putting together the Centennial subcommittee?

The photographer complained he was losing light, and Karen had no choice but to give him the green light. He stood up on a bench and, after fussing and tweaking to "fit" everyone in, he snapped a group shot with a wide-angle lens.

On her way to the buffet table, noticing that there was a lull in conversation, Karen stopped and addressed the guests again: "The Holy Roman Empire was neither holy, nor Roman, nor an Empire. Discuss!" she told them, to scattered laughter.

When most of the guests were seated inside the tent with their dinners, Frank shuffled up to the podium to make some preliminary announcements.

Just then, Rick entered the hall with Meg on his arm, and the electricity in the room seemed to have been amped-up as all eyes turned to them and couldn't look away. Meg wore a sleeveless black dress, a V-cut in the front revealing a startling bit of cleavage. The cut of the dress was straight across the shoulders, and a wide waistband and subtle flare of the skirt gave the clever illusion that Meg had a good figure. Maroon lipstick accentuated the alarming lack of color in her skin, which hadn't been aired in a while.

The sharp contrast of Meg's pale skin to her lipstick, and the black hair and dress caused Blake to mutter that she looked like Anakin Skywalker when he took off his Darth Vader mask. Some adults in the room thought, however, that in the sexy but classic number, Meg looked the sharpest they'd ever seen her.

If there was a difference of opinion about Meg's presentation, there was none whatsoever about Rick's. For a man who managed to look elegant in polo shirts and khakis, in his tuxedo he outdid any British actor walking the red carpet to an awards ceremony. Conscious of the effect they had created, the Silvermans lingered at the tent's entrance, while the others imagined flashbulbs going off and escorted them to their seats with admiring gazes. Only when they were out of sight, hidden among the guests at their table, did people turn their eyes back to Frank, who was waiting forlorn and superfluous at the podium.

"Well, Rick has come just when we needed him," Frank said after a pause.

The chef wheeled the Centennial cake out into the hall. In the shape of a cowbird, the cake had a chocolate head and a glossy black body. When the cake rolled past Dana's table, she looked on in shock. "That woman never gives up," she said.

Sitting across from Dana, the Egret shook her head. "She doesn't know the meaning of the word *quit*," she added.

After Rick's arrival, the opera director was at her peak. Karen motioned Frank to invite Jim Skua to the podium and signaled to Rick the appropriate moment to step forward and accept the Cowbird Award. Skua made a short speech congratulating A.B.S. on their historic Centennial, and then proceeded with the presentation of the award.

Karen had been waiting for this moment.

"Is there any lettuce in my teeth?" she asked at her table before going to the podium.

Just as Rick was about to return to his seat, Karen caught him by the sleeve of his tuxedo.

She announced to the flock that she had written a poem in honor of Rick's contributions to A.B.S. The poem was a parody of "The Raven" by Edgar Allen Poe, and she recited a couple of stanzas of the original before she launched into her version, turning from time to time to notice the effect her recital was producing on Rick, who fluctuated between embarrassment and a sort of hapless pleasure.

"It was the Cowboy Rick at my door."

"He said, 'Can we go birding evermore?' "

Laughter spread through the audience, and the performance piece grew more ridiculous. Karen's voice took on a Victorian prissiness, her face displayed a catalog of expressions, her hands fluttered and soared to describe the movements of the various birds mentioned.

"The award might be given in jest," she said over the applause, preventing Rick from leaving the stage one more time, "but the sentiments behind it are real." She hugged him, patting his back as she did so. Then she kissed him meticulously on each cheek.

All this while, her husband, Oscar, watched from the farthest corner of the room, across from Luna, who had been cued to play a soft background melody during the poem. Oscar was as quiet as Karen was ebullient, as absent as she was present. When the guests had arrived earlier in the evening, he greeted not a single one, and when they congregated in circles in the courtyard, he joined no one, but was content to sit behind a table and hand out raffle tickets or do whatever else was necessary. And when Oscar chose to speak to a person other than a family member that evening, he chose the Mexican chef, whom he sat with in the courtyard while everyone else was noisily enjoying dinner inside.

As much as Karen needed her husband to be her audience at home—and he was the perfect audience (the way he listened to her with his calm, intent face; the way he offered his comforting shoulder for her to cry on; the way he showed determined concern when the welfare of his children or wife were in any way threatened)—it was just as necessary for her to have one perfect audience member among her friends and adversaries in A.B.S. for whose benefit she performed. And it was obvious to her now that if A.B.S. were going to be her stage, she had to outgrow the role of Hospitality Chair; the role of president would suit her much better.

And so she could not and would not let Rick retreat from the spotlight. She would stoop to anything, even presenting him with an award she had invented, even making an utter fool of herself, to shame him into staying by her side. His presence was what made her performance seem worthwhile.

Blake looked on, feeling nervous about the elections. The Centennial event was stretching out a lot longer than he had expected. His mom had said they were running at least an hour late. Blake had done a preliminary ballpark count of the votes for Frank and those for his mom, and it wasn't clear that she was ahead. It seemed to Blake that they were split about evenly. He didn't mind Rick getting the Cowbird Award, but he wished that J.K. had accepted it in the first place. He was sure that J.K. would have voted for his mom, but J.K. was off somewhere living in the forest like a wild animal, his mom said. Blake would have liked to have spent a weekend out there with J.K., camping or whatever, but his mom vetoed the idea.

"We have a fine set of officers running for elections this year," Rick announced. "As many of you know, I resigned as president earlier this year. It was nothing to do with A.B.S. My wife needed me, and I had to give up what she called 'my demanding mistress'—though she said it in French."

Rick waited for the laughter to subside.

"The good news is that Frank took over as acting president and saved my marriage, and I think he's shown us already that he'll make a fine president. But this year we're lucky. We have an embarrassment of riches. There's another person who's interested in this position, and many of you know her as our fabulous Hospitality Chair, Karen Mercer."

There were gasps in the audience, and some octogenarians looked as if they'd been Tasered. In the countless years these people had been members of the Alpena Bird Society, none could recall the position of president being contested.

Karen sighed. Clearly these people had not bothered to read the color fliers she mailed out to the full membership two weeks ago at her own expense.

"And that's not a bad thing," Rick chided. "It's good to have some healthy competition. Now, each of you has a ballot at your table. I'm going to ask you to fill it out and drop it off at my table, and then we'll count the votes while you eat dessert."

There were uneasy giggles in the crowd, followed by sounds of the stubby pencils that had been distributed scribbling against paper. The votes were being cast.

Feeling too nerve-wracked, Blake wandered out of the tent and began listening for night birds. Maybe he could score a nightjar. Instead, he heard two voices. He recognized them right away and ran in that direction. One of his shoes hit a stump and flew off his foot.

J.K. and Paul Little, looking all beat up, like they'd been to hell and back, were walking up to the tent.

"You guys all right?" Blake said, putting his shoe back on.

"I probably have a fever or a head cold or something," J.K. said. "And Paul here got some mean scratches on his neck from a friendly kitty cat."

"My mom needs you," Blake cried. "They're voting right now."

"That's why we're here," J.K. said. There was a glimmer of resolve in his eyes. All these months it seemed to him that he was done with life, but maybe life was not done with him yet. There were people like Karen, Blake, and even Paul Little, who still needed him, even if in a weird, self-centered way. And then Karen's ascendancy to president might actually help both cowbirds and vireos, and save Joss Canyon from development. Once a birder, always a birder. If he couldn't have a career in physics, could he figure out a way to make birding his livelihood?

"We were hungry, man," Paul Little said. "We figured you had leftovers."

"We have a ton of food," Blake said. "But you should vote first."

The trio hurried into the tent, and Blake steered them to a table that had a couple of empty chairs.

Dana looked over and walked up to them as Paul Little pored over the ballot.

"He can't vote," Dana said. "Members only." Then she looked at J.K.'s untidy state as though he were turning into a vagrant just like Paul Little.

Paul Little pulled out an application form that was filled out in J.K.'s handwriting. Then he began fishing an assortment of nickels and dimes out of his fanny pack.

"We don't have time for this," Dana said, disgusted.

"You keep that stuff, man," J.K. told him. Instead he pulled out three worn ten-dollar bills from his pocket. He thrust the money into Dana's hand. She was Membership Chair, and now that dues were delivered, she had no further grounds to deny Paul Little voting rights.

"All right, then," Dana said. "I don't know if there's a rule barring people from voting in such cases, but there ought to be."

There was a silent auction during dessert, and while the members surveyed the bird books, posters, and jewelry, and wrote down their bids, Rick and Zanne counted the votes.

The guitar music grew animated. In a blue crepe dress and pillbox hat, Luna was the most attractive J.K. had ever seen her. Her music was a mix between The Romeros and Paul Simon, but with an edgy spark of her own. J.K. approached her.

"Surprise!" Luna said, continuing to play the guitar. "I thought you'd never come."

J.K. grinned, hoping he wouldn't jam up this time. He grew aware that his checkered lumberjack shirt was torn in places, on the back where a thorny bush had snagged it and along the elbows where it had simply given out. "I wasn't planning to attend. That's why I'm in rags."

Luna looked him over and nodded, knowing he'd have some explaining to do later. "Rick offered me the gig. I'm glad I don't have to sing."

"But you have a good voice." J.K. looked away. He had meant the praise. He hoped it hadn't sounded lame. Blake was motioning to him from the other corner of the room, but J.K. ignored the boy. "It looks like I'm driving to San Francisco tonight."

"Cool. My best friend lives there," Luna responded.

"The hat-maker. You said you'd like to visit her. Your other friend, Paul Little, is making me go. We could give you a ride."

"Seriously? That'd be fun. But I can't leave work."

"Think about all the Chinese food you could eat."

"Mm-hmmm. But my manager at the café won't be happy."

Luna glanced into his eyes. Her fingers strummed the guitar strings more softly, it seemed to him.

"I thought *you* were the risk taker," he said. "What was that quote by Elvis Costello?" His father had told him that in his day, girls were ready for adventure at the drop of a hat. But Jake had picked Antonia because she was more sober than the rest; Jake figured she'd be more likely to stick with him in the long run. J.K. was glad, in a way, that Luna was resisting, but he hoped she'd give in already.

"How long are you going for?" Luna said.

"I don't know."

"You don't know?" She chuckled. "That's interesting."

This time their eyes lingered.

"I'll call my girlfriend, ask if I can stay with her. I might be able to come in a few days."

"That's cool," J.K. said. "You'll miss out on our road trip, but that's probably for the best. We'll stop and look for birds."

"I'd wanna take the train anyway. I like looking out train windows and thinking. That's when new songs come to me."

Their conversation was going in the right direction, but so tentatively; one wrong word or look might puncture the cool plans they were hatching. J.K. was relieved when Blake, who seemed unable to wait any longer, walked up to him.

"You gotta talk to the professor," Blake said in an urgent voice. "He needs someone to count parakeets in South America."

J.K. slapped the boy's back. "You're messing with me!"

"Nope—ask him yourself."

Even Luna thanked Blake for interrupting. "I can only play the guitar *and* make travel plans for so long," she said.

Kern was at the dessert table, cutting a piece out of the cowbird-shaped cake—the chocolate head was all but gone and only the glossy black body remained. J.K. hesitated to go over. He remembered Kern eating butter cookies at that dispiriting tea when J.K. had told Kern about his problems and Kern hadn't seemed interested. J.K. swallowed his pride and walked over.

"Cake?" Kern said, offering him a plate.

J.K. ate the cake too quickly; it cloyed his empty stomach. Kern cut himself another generous piece. Then J.K. asked if it were true, that Kern needed someone to count parakeets.

"I've decided to give cowbirds a rest," Kern told him. "I need to sort through some things first." He made himself a cup of green tea, moving like he had all the time in the world. J.K. waited impatiently to hear more, but Kern said nothing. The schoolteacher, Wynn, bee-lined to the cake. J.K. paid no attention to him. Crystal ran around chasing a squealing boy. Two middle-aged women were comparing nail polish. Grimsby's teenage son leaned against the dessert table, acting oh-so-bored.

"Blake told me you need someone to go to South America," J.K. repeated.

"Why? Are you interested?" Kern said, acting surprised.

"Sure. I'd like to know more."

"A colleague and I are planning a study on the distribution and habitat of certain types of parakeets in parts of Brazil and Argentina." Kern told him.

"We'll need someone to go to a few hot spots—to start looking at topography and climate predictors."

"That sounds cool."

"There's no salary. Maybe a tiny stipend. But I can't promise that. We'd pay travel expenses though."

J.K. felt lightheaded, barely able to believe that Kern might take him on. He was glad he hadn't told Kern off at the Faculty Club tea, as he was tempted to do.

"As a matter of fact, we could use someone good with math," Kern added, "someone who can generate pretty plots and a preliminary model to plug into our grant application."

"I can do all the plots and models you want," J.K. said. "You won't be sorry you hired a physicist." Maybe there was a way out here, a way to figure out how to transition from physics to biology, but J.K. wasn't ready to bring that up yet. Kern was too flighty, and J.K. didn't want to stir the pot just yet. He decided he was going to be an asset to Kern's team, and not just a tag-along. He felt like his run of bad luck was changing, and this lifted his spirits enormously.

"I'm leaving town for a few days," J.K. said. "Just let me know when you want me back. I don't have a cell phone, but I'll check my email. I can also give you my parents' number. I'll call Sundays in case there's a message from you." A smile flickered on his lips. "That's more than I've called in a while. But I just had an encounter with a mountain lion, and I thought . . ."

Kern was fascinated hearing the mountain lion story. He assured J.K. that he would pack him off to South America as soon as he got clearance on the travel funds. J.K. was just the sort of guy he needed.

Luna was done playing the guitar; she pulled off the hairpins that attached the pillbox hat to her head. She found J.K. and Paul Little in the makeshift kitchen. Her blue crepe dress swayed to the air of a table fan as she stood watching them. The guys were devouring mashed potatoes and chili stew as though they hadn't eaten in weeks.

"That's real attractive," Luna said with an edge to her voice.

J.K. smiled sheepishly; he wiped his face with a vireo napkin and pushed away his plate. Then he told her about his conversation with Kern. "I don't think the job's a done-deal though," he added.

"See!" Luna said. "I knew you'd figure something out."

"It'll involve me vanishing into the forest for a few months."

"Why not? That's what you're expert at." She paused, and then grew serious. "You know, I'm saying that, but for me, S.F. is kinda like a forest. It terrifies me. I've wanted to explore the music scene there for a while, but . . ."

"Now you will," J.K. piped in. "Why not?"

"*You're* giving *me* a confidence boost?"

They laughed. He took her hand, pressed it. She brushed her mouth against his cheek.

Paul Little let out a loud burp. "Excuse me!" he muttered, looking them over. To J.K., he added, "Didn't I say Luna digs you, man?"

"Paul, you've gotta be the most annoying dude on the planet," Luna said.

"I won't interrupt you lovebirds," Paul countered. "Right now, I need to go get me a piece of that cow-birdy cake."

The Egret reddened as the tally grew close. When it seemed that Karen had won by one vote, she suggested they do a recount just to be sure.

The elderly voters were getting drowsy and restless. Some of the younger birders showed signs of having too much to drink—neckties were loosened, shirts pulled out of trousers, the women had drunk up their lipstick and not bothered to reapply it, and their eyes sparkled unnaturally, or were nearly vacuous.

When the results were announced, Frank looked on sheepishly. He was shocked that the membership should have chosen Karen over a solid candidate like himself. But to save face, he walked over to Karen and congratulated her.

Karen shook his hand with a triumphant gleam in her eyes, her mind full of all she would achieve as president, over the objections of the old guard, if necessary. The cowbirds would have a trusty friend in her and in the bird society. Indeed, all the birds in Alpena would fly freer and chirp sweeter because of her efforts on their behalf. A golden age in Bird Education would no doubt dawn in Alpena schools. As her elated children and husband, and Rick, surrounded her, she sighed with pleasure. She was still not quite able to believe that she had at last brought together so many of the loose ends in her life. All those days she had spent birding, which could have so easily been frittered away, had, because of her resourcefulness and vision, strung together like pearls in a glowing necklace of victory.

When Rick moved in to hug her, Karen looked into his soulful brown eyes and dismissed his investment-related transgressions as a momentary lapse. She imagined their future as loyal friends, working hand in hand to elevate the oldest birding society in the United States. One day, maybe, even the whole country would be proud of her.

As Karen was being congratulated by well-wishers, Dana and Zanne lingered behind, looking quite pale.

"If she's thinking of shifting our money to some hare-brained cowbird fund, that ain't gonna happen," Dana said.

"Yeah, over my dead body," the Egret vowed.

# Colophon

This book was created using using Quark XPress.

The text is in Bodoni, the name given to a series of Didone category
of serif typefaces.
It was first designed by Giambattista Bodoni in 1798.

Bodoni was the favorite typeset of UK Poet Laureat Ted Hughes,
and is used in Vogue Magazne.

The display typeface is Zafino, a calligraphic typeface
designed for Linotype by typeface designer Hermann Zapf in 1998.

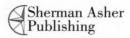Sherman Asher
Publishing